Following
Shadows

Book One of the Finding Home Series

Janneke Jobsis Brown

Following Shadows

Book One of the *Finding Home Series*

Copyright © 2017 Janneke Jobsis Brown

All rights reserved.

Cover photo - Java; boys in Kamp Ambarawa 5-6 weeks after liberation

Published by EA Books Publishing a division of
Living Parables of Central Florida, Inc. a 501c3
EABooksPublishing.com

As the editor and author of *The Defining Years of the Dutch East Indies, 1942-1949*, it touched me greatly to "meet" the Vanderveers, who slammed the door on these years. As mind-blowing accounts of true history and suffering are revealed, a beautiful bridge is formed: spanning three generations of a family saying what many, who experienced these times, wish they could.

Jan A. Krancher

Reading through the story of several generations of Vanderveers, from the Dutch Indies in World War II to Texas fifty years later, with many stops in between, is like reviewing a case of multi-generational war trauma. We can see how the initial internment in a Japanese prisoner of war camp sheds its repercussions down to the present. Janneke Jobsis Brown has woven together love and war and loss superbly to not only offer us a fine historical novel, but she has also shown how a single person's psychological trauma carries us forth into the lives of several generations.

Lewis Aptekar, PhD, author of *In the Lion's Mouth*,
Clinical Psychologist, Professor,
Counselor Education, San Jose State University

Following Shadows takes the reader on a family's around the world journey. Flashbacks from the father's boyhood years spent in a Japanese concentration camp during WWII are masterfully woven into the present dynamics of the family drama. The daughter's quest to understand and unravel the past helps her to explore her present-day struggles, bringing her closer to her seemingly distant but loving father.

Azadeh Tabazadeh, NASA scientist and the
author of *The Sky Detective*; named by *Kirkus Reviews*
as one of the Best Books of 2015

In memory of Adrianus Cornelis "Kees" Jobsis

Your shadowed World War II years,
were vastly conquered by your bright spirit and love.
The memories I treasured with you,
led me to pursue missing memories and
affirm the unbreakable bond of love among
three not-so-distant generations.

And dedicated to

Boukje Jobsis de Vries:
for your courage, steadfastness, wisdom and love

Anna Mechtelina Jobsis Johnson:
for all we shared, your insight and your love

ACKNOWLEDGMENTS

What began as a simple act of writing down the little-known story of the concentration camps of the Pacific — the Japanese Concentration Camps, and the generations that followed — launched me into my own decade-long journey. Deep sorrow, fear, anger, and heights of joy accompanied me along the way. Some art, such as novel writing takes a long time, and required finding soulful companions as I traversed the peaks and valleys of storytelling.

The people with whom I crossed paths — in writers' groups, at the Mount Hermon Christian Writers Conference, San Francisco Writers Conference and the Iowa Summer Writing Festival, and still others — all encouraged me to never give up. Denise Martin and Margaret Cretzmeyer you both inspired and empowered me.

After an uprooted childhood, I put down roots in the process of telling this story. My life has become intertwined with people I am honored to know who provided reading, consultation, the international perspective, and amazing support. Thank you, Rosa Apodaca, Peggy Tuite, Willie Z. Holmes, and Michael Brownkorbel.

My Agent, Leslie Stobbe, never gave up on a long creative process and gifted me with the conviction that WWII stories need to be told. The intrepid team at EA, Cheri Cowell, Bob Ousnamer and Dawn Staymates, made publishing my book a reality. Writers are a wonderful tribe. A trio of editors/writers/coaches ensured completion: Jordan Rosenfeld, Cindy Coloma, and Robin Shepherd. Fellow writers are generous. Thank you to Barbara Wilson for connecting me with your Dutch-American family, and

Azadeh Tabazadeh for leading the way with your international memoir.

Writers' groups believed in *Following Shadows* when my belief in a finished novel was shaky. Thank you for the creative partnership: Nancy Benich, Constance Doty, Ann Starke, Linda McGinnis, Kay Ross Leach, Lewis Aptekar, Lynn Morgan, Debby Kantorik, and Nicole Moore.

War is indeed hell, and no one is spared. We only have to look at history and the arts to find the evidence. I hope our world will have the wisdom to learn from the past, and the grace to honor those who did what they could to end war and bring peace. The Allied Powers, including America, were the great hope for those in the *kamp*s. We are living in times when recognizing the precursors of war and suffering are at the same level of urgency as eighty years ago. As someone who has experienced the effects of intergenerational trauma, I used to compare my suffering with that of others who "went through so much more." I learned that such comparisons are pointless, and compassion is the point.

Let us remember that World War II created suffering around the world. Nazi genocide not only cruelly exterminated 6,000,000 Jewish people, but 11,000,000 more civilians. In Indonesia, four to six million people died, including thousands of laborers forced to work to their death — *romushas* — by the Japanese. In the Netherlands, more than 20,000 people died during the Hunger Winter of 1944-45. Food supplies were cut off by the Nazi Regime as retribution for a Dutch Railroad Strike in September of 1944. All told, 200,000 civilians and military lost their lives.

Russia lost 22,000,000 soldiers and civilians during the war. In the Philippines, almost 1,000,000 civilians and military lost their lives. Canada lost 453,000 soldiers, and America 400,000 soldiers. National fear after Pearl Harbor caused 120,000 Japanese-Americans to lose their homes, land

and possessions before being imprisoned in internment camps.

May we focus on compassion, strive for a true "never again," and advocate for those still waiting for justice.

CONTENTS

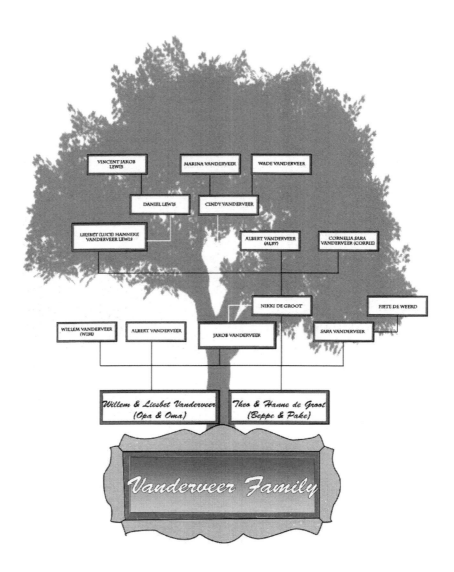

CONTEMPORARY MAP OF INDONESIA

Jakarta was previously named Batavia (Tjideng and Grogol vicinity). Tjimahi *kamp*s were near Bandung.

PART ONE

The past is never dead. It's not even past.
— William Faulkner

CHAPTER 1

Luce

Calabria, California
September 2004

"Lucie?" A late night voice rasps over the phone.

Only one person calls me Lucie—Papa. I have gone from my Dutch given name, Liesbet, after my grandma, to Lucie as an Americanized teen. And for decades now, just Luce. The name Luce (pronounced *loose*) amuses me, as if in all my recent years with one home town, one home, one family, one job, I am a loose woman.

"I didn't want to call you last night," he says. "It was so late already. And now it is late again."

"Papa." I click off the music, letting my writing journal clatter to the floor. "What happened?"

"Ja-akob!" I hear Mama in the background. "It's not good for you to call her up so late; it can wait for the morning."

"*Stil* and quiet *nu*, Nikki. We must do something, make a plan."

"Hey Papa, no fighting between you two now. What's wrong? Are you sick?"

"No, not me."

My ears buzz. "Mama is sick? What's wrong?"

"Albert," he breathes out.

Not my brother, not again. This has to be bad. It's midnight in Houston, and two hours earlier for me here in California. "Alby? What happened?" I ask. "Are Cindy and the kids okay?"

"Well, he's in the hospital. The family, ach, all in shock I think. Your niece was alone with him at home when it happened yesterday. She had to call nine-one-one."

Mama picks up an extension, her tone soft. "*Liefje*, I don't want Papa to keep you up so late now. Jakob, there's nothing Lucie can do from there so late at night."

Liefje. Little love. *Help, help, help,* begins a prayer in me. "Ma-ahma," I try.

Papa interrupts. "I didn't know if he was going to live until two a.m. this morning, and then after that, all the calls."

"Live?" My voice is shrill. "Mama, I'm wide awake now, and I still don't know what's wrong. Let us talk now and then we'll all get some rest."

"Off the line," Papa orders Mama. "I'll be to bed in a few minutes."

"Both of you, don't make yourselves too tired. Alby is fine for now." She had to get the last word in.

"Back to Alby." I sigh. Papa's meticulous retired-engineer habits are failing him. I have no coherent story yet. "And yes, why call so late?"

"Well, first I thought, what can you do from California? But then, you know me, I got to worrying and I know my daughter, you would still be up. You're tough. And ... you need to jump on this first thing in the morning." His voice sounds proud; he always thinks I'm strong.

"Okay. And now please start at the beginning." At forty-five, I flush like a ten-year-old to think he's proud of strong me, while my eyes well with tears. My little brother, the one whose hand I held in each and every move across the continents of our lives. What if he's near death? *Help, help, dear God, help.*

"We found out Cindy's had a tough time of it with Alby lately, and didn't wish to scare us, until she had to call. She was at the grocery store when your niece had to make that nine-one-one call. We had no idea your brother was so bad again. I had to talk to Marina today, the little *liefje*—

4

sweetheart. She thought her daddy was asleep, but then she couldn't wake him."

"She's only thirteen. That must have been traumatic for her."

"*Ja*, and happy-go-lucky she called emergency so quick. When Cindy rushed to the ER, Marina was all alone in the waiting room, shaking and crying."

"Which hospital?"

"He's in … how you say it … the *intense* unit, right next door to a new treatment program. *Feasta* something." He inhales and exhales haggardly. I wonder if he's smoking again. No he quit smoking twenty years ago, "That's where he's going next, same hospital, *Feasta*." Two decades after retiring and tired as he is now, Papa slips into more and more Dutch-English. He sounds a decade older, overnight. Usually he's upset over the details of life—lateness, wasted food—and calm during crisis. Now this. A real crisis and it's hitting him hard.

Our talk has no anchor for me. I know nothing. I ease my grip on the phone. After all, everyone's alive.

"So he's in the intensive care unit … ICU? What was it, the drugs? Are you okay?"

"Oh, *ja*. Fine," he says. "Yes, it was the drugs. Pills and an overdose. They think it was no accident, but a suicide attempt." Papa's breathing stays choppy, but his words even, as if he's trying to hold it together for me. I can see his white-gray hair, his sagging face.

"I bet it's both. Too many pills and wanting to die." I kick away the pen at my feet. He could be dying, and so selfish, letting Marina find him. None of this had to be. "Ach, *ja*, stupid brilliant Alby. Why is he so stubborn with getting help?"

Papa wheezes. "I tried to tell Alby, 'Enough already, stop it.' But he and I couldn't really talk well today." He exhales, sounding *zielig*. The Dutch word for pitiful, sad, wrapped around the word *ziel*—soul. His soul is hurting, not that he would ever tell me that.

"It's been a long time since any of us have talked well with him. Don't worry so, Papa. He's the one who has to be ready in this treatment program, not you."

"And you, you have worked for these so-called treatment programs," he hisses in accusation. "We need your help. Why don't you get this *Feasta* outfit to do a good job this time, make these people earn their living, make him really think and stop his nonsense?"

"Papa, he does think. They have to help him think a different way. You know I believe treatment programs work, if *he* wants to work. You went with me oh so long ago when I was a teen, to HOW meetings, remember? I was ready. So it can work out great for Alby. But he'll think he's the smartest one in the place, and that's when he stops listening."

"Well, he is the smartest. Who else there has patents for their bioresearch medications?"

"Really?" I growl. "Plenty of smart people other than him get help." *Like me.*

"*Liefje*, stop it with worrying about your stubborn brother taking it all in." Like always, his voice rises. "We'll make him. What we have to focus on is he's not just landed himself in some other lousy chicken-outfit rehab. That's my worry."

Here it is, Papa and *ruzie*. He calls me late at night to do what he's always done, fight and rage. I squirm back in my easy chair, determined to be clear. "You asked me, so I said what I thought, Papa. He needs one more rehab. What is this, number three? This has to be the one where he doesn't leave."

"According to Cindy, he wasn't even conscious until late yesterday. The doctor told her he had liver damage. Doesn't that mean he's ready to listen?"

"For most people, sure. Has Corrie been to see him?" I think of my baby sister, how she is usually right in the middle of things and way easier to talk to than Papa.

"I'm sure Corrie will see him soon. But what good will it do?"

Familiar words for the Vanderveers — *what good will it do?* "If he wants help, our visits," I repeat, "the treatment program will do a lot of good." Then again, might as well stop repeating. Thirty years ago in HOW meetings, I gave up my own magic elixir, alcohol, and at first told our parents nothing. When there is a problem, it is worse once Papa or Mama make *ruzie* over it. I recall roaming the dusty church halls where I attended my HOW rehab meetings, one of the kids with no family, until I dragged Papa along.

I know Mama can't sleep now, and Papa will worry endlessly. I hate for them to have this pain. My head swims with rage and worry. Alby will live. Alby will die. Either way, my brother's been gone from us so long. Whether here in Calabria, or in Houston, I can connect with Cindy and the kids, not Alby.

We've been silent awhile; I hear my own asthmatic breathing. This is another family thing, the silence with words screaming to be said. I aimlessly say, "Corrie and I have wondered for years. He's looked so bad."

"Oh *ja*, I think your mama thought everything was fine these last years. To me, no. He just looked too … how you say … *sieke*. Too sick to be okay." He raises his voice. "I didn't go with my *insinks*. That crazy bioresearch and Alby being in charge of the project exhausted him. I told myself that's why he looked like living death — not that he was still on pills." His fist thuds down on something. Sounds like he's working himself up again.

I feel the familiar tightening of my gut when Papa is riled up and *ruzie* could take us both down. One of the most frightening things is when I rage into the *ruzie* too, after promising myself to be calm. "Well, at least he can't check himself out of treatment since he's so bad off."

"*Liefje*, I'm just worried. He came" — he coughs — "so close to dying." No pounding the furniture. Maybe he's crying. I wish we could cry together. He tries to order me around and sounds so strong, but he isn't. He's seventy-five and frail after the accident thirty years ago. If I were with him, he'd be often looking away, as if he sees things I don't. "I asked Cindy to not tell Mama about the liver damage yet."

"Oh Papa, might as well tell her. I'm sure this time will be different." I bump a cup of herbal tea gone cold. I don't believe my words.

"I thought you should know, and that's why I had to send Mama to bed." I hear a click on their line. So she's heard everything. "The people from this *Feasta* program have been calling the rest of us too. I don't pick up, just let it go on the answering machine. What can we do? But you, you can make those people shape up."

"No, I can't make them. But I can check them out, Papa. And of course you must talk to them."

"You will call *Feasta* first thing in the morning? We have little time."

"Okay." I sigh. "I will call if you also call the *Feasta* Family Program people back." To agree has always been the only way to buy brief peace from Papa.

He's silent for a long while. "Yes, okay. And get some rest."

"I love you, Papa."

"I love you too, *liefje*."

He doesn't always do the *I love you* reply, and his love doesn't settle me. The scariest part of this call is Papa trying to sound like his old self — demanding. I heard the effort in each and every word, his exhaustion.

The phone receiver is still against my ear. First, dial tone, then the screeching phone-off-the-hook warning. I drop the phone on the hook. A whirring outer space noise rings out.

The printer. Next, nothing, silence. The room collapses into darkness. My heart pounds and I feel paralyzed. This is just one of our usual California power outages, yet my throat and chest burn with panic, and I gasp for air. The digital kitchen clock flashes green—an upside-down four and ones almost spell *hell*, as if warnings come from California power glitches, and bad news comes from Texas.

Hell, help, help. I go back to prayer.

I force slow breathing, long on the exhale, like I do with my counseling clients. This one's bad, so I lower my head from the dizziness.

Keep breathing.

Finally, my brain stops screaming panic and I concentrate on deep slow breaths. The asthma wheezes also stop. I lean forward to gather everything at my feet and find the flashlight in the drawer next to me, just as lights come on, the refrigerator hums, the printer stutters, static music plays. So it is over.

I reset the clock. It's midnight and I'm tired.

Forty-five suddenly feels old. Alby is old too. Forty-two is too old to have a death wish and not know how to live. Thirty-nine is too old for my sister, Corrie, to let Papa be the one to inform me, instead of warning me herself. She knows we're all worriers and none of us needs another shock. I have had enough shocks in my life.

I think about calling my AA sponsor, Kemble. She's a night owl and would be up. It's been decades since my last panic attack. Back then and now, calling is not my way. No one, not even Kemble, fully understands. Our parents' *ruzie*, multiplied today with the fact that Alby could die, is all too crushing. A thousand miles away from Houston, I'm surrounded by their stress, and my own words choked down like bitter bile—never said.

I touch a soft wall tapestry as I tiptoe to my teen son's room. Another trick I teach my clients is ground yourself, touch your world. I slowly pry open the door as Vincent's snores greet me. His flashing clock glows green on his face and longish curls drape his pillow. Like always for Vanderveer problems, I see my Vincent and believe all is well.

I head for Daniel, his comfort. Chilled autumn air fills our bedroom from the open window. I wish I could wake him to talk. He wouldn't mind, yet I don't want to try out the words with him: *This time Alby almost died.*

Moonlight from our window casts a silver glow on the photo Papa sent us. Verdant terraced rice paddies, like gently curved stair steps for a giant, reach up to steep hills.

"*Ja*," he had said, "so beautiful, not my home island of Billiton, but Java. I had to take this picture for you kids when Mama and I went on that world cruise. We have one too. Almost home, almost home."

Until recently, when I did my internet research, I had always wondered why he said some words twice out of habit. If you say a word twice in Indonesian, it is plural.

His homes, almost home.

† † †

For several nights I sleep, but never soundly, dreaming of lost packages, lost passports, and the worst—lost babies, children, sisters, brothers, parents, grandparents. I'm sent back at every border crossing to countries full of shadows and danger. I never have my papers, never am I ready, never do I have a home.

Then I wake up in my country, in familiar cold-weather flannel sheets, and recognize the return of the dull ache where all my family pain lives. One way or another, my brother is dying.

Maybe, maybe this time he won't leave.

This is a lot to shake awake from. So I find Vincent as quickly as possible and ask to check his homework folder. I open my calendar to ordinary days with lists of clients. No Vanderveers have called. I find time to do reconnaissance, and my ex-colleagues in Texas report that the "*Feasta Something Program*" is Vista Treatment Program, a well-respected rehab south of Houston. Well-respected, so *no more calls*. I break my promise to Papa to "shape up" *Feasta* Treatment Program. Maybe if those *Feasta* people call me, I won't call back either. This time around I'll have no careful notebook with lists of names and numbers, no calls from me as an ex-clinic director to Alby's clinic director. I tried in the previous hospitalizations, and what did I learn? That a therapist can't help her own family.

When Papa calls me back about my supposedly urgent call to *Feasta*, I will have no report. I'll challenge him. Did he call the family program? I grin and shake my head—no chance of that.

Papa loves us deeply, obsessively actually. But the family program, he and Mama would need to be part of therapy. For Papa to talk about the past, this he will never do.

Unless, and here I think for a long moment, magnetized into two family photos propped up before me. One shows Albert and I with our special grandparents in the Netherlands—Beppe and Pake. Another photo shows my other grandparents: *Opa* Vanderveer, who we never knew, and my Oma who was so silent every time we visited her. They lounge on the veranda of their tropical home, smiling into the camera. Young Jakob, his brothers and sister pose around them, with their Indonesian nursemaid. Papa's beloved Baboe.

I feel dizzy with wonder. Would Papa finally reveal his deeply buried story about losing this beloved home, never to return? Would he, if it might save his son?

CHAPTER 2

Jakob

Billiton Island
Dutch East Indies — Indonesia
December 1941

Jakob knew that Mollie was not beautiful to everyone.

Others might have picked her litter mates. Perhaps the orange-striped kittens, or the lone black kitten with white paws. They would end up with ordinary names such as Tiger or Socks. But Jakob noticed the powerful and mysterious gray kitten and named her Mollie. Her fur gleamed like dusky silver and she purred from the moment he first held her close.

She was his, and she was the most beautiful cat in the world.

Mollie had been with Jakob since he was five years old. When his big brothers Wim and Albert were in school, their housemaid, Baboe Min, asked Mammie for permission to take Jakob to her kampong — village. He remembered every moment.

† † †

"*Mevrouw*, I can take Jakob with me now. The kittens are old enough to go to their new homes."

Mammie was in the kitchen, and looked up from meal planning with Kokkie. At first she frowned, but then her eyes crinkled with a smile. "Oh, the kittens. A cat trains itself, so not much trouble."

"*Ja*," Min nodded.

They were out the door as Mammie called out. "Watch him every second in the kampong. Remember, no foul water or food, only clean!"

Jakob danced along with the excitement. Going to the kampong chased away the longing to be big enough for school. He loved Baboe Min, holding her hand, hearing her Indonesian fairy tales and hearing her sing. They sang together on his favorites, *I am a Captain* and *I am Happy Everywhere*.

The children saw Mammie mornings and afternoons for an hour or so. They would join Mammie and be on their best behavior to make her happy. Best behaviors or worst behaviors, Min was happy, and loved him all the time.

Now that he was thirteen, and Mollie eight, they skirted the edges of their home's large rooms, mostly to stay out of Pappie's way. Pappie was important and busy, and not to be bothered when home for the afternoon rest of *tidur siang*—or most other times.

† † †

Jakob rushed in; Mammie's piano playing beckoned him indoors. He skidded across the veranda out of breath. Once inside, he scuffled along cool tile, purposely switching to tiptoe as he entered the thick-walled coolness of the living room. Catching his breath, he eased himself onto a carved teak couch, his arms resting on an orange cushion. He tried to copy Mammie's long hands flying over the keys. Mollie jumped up, knocked his hands off the keyboard pillow, and settled into his lap, purring.

If he stayed very still, he could remain alone with Mammie. Jakob filled up with her music, noting her feet on the pedals as notes crept louder, then softer. Mollie dug her claws in and leapt off his lap. Jakob's jaw clenched and the back of his neck prickled; Mollie never clawed. Something was wrong, very wrong. As wrong as when Pappie was furious with him all day, working up to punishment. But this was a good day, Sara's birthday.

The veranda drew the best of the cool breezes from the sea a few kilometers away. Voices and dishes rattling told him the servants were preparing Sara's birthday table there. Soon they would all congregate to clap and sing. Their cook Kokkie called, "Ready!"

Mammie walked away from the piano, her hand trailing over Jakob's shoulder. She knew he was there all along. Jakob followed, still struck with unease, a tingling creeping down his spine as the family gathered. Sara's cake with sliced fruit all around stood ready. Jakob edged closer, hoping for a taste of the syrupy goodness soaking into the buttery pastry below.

Fourteen-year-old Albert settled quietly at the table. The empty chair, today decorated for Sara, used to be for their oldest brother. Sixteen by now, Wim was still stuck in the Netherlands—with no communication since the German invasion in May 1940. Two long months later, Radio Orange broadcasted for the first time via the BBC. Exiled Queen Wilhelmina spoke of hope and strength, but that didn't mean that anyone knew where Wim as.

Jakob scrunched his eyes, until everyone at the table became blurry, trying to imagine Wim there. But all he could see was the cruel goodbye, Wim being handed his photo album at the last minute; he'd been given no warning. Like many Dutch Indonesian children, he was being left in the Netherlands for his high school education. Jakob recalled leaning on the ship's deck railings and his own excitement on the voyage back from the Netherlands when Pappie handed over an important gift for him alone, a compass.

Every day thereafter, Pappie and Jakob plotted the ship's course home. They visited the bridge during the day, rolled out the map, and used a sextant at night to navigate by the stars, verifying their plotted course with the compass. The only time Jakob felt at ease with Pappie was during their time at sea.

About Wim, Pappie said, "Our clever firstborn," and Sara he called "our darling one, the light of the family." In the ship's dining room, Pappie had presented Albert with a gift—a botany book. "Our scientist," he said. "And you," he said turning to Jakob, "you are our adventurer." Pappie knew him on the trip home, knew he wasn't always a troublemaker—he truly was an adventurer.

† † †

Sara jumped up and down next to her chair before bending to blow out the candles on her birthday cake. Pappie steadied her chair. "Sit, sit. Sit now." But he did not force her to sit down. Sara whirled around in her new sailor dress, lifting the broad collar that matched her blue and white hair ribbons.

Mammie cried out, "Time to sing!"

"Daar is er een jarig, hoera, hoera, dat kun je wel zien dat is zij!" There is one whose birthday is today, hurray, hurray, you can see it is she! The song ended with everyone pointing at Sara.

Pappie patted her hand. "Ah, you are eight."

The white ribbon almost fell from her hair, and was caught up precariously by her ear. Sara grinned wide and clutched the table edge as if otherwise she might fly away.

With some effort, Sara calmed herself and sat down to open her gifts, saving the biggest for last. She playfully elbowed the tallest box as she opened the other gifts. Each time its oblong length trembled and almost fell.

Jakob stared. Even at age thirteen, waiting defeated him. He would have opened it first.

At last Sara grabbed the mystery package, tore it open, and peeked inside. "Oh, so beautiful!" She scooped her hands around decimeters of blue and white fabric, and all leaned in to see. Out came a pink doll, not porcelain, but

15

with real-looking pink skin. "She's dressed just like me—her new Mammie." Sara blushed and pointed at herself. "I will call her Tina." She angled Tina back and forth causing the doll's blue eyes to flash out from moving eyelids. She cradled and rocked Tina as she ate her cake.

Jakob wanted to hold Tina but didn't dare ask in front of Pappie. He wondered about the mechanics of her eyes. Perhaps he could see how they opened and closed. His fingers itched to find out. Instead he reached for a second piece of cake, which he justified as his since Wim wasn't there to claim his share. Mammie shook her head at him, too greedy. Every morsel dissolved in Jakob's mouth. His jaw ached from the sweet fruit. Good.

Just as Pappie gathered his work papers and went inside, the children all ran out to play. Sara stripped off her dress on the veranda and raced into the yard in her white under-slip, Tina tucked securely under one arm.

"Come in soon," Mammie called. "Afternoon rains are about to start."

"I'll be a soldier," yelled Jakob, "You Indians hide." He stopped at the edge where the machete-trimmed lawn edged into rainforest shrubs and trees. The Indians ran in that direction; he could still hear their progress crashing through the foliage. One eye in each direction like a snake, he surveyed their home and the jungle. Their house stretched out friendly, the verandas on either side like hugging arms. Albert and Sara were quiet now. They must indeed be hiding in the growth, Jakob, thought, not doubling back to sneak into the house. Only Adri, their house *djongos* and chauffeur, crossed the lawn. An ocean breeze caressed Jakob's shoulder blades and cooled the sweat dripping down his back. Perhaps tomorrow he and Albert would take a native prow, a sail-rigged canoe, along the coast. The outrigger would skim along, while they turned in and out of harbors for a swim.

He leaped up—time to capture the Indians. Seeing a flash of white, he grabbed Sara's wrist and tried to grab Albert, who pulled back hard just as Kokkie screamed. "Aieeh! *Oeler* snake!" The whole house emptied. The children dropped hands and clustered close to Mammie and Pappie on the lawn.

Adri carried two hoes and a machete from the garden as weapons. Min stood nearby, her sweet round face calm. Kokkie stood tall. The snake had been after their food, her food. Her chin jutted out as she readied herself to go back in the house.

Jakob whispered in Sara's ear: "*Oeler*s always travel in pairs."

She nodded; this was well known. Holding Tina close, the doll's head tucked under her chin, Sara whispered, "Still now Tina. All will be well."

Adri stood in front of Papa. Skinny, brown, he looked like a palm tree to be climbed next to Pappie's sturdy roundness. Adri nodded at Pappie's whispered words. The family never spoke much once snake-in-the-house maneuvers started. It was the one time Pappie did not yell. Jakob dug his feet in the dirt as Adri, Kokkie, and Min crept into the house. A bird called in the distance, and in the silence, it was like a gunshot. A whack sounded in the house and everyone jumped. In a moment, Min yelled, "Here!" Another thump. Soon Adri emerged, thin rivulets of blood on his hands. He Hoisted two heads with long bodies twitching, trailing in the dirt.

Jakob and Albert rushed up to Adri, and Sara ran to Baboe.

"See how they are camouflaged killers." Albert tapped the still-twitching cobras from behind as the children followed Adri to the servants' quarters. Strange how many times they had found snakes in their home, but never cobras. Jakob's sense of unease returned. Dark came quickly every day of the year. Within minutes, outdoor lanterns were lit.

Shadows flickered in yellow light as the sharp knife in Adri's skilled hands finished the beheadings.

The boys squinted into a halo of light as Adri carefully skinned each snake. Tools hung on the walls. Friendly smells emerged: oil for hinges, petrol for the car, and a wheelbarrow of fresh machete-cut grass to be hauled away. Adri tacked each long skin against the wall. A happy shiver ran down Jakob's back. "Let's ask Pappie about the time he shot the huge python." He leapt up and ran toward the house.

Jakob dashed into the living room ahead of Albert. Mammie and Pappie's heads huddled close to the radio. "Pappie!"

"Not now." Pappie's hand swatted him away, stinging his wrist. Albert caught up and jerked him further back, pushing in front of him. Everyone always wanted him out of the way, because then he was no trouble. The grown-ups attended to war reports every night now, especially the broadcasts of the BBC's Dutch Radio Orange from their exiled *Koningin* Queen Wilhelmina

The boys paused long enough that Mammie and Pappie turned their attention again to the radio. After a bit, so patient, Albert whispered, "What is happening?" He ventured towards the radio. They heard *America, attack, war.*

Jakob yanked him back, surprised Albert would now be the bold one. Grownups never responded to war questions.

"Our Governor-General van Starkenborgh's report. Nothing for children," said Mammie. "Off to sleep. All will be well."

Oh, if only Albert hadn't spoken one more time. Then they could stay up longer, and overhear every word. They could work out their own puzzle about Royal Dutch soldiers, allies, evil Japanese, and bravery.

They walked away and Pappie called after them. "Never mind boys, you may as well come in."

Pappie clicked the radio off, and pointed for them to sit. "First a year and a half of no contact with Wim because of Hitler, and now Hirohito bombed Pearl Harbor in America's Hawaii. The United States declared war on Japan, as has Queen Wilhelmina from Great Britain."

The boys sat, stunned. "Will we be fighting now?" asked Jakob.

Pappie nodded. "Boys, we are prepared. We could be next, along with Borneo. The Japanese have no natural resources of their own, they will want our oil."

"And now, off to bed. Like Pappie said, we will be safe."

Baboe came to check that they were in bed. "Boys, stay." She spoke in musical Malaysian, which could never sound stern. They stayed put for her; Pappie would be mad at Baboe if they got up again.

Jakob pulled feathers from the seams of his pillow and punched it hard. He whispered, "Do you think we could kill two snakes on our own? You and I, the garden *patjols*?"

Albert's white-blond head remained silent in the silver moonlight. He had the annoying habit of pausing, then sometimes not answering at all. Finally he said, "*Ja*, we could. We would do it together."

"*Ja*," Jakob echoed.

With Albert's rhythmic breathing and no longer hearing Mammie and Pappie, he knew they were all asleep. Being the last to fall asleep was almost as interesting as being the first awake in the morning. Crickets chirped. Tjik tjak lizards soft clicking told him they were doing their job, catching and eating all insects which might buzz about.

The door creaked. Jakob jerked from almost asleep to fearful wakefulness, his imagination wild. Could a snake find its way through the house at night?

"Mew." A paw tapped on his mosquito netting. Mollie usually hid mysteriously at night, not appearing until dawn, but here she was.

"Oh, are you scared?" he whispered. "Come on in with me." He pulled Mollie inside the klamboe netting, turning on his side. She curled against his chest, purring. His pounding heart eased. *The Japanese will not attack, that's what the Americans used to think. We will be next.* But tonight he had Mollie, and all was well.

CHAPTER 3

Luce

Calabria, California
September 2004

Dr. Ingstrom leaves a message on my work voice mail before more updates come from my family members. "Hello." Her voice lilts with some kind of European accent, probably Scandinavian, not Dutch like us. "Luce, this is your brother's doctor. Call me; it is crucial for his recovery."

Her message is so direct, just dumped right on my office voice mail. I guess doctors don't have to think about people's feelings. She has no idea how many crucial-crisis family calls I have had. And this one is like an attack on my work day, an attack I don't need, in between appointments with clients.

First, she should establish that we will talk, and then spring the urgency on me. I'm a psychotherapist and treat people too, although no longer at rehab centers. You're supposed to mobilize the family and get each one to communicate by putting pressure on the key players, challenging them from the beginning to pull each other into treatment so they can relate in a new way. I know why she calls me herself in place of the key players, my brother's wife, Cindy, or our parents, Nikki and Jakob. No matter the stakes, Vanderveers don't ask anyone into a therapist's office. We just order everyone to heal, to shape up. As if that works.

I have only minutes between appointments. The shelves around me have hints of everything I am, for my

21

psychotherapy clients to pick up on. The Black Madonna for transformation and redemption in life, pottery bowls to contain all the feelings and life stories which come here, and stones, fabrics, worry dolls from Guatemala. I am surrounded by the international, just as I grew up.

I'll get rid of Dr. Ingstrom's request by calling her. And at the same time, I can keep my *Feasta* promise to Papa after all. To my surprise Dr. Ingstrom picks up herself, and to my greater surprise it scares me. I steady one hand on my desk, and after a quick hello, she says, "Come, here to Houston. Come to a *fightal* ... family appointment." It takes me a moment to realize she means "vital." Yet *fight-all* is more like it.

"Why would that be necessary?" My voice rises. "I've already been to a family week, during rehab number one. I've already been reminded to take care of myself, instead of him. I've already lovingly confronted. I've already seen his kids miss him, his wife cry during rehab number two. He's either going to recover or he's not. Why should I come?"

My eyes rivet on the glass shelves. The objects tell therapy stories too, like the one where the character is cursed, frogs and toads spewing out of her mouth whenever she speaks.

Dr. Ingstrom's tone remains unperturbed. "There are aspects of your family life that you all need to discuss so you can sort out a new way to support each other. There are huge gaps, questions in your family history for mental health and, I believe you would know, war trauma."

I'm hypnotized by her voice, the grammar and pronunciations just like my parents, without the arguments. The calm cadence of her words calms me.

"What do you mean 'war'?" My voice sounds far away, as if someone else were speaking.

"The trauma of what your mother and father experienced. How could they describe it? For your father, those Japanese concentration camps, they were brutal. So much wasn't said. Surely this had an impact on how everyone did not talk about feelings in your family. So now, your dad, Jakob, I think he will talk."

No, he won't. His words for the past are locked in a black box like those found after airplane wrecks, but with no hinges, no keyholes, nothing. Yeah, he'll talk, but not about the war years.

"Can I ask you what your credentials are?" I challenge.

"I'm the treatment director here, and an addictionologist, MD. My license to practice medicine is in family practice. Once I learned about addictions recovery twenty years ago, I made it my *bisseenuss* to learn all I could about family therapy."

Her voice sounds so self-assured, first a slightly deeper warm tone, then rising again. She has taken time out of her day, bringing up what no one ever brought up before, Papa's Japanese concentration camp years. In my experience, however reluctantly I think so now, the main credential is: does my helper care? She does. She's tying everything up in one caring package—past, present, my pulsing heart. I could trust this caring voice, and that terrifies me.

"Okay, so why come all the way out to you … from California? When and who will we be meeting with?"

"Me."

She's the director, and she wants to meet with us herself?

"Your brother's wife, Cindy, and your sister, Corrie, have agreed. I think your parents are ready to meet. Alby is still physically suffering from the overdose; I do hope he can join us. Soon would be good. I can see you next Wednesday."

So soon, a week from today. Just to help Alby, who I'm sure doesn't want help. I yearn to explain, to hear her voice soften again. I always go to him, he never comes to me. Month by month, year to year it's as if I don't exist, and now she wants me to drop everything, and buy an expensive last-minute ticket to go see him for "fight-all" Vanderveer time? I don't think so.

I've been clutching an obsidian shard in my hand, culled from the nature shelf of the wall unit—its pebbles, rocks, tiny shells. As the ragged edges dig in, I see us as children on one of our meet-the-people-in-yet-another-new-home walks, side by side. I see us as teens at the first Texas hospital thirty years ago, my warm hand in his cold hand, tubes everywhere. Corrie too somewhere, lost in it all. Alby could have died then. A part of him did die then, and I'll never forget. I can't let him die on my watch.

I hear the faraway voice again that's mine. "I'll come."

We say good-bye.

It's Papa I think of when we hang up, not Alby, because I did it now. I'm crazy to go again, but I am. Surely brothers in their forties don't really die I try to reassure myself, but Papa? He always acted as if he would die if he told of his war years, his family and home country he lost forever. By claiming that Papa will tell of his concentration camp—kamp—years, it's like she's telling me he'll die. When Mama told of being eight years old when the Germans marched in, about bombings, about knitting needles in blocked electric outlets, of malnutrition and abscesses, and savoring fleeting times of good food, we always turned to Papa expectantly.

Nothing.

Once I asked him at dinnertime. Chopped up words sprung from my tight throat, half Dutch, half English. "Please tell us a story about the oorlog—war."

His hands trembled as he reached for more food, spooning a mountain of Indonesian nasigoreng rice on his plate. The light in his eyes dimmed as he made neat stacks of his food, lifting large forkfuls of meat, rice, cucumber to his mouth. He miscalculated. With only a few bites his plate was clean.

"Papa," I said, "what about … "

His fist pounded the table, his water glass shook. "Enough!"

He was often mad, but about this? He glared at me, ate several bites, then glanced at me, as if he was sorry, which he would never say. "How about I tell you about our pet monkey before the war."

Corrie cheerfully chomped on her own spicy *nasigoreng*, the only one of us who liked the Indonesian rice dish. "Papa, you already told us about the monkey."

Silence.

I had lost my appetite. Papa never lost his.

† † †

I lurch to the couch, clutching a pillow to my heaving belly. Sobs rumble up as I press my wet face to cool leather. I just told a stranger I would come to Houston for a week, without consulting my husband and son. And this stranger called before anyone in my family reached out to me again. I hold my breath, glance at the clock—two minutes to quell tears so I can meet with my next client. I scribble a note that says, *Luce's appointments will be running five minutes late all day.* I jostle open the office door with paper and tape in hand.

Fortunately, or perhaps another force is working it's will behind the scenes, the waiting room is deserted. Crumpling the note in my hand, I check the rest of my voice mails. Gene, who never misses appointments, called to say he can't make it due to an emergency work meeting. A whole hour to myself now. Grace, a God-gift for this strangest of times.

The war, World War II. It is a rusted over, dead ache inside of me that tears my heart, my soul and won't let go. Maybe I too have guilty secrets. I abandoned them all before at that other hospital. Now a generation later, if they will gather one more time at a hospital, I have to as well. So I want to go. I catch myself. Want is too strong a word. It's what I do, I *will* go.

I gaze at my office door, the emptiness beyond. I guess I believe that if I show up from far away to Dr. Ingstrom's waiting room, that we will all get there. There's no ocean in between California and Texas, but there is great distance, and traveling, this the Vanderveers can do.

If we had never left Holland, maybe none of this would have happened. No Alby emergencies, or let's face it, no emergency with my own alcoholism. No Corrie proudly focusing on professional life, with no family to come home to. That's what Mama always yelled at the end of every *ruzie*—argument with Papa—*if we never left* ... I know the script. I hated her words, but deep inside I wonder, *Is it true?*

I am safe from *ruzie* here in Calabria, a thousand miles away from my family. Most days, my life with Daniel and Vincent feels secure. This small farming community next to a big city has become America, Dutch farm country, and home to me. Yet to know we are all safe, to bring all of us home, to feel safer inside, this is what I long for.

Family secrets pull on me, like they always did. From my earliest U.S. memories, we went to the library weekly, filling satchels of books. All of us spent up to an hour in Houston's Braeburn Library. Corrie plopped down on the rug, leaning against the picture book section. Alby roamed back and forth in Children's Nonfiction, finding cars and planes in the encyclopedia. I, as a lonely eleven-year-old with few friends, had exhausted the children's sections and perused Adult New Fiction, Young Adult, and my favorites: *Time Life* books. Something about one cover drew me in. Grainy gray photographs, skeletal ghost people.

Quiet footsteps approached, a velvety voice asked, "Are you sure you want to look at those pictures?"

I closed the book with a snap, as if I'd been caught with the worst book in the world. I had been found out— witnessing the horrific. Hot guilt flooded me as if I'd hurt and killed those people, or defiled them all over again by finding their pictures.

I looked away, my eyes stinging. "Yes ma'am, it's okay with my parents."

"Do you know what this is?" she whispered. Her perfume drifted to me as she bent down.

"Yes, I know," I whispered back. "The Holocaust, World War II. The Nazis killed millions of Jewish people."

"My people honey, my people." Her eyes glowed, her mouth looked sad. She patted my shoulder, then walked away.

My heart beat fast. She wasn't mad at me, but I didn't need to open the book again that afternoon anyway. Pasted in front of my eyes were gray photos of lifeless bodies loosely held in striped clothing. If they were standing or sitting, you could tell they were alive. If lying down, stacked, then they were dead. How could a skeleton person escape, with or without the prison clothes? So few survived. How could six million people die?

I moved with purpose when we got home, bumping the book bags into the closet, where they lived, to be read throughout the week. The *Time Life* books weren't stored there; they couldn't be checked out. All the better, they were my secret. I could find them again, every library visit. As I shoved in one more bag, I found the Dutch rubber boots Beppe and Pake still sent each year. I pulled on my pair, wiggling my feet down the felt lining, noticing how good they still felt. Tugging them off and returning them, I touched something old and worn in the back corner. I ran my fingers over cracked leather and pulled out a bag.

"Papa, did you forget this bag?" I called.

He hurried over. "No, this bag is not for you. You leave that alone." He jerked it away from me, bumping my mouth. Then he was gone.

Caught again, all in one day. I touched a little drop of blood on my inside lip. I shouldn't cry, I shouldn't speak. He hadn't intended to hurt me. The bag was gone.

† † †

Mama may have seen something, she often saw so much. That night she explained to me, again, about the Holocaust and concentration camps in Europe.

I felt we should whisper, like the librarian. "Did you and Beppe and Pake — my grandparents — go into concentration camps?"

"No, for two reasons, *schatje*," said Mama, calling me her little treasure. She didn't bother to whisper. "We were not Jewish. We only hid a few Jewish people early in the war, on our farm — *de boerderij*. Soon Pake said he wished we could do more, but couldn't risk it. He had to keep us alive." Her eyes became somber and peaceful at the same time. "Secondly, Pake never was caught. The Nazis sent all the able-bodied men to labor camps, almost as bad as concentration camps. We always had a warning and hid him just in time."

"Was that hard?" I asked. But I knew the answer was yes. "And how did Papa end up in concentration camps then?" I did know Indonesia was my father's home country. But had always thought it was Holland that he missed, not the tropics.

Mama's words became more precise. "Indonesia, then, was called the Dutch East Indies … or Netherlands East Indies. All the Dutch and Europeans had to go into Japanese concentration camps. Many people died." This is what I got sometimes — a history lesson but not a family lesson.

"But Papa and his family didn't die."

"Oh *schatje*, of course not Papa, or you wouldn't be here. But some of his family, yes, they died. You know that. You never met your *Opa*, Papa's daddy, or *Oom* Albert, your uncle."

The chill of real people dying, not the history lesson. My *Opa* and *Oom* Albert — Alby's namesake. "What happened to Papa and to them? Will he tell me?"

Mama shook her head. "First, he was in a concentration *kamp* with family, then later all alone. He will never want you to know that pain."

But all I heard was, he will never want you ... to know.

††††

Jakob

Billiton Island
Mid-December 1941

At night Jakob wondered about Tina's eyes, how they flashed and turned inside her soft plasticine head. Finally, on this full moon night, he forced himself to stay awake. He waited until Min had left Albert and him to sleep. Pappie snored steadily, so he could make his hushed way to Sara's room. Soon he had Tina in the kitchen.

In the moonlight his fingers probed how Tina's eyes flicked back and forth. When turned this way and that, her blue eyes clicked closed, then opened. Just as he spied the dark gap behind Tina's eyes, he heard a noise and stopped. No further sound, except an eye click from Tina. He took a breath. *I will be ever so careful.* Using Kokkie's kitchen screwdriver, he poked gently into the space just behind the whites of Tina's eyes.

Another noise, padding feet. He froze. Pappie would hate him.

"Jakob, what are you doing now?" It was only Albert, who rarely woke up easily. Albert spotted Tina on the drain rack. "*Ai*, you are hurting the doll."

"No, I'm not. Just learning," hissed Jakob.

"*Ja*, see." Albert jabbed a finger at Tina's face.

A dark scratch had appeared by Tina's left eye. He must have hurt her with the screwdriver. Her pale flesh had the look of a tear as if Tina were crying. Jakob rubbed the spot with a dish towel, still there. He pressed his finger into

Kokkie's flour tin and rubbed it on the mark. Still there."Oh, it won't go away."

"Maybe no one will notice," Albert said. "Quick to bed."

Jakob eased the lid back on the flour, wiped the screwdriver, and put it back in the drawer. He still knew nothing about Tina's eyes. And worse—Sara would notice.

Albert kept watch as Jakob tiptoed back into Sara's room, heart pounding. He eased the mosquito netting up from Sara's bed and tucked Tina next to her. Holding his breath, he draped the klamboe down. When Sara noticed in the morning, he would make it up to her. He would tell her she could come to his secret hiding place; he would push her doll carriage if only she would not cry. He could not tell which was worse about the morning to come: to hurt Sara's heart, or for Pappie to be mad and start yelling and spanking.

† † †

Jakob was hardly asleep when the dawn light crept in. Of the three children yet at home, he always awoke first. He liked his reconnaissance time to greet or avoid Pappie and then find Kokkie and Mammie. Today he could hear the staccato voices of the radio already.

Pappie yelled, "Liesbet!" for Mammie.

Sara must be up already, crying over Tina.

Albert mumbled, "What," opened his eyes, and turned over. Even half asleep, Albert knew he was never the one in trouble. Jakob glanced at the third bed, already empty one and a half years. No Wim to grin and say, "*Hoi*, come on."

He was left to wonder. Now Pappie knew that Jakob was this kind of boy, always the bad one. The punishment would be severe. Jakob left his room and pressed back against the wall. Strength, he thought, and clenched his fists. If he thought like a snake, or like the Indians in his American-West books, who thought like their prey, he would become a better fighter, even a soldier.

He strolled into the living room. Pappie and Mammie looked serious, not angry. Pappie's hands gripped the radio table.

The radio announcer spoke in an urgent voice. "The Japanese invaded Borneo."

"More, more, more," Pappie said. "All these countries falling, and they want us. Oh, they want us. And the British, we have to depend on them to fight to the finish for Northern Borneo. If only we could rely on the courage of the KNL for Dutch Borneo.

Mammie stood straight in her nightgown and dressing gown, her hands on Pappie's shoulders, murmuring, "So Willem, we will make our plans."

He lifted his hands to hers. "The Japanese are ever so much closer."

"What? Will we be fighting?" Jacob interrupted. "We can beat the Japanese!" He wondered when they would grab their rifles.

Mammie turned to him, pale, but her eyes were warm. "The men may fight; you, never. War is not for children."

When Mammie went to Kokkie, Jakob followed, as if he would go to the breakfast table as usual. But instead, he diverted his route to sneak up behind Pappie. Keeping Indian-scout quiet, he matched Pappie's footsteps further into the darkened room. Somber shutters blocked the warm sunlight and let cool air in. The left wall sideboard looked like Oma and Opa's in Nederland, porcelain dishware inside and a plush cloth cover he ran his fingers over—the best kind. Then he slid his fingers over the cool, smooth piano too. Nearing Pappie, he yearned to touch and stroke his red hair, but kept low instead. This was the rare chance to sneak to the gun cabinet wall. He stood stock-still when Pappie lifted his key to the lock.

His neck prickled, a whoosh of air and motion and his cheek stung. He turned to see Mammie, her face tired and angry. His eyes burned with tears. She had never struck him before.

Mammie gripped his shoulders, "Stay away from guns and fighting. War is not for children. We will be safe."

† † †

I rub the cold leather office chair I'm curled into, to come back to the moment. I check my face for the flushed look of tears and sorrow, but believe I look normal. Just like Papa, not showing pain.

This one hour felt like a day or a lifetime. My whole body aches with fatigue and I, usually not a nap taker, want nothing more than sleep. This pull of the past is exhausting me. Only two sessions left. Later, I drive home in rain over hissing country roads.

† † †

Vincent's bicycle lies abandoned on the hedge and Daniel's work truck dominates the driveway when I splash up to our home.

I drop my work bag just inside the door. "Phew!"

"Honey, if you would always put your stuff in the same place …," Daniel chides.

"You wouldn't lose it and go looking for it later," Vincent finishes.

"Yeah, yeah, yeah." I move my things to a living room chair. "Go put your bicycle in the garage where it belongs," I say gruffly.

"What's wrong?" Daniel asks.

"Alby's doctor called. I've been asked to go to Houston."

"You're kidding! You've been out to Texas a million times for your family. Is he that close to dying?"

"Maybe. That, and this doctor is so different. It's like she knows our family already."

It's our family night, the rare time we three sit down together for dinner. I head into my home office, avoiding topics like how I've already promised I'll go and how expensive my last-minute ticket will be. I have one desire — to search the bottom of my old metal file cabinet and find the farm coveralls I wore as a child and touch their soft, ink-blue cotton.

"I'll show you what I mean later," I yell.

No response from Daniel, who can't hear from the other room.

After dinner I pass around the coveralls. Daniel and Vincent admire my embroidery handiwork. A sailboat, a farmhouse and two farmers — my grandparents Beppe and Pake.

Daniel caresses the weave, touches an old KLM Royal Dutch Airlines patch Mama had sewn on before my own artistry. "Ah, the coveralls."

Vincent tips his chair back. "What's the deal with the coveralls?"

"Chair, Vincent, it's going to break." I reach out to pull his chair down. "When I was a teenager, I still had these, the last pair from being six years old on the farm with Beppe and Pake. I discovered if I cut off the legs, I could still squeeze into them as a jacket. I was skinny as a teenager, and Mammie bought all our childhood clothes in enormous sizes so we could grow into them. I loved the coveralls because they reminded me of life at the farm, before we had to leave our homeland for another country and then another. I'll show you more."

I jump up, almost knocking over a water pitcher that Vincent grabs, rolling his eyes, and go pull a photo album out of the same file cabinet. Images of Beppe and Pake's Dutch farm fill page after page. In one, I'm sitting on the farm wagon next to Pake. "See, this is me in the coveralls, helping Pake in the fields. Those captions in Dutch were written by your grandmother, who recorded our moves from country to country."

Vincent flips through more pages. Palm trees, desert. "This isn't Holland."

"No, there we are in Iran, where Uncle Alby was born."

"Mom, you've got him on your lap like you're going to drop him on the ground."

Baby Alby looks off balance, yet happy. "I would never have dropped him." I smooth crisp pages of photos, rice paper in between, turn the pages. "We went back and forth: to the Netherlands, then Iran again, then the Netherlands to wait to immigrate to America. Here we're in Utah and that's baby Corrie. I wish she would call me."

"Mom, you had cowboy boots!"

"Oh yeah, I wish I still had those."

"Why don't you call Corrie?" Daniel asks.

"Because I want her to call me," I snap.

Daniel raises his eyebrows. I know what he's thinking: I'm being loud just like a Vanderveer.

I want my brother to be well enough to call me. I want my sister to want to call me. She and I used to call each other regularly, and now a wretched reserve on her part.

"Guys, I do want to go to Houston. I'm sorry it's so sudden. I think I'll be gone only a week."

"So they never call you, and yet you've decided to go," Daniel says. He knows I'm avoiding discussion and presenting my decision as fact.

"Yeah, or I'll worry."

Vincent slowly tips his chair back, looking right at me. "Oh yeah, Mom, we wouldn't want you to worry."

"Okay, Vincent, I get your drift."

Daniel looks at me. For moments where I expect only his frustration, we connect with tired eyes. He shrugs his shoulders. "Come back to us well. Come back to us, way over all of this worry," he singsongs.

"No problem." My stomach clenches, because this visit will be all problems, and apparently, all different.

CHAPTER 4

The great thing about my nighttime journaling habit is that it's every night. Some people call their mom every day — I journal.

September 23, 2004

I do know where the worry comes from. If I could talk to Alby right now, or if Corrie really wanted to talk to me, this is what I would tell them. We were there when our papa was a little boy in the wrong kind of camp, lying in mud, full tropic sun, in his own blood, scrambling up, running away with a crust of bread, leaving teeth behind. He had won. But there was no victory to celebrate when one lived and so many died.

We were there when our mama was a little girl in darkest winter. Frozen and quiet, she kept her eyes straight ahead as she was told. Her father hid under the floorboards of their Dutch farmhouse, while her mother did the talking. The German soldiers stared at little Nikki. They always talked to Mem, while looking down at her, in a way that made her tremble. Even the slightest twitch of her eyes could give Heit away.

Our parents met years later, in the Netherlands, where Dutch Indonesians who had lost their country came. My father found a home in my mother's heart.

Four years later I was born. First I became the focus, then my brother and sister in turn. I saw all of Papa's photos of us today — from the Netherlands, to Iran, back to the Netherlands, to Utah, and then to Texas. There we were, as kids, grinning always. Our bangs were perpetually crooked, suffering from Mama's home haircuts. The bangs became more skewed and shorter every time Mama tried to fix them. Alby and I didn't care. Corrie, however, ended up wailing in front of the mirror at every snipping episode. Finally Mama gave up and took us three to her salon; an ecstatic Corrie going first, indifferent me next, and a scowling Alby last.

Papa's sorrow was covered up by our smiles, beaming again for each snapshot. When he did smile in photos, his mouth was as crooked as our bangs, partly due to the bridge in his mouth from those teeth lost fighting for bread; partly from his unnamed sorrow.

So many memories. God, I would like my own crooked smile to go away. I would like to feel that spark of joy I had before the phone call. Must that joy be so fragile? I yearn to feel and fan the spark of hope I felt when Dr. Ingstrom said Papa would talk.

† † †

A few days later, I'm packing.

Fifteen-year-old Vincent leans against the doorjamb, his head almost to the top. In his black jeans and black T-shirt, his skinny body barely blocks the doorway. "Why are you going again?" he asks.

"Well, your uncle really did a number on himself this time. His doctor wants us to try to help him in a new way."

"Why do they need you? I can't believe you're going again."

"You would help your cousins Marina and Wade. I think he can change, and maybe this time we can say things that no one has ever said before in our family."

"All our Houston family ever does is say stuff, fast, interrupting each other, and laughing. Keeping us poor kids up late at night."

I glance up at him with amusement. "As if you care if you're up late."

"It's true. They talk all the time and no one can get a word in. Is this doctor like—aaieeh!" He leaps, Karate-style, his

36

arms cut the air as if breaking wood. "Now you talk, now you, ai-yah! Then maybe she can get them to take turns talking." He kicks the closet door shut.

I laugh hard. "Oh, honey. Yeah maybe, she'll have to be like that." Maybe I'll have to be like that.

"Mom, I think you could help out." He has the simple confidence I lost, that a family can change. He's too old to say he'll miss me, but I can see it in his eyes. I pat the spot next to me and he bounces on the bed.

"Well, if anyone stops talking long enough to listen, I'll try. Maybe Dr. Ingstrom will get the family to talk, to be open, even about the war years."

He straightens up. "I thought they didn't talk about that stuff."

"Well, I guess we will now."

Vincent is fascinated by World War II history. When Holocaust survivors came and talked to his classroom, he told the class that there were Japanese concentration camps too, which his grandfather survived.

Daniel comes in and joins us on the bed, leaning over the stacks of clothes to hug me. His glasses bump mine. "You look tired."

I lean into him. "I am." How does he know I'm not sleeping well?

He jumps up readily for a man in his fifties, pulling Vincent off the bed and wrestling him against the wall. I hear bonking bodies still thudding into the walls as I trudge out to make my last-minute phone calls. I wish I was still thin like Daniel. I pat my fortysomething plump belly. No one seems to mind the extra pounds, except me.

I call Corrie, who is on her way to choir practice. I can't help but count it up, two weeks now with no calls from family. My disappointment is a chilled sadness inside, with instructions. *Don't speak up, you'll be hurt worse.*

"Glad you're coming, Sis," she says. "I'll pick you up at the airport." No note of apology in her voice.

37

I slowly punch in Mama and Papa's phone number. My parents, perhaps because they subjected me to moves from Nederland to Iran, and back again, and then to America, never questioned my living far away — first in Colorado, and now in California.

As we talk, Mama asks in her most fatigued tone, one I recognize as part of all our Vanderveer struggles, "So who will you see while you are here? What are your plans?"

Once I arrive in Houston, I am expected to designate virtually every minute to family. There is no understanding of a balance of time to be with friends, or alone. The question means: Don't go, be with us. You are with us, or not.

"Yes," I say, "I will be with the family."

† † †

In the early morning, Daniel and I rumble along in his big truck. I have the first San José-Houston flight out of Mineta International Airport. Large work trucks can't be in the carpool lane. Instead, as the traffic hour builds, we merge into the slow lane, which makes me grit my teeth. On and off, I remember to pray.

Like Papa, I am a nervous traveler. All I know of my journeys with him is hurry up, arrive, collapse. At the end of trips to Houston, I always lie to Papa about my departures, saying flights are scheduled later than they are. When I leave, we hug calmly at the door because of my clever lie. He loves to know I've left early enough to be prepared for every possible disaster.

Sometimes I imagine Papa gathering every potential calamity to him as if he were conducting an orchestra of worriers. He stands, directing all the instruments. The violinists pluck their strings, bowless at first, while the timpani drums build fluttering heartbeat taps. The tension builds. He closes his eyes, and then looks up glaring, ready to bring in an entire section of violins or brass for the disaster sure to come.

Me, I wanted to escape, not conduct an entire orchestra. There is a chamber ensemble in my head—acoustic guitar, flute—going for the harmonic peace that would transcend it all. The peace inside doesn't always work, especially on the way to Houston. Especially when it's too late to turn around. I'm committed.

My vision narrows to the dashboard. *Now you've done it. You're really leaving; You spent eight hundred dollars on airfare. You're always leaving. This marks six years of trying to help your brother.* My pulse is timpani-drumming with a *whoosh-whoosh*, faster and faster in my ears. I press myself back against the seat, and do the breathing trick. I exhale slowly to a count of *one, two, three, four, five* and inhale slowly to a count of *one, two, three, four.* My brain is screaming in panic. I stretch my legs out again, my back's hurting too.

Daniel puts his hand on my shoulder. "Are you okay, honey?"

"I'm great. I'm glad I'm taking this one last flight." Tunnel vision widens. I won't let Daniel say *I told you so,* about this panic attack. Besides, both he and I thought they were long gone, and now—one a week. I can conquer this.

Breathing, breathing. Eardrum timpani drums subside. Daniel's favorite '70s rock and roll seeps in, only slightly louder than the roar of the diesel engine. The heater kicks in and warmth seeps into my bones. *I'm scared ... but of what?* My anxious gasps shift to normal breathing. Looking out the window we see gray hills turn green in the early morning light. Daniel points out distant deer to the west. What he sees easily I strain to discern through my bifocal glasses. At last I can see the deer, white tails bobbing as they make their way into a ribbon of dark-green trees.

Highway 101 leaves the hills, cuts through neighborhoods, and enters the city as we near the airport in San José. I tense again, counting the minutes between every street and freeway in my mind. I can notice my ragged panic-style breathing, and slow it down, but can't help naming each exit silently as if this means I can hurry our progress along. I am so edgy that I wish I could have lied to myself about the actual departure time.

Near the airport I turn to Daniel, speaking loudly above his rock-and-roll-damaged hearing and our noisy ride. A stranger would think I was screaming angrily at him. "Will the truck fit through the overhang in the drop-off zone?"

"Of course it will fit; you are such a Vanderveer. Relax. You have lots of time." He squeezes my hand.

I look at the dashboard clock. He's right, yet I clench my knees again around the luggage at my feet.

Finally, we pull in next to compacts and SUVs. Daniel sprints around the truck, grinning. We hug and he says, "I know you're stressed out, but chill now. I love you. Call us."

His directives sound possible this morning. I can chill now. I am on time, a common yet necessary miracle for a traveling Vanderveer. I lied to Daniel too, told him the flight was earlier that it really is; my on-time is two hours early, his is a mere hour. Clearly he is not as well trained in the ways of disaster as I am.

† † †

Like my papa, the jitters subside once I reach the true first step of the journey, gate 62. A family is traveling together with a toddler and baby. The husband holds his squirming little boy, and then lets him run around with a kiddy leash connected to his wrist. Usually I wonder about such restraints; today it looks like a great idea: no danger, no one lost.

I call Corrie on my cell.

"Hey, Luce!" She sounds so pleased to talk to me. I guess she's happy to sit around and let me to do all the calling.

"How is Alby?"

"Oh, he's in bad physical shape, but talking up a storm and insisting on leaving. The staff put him on another seventy-two-hour hold for trying to leave when he's paranoid. He called one of his board members and said their competing bioresearch company is plotting to keep him locked up. So now the treatment program took his cell phone away, but he still manages to make more calls."

"He's always determined. There's no stopping him. So why am I coming out again?"

"You're coming out for me, right?"

"Yep, just for you." Funny how she thinks the joke is I'm coming out for her, not Alby. Ha-ha. But I'm really coming out for Papa, to fill that big gap inside him, or is it to fill the gap between us? I know Papa was like a force of nature while we were growing up, demanding great grades, great accomplishments, yelling, cajoling, nagging. There was much he expected of me as the oldest. But what I expected of him, to know the gap once filled with unspeakable years of captivity, that vacuum is still there. A therapist colleague once said to me, "The greatest loss we can ever have is the loss of what we never had." I never knew about Papa's journey from childhood to adulthood. For years, his only comment was, *it is too terrible to tell you.*

I shake my head, trying to listen carefully and focusing on the leashed toddler crawling onto his dad's lap.

"I don't know if anyone's getting through to him," Corrie continues. "Dr. Ingstrom told him about his liver. Even I could see his abdomen is swollen on one side. But he doesn't want to talk about that, just work."

"Great, the competing company must have attacked his liver too. Maybe he'll have himself discharged by the time I get there."

"You sound as gloom and doom as Mama. Actually, you sound totally burned out on Alby. This is life and death, Luce."

"That's why I'm burned out. Doesn't he get it?"

"It's a *seven-tee-two*-hour hold, and no matter what we do, Alby will either *ixcept* help or he won't." As the youngest, Corrie absorbed a Texan drawl, the last of the travel accents.

"Yeah, and what will you do if he leaves the second he's off the psychiatric hold? Just *ixcept*?"

"Ha-ha, my accent's not that thick. I don't know."

"I don't know either. See you, love you."

I should relax. Most people would feel secure to have their brother on lock-down with hospital staff all around. Maybe that's why Dr. Ingstrom wants Alby and Papa to talk over old secrets, to corral one and free the other.

† † †

I pass the four-hour plane ride trying unsuccessfully to doze. Ever since the Alby-in-crisis-again call, I've struggled with endless fatigue. As the plane drops for descent, nausea hits. Saliva pools in the sides of my mouth. Tired of the buzz of the plane, I remember loud prop-plane landings whenever we landed in Iran when I was three, four, and five. Then I knew we would return to Nederland again. Beppe *en* Pake, the rootedness of their farm waited for us.

As I rest my forehead against the icy plane window, tears sting my cheeks. So many losses and moves for the little kid I was. First, we made our home in Nederland's winter cold and wet clover-green spring, wildflowers and chilly days at North Sea beaches like Scheveningen. Then, in Abadan, Iran: always baking hot, school, the relief of the cold swimming pool. Next, a few temporary homes again in Nederland, apartments stretching out into the gray wintertime. We left in January, in the midst of that gray wintertime. Beppe and Pake had waived good-bye at the *boerderij*
, our other family at Schiphol Airport, Amsterdam. Then, there was Utah, easing into four seasons; the first snow always fell on our new American holiday, Thanksgiving. Finally, the irony of our last home, Houston—no lovely seasons. The sodden, gritty heat of the Gulf Coast mixed with wet winter cold. Spring and fall each spanned a couple of days. I know now, that although not on the equator, half the Houston year mimics the Indonesian islands' weather

patterns: heat, heat, sweat, rain, baked dry, occasional cool, repeat.

I grab a damp cocktail napkin to wipe my tears. The plane breaks through the cloud floor to glide above dark-green woodlands. To the north of the runways, flooded rice fields and lakes shimmer. I reluctantly made this city my home for twenty years, yet never touched those particular lakes.

Houston is fertile; everything grows. Moldy odors rise on bath towels within a day. After extended rain and flooding, the more sinister black mold takes hold in walls and creeps through homes. Unwanted foliage is thick—vines choke trees. Stubbly grass pokes bare feet running across lawns. The wanted growth struggles in the claylike soil: roses, flowers, vegetables all must be pampered to take hold and grow. Dutch tulip bulbs go in the refrigerator to fake winter cold, then into the soil, blooming once in the spring. They must be replaced annually with another refrigerated generation.

† † †

At the luggage carousel I see Corrie talking away on her cell phone. She hangs up when she sees me. We grab each other hard; I like how she folds into a hug which makes me miss Alby. The wish for him to be okay, to be reachable, is like a physical ache.

Corrie is compact in her petite-size jacket with gold buttons. Watching her teeter in her high heels to my suitcase, I am reminded that Alby and I have the solid build in the family, she the slender. Her wispy wrists bend as she makes a gesture to haul my suitcase to her side.

I wave her away. "I got it." I am tall and sturdy with an incongruous round face at the top of my length. On my bad days, I believe I look like a bobble-head doll.

In her new VW Passat, Corrie expertly spins down the spiral driveway out of the parking garage and gets us on the freeway. "Let's stop for some sustenance on the way to the parental units."

I smile at her parody of old *Saturday Night Live* episodes. "No, we'd best go directly to the parental units." I press my aching back into the seat. "And how are they?"

"What do you mean 'go directly'?" Corrie says in her negotiating-a-marketing-deal-at-work tone. "I told Papa you and I would stop somewhere together, just the two of us."

My cell phones rings. It's a number with a 713 area code — Houston.

"Papa," I observe. "I can't believe it." We both laugh, and I answer, "Hi, Papa. Yep, your *Eagle* has landed."

"*Liefje. Toe nou.* Come on now. And don't stop like Corrie said you would. You'll be exhausted. Mama worked all day on a nice meal."

"Don't worry, Papa," goes the familiar refrain. "We'll be home soon, *liefs*."

"I love you too, Liefje. We will wait." Guilt. He can't stand to wait.

Corrie rolls her eyes at me as she pulls up to the next traffic light.

"Hey Corrie, this would make a great song, we could call it 'Don't Worry Daddy, Everything Will Be Alright.'"

We spontaneously break into the song, first both of us on melody, then Corrie breaking into perfectly pitched woo-woo-woos.

She throws an arm over my shoulder and breathes *ahhhh*. She says that she, too, has been stressed, and now we laugh. "Luce, don't give in so easy. Let's go have our private moments. You know how it will be once we're in the hubbub."

I hate being a mood breaker, but I want to give Papa his win, and arrive home quickly. "I'm tired. I really would like to just go straight there."

"Come awwwnn," Corrie says.

"I just can't handle them waiting. I'm too tired and stressed. You come on," I say.

"You treat them like they're going to break. There's no pleasing them no matter what we do."

"True, but Corrie? You know you could have called me to go over stuff before I ever came."

She brakes hard and sighs just like Mama. "Okay, twist the knife. I just couldn't talk then. So 'later, gator' on our talk. Would you relax, please? I'll get us both there."

I jostle one of the Cokes we picked up at the airport. It spills on my hand and up my sleeve. "Oh, no! I'm so sorry. It's on your floorboard. Your brand-new car. I bet these floor mats haven't seen a fleck of dirt."

"Luce." She sighs. "Just use these napkins. Stop worrying and being so sorry all the time. It's going to be okay. I'll just have to tell you the short version of the new man in my life. He's taking me to early breakfast tomorrow before our family meeting."

Usually she talks a mile a minute about her marketing work; now she's talking to me in measured slow words, and I wish we had stopped for a long enough visit, before being pulled to Vanderveer Central. But changing my mind again would be even worse.

Rain starts as Corrie whooshes us through empty Sunday streets. She gently brakes, changing her wiper speeds for every variation of rain.

"So, okay, tell me about the guy."

She glances at me. "You look like you're not feeling well."

"I feel great. I just got nauseated from the plane trip." My hands are sweaty around the cold Coca-Cola cup. I'm worrying of course, and I can't fool her.

"Nah," she says. "Actually I think it's your gloom and doom thing."

"Thanks, you make it so nice to be with you."

She cracks up laughing and spits some Coke at the windshield.

I burst out laughing too. "Ooh, this poor new car."

"There's that wild laugh of yours," she chokes out, while I smear her view trying to get Coke off the windshield.

We arrive. Papa is on the doorstep already, and the dogs explode into barking behind him.

"*Heh, heh*, here you are at last," says Papa, like it doesn't make an impact that we hurried straight here. Since I last saw him, his cheeks have sunk down, his eyes are sadder. His small advantage in height over me has disappeared, leaving us eye to eye. Pink scalp glows through his white hair. He grips the aluminum cane he always refused to use before, and his other trembling hand reaches for my suitcase. "Come on, come on. Give me the suitcase."

"I'll get it. Look, it just rolls."

Mama scoots in behind him from the kitchen. Covered with a film of sweat from cooking, her cheeks are as round and high like Beppe's were. When she squeezes me in a hug, she strokes the back of my head for a moment, as if I am here to be comforted, not to help. "Corrie said you'd be a little later, but dinner will be ready soon."

Corrie elbows me. "See?"

Papa captures my suitcase. "This way." We dodge the cockapoos, who are now licking my ankles. He breathes heavily by the time we get to the guest room. "Look, I fixed the suitcase stand, so one side is propped up." He hasn't stopped tinkering with things.

Mama yells, "Oh Jakob, let her rest. Don't fuss."

Defying Mama, we hang out as I unpack and Papa shifts himself to a chair, grimacing as he sits. Alby masked his injuries and pain from their accident when he was a teen, not Papa. After the accident, his pain was on display, as if his defense for foolishly going up in an experimental ultralight plane with his son was, *See, I am still paying the price for what happened.*

Within ten minutes, we are at the dinner table, and Mama fusses. Steam rises up from my favorite Dutch soup, the simple one from our childhood, vegetable with meatballs. "You girls already ate?" We shake our heads. "So who just wants soup and who wants a whole dinner?" Automatically Mama puts a soup bowl down for Corrie, and a plate and bowl for me.

Corrie unsuccessfully waves her hand over her bowl. "Just a little." She gets a full ladle.

"Sit, sit," says Mama as I try to enter the kitchen to help her. Her wispy hair is plastered to her round face. She brings in roast beef, green beans, salad—everything healthy and simple. Real butter melts on the beans. We pass around a nutmeg grater to bring out their flavor, signs of home.

"I can't stay long," says Corrie. "We all have an early appointment tomorrow."

No crazy fast talk yet. No talk about what's really going on.

"So did you hear anything new about Alby?" I ask.

A pained frown crosses Mama's face. "Well, he's still there."

"I keep worrying he'll leave, like always." I slurp my soup.

Corrie rolls her eyes.

"Ja, when we visited him this morning," says Mama. "He said nothing about anyone else, only himself. He went on and on about the corporate competition this, the competition that. They're the ones who put him there. So he tells us."

Papa's fingers tap on the table, an imaginary allegro piano passage. "I told him it was nonsense, but he didn't want to listen."

Mama jumps back in. "I told him he could still pass the mustard at work if he would just stay and get better. He had nothing to say about Cindy, the kids."

"Well, maybe he will be more ready day by day," I say, hoping to soothe her.

Mama smiles at me for the first time this day. "Remember how he always needed a lot of comforting? I tried to comfort him."

Papa pounds his hand on the table, and Corrie and I jump, just like when we were little. Everything rattles with the force. "I told him, 'Enough now!' One of those nurses came over, said to stop yelling. What does she expect? Nothing gets through to him. Finally we just left."

The lump is back in my throat, choking me. I have no words for Papa now, even though I tell counseling clients in my office not to yell.

"*Heh* Jakob, this is why I hate for you to get worked up," says Mama. "First you upset the nurse, now the girls. Stop now."

Papa stacks a neat forkful of beef and beans and lifts it to his mouth.

We're all supposed to ignore the outbursts, so we do.

He turns to Corrie with his typical complete gear change to neutral. "Liefje, you look like you need some rest. You always do too much at that job."

Someone's always saying, *Stop now, rest.* If only it were that easy.

"Oh ... kay," says Corrie. "You know, I think I will go rest up now."

I follow her out.

"Aren't you glad you got here nice and quick?" She leans tiredly against her car, as if following the instructions to need rest.

"Ja, Ja. Enjoy that early breakfast with the new guy. See you in the morning."

"Craig is his name," she says. "He is making sure we see each other early in the morning tomorrow, because he's just that sweet." Her eyes pool with tears. "He knows I'm nervous about tomorrow. If you're good, I'll tell you more about him."

So far, I haven't been good for her at all. I stop to lean against the small gateposts myself. More tired now than before.

After dinner we three sit together companionably with stacks of books around us, each of us reading, as if no nagging to be on time or beating on the table ever happened. I feel niggling shame that I said nothing about Papa's fist pounding. "Let's take the dogs for a walk, Mama."

Sadie and Tutu, named by Marina and Wade when they were littler, trot briskly. I storm along faster with my athletic mama than we could with Papa along.

She reaches for my hand, and we hold hands, each with a leash and a dog in the other. "You know, liefje, Alby did call me several times in the weeks before this overdose. He said he was talking to a new counselor, and would get more help as soon as he conquered a research breakthrough at work."

"He called me too," I reveal, "but in the middle of the night. I saw his number on my cell phone, I called him back in the daytime, and he never picked up. One odd call, his breathing and his pacing. That's what I woke up to."

We drop hands. Sadie and Tutu's leashes are tangled, of course.

"Do people who want to die make calls like that?" asks Mama.

"I hope not. I hope he finds that fighting spirit to live." I stoop down and the leashes are unsnarled.

"Ja, for him to want to live *and* without all this destruction he causes," says Mama.

For the rest of the evening, we read. Papa keeps plopping down his book to write inside a folder balanced on his lap.

"What's that?" I ask.

"Oh, nothing much. It's for Dr. Ingstrom tomorrow." He folds the paper back into the file, reminding me of myself as a teen, hiding my journaling.

Later, with few words, we get up, turn off lights, then pass Papa's treasured carvings from the Dutch East Indies, followed by photos of our young family, the Utah Rockies bathed in light.

Papa stops in the hallway, carrying his folder in one hand. "Come on in, I have something to show you."

I follow him into his study step by slow step. He propels the cane forward, then drags his bad hip up, swings the other leg, then moves on. I put out a steadying hand as he falls into his chair. His hand folds over mine.

"There," he says, pointing next to his computer. "See, Billiton Island, the beach. We are all just out of the waves. Wim, Albert, me, and little Sara. Before we went to Nederland to leave Wim behind. Before it all changed."

Within the chipped wooden frame, four children in old-fashioned wool bathing suits glisten at the ocean's edge. The black-and-white photo is grainy and worn. The faces mean nothing for a moment. Then I see that the youngest boy is Papa, his round head much like mine. The older ones with narrow faces are Oom Wim, then Oom Albert; the littlest, a girl, is *Tante* Sara. She looks boyish in her identical old-fashioned wool swim suit with sagging shoulder straps. She has the widest mouth and grin, the same grin I saw on Corrie's face at the airport.

Of these four children, two are dead. The oldest brother, Oom Wim, died ten years ago after a battle with emphysema. Oom Albert died in the camps, as did the ghost photographer, my grandfather Vanderveer. Little Jakob and Sara in the picture have open laughing mouths, but they don't talk now about the four missing war years. Or do they? I turn to Papa, ready to learn more.

He is heaving himself up out of his chair. "*Welterusten*, good night."

I put out my hands to lift him and hold him here in the room, jarred again by being as tall as Papa. "Please tell me more. What made you bring this photo out now?"

He looks at me surprised, as if I should know. "I have to remember now, and I have to hold us all close to my heart.

Then I can reach Alby, bring him back in. Like I couldn't ..."
He shrugs.

"Couldn't what?"

He points at his brother Albert, almost as tall as Oom
Wim, looking away from the camera with a hint of a smile.
"The things the Japanese did. Ja, you could say they
murdered him right in front of me. He died, but our Albert,
Alby, he's right here. I can still save him. I will."

I feel a chilly blast of Houston air conditioning. I'm used
to Papa's pronouncements, his belief that he can make
everything happen: happy children, kids who all went to
college. Also his belief that if the worst happens, it's gone,
over, we will say no more. Death has crept in like a dense
California fog. He's picked up the photo, and his back is
turned to me.

"Nice, the four of you," I hazard, "and the three of us." I
wonder if the ocean scene makes him think back to our
sailing days, the moment of entering safe harbor, letting
loose the sails just right, to ease into the dock without
bashing it.

He touches young Albert in the photo. "There were
beatings, so much blood," he says hoarsely. "You try and try
to keep everyone alive, hold them up in those horrible
forced lines, half dead, and then they're attacked anyway,
and die."

"I'm so sorry, Papa." The huge growing lump in my
throat, threatening to cut off my breathing, must be one-
hundredth of what he's been through. He says good night to
me as if his eyes see nothing. He is too spent for me to say
anything else but, "Papa, we will, we'll bring Alby back in."
Terrible words that an irresponsible doctor, Dr. Ingstrom,
has me saying now too. How could she feed him false hope?

Alone, I touch the old photo he so carefully placed back
on the desk, knocking it down. My heart pounds as I pick it
up. What a relief — there is no glass cover to break. I glance at
a familiar photo on the wall, the one Papa took of my high

school graduation. We three kids are standing in a row in order of age, just like our aunt and uncles.

Months from now, will I look at this photo to see that one of us, Alby, is dead? Will Papa, our unseen ghost photographer, also be dead? The air-conditioning chill tightens my aching back. Too much sorrow. This much I know, Papa came from a generation of death. Papa and Alby have to go one way or the other: live fully or die. Papa must face that Alby may never be safe again. Papa could keep me safe and secure, by letting me help him face his past. I don't know why this is so. I just do.

I carefully right the wet, happy children in the Billiton photo, angling them to face the three American teenagers on the wall. For a moment I touch a photo on his desk I've long remembered. Papa as a boy holding his cat. Oh yes, Mollie I recall.

† † †

Jakob

Billiton Island
Third week of December 1941

Jakob still knew that Mollie was not beautiful to everyone. To others she was ordinary. But he had picked her out of the litter, passing up the striped kittens, and one all black kitten with white tips. Mollie's dusky gray gleamed as she rubbed against Jakob's legs, purring louder than crickets or frogs just for him.

She was his, and she was the most beautiful cat in the world. Lately Sara, if he and Albert wouldn't play with her, held Tina and talked to her. Tina became her *vriendin* — girlfriend. When troubled at school, or in trouble with Pappie, he did the same, holding Mollie and talking to her.

Just like Jakob, Mollie often skirted the edges of rooms, staying out of everyone's way, except Kokkie's. Other times

Mollie boldly presented herself. Kokkie scolded Albert and Sara out of the kitchen, but not Jakob and Mollie. Jakob was Kokkie's favorite, but nobody else's favorite. Well, perhaps Sara. Pappie liked Wim best, and admired Albert's studiousness. Albert was Mammie's favorite, and Sara each family member's darling. Since Pappie liked Wim best, Wim disapproved of Jakob. This left Jakob still rich, he thought, basking in the attention of Kokkie, Adri, Mollie, Albert, and Sarah.

Mammie knew he helped Kokkie with dinners. The best was delicious pork marinated with *ketjap*, to become saté served with peanut sauce. But he wouldn't let Pappie find out. He suspected Pappie wouldn't like it.

† † †

One morning, much like all weekday mornings since Sara's birthday/Pearl-Harbor-Radio-announcement day, Jakob awakened to no school, Mollie, and the steady rain of the wet monsoon season. Constant spattering on the roof had rumbled the family to sleep and rat-a-tatted him awake now. Mollie came in, with only her fur tips wet. She bypassed Albert's bed and came straight to him as he stretched out from under mosquito netting to pull her in.

He rolled them both out from under the mosquito netting and then, while strolling to the kitchen, draped her over his neck like his mother's fur stole, the kind she wore in Nederland. Kokkie served his favorite breakfast: rice and coconut milk. The same deliciousness served to children in the kampong—village. He pulled Mollie up snugly to his chest with one arm, just the way Min burped new babies. In the middle of his bowl, Indonesian brown sugar—goela jawa—melted like a golden island.

If Pappie were here, he would growl, "Dirty cat at the breakfast table," and make a face. Mollie would race from the room. Yet Pappie liked Mollie too. He always smiled after he said, "Dirty cat." At night, in the living room, there Pappie would be, petting Mollie.

What if he, Jakob, became Pappie's cat? Then Pappie would pet him, smile at him, just like Mollie.

Kokkie waved her hands as she left the kitchen. "Play, play."

Jakob scraped his spoon over the last of his rice and licked the plate.

Mollie leapt up on the table to lick the plate too. A damp, cool breeze wafted in and she sniffed the air as if on a mission. In seconds she ran to the veranda and disappeared. Mollie's gray camouflaged her perfectly in the rain.

"Mollie!" Jakob yelled. He would have to be a sharp tracker.

He ran, thinking maybe Mollie would show him her dry spots in the wall of rain. He cut across the grass, ducking under trees and fronds, the no man's land where he could hide. Looking ahead, deep back under a frond, dark-gray fur waited for him. *Eigenweis* — independent — the word everyone said defined cats. But for him, Mollie listened and waited. They could be *eigenweis* together.

"Good Mollie," he called. Mollie bolted ahead. Oh well, he followed.

A wise runner never slipped in the foaming mud rills in the middle. He planted his flashing feet wide, in the verdant green, dryer foliage on the edges of the path. On he ran, like a fast duck speed-waddling from side to side. The dense growth had soaked up all the moisture and turned brighter green. Mollie paused and dashed off again. Following, he found a narrow animal path. Wild boars. A cold chill ran up his spine.

Mollie slowed, the tip of her tail disappearing under fronds. He pulled under next to her; no wild boars in sight. Somehow she was less wet than he. Maybe her fur was like a raincoat. He'd grab his raincoat next time. But still, he was pretty dry, like a really fast Indian tracker, knowing every path.

Heart pounding from running, he tried to catch his breath. They rested on the slightest of slopes, under one large tree here, small ferns joined together around the trunk. A dry house, just for Mollie and him.

Just yesterday his heart had pounded as he longed to hide, sure Pappie had discovered he had wounded Sara's doll, Tina. But Sara had done nothing after kissing the hurt eye. He waited for Mammie, Pappie, or others to notice the scratch. Eventually he reminded himself, grown-ups didn't see such things.

Albert, Sara, and he had caucused on the veranda in whispers. "Don't tell Papa. Jakob will make it up to you," said Judge Albert. And he had. Mollie, Tina, Sara, and he had a tea party, with Albert, who always did what others wanted anyway, as their guest.

A lonely cool droplet fell on his neck, while rain sheeted all around. This would be the place to hide from the Japanese. Close enough for a quick getaway, far enough to be safe. He would tell everyone else. Pappie would smile, like when he gifted Jakob with the compass. They could hide the whole family here, except for the men, who would be courageously fighting the Japanese.

"We'll go back," he said to Mollie, "and load up supplies." It's all anyone ever talked about—how to be prepared. He crouched under the fern and breathed deeply in readiness for his sprint, just like the Houdini escapes Pappie told them about. *Breathe deep and hold your breath. That is the key*, he always said. *Exhale to wiggle out if you are trapped. Otherwise, breathe deep and run.* The deep, earthy dampness smelled like home. *No, not Houdini, like an American Indian racer sent to the Olympics, because I am the fastest in all the land.*

"One, two, three, go!" he shouted. Running, he jumped over small water troughs turning to raging rivulets along the paths. He then catapulted along the pouring mud between his steps.

His elation grew as he thought of gathering supplies, and the brave fighting to come. Everyone knew the Japs would invade soon, and that they would not conquer Indonesia. They had taken too many countries already: China, Malaysia, and attacking Borneo. These islands, Billiton, Java, and Sumatra, this is where they would be stopped. The Japs were coming in more pairs than snakes. An army, naval forces, air squadrons.

They must be stopped.

He crossed the grass clearing to the house and threw himself into a chair on the veranda. No, he wasn't soaked through—just moist. Mollie plastered herself against his damp arms, then licked him with her sandpaper tongue. He leaned back, thinking of mango for snack.

When war—a vague, loud, dark thing—came, he, too, would fight. Bravely, to the death, yet he would survive. He would be scouting in the jungle with Mollie. Noise in the distance would warn him. Mollie could not fight and would be left in their hiding place alone. He'd run for the house, not shouting yet. Just inside he would yell, *"Japanners, Japanners!"* Sara and Mammie would barricade themselves with Kokkie and Min in the kitchen storage. Albert would protect them and Jakob would help fight.

Pappie's companions had trained weekly for battle. He could see who would do what, like the one Hollywood Western movie he had seen in the theatre on Java with Cousin Ankie and their family. He would be the boy who guarded all the ammunition and handed the men their loaded weapons, one after the other, to keep the raging battle going.

Steam rose up as sun rays warmed his damp shirt. He imagined what could happen.

† † †

Pappie broke out a window with his rifle, as did the other men. They shot over and over, felling rows of angry soldiers in red uniforms, red like the sun on their flag. Jakob slid down next to the gun cabinet, reloading rifles, throwing them out to the men, always keeping one on hand. Pappie turned to him time and time again, and up Jakob threw the next loaded rifle.

Deafening shotgun blasts roared all around. A Jap broke a side window, snarling, his bayonet raised to stab Pappie from behind. The little man in red hadn't reckoned with the quick reflexes of a boy. Jakob leaped out, his chest on fire with courage. The man turned, his mouth an oh, terrified to be eye to eye with such fierceness, a pistol in his hands, a pack strapped to his back.

Jakob swiftly brought his hand up and shot the man through the head. The Jap fell with a thud that echoed beyond the ricocheting firearms. Another soldier leapt through the same window, yelling what must be the Japanese battle cry. *Aieeh!* Jakob wheeled around, cracking him in the head with the butt of his pistol. *Oof.* One enemy lay in a pool of blood, the other motionless. The horror of red blood gushing from red uniforms washed over him, but the bad guys had to die.

The rounds of shotgun fire stopped. Pappie turned around, his round glasses dirty and askew, then wiped the sweat from his brow. In the sudden silence, he gasped at the two Jap soldiers at Jakob's feet. Then he winked and signaled thumbs up.

The battle done, Albert came in. "The rest all fled, they won't trouble us anymore," he said admiringly.

"Our hero," cried Pappie, raising Jakob's arm in victory.

CHAPTER 5

Luce

Houston, Texas
September 2004

"We'll be late," says Papa in the driver's seat. We are heading to Dr. Ingstrom's office.

I flinch every time he brakes too hard. He has a terrifying habit left over from his stick-shift driving days. His right foot is on the gas, his left foot on the brake. My bobble-head moves with each stop. Vague nausea starts. I pick spots on the road ahead to look at, purposely drawing on memory, just as I drew on happy Beppe and Pake memories all the many times I felt lonely here in America.

† † †

On my thirteenth birthday, I asked again for a missing story, a missing part of him. *I'm almost a grown-up now.* Alby still played with Legos, but Papa and I sailed together. Alby crewed, and we could boss him around. Mama loved sailing, easily ducking and gliding from one side of the sailboat to the other each time we turned against the wind. We all poised while the boom snapped across. If Corrie was there, her head was down most of the time, waiting for stability. As soon as she could, she and a friend would return to shore and huddle there, waiting for the day to be over.

I told myself I'd be like the daughter in fairy tales who could not be denied her one wish, once alone with her Papa. I always felt as if I forced my way through the *Starship*

Enterprise's force field on our favorite TV show to bring up his teen years.

"Tell me about when you were a teenager like me … about the *kamp*s."

Papa's prematurely gray hair, lion-like, matched the silver anchor necklace around his neck. His face went flat behind his glasses.

I believed I hurt him, no way could I stop. I held my breath.

He shook his head, opening his book again. He dismissed me without a word, and it was my birthday.

"Come on, Papa. Tell me a little, tell me anything."

He slowly closed the book, not bothering to mark the page, then looked at me as if he didn't recognize me, as if I were brand-new to him, not his daughter at all, not me. "Come sit with me."

I awkwardly squeezed my budding hips into the chair with him, in Corrie's territory of cuddling with Papa and glad for it. I would hear his story at last.

Instead, he sighed, "I can only tell you before the war, when Billiton Island was like paradise. All of it, the cruelty, it is too much for you, as it was too much for all of us. Only Oom Wim in Holland, Tante Sara, and your Oma survived."

I turned away, tears in my eyes. I couldn't tell anyone about the books in the library, I couldn't tell anyone, not even Papa, that his past would be a gift to me.

He surprised me by turning my head and putting a warm thumb where the tears ran down. I wanted to run away in embarrassment, such a big girl crying. "I'll tell you one more story, liefje, but not about those *kamp*s." He hugged my shoulders hard, and I felt him relax. He told of being on the ocean when they evacuated, seeing Billiton disappear.

† † †

As we careen into the parking lot, I'm shook up by the memory. How many times did Papa tell us a story, and I didn't recognize he was giving part of himself?

We arrive early, of course, and so do the others.

I savor the chance to breathe away the car-ride nausea when I step out. I see my sister-in-law, Cindy, as tall as I, hugging Corrie and everyone and then standing off to the side. I go to her. She links arms with me, which she knows is a Dutch girlfriends' habit, and off we go.

Dr. Ingstrom's lips curve gently as she greets us. Her hair is dark with streaks of gray, clipped back on either side as if she were still young. She looks to be in her late fifties. Most of us have thick coarse hair. Corrie ended up with the silky gold-spun hair from Mama's side of the family. My wiry, thick dirty-blonde hair is pulled back with a scarf today.

We crowd into her relatively small office: me, Papa Jakob, Mama Nikki, Cindy, and Corrie. It looks like Alby can't join us. A small cross, made of bits of mirror, glints and reflects on one wall, catching the light coming in through the window where a magnolia tree blooms, each white flower a glowing lantern.

Dr. Ingstrom's eyes roam our faces as we all stand awkwardly in front of her. Vanderveers are bold yet polite. None of us are sure where to sit. Her glasses soften her eyes, making them look kind. Everyone in my father's family wears them. I have never seen a Vanderveer bother with contact lenses. "I made tea for everyone," Dr. Ingstrom says. "Serve yourselves, sit anywhere."

An aged blue porcelain teapot resides on the sideboard, stained dark around its gaping sparrow mouth. Just like our family teapots, no one tried to make it perfectly clean. After generations of use, it is here to pour into all of us who funnel through this office.

She speaks to me. "How was your travel?"

"Fine." A matching delft cup and saucer rattle in my trembling hand as I take my turn jostling by the sideboard. I

60

abandon the saucer to hold a silent cup. I clutch the teapot; the dark spout fills my cup as I give up on the milk and sugar, which I favor.

Just need to sit down.

I start to feel acutely present; the wave of presence is good. Glancing up at the cross, I inhale it as an omen, a foundational reminder of my own steps of faith: leaving my home country pumped full of grandparents—Beppe and Pake's faith, losing faith in the hatred of too many moves, finding faith in nature, returning to belief due to my own sobriety as a teen, finding a church home in Calabria.

As the mirror bits sparkle, every color in the room brightens. Papa fades into gray, with white hair, silvered glasses, a gray shirt on today. He can look charming, in one of his many ocean-colored shirts, but today he has forgotten charm. This has to be the only drab gray shirt he owns.

Corrie, typically dressed up, is in a similar drab state, in old jeans and a poncho.

Cindy is balancing her cup with what looks like her list for today. Surely her warped pad of paper was once left in water at their barn. She is not in her usual out-about-town silk blouse, but in a feed-store T-shirt and jeans. She smells faintly of horses. Mama, the farm girl, leans into her; she likes horse smell. I wanted to be a Dutch farm girl too like Mama, but then we left for America.

Mama looks lovely in an aqua cotton sweater, although her face is worn down, as if she couldn't sleep last night. Her breathing is uneven, asthma starting; I wish I didn't always take her emotional barometer. I am waiting for her to snap. She not only wheezes, but she sighs.

Papa coughs. Maybe the heavy air around her is why Papa faded into gray today. Perhaps his fallen face is why she is tense.

I look at Dr. Ingstrom; I wish she would get on with it.

She pulls out a file. "So Marina, ten days ago, could not wake her dad up. She was the one who had to make the nine-one-one call."

Okay, so she dives right in.

"Yes," says Cindy. "Marina hasn't gone anywhere since. She just sits in the house. Yesterday she told me sometimes she hates her dad, sometimes she loves him. He had just promised her to go back to Alcoholics Anonymous before she found him."

Dr. Ingstrom sips her tea. "For families it is hard to understand an addict's self-destructiveness. Why not just go to meetings and stick with help? I asked all of you to gather together, because truly this doesn't make sense. Sometimes he has faith, attends church, goes to Alcoholics Anonymous meetings. He likes his job. He has a wonderful family."

I recall a few weeks of faith-based talk years ago, when Alby and Cindy found their home church. He liked the words of John: *In the beginning was the Word* ... Yet there's something white-hot in me; maybe it's what keeps turning my stomach on this trip. "But what has he really tried, I mean, really tried?" I break in loudly.

Mama snaps her head around to me. I'm not usually the loud one.

"AA, rehabs, church. None of it works just because you step through the doors."

Dr. Ingstrom turns away from me, towards Cindy. "A good family," she repeats.

I feel chastised, shamed. I hate how my emotions attack so viciously lately. I'd rather not feel ice-pick tears behind my eyes. Mama puts her cup down, rubs her hands up and down her sleeves, and looks as if she would like to hug herself and then disappear.

Cindy relaxes back against her chair and flips the warped pad open. "Okay, Dr. Ingstrom, he did try all of this, the different psychiatrists, AA and NA. We met with our pastor ... everybody."

"Dying's trying," they say in AA. *What do these two want for Alby's trying — a prize?* "Hey, there's gotta be a few people you haven't met with," I blurt out.

Corrie laughs. No one joins her.

Dr. Ingstrom turns to Cindy. "Together, you felt times of love and hope. How open is Alby? How well does the family know him?"

"Well," I jump in, aware they're not talking to me, "it's not like we're used to being open with our parents. They haven't known our deepest problems. He needed a therapist."

Mama and Papa both look away.

Cindy rips off the top page, repositioning it on her pad. "He did therapy. A lot of money and little help."

I hadn't known. Sounds like he did go beyond trying, some doing. He should never have given up.

Dr. Ingstrom leans forward. "Here's what has not been said to all. Only some of you. He has abused pain pills for years, including opiates, a very serious addiction. He may be having mood swings. We don't know yet if his paranoia about competing research scientists is from the drug abuse or his psychiatric problems."

"Psychiatric?" Mama says to Papa. They gaze down at the blood-red pattern on the Persian carpet at their feet.

Cindy raises her hand like she's at school. "Yes, we know little. How long is he going to need help this time? He always comes back and does the same after rehab. Has big plans, but soon he's avoiding AA, doing his disappearing act again. I know I make things too easy for him, by covering all the bases. I don't want to do that anymore. He needs to show some responsibility from the beginning."

I turn to Cindy, thinking of my own years of sobriety and working at rehab. "The doctor is just finding out what he needs right now. It's too soon for that question."

Cindy glares at me. "And why for my first appointment did you invite *all* of them?"

Mama flinches; I am shocked. Cindy, who is usually so even tempered, is the loud one now. Sounds like she hates us. My eyes ache with the held-back tears; I can't focus. I feel I could mess this up. I tell people all the time to not feel so powerful, to not believe in the power to either heal or harm your own family. Yet I feel I've harmed them. I catch Dr. Ingstrom's eyes. She gives me a knowing look I already hate. Is she going to say I'm playing counselor too much? Am I?

Ingstrom coolly says, "We do have recommendations for his recovery and when he needs to return home."

Mama exhales loudly. "Doctor, you asked us to be here, but for what? What good does this do?"

Now everyone hates Dr. Ingstrom. This I expected.

"Jakob, you and Nikki do know why you're here. All of you do. Remember, it is addiction and secrets you are angry at. Maybe mental health secrets too, not so much Alby ... or each other." She hands a cloth napkin to Cindy, who wipes away tears. "There is a loosening up, an opening about the past that only you elders can start, especially a father. That's why you're all here together. I have been able to interview Alby, as angry, frail, and mixed up as he is. There is a lack of agreement among you. But in all families"—she looks away—"there is a true voice and it goes way back. In your family, it is the legacy of the other Albert, the deceased Albert."

Silence.

She goes on. "Jakob, as one of the most wounded ones of World War Two, you survived Japanese concentration camps in the Netherlands East Indies. You never talked about it. Your old legacy is one of secrets. Alby keeps secrets too. Let's have you make a new legacy. No secrets."

Papa clutches something, the folder from last night. "And why?"

"Because Alby has plenty of secrets and of course he's not the only one. Only honest and open people can recover." She smiles radiantly at me; I drink it up like her tea. Something's happening; I can listen again.

"I have started to talk," says Papa. "These are the kids' thank-you letters from the elementary school I visited, when Alby's son, Wade, asked me. He and Albert were both there. They heard."

Every year I asked and he never did this for me. Now he talks for Wade, a classroom, for Alby—who probably barely heard it all too—and only maybe for me. I want to scream, but I never do anymore. I study the magnolia tree. We have been here so long each blossom is darkened into shade.

Mama's face softens. "*Ga maar*, Jakob." Go ahead.

Papa looks at me. I'm glad our eyes meet. The way he looks past me, and then pulls his eyes back to me, I can see he remembers the times I asked, and how he never answered.

"I always thought happy-go-lucky," he begins. "I never have to think about that horrible time again. In January of '42, my mother, father, sister, brother, and I had to leave the beautiful island I grew up on, as the Japanese were coming. I didn't know then that I would never see Billiton again."

Stretching out the word *Billeehtohn* melts his face and reveals him—strong, calm—before the war. Did the before-the-war Papa die away? I never thought about his not-talking that way until now. Both his hands tense into one doubled fist.

"My father stayed behind to sabotage the mine. The rest of us went to the big island of Java for our family evacuation, having been told to bring only a little along. It was considered bad for morale to have the appearance of moving for the long term. ... Bad for morale," he spits out. "What could be worse than escaping without enough, on the eve of war? Fortunately my mother was smart. She packed medicine and jewels. Even we kids were smart. We had our rucksacks from all the times we trekked the island with Pappie. All my treasures, they were in this one rucksack."

He stares at the wall. Mama touches him again. She knows to bring him back from there.

"Since Pappie had been ordered to stay behind to sabotage the mine, his escape was with a convoy of ships. They were bombed and sunk by the Japanese in February of '42 in an incredibly uneven naval battle. A few mostly antique Dutch and Allied ships were no match for Japan's well-prepared war machine. It was called the Battle of the Java Sea. How he survived, at least for a time, is another whole story. Since our oldest brother, Wim, was in Nederland, Albert, my one-year-older brother, and I became the men of the house."

"And when you all packed your treasures, did you somehow pack the treasure of your family life?" asks Dr. Ingstrom.

"Treasure?" Papa regards her interference. For a moment, each with wavy hair and glasses, they look like family facing off. "We spent months on Java, first in the cooler mountainous area of Bandoeng, renting a house provided by friends. There we stayed with Tante Ankie's family. Later we had to move to Batavia, Djakarta, they call it now. Our families shared a house, living in yet greater danger. The Japanese could raid the house at any time and did. There was nothing we could do."

Dr. Ingstrom arches an eyebrow. "And your family?"

"My *familie*?" He blinks. "You know that of the five of us in the *kamps*, two died. My pappie had always been such a strong man, sometimes a frightening man. He had, you know, the hands of iron. I so admired my pappie, though. By the time Tjideng had become a ghetto, Pappie was in a men's *kamp*. After three months, before we were also imprisoned, all the families were allowed one visit to their men.

"I saw all those men lined up, starving as we would be soon. My redheaded father was crusted" — he gestures to his arms and head, his eyes filled with tears — "with sores from surviving in the ocean after the battle, and then life in the full sun, blisters oozing yellow against his reddened skin. I couldn't imagine why all those big men, my heroes, didn't fight back. Yet I knew they could not. I had already seen people shot down in the street or beaten for not bowing down."

"And how did you feel?" asks Dr. Ingstrom.

"Well, it was so disturbing. All those men *krachteloos* ..."

"Powerless?" says Dr. Ingstrom.

How does she know this Dutch word?

"Ja, powerless like that. What you need to know and what I want to let our Alby know," says Pappie, turning to us, "is that eventually we lost everything and I ended up all alone. I don't know if I ever taught him" — he looks at Cindy — "to get help, to be at home with anyone."

I reach and touch his hand. My chest feels warm, and I see a boy like my Vincent, held captive, having lost all that was familiar.

† † †

Jakob

Kamp Tjideng, Batavia
July 1944

Mevrouw — Mrs. — Bevins went silent now that she was alone, her only son gone. The Japanese proclaimed boys sixteen and older were men, a threat to Hirohito's power, and transported them away to a men's kamp. Jakob noticed her words didn't come back. Her silence stayed and turned to delayed movements. Being slow was a constant danger around the Japs. Beatings were bound to follow. Thankfully, so far, she had been left alone.

The kamp, first a crowded ghetto for Blandas — the Dutch — and then a still more crowded concentration camp, was divided into sectors of stifling houses and garages packed with thousands of women and children forced behind woven bamboo and barbed wire. MevrouwTineke Bevins and others were in with Mammie, Albert, Sara, and Jakob. He studied Mevrouw Bevins in the long line for a carefully meted out bowl of broth, a fish gut lump, and some strange tapioca. This was dinner. Mevrouw Bevins just held her bowl. Now she didn't eat either.

Along with everyone else, Jakob chewed each watery mouthful up to one hundred times to pretend fullness and sustenance. The chewing ached his jaws as his mouth watered, wanting more. Mevrouw Bevins' bony shoulders poked out of a blouse made front and back from two dishcloths. He touched her wrist. In their early days here, he could make her laugh with faces, or fake piano duets with her son, Siebe—before he was taken. Now she did not respond to Jakob. He was uncertain whether to cajole her to eat, or to hope that she would pass her bowl to him. His stomach cramped as it did every day.

Once he had taken a bite from Sara's bowl before handing it to her. She threw her spoon at his head, but had not given him away to Mammie; he still felt guilty. He knew he was still this kind of boy, often being bad.

Mammie approached. Gray broadly streaked her hair since being here, her face deeply ravined. Sometimes she still smiled, like now. Did she want Mevrouw Bevins' bowl too? "Hey," she said loudly, as if her words had to break insulated walls of silence around Mevrouw. "Tineke. Time to be alive again, eat. We may as well live until we are liberated."

Jakob looked up at Mammie. She had not been one to talk about liberation till now. Life was day-to-day survival. Mevrouw looked at no one, her spoon still in her bowl.

The twenty or so others turned away; for this was the only way to give privacy here. But Jakob looked. Mammie sat down next to Mevrouw, one eye on Albert and Sara, who sat still dipping into their bowls.

Jakob had to strain to hear Mammie whisper, "Stay. Stay alive for your son, Siebe, for when we all survive. Imagine it. One day we will leave this life of being crowded like rats. Siebe and your husband will come looking for you. They will need you."

Mammie reached for Tineke Bevins' spoon. Jakob was surprised. *She wants her food after all.* But Mammie lifted it not to her own mouth but Mevrouw Bevins' lips, pressing against her sealed mouth. "Finally, Tineke," Mammie said as the compressed lips parted, swallowed, laughed. Mammie reached the spoon again, singsonging now, laughing too. "Here comes another worm to the baby bird on her own."

"Worm is right," muttered Mevrouw. Her shoulders shook with spasms of tears and laughter. Then she reached for the spoon and ate, skipping chewing.

During the endless days that followed, Mevrouw Bevins stuck close to Mammie, while Jakob stuck close to Mevrouw. Soon he would make her smile again.

† † †

After she had helped Mevrouw Tineke Bevins, Jakob saw Mammie with new eyes. She touched them more than in the days when the servants, especially Min, had done everything. She was exhausted, yet she told stories, chattering on for them during the endless lulls of captivity. Sometimes, Jakob came in, then collapsed in the shade from playing soccer with a ball made from bound-up twine.

"Rest," Mammie said. "You must listen to me, be still. You cannot burn so much energy here, with so little food."

They played cards, watched Sara play with her doll, Tina, who survived thus far, and made carvings from the chopped-up teak furniture dumped as firewood in the compound. They all slowed in the rhythm of their days, waiting for even worse or for another hundred days until liberation.

At first, Mammie showed no sign of worry that Albert, his older brother, would be taken next. Recently she fussed how, with so little food, they still grew and grew in height, and it was hard to keep them in decent clothes. She had to sew rags together, she mumbled. Then, silences crept in, just like Mevrouw. Years ago no one had spoken of Wim being left behind either. Could their oldest brother still be at school with the German occupation? Or worse, much worse?

Everyone peeled away, Jakob thought, as he struggled with counting off the years correctly. First Wim, in 1939, then Pappie in 1942, then Siebe Bevins, and soon Albert. Having Siebe with them as a friend had been great. Together they sat by a board painted like piano keys, and Jakob learned scales, sharps, flats, chords. They sang the piano notes, made toys, told stories.

Now that Mevrouw Bevins talked again, she and Jakob joined women's conversations about food, while Albert usually carved. His latest was to try for a toy airplane with moving propellers. Mevrouw and the others fantasized whole meals, and traded recipes back and forth, as if they themselves had prepared food all those years, not their servants.

"Ja, with *rijsttafel* dinner, you soak the rice, then arrange the *kruiden*, and set them aside. Meanwhile the saté can marinade."

Jakob squinted his eyes to remember years back, his whole family out on the veranda, a cool breeze, waiting in full assurance of food. Albert reading a botany book, Sara holding Tina, Mammie's piano music drifting out from the house.

†††

One day Jakob and Albert hunkered together ready to leap up if necessary, as they shared the only spot of shade near their garage-corner home. Tjideng was completely fenced in now with *gedek*—the bamboo and barbed wire wall that surrounded them. In their spot of fleeting fresh air, Jakob wondered about the darkened hushed paths in the jungle, the ocean only kilometers away. *The women have their food fantasies.* In his mind he was in a *kano*—ocean canoe—with his friend Matteus, free. He missed him like pieces of himself were gone, and this is how people tore away from you in the kamps, first neighbors, then forced moves, then gone.

Pain cut into his stomach more than usual. He had just alleviated the last cramps by running to the outhouse ditches. Since they ate so little, it was a mystery where the pain and the runs came from. He knew his insides were hollow. The breeze shifted and the stench of the always-overflowing sewage surrounded them. Even breathing through his mouth, the rancid air sickened him. He went the short distance to their garage room. Their mattresses were outside in the sun, to chase the lice out. Not much good it did.

Mammie hummed as she sewed numbers onto their small stack of clothes. Sara was at her side, pretending to sew more doll clothes for Tina. Everyone had to have a Japanese prisoner number and everything was recorded by the Japanese. They knew the age of each child, especially sons. Beyond Mammie, light from the broken roof danced, bringing ragged light onto the narrow areas where at night they slept. They barely had room for a path to relieve themselves at night. He squeezed in next to Mammie.

"*Dag*, Jakob."

"The cramping, the pain. I'm so tired."

"Ja." Her hand moved to her own abdomen.

Darting his eyes around first, he dug into the hole he had made under their one surviving suitcase and pulled out his copy of *The Jungle Book*. Their best rucksacks had been snatched away early on.

He looked up to see Marijke Westen in the open part of their garage. Her lips curled up, one on her rare smiles. Her eyes were always sad; he was ready to read to her. She, his Billiton Island school friend and class gymnastics champ, was still silent after her own ordeal. Everyone altered here. Now-quiet Marijke had been one of the most talkative girls in school with her pale skin, blue eyes, and long black braids with matching ribbons at the end, flying behind her when she did cartwheels. Ever the adventurer at school, now she stayed close to her mother. He sat down next to Marijke, and as they usually did, read the part where Mowgli first meets the wolves.

Cries rang out. *"Appel!"*

The lineup for an extra daily rollcall formed hurriedly. Jakob stowed his book, everyone hobbled or ran to their places. Sara ran to Mammie's side, then Albert and Jakob. He moved the hinge of his hips forward into the slanted L-shape bow. Those who had the cramps and runs stayed in line or they would be beaten as shirkers. He saw Mammie sway, and he bit his lip, holding his breath.

Fat Nose, Ienega, was striding by. His short stature and quick movements reminded Jakob of a cartoon film. Fat Nose had never been as cruel as some. On rare occasions he gave Sara an egg. As by the unwritten rules of kamp life, she had brought each egg back to their garage to be shared. They each had the tiniest bit. "Protein," said Tineke Bevins the last time, with her newly refound voice.

In front of other Japs, Fat Nose would be mean, however. Through the sea of legs, Jakob could also see their kamp commandant, Captain Kenichi Sonei, watching and pacing. Mammie moaned softly. Jakob saw Sara's perfect low bow and her tensed hands as Mammie moaned again. He had the prickly feeling in his neck warning him of a sudden change in the wind when sailing, or of danger now.

Mammie swayed again, Jakob bent deeper as Fat Nose-Ienega, neared. Had he seen Mammie sway?

Ienega kicked Jakob's shin. "Respect!"

Tears pooled for a moment in Jakob's eyes, but didn't last. In the brutal heat, teary eyes dried instantly, like laundry on the line. Hips set, eyes dry, he pondered. *Sometimes Fat Nose, who brings an egg, sometimes Ienega, who briskly walks away as if blows and kicks never happened. Maybe this tenko line-up will be quick.* Captain Sonei's recent start at Tjideng marked the Japanese ruling that all kamp administration would now be by military only. Thus brutality, cut rations and tenko as punishment had increased.

Suddenly Captain Sonei strode closer by. Jakob's heart raced. Could Fat Nose's kick have been meant to deflect Sonei's rage? The pain in Jakob's stomach tightened, the silence so acute, a calling bird from the jungle a kilometer away echoed to them.

Sonei went back to the center of the square, yelling along with a Malay translator, "Transport! All boys twelve and up, men's camps now, first thing in the morning." He handed the list over and all the names were read. So he and Albert would both go?

"Albert Lucas Vanderveer." The Japanese pronunciation, since no Dutch was allowed, made it difficult to understand.

Mammie swayed, but did not cry. Jakob tensed. He had seen so many women hit, but never his mother—yet.

A woman cried, "Babies! You said sixteen and up before!"

Jakob quivered, and wished he didn't. It was an ugly and constant defeat to tremble in the face of the enemy. The tension ate away at his insides, the acid in his stomach threatening to come up into his throat. Sonei could erupt and attack at any moment. His violent tirades were worst during the time of each full moon.

Screaming announcements went on. "Now! They will be men!"

Inexplicably, he would not be going along, another brother peeling away. Then more names, and at the end, oddly, "Jakob Gerrit Vanderveer."

"What? No, not both!" Mammie's voice rose. Tineke Bevins arm rose to hush her.

He ran to Albert's place in the line, a brief freedom of cool air rushing against him. "We will go away."

"Ja, hurry, we will help each other." It was just as it was last time for Siebe, only one night to get ready.

Not both, rang in his ears. Mammie and Sara would be left alone.

They all strode to the garage-shed room, to their small hidden supply. Once there, even Sara was wise enough to reach with slow movements for their hiding spots. Sara stuck close to Mammie, her face pinched with worry. Recently Captain Sonei had come upon some young children, they bowed carefully, but smiled nervously. Sonei had raged, had their mothers hauled out of their homes, and beat them viciously for their children's supposed disrespect. When Jakob had tried to comfort Sara that night, she said, "Well, it's not so bad. You see, no one I love has been beaten yet." Oh how he wished he could protect.

On Billiton, Sara's hair was always to the side, just so. She started the day with a tied bow, in different colors, often gone by dusk. Now long gone. "Not Albert *and* Jakob," she cried.

Mammie's face was wet, and Albert patted her shoulder. Her eyes darted wildly this way and that with panic Jakob hated to see. Albert stayed calm, grabbing a cloth to bundle what little they had. With no rucksacks, bundles were the way to make do. They grabbed mosquito netting, tin cups, and a spoon.

Mammie's hands hesitated over the only knife they had, laid it down and pulled Albert to her, in a way that had been rare on Billiton Island. Most hugs came from their baboe and servants, except for weekend morning pillow fights and laughter, when bumping up against Mammie and Pappie was fun. Jakob had loved those mornings, when he could be within arm's length of Pappie, no fears of stinging slaps or yelling, no matter how wild he got. Jakob ran his finger over the dullness of their extra knife. Those mornings and rare hugs were from when he was little, back when he was a kid, not a man of thirteen.

"Ik ga ook!" declared Jakob.

Mammie turned slowly, her brown eyes swimming. "Ja, oh. You are going too." But she didn't reach for him, and snatched one gold ring from her own pack, passing it to Albert. "This is for trade, for greatest need. *Voorzichgtig.*"

The ache in Jakob's stomach traveled up to a spot between his shoulder blades, the way it had when he knew he would never see his cat Mollie, again. He reached out his hand for Mammie and Sara.

Sara was so bony now. At nine years old, she looked younger. It had been a long time since her hair was combed to the side with a bow, tied to look like a butterfly. No one ever said to her, as they did to Jakob and Albert when they were young, "Oh, Sara, you are getting so tall."

It hurt Jakob to see her-tear streaked face, all sunken in like Mammie's. He would have loved, even for an instant, to see her in a fresh white cotton dress. He thought of their oldest brother trapped in a Nederland boarding school. Perhaps this was a day that Wim had pap porridge, and more. Sara had so little.

One way the Japs are correct. *We are men now!* Wim, Albert, and him—no longer boys, but grown men like Pappie.

Albert's bundle grew. Mammie's eyes widened when Jakob reached for a second knife he had stolen and hidden, giving it to Mammie. She had a hint of a smile at this discovery. Jakob thought that Mammie must be proud he could do such things. Each duo would need a knife. If you didn't have a tool for forced food gathering, you could be refused food. He leaned forward, anticipating a hug from Mammie for her youngest son, but only their shoulders grazed as she swiftly hid the knife.

For a moment she smiled. *"Goede jongen* — good boy."

Such rare words.

Sara clutched his hand, then let go. Mammie murmured a series of last-minute instructions to Albert.

With an ache in his chest, Jakob wandered outside. He would not be missed as much as Albert.

Marijke was in the yard, quiet and bent over. Was she thinking about the horrors done to her when the Japanese seized her and other girls?

No, she smiled shyly up at him, then at the package in her hands. She dropped a neatly folded blue cloth into his hand. Unfolding it, he saw the words *Marijke, Tjideng* embroidered in white cross-stitches. He beheld the wonder of her clean hands against the clean cloth with its tiny stitches. It had been a long time since he had had a reason to smile. *"Dankje wel* — thank you. We will always be friends."

"Always," she whispered.

While others averted their eyes, they strolled away, hoping for a few moments of privacy. Finally, they sat on the ground and pressed their backs against the garage wall of the home where Marijke was staying with her mother and many others. Jakob touched her soft cheek. She turned to him, her dark-brown hair tucked behind her ears and the blueness of her eyes always surprising him in her burnt brown face.

There is no way to say good-bye, he thought.

Her eyes closed and he pressed his lips against hers for the first time. Her breath tasted fresh, as if she somehow had eaten fruit. Impossible here. He felt sharp joy jump below his stomach — a moment of deepest pleasure. Did she feel it too? He pulled away to look at her face. He would love her always.

As he walked back, Mevrouw Bevins was outside too. She had been standing apart to give the family alone time. Suddenly her arms opened, and Jakob sunk in deeply, not minding her sharp bones, knowing she would miss him, and he her. "Maybe I'll see Siebe."

"Maybe," she said, her voice cracking, as if words were still a strain.

"I'll send your love."

"All my love."

† † †

That night Mammie surprised Jakob by pulling his mattress next to hers. "Oh, I will miss you," she said.

Jakob woke up hourly feeling as if he had warm grit inside his eyelids. Each time he would see Mammie, curled up tightly, awake. One time she was sobbing. Her eyes widened as she saw Jakob looking and she turned away, only her shoulders heaving. Those heaviest tears were for Albert, not him.

Morning breakfast had a bit more gruel. The women rising at dawn to stoke fires under the oil drums had somehow managed to put in a little bit more. Albert and Jakob ate silently, side by side, chewing each bite one hundred times.

"One hundred more days now," Albert said, "and America will liberate us. We'll be back."

"Just one more hundred days," Jakob said. It was what they believed. The only belief left.

Sara sat close to them.

"Here," he handed her *The Jungle Book*.

She smiled wide.

"For you," he said, "but never risk your life for it. Turn it in if you have to. You are worth more than a thousand books."

She nodded solemnly and looked tired, like a girl-child turning into a soldier. She would read about Mowgli and think about their wolf pack. Then she would smile.

The trucks started up, roaring, as did the guards. *"Lekkas, lekkas!"* Always they screamed to hurry.

Jakob's heart pounded, he felt he was tearing apart inside. They had to rush and grab Mammie and Sara for their good-byes. They joined rows of silent, stone-faced boys who then ran forward. Most appeared too shocked to cry. The women and children sobbed.

Most of the newly made men moved clumsily; one clutched a teddy bear. A yelling guard's bayonet point grazed a boy's shoulder. His mammie cried out and reached for a rivulet of blood as if she could put it back, and her son jerked away trying to be brave. Everyone hurried, yet Jakob felt like a slow-film camera. A shot of the mother's bloody hand, raising it to her mouth. His own arm almost wrenched away from Albert.

Jakob grabbed Albert's wrist and they leapt forward into a truck as more and more crowded in behind them. Soon they could not move. Jakob kept one hand on his bundle and snaked his other hand up, determined to wave. "We will see Pappie," he shouted to Albert.

"I wish."

They gazed out at the sea of women. Jakob's eyes found Mammie, swaying, with bobbing children all around. Mevrouw and Mammie were together, holding Sara in the middle. Jakob's eyes held Mammie's for a long time. He felt a cord of love from her eyes to his, sending him her strength. Sara looked up, spoke to her, and tugged her hand. Mammie never looked down at Sara; no words to zusje. Mevrouw Bevins stood on her other side, with no Siebe to hold, two women silent in a sea of tears.

††††

Luce

Houston, Texas
October 2004

Doors whoosh open on my lone journey away from Dr. Ingstrom's office. Everyone else has already made their treks to visit Alby.

I am consumed by the suffering in the Japanese camps. Pake used to tell us, when he was close to the end of his life, that the cord was growing stronger, meaning that he was being pulled to heaven and his reunion with Beppe. The life cord became thin filament and the heaven cord a rope, by the time the camps were liberated. But I don't think many focused on heaven; too much of hell had been lived to allow for God's grace and heaven.

The usual hospital surroundings I know all too well all rise up along one long hall, and pull me back. Antiseptic smells, pinging bells, patients calling out, intercom announcements *(Code ...)*, odd wall signs — not helpful. I could get lost here and need to stumble outside for a dose of reality. But I should stay inside. Muted colors, too-cold air-conditioning blasts, staff in white lab coats strolling, visitors with stories in their eyes. I rush along and feel otherworldly as if I have to absorb as much terror as Papa's family did at Kamp Tjideng all those years ago. I must find my way to this next, and I hope last, hospital room. It's as if I'm rumbling away on the boys' truck, crammed in, looking for my brother — a scared boy.

Through the hallway window, I see clumps of family in the parking lot. Corrie hugs Cindy. In their closeness I can see frustrations melting away. Mama and Papa head toward the hospital cafeteria to wait for me. I'm puzzled Dr. Ingstrom never mentioned Alby again, and didn't offer to come with me to connect us. No one has really prepared me for what to expect. I imagine he's hitting rock bottom because he's tired, because he's glad I'm here. I pause to lean against a wall, hating that I feel abandoned by Dr. Ingstrom — Clara, her office sign said. I am not the patient, and this isn't about me. Ironically, thirty years ago in my own recovery, I didn't allow my family to have it be about me; I had my secrets to protect.

Wavy generic paintings, like desert sand dunes, lead me past the ER, with Vista-*Feasta* signs beckoning beyond. Double doors bang open as medics jump out of a wailing ambulance. They swing out with a man on a gurney, brace around his neck, an IV on its pole, just like in the movies, just like Papa and Alby thirty years ago.

This must be where Alby came in, almost dead. I hasten my steps, ready to escape the urgent cases. A woman moans, "Nurse, nurse." My shoes squeak on linoleum. All doors have metallic-streaked scratches from scraping of gurneys, laundry, meals. I can't get away quickly enough. Soon, I'm by the signs: Hope Vista and New Vista. I think of Mama and Papa's *feasta* pronunciations and grin. One of these wards holds Alby.

I stop at the next nurse's station. A nurse sits there between one world and the next. Half of her window opens to me. The other half opens to the unit beyond. So New Vista must be official rehab, and he's not there yet. Do they check patients for readiness for the next unit by seeing if they can keep the names straight? If so, I wouldn't make the transfer.

I reach for the door handle vigorously and my hand jerks. The doorknob's stuck.

"I have to buzz you in, dear. Hope Vista is locked."

I should have known. This is why I was grateful when Papa first called to say they have him locked up. I count room numbers and find him, silhouetted in his room. He's reading the familiar dark-blue AA Big Book, the one your first sponsor or rehab has you read over and over to help you work the Twelve Steps of personal recovery. "Hello, Alby."

He turns to me fully and I shiver. His shadowed eyes and hollowed cheeks show he's emaciated to the point of looking like one of the skeletal boys leaving Tjideng. Wet, combed-back hair drips onto a faded turquoise-blue polo shirt. Don't they give them towels here? He looks like an earnest little boy, doing his best. I realize with a rush of shock that I feared a strong and rebellious Alby, not this guy.

"*Dag,* Alby." Switching to our Dutch greeting holds many nuances. Dag means here you are, hello, good-bye all in one word. I come between him and the window. There is nowhere for me to sit, as he's on the one chair. It will be either the bed, or the broad windowsill.

"*Dag,* Luce. You're here."

Funny how even Alby emphasizes how I'm here, echoing our parents' admonition, *don't go anywhere, don't run off to talk to friends.* "Yes, I'm here."

We both grin big. This may be the first time we're happy to see each other in five years. Quivering joy and light warms my heart and collides in an ache in my throat, bursting to talk, to challenge, rather than fall for the tricks of loving Alby, only to be hurt again.

When I touch his neck, water drips from his hair to my hand, like a sad rivulet. "So you do want to live now?" *There are places worse than here. The ones you don't come back from.*

He stands and flinches when he puts his weight on his bad left hip, wobbling and resting one hand on the chair.

I grab his other arm, trying to help. I realize my immediate directness unbalances him. I clench my jaw. He is frail. Just as frail as Papa, during World War II or now. "Oh Alby, you're in pain. I've been so worried about you."

"Worried? Great. Worry's like a love song in our family," he says tiredly.

"Oh Ja."

We smile again, and I think about Papa's continuous worry cycle, which was always his off-kilter love song to us kids.

Alby grimaces as he drops back into his chair. "No pain meds here, of course." He pulls himself straight up.

I pull a chair in from the hallway, screeching it along the floor toward Alby. He flinches again. He must be on a long detox, every nerve on edge. He's shoving something behind his back. Oh, he has a cell phone again; how does he keep smuggling them in?

He sees my look and juts his chin out. "Luce, don't visit me just to be a pain and a detective. I want to live. I never stopped wanting to live."

"Great. I'm so proud of you, so proud of Papa for starting to tell us all more."

"What?" His eyes look puzzled.

"Oh yes, Papa told all about entering and leaving the first kamp."

"Tjideng," we say together.

I feel relaxed for the first time since getting off the plane. This is good. "Hey, Daniel and Vincent say hi, and I have an AA meditation book with me. The same one we read all those years ago, so we could read together."

"Nah." He points at his own meditation book. "So let me tell you about my work. Exciting things are happening. I had FDA approval for my third medication patent right before the accidental overdose."

So that's how he's playing it.

"I have job security up the wazoo. But the board needs me to move quickly out of here; they'll only hold on so long. Timing's everything with a new medication release."

This doesn't sound true to me. What is he, the main salesperson, not a top project manager and researcher? "Okay," I interrupt, trying to beat him at his own game. He could always talk faster than any of us. "So workwise, everything is fine."

He waves his arm back to the psych surroundings. A Doctor Green is paged overhead. "Well Luce, this isn't all there is for me. I do have a life to get back to."

"And I have a life I'm away from," I snap, and I leave the peaceful eye of the hurricane for the crazy outside of *ruzie*. "So for you, every moment of coming here, everything is wonderful in your life? Maybe I shouldn't worry about you, or love you." I intended to be nice, but I'm standing up, waving an arm too. "Can't you see where you are? In the middle of a psych ward this time!"

He opens his mouth, closes it again. He's not fighting back as hard as I'm used to with him.

I ease myself back down. *Try, just try. Don't give up now.* I go on gently, almost reverently, wanting to see the light come back into his eyes. "I thought you'd realize that you could die. I thought you'd realize you scared everyone who loves you, especially Marina finding you and thinking you dead that day. I thought you'd put first things first like they said to both of us when we got better together in the HOW program, like they also say in AA."

I turn, and he's dropped his Big Book on the bed and is fiddling with the contraband phone. "Come on, Luce. You bring up HOW from a century ago. Really, I suppose the Honesty Openness and Willingness and its slogans helped us then. We were kids, we could be idealistic. I never asked you to leave your life and come here. And I've got real world work issues, as a director, to get back to."

"Drop it about work. There are more important things," I hiss.

He struggles up again and bellows. "You never call me, you hardly visit, and I can't say one thing about work, one huge thing like FDA approval." His belly bulges on one side — must be the liver damage.

I grab his bony frame in a shoving kind of hug, and find myself holding him up. Although he's tall, he feels like a wisp of a man.

He pulls back and glares. "So you may as well leave. You do that well."

"Fine!" I yell.

If I leave now, he'll feel the loss I've felt all these years. In one minute he's turned it all around on me. It's senseless to tell Alby that he's the one who's always missing. He never gets on the phone. We Lewises visit Texas all the time. He never visits us in California, even when work brings him to nearby San Francisco.

When my sneakers skid and squeak again on the polished linoleum it brings me back, catching myself running away. I stop and lean against the wall, staring at the New Vista and Hope Vista signs. The deadened joy-light lump in my throat is huge. I imagine he's sitting in his room in shock, a longing look in his eyes. I don't know if he understands or can name the closeness we used to have, and he doesn't want to hear the deep need inside of me. I miss him as much as always, even though he's near.

This is our chance. I will my angry heart to stop pounding. To not count up this third chance like an accusation. No, this right here is our chance. Just like it was an emergency when Papa and Alby had the ultralight plane accident when he was a teen, and I did all a scared teenaged girl could do, this is our only chance now. Furthermore, if he leaves *Feasta Whatever*, I'll always worry it was because of me. I groan. Am I really thinking, *what will everyone think about me*? Yes.

Voices murmur from the nurse's station. A nurse, Endurance I see by her name tag, strolls by. I almost ask her for help, but watch her back instead, beautiful regal bearing, tall, ebony skin. Why isn't Alby out in the hall? *So that's what I wanted, like a big baby — for him to find me.*

His body is weak, his central nervous system shot. The guy in the room is not fully my brother. I have to remember, not a thought in his head makes sense. I should have stayed. I rest in the patient common room, a place with big windows and posters about change. Why do I always end up feeling like I'm wrong, when he is the one not returning phone calls for a year, not talking to my son—his nephew, not caring if I am in his life at all? I trudge back.

He is curled up on the bed.

"Hey," I say.

"Hey," he says, not moving.

I take his damp chair and pull close to him. "I can't handle you going on and on about work. That's all I get from you: only what you want to talk about ... or nothing."

"It's really been that bad?" He hugs himself, shivering.

"Yeah. For instance, do you know how old I am?"

"Forty-four," he says.

"No. Forty-five and my birthday is a month and two years before yours, so that's not hard, Alby. Everything is off for you. I get your work, that you're a brilliant research director and patent guy. Because of that, you need to stay here, to get it together."

"I'm not going anywhere."

I touch his cheek. "Then why do you have to talk like you do? Get better. I love you; I do want to be with you. People enter rehab so they actually feel better, you know? What do they call it here? Uh ..."

"Hope *Feasta*." His shoulders shake with the same joke playing in my brain. He sighs. "I might as well stay here in Hope Vista, but you know how's it's been. Rehab doesn't work for me," he says woodenly.

"Of course it works," I reassure. "You're still detoxing, remember? You're going to feel like hell right now."

"Well, work really is going good." He reaches next to him.

"Got it!" I grab his cell phone off his bed. "Focus, Alby. You can do this. We struggle with depression in our family, and some of us struggle with alcoholism, addiction. We act as if we're unique, us Vanderveers, the little foreign kids. You will get better just like anybody else Alby, really. You have so much to live for. Don't play this game with me like I'm the one who's a million miles away. You are too."

"Luce, you're crazy! Who are you, the police? Give me my phone back. You really are a million miles away. Like here you are lecturing me, and I know nothing that's going on with you."

My chest burns, and I grip both hands around the phone like I'll never let go. "Funny, Corrie said the same thing."

"Yeah, so sit with me for a while. And it is important for you to know that the new biomedical chemical we're developing is a ..."

I leap up, relieved to leave with kinder words. "Soon Alby, we'll have that long talk. I love you, gotta go."

In my haste I almost run into Endurance. "Sorry." My eyes are blurry with tears. "Did you know he had this?" I hold up the cell phone.

"Nope." She grins.

Either its amusing to her that I'm just another raging family member ready to leave, or hilarious that he got away with smuggling in one more phone — his lifeline to work. He's just a typical addict. If he puts half the energy into recovery that he puts into rule breaking, he'll do fine.

I walk the maze of halls. Before I left Calabria, I contemplated every day how fragile Alby must be, and imagined him cradled in God's hands, not mine. I imagined how caring we would be, how we would just sit together, without words. Yet the second I arrived, an ancient anger hit, which trumped his frailty. Then I walked in one more time only to seize his phone.

I meet Mama and Papa in the cafeteria. They are holding hands, such a contrast to the old days of frequent *ruzie*. Mama reaches up to my face. She can see I've been crying.

"*Heh-heh*, that was quick," says Papa. "Go back to him, he needs you."

"No, I'm done," I say. "There's just no use in trying to get across to him."

Mama's face falls. "Why did we all even bother to come today?"

"It's good we bothered. Really, it's doing a lot of good, Mama." I try to sound convincing and touch Papa's folder that he's still carrying. "You're both helping him. I just need to be more patient. You're for sure helping me."

Mama has a questioning look on her face. "Helping you?"

I feel guilty for having been the one to drop the familiar family line, *it's just no use*. No wonder I chose to live so far away from the whole family. They're exhausting. I tell the people I counsel that they are not responsible for their family's painful feelings, but I also tell them to be kind. I have failed at both.

All the way home I jerk and bump along with Papa's driving. When we pull up into the driveway, it occurs to me that I didn't say how Mama and Papa are helping me with their revelations. I feel the strange elation of a good cover-up. Maybe I'll pretend everything's "hunky-dory," as Mama and Papa would say. But it's not hunky-dory. It scares me that I walked away twice. Surely he won't stay this stubborn, nor will I. He's got to get better.

† † †

The next morning I read my Bible in bed, sipping water while longing for strong Dutch coffee. But I don't want to get up yet. My stomach clenches, and I remember how I treated Alby, and how I came to hear more of Papa's story. I read my favorite worn AA meditation book. Maybe Alby's reading his. I hadn't wanted to be gone long when I planned this trip, so I arranged for only four days. But now I yearn to stay longer. My anger at Alby abated overnight, and the sense of Papa as a boy is back. I pull out my journal and write, *I will return*, which strikes me as dramatic and motivating, like General McArthur saying he would return to the Philippines after defeat on the Bataan Peninsula. No, just me, needing second, third, fourth chances—just like Alby.

I need to appear fully dressed. That way I can choose between hanging out or escaping for a walk. From the hallway to the kitchen, I hear loud voices and automatically slow down. Papa and Mama are always more intense in pairs, like snake number one and two in Papa's story. Easier to slip into the old habits of spying on my parents when I'm still hidden from view.

"That doctor, she is crazy to cover so much in one appointment," comes Mama's strident voice.

"Ja, *wel*, the Norwegians always were a stubborn bunch, and they didn't suffer as much as us during the war. They had their bravery, but less deprivation than the rest of Europe ... or Indonesia."

"And Alby, he was not even there with us."

"Ja, I talked to him this morning. He thinks everything is wonderful. He insists he'll leave in two days. I will not say more to him or that doctor about my life, all the pain. That boy is impossible."

I stifle a gasp. Papa will shut down again.

"You know, maybe that doctor is crazy, but at least she has a plan. You will talk, Jakob."

Mama championing open communication — amazing. The blanket of warmth from yesterday steals over me. I venture in.

"Good morning," I say loudly.

They both jump.

"How did you sleep?" asks Papa. Dutch people always want to know how you slept. He looks rested, not guarded. He's makes a show of loading the dishwasher. Cane and all, he drops in one item at a time. I picture him when he left Kamp Tjideng with Albert, anticipating adventure in the midst of chaos. He was not yet the methodical fix-it man he is now.

"I slept well. And I would like to know more about you and the kamps, Papa. Remember how I always asked?"

He shoots me a knowing look. He knows I was spying.

We sit for my late breakfast. Mama and Papa have their coffee. Mine is a perfection of strong grind and warm milk. *Kinder* — children's — *koffie*, we call it. I look at Papa expectantly, willing him to talk.

"You know, all this has me thinking," he says. "*Bersiap* is what happened upon our liberation, when no armed allied forces had arrived. *Bersiap* meant get ready for a huge revolution, a revolution like a flood, all of Indonesia back into turmoil. The kamps were 'liberated,' but our captors, the Japanese, were ordered to protect us. Young Indonesian rebels with Japanese weapons, or anything they could hold in their hands, went on the attack." He goes on and on.

I take mental notes, terrified that taking real notes or, God forbid, finding a tape recorder in Papa's study, would stop him. I'll remember all that Vincent and Daniel will want to know. I then glance at my watch. I had planned to see Alby one more time. But I can't leave Papa now.

"*Bersiap*," says Mama, "the chaos of the end for you, reminds me of the chaos of the beginning for us. First the grown-ups believed they shouldn't warn us. You know how it was, don't worry the children. Then one day the Nazis marched into the town square of Leeuwarden."

Leeuwarden, like home to me, so near Beppe and Pake's last farm.

"All of Nederland had fought briefly. You know why? The Germans were bombing our dikes and flooding the country. In the province of Friesland we had to surrender immediately. Within the year, Heit, my father, had to hide all the time against the *razzias*, when the Nazis rounded up all able-bodied men and sent them to labor camps."

"Labor camps like concentration camps?" I ask slowly.

She nods. "Almost as bad, we heard. By that time our farm house had no heat or light. Towards the end of the war, I had abscesses from poor nutrition. Yet, we were lucky. Being on a farm, we suffered malnutrition but not complete starvation in that last hunger winter. I remember twenty-thousand people died." Her face has the red spots which flare on her face for deep emotion. Sadie and Tutu come running as if they know she's upset. "The most lucky is I lost no family. Not so for you." She looks at Papa.

Usually when she is sad, brittle angry words break out, as if she would snap in two from surrendering to grief. Today her face looks the softest I have ever seen her in sorrow. I reach for her hand, and I don't have to ask questions.

Papa slurps his coffee, plunks it down. "Yes, I lost family." His face grows paler, and he and Mama put their hands together, clenched. "By the time Albert died in 1945, bodies were taken away stacked, only occasionally sewed into burlap bags or put in coffins, but Albert did have a funeral of sorts. Young people died less than the old ones … Everyone was sad. The Japanese were so brutal. They were nice occasionally to the young children at Tjideng. But in the next camp, right away we were treated like men. Forced labor, everything."

They must have beaten Albert for some imagined or fabricated crime. Finding food should never be a crime. He may have grabbed extra food, smuggled it in, or allowed himself to be the scapegoat for another prisoner's mistake. The beating must have led to Albert's demise. I still can't help feeling that it's too horrible to ask Papa for details, because in doing so, it would be me causing him pain, his memory of war.

I see a poor broken body wrapped in burlap, or maybe a makeshift coffin. My young Papa assaulted by the worst good-bye.

He says somehow there was a violin player, a ritual few others had.

Moments pass, then Papa swings to his feet with his habitual grunt of effort. He wants to show me something and goes off to fetch it. He returns with a photograph of himself and Mollie.

I peel an orange from the bowl on the table, and admire the photograph. I put my arm around Papa. "Thank you," I say. "I wish I could take all the pain away."

"Well, I always pretended the pain was gone."

"Except for your nightmares," Mama says.

"And now we'll talk a bit more, because Dr. Ingstrom is right. Telling does make pain come up like a crashing waves. But you dive through them and the pain ebbs away."

CHAPTER 6

Jakob

Billiton Island
December 1941

Jakob stood panting on the porch; Mollie had won the race once again. Rain slowed from a constant snare drum to a faint pitter-patter. Sun broke through the clouds. It was going be a warm *tidur siang*—nap time. Just then, the family car, referred to as the Henry Ford, pulled into the driveway.

Our hero! The words rang in Jakob's ears as if there truly had been a battle, and Pappie had crowed the words out loud. Pappie got out of the Henry Ford and hurried inside while the chauffeur drove the car to its place behind the house.

Jakob raced to the *goedang*—kitchen pantry room, and automatically checked for snakes. He dried off with a rough warm towel and pulled on dry clothes, leaving his mud-spattered outfit for Baboe to find. His mission was to make it to the living room without being detected by Mammie and Pappie.

Although Indian-quiet, Pappie still sensed him. "Not now, Jakob," he said without turning his head. "We are busy. Go see Min."

Jakob opened his mouth to protest. Why was Albert allowed to stay? Albert sat quietly on the teak bench, bent over his botany book. He caught Jakob's eye, shaking his head as if to say, *don't make a fuss. They have forgotten all about me.*

Jakob scuffed his feet as he wandered away. Pappie always noticed him first, then everyone else. He retrieved one of his favorite books, *War of the Worlds*, and headed into the kitchen. Kokkie and Min murmured while they worked. Sara was making tea. Mollie purred in the corner. Despite having run through the monsoon rains, only the tips of her tail and her ears were wet.

Jakob imagined the Japs could be lurking along the shoreline, with knives in their teeth, right now. No, not onshore yet, just out of range on a great battleship, planning to invade by sea and air. He felt a chill up his spine. *Yes, we will all be prepared to fight.* He would have to wait patiently until Albert filled him in.

Min smiled as her darting hands laid out the children's tea set, next to the doll tea set, on the smallest veranda table. Dark storm clouds ruled the sky, rising taller than the great ship they had sailed to and from the Netherlands. A Japanese carrier could be that vast. Jakob kicked the table impatiently. Maybe he could sneak down the hall and hide just outside the living room door to find out what Pappie had to say.

But he couldn't leave Sara alone. She settled in with Tina, touching the little gray scar. Tina and she wore identical little-girls' outfits, skirts with crisscross shoulder straps, over white blouses. Sara lifted two tea cups in turn, first the play cup for Tina, then her own. Each time she switched, Jakob kicked the table again, rattling the dishes.

Finally she frowned. "Be careful! You'll spill Tina's tea."

Jakob rolled his eyes, but didn't dare protest. Pappie and Mammie still didn't know about Tina's wound. Sara had been wonderful about not telling. This waiting for Albert was too hard. The delay was worse than sitting in school with a history textbook, the teacher droning on about changes from one century to the other, then writing an endless, boring paper, with only one illustration to have fun with. And who cared about the Romans anyway, or the

Greeks? But this was war. When would he finally know more?

He lifted out of his chair to sneak back into the living room, just as Albert finally appeared, his eyes wider than usual, moving with purpose. They all bumped their chairs in close to the table. His description was soft and intense, like the scariest of stories told by their favorite uncle, Tante Ankie's husband. "Pappie said to Mammie, 'The Billiton Mine Company believes we have been here for generations and will be here for generations to come,' and not to worry."

Not to worry. So it was time to worry. Even the powerful company thought so.

The evening sky darkened, and they heard the scurrying *tjik-tjak* house lizards starting their nighttime hunt for insects.

Albert went on with his exacting memory and Pappie's commanding tone, "Liefje, there are so many parts to this massive Japanese war machine. I would like to tell you we will defeat them, but we are backed by a home country already conquered, and there our Wim is. So the company says no panic, no big moving operation. But be wise. Who knows when we will return to Billiton? We'll put some valuables in hiding now to our most trusted family, Kokkie's. Pack cleverly. No one can ever prepare fully for war. Take provisions, take some of everything."

"He said the Japanese war machine is huge?" Jakob envisioned a towering machine moving about the earth, like the alien space ships in *War of the Worlds.* "What huge machine?"

Albert chuckled exactly as grown-ups did. "He means the Japanese are powerful, like a big machine. We can't be sure to win when they invade."

Jakob's cheeks flamed with embarrassment. "And he told Mammie what to do?"

"He said Liefje. They held hands. He said pack carefully, but not too much. She has to pack just right. We all do."

Was it wonderful, his father being gentle, and firmly telling him to leave the room, but not yelling? Or was it strange and terrifying? Pappie held hands with Mammie, said Liefje, quietly listed plan after plan. Pappie, just like he and Albert now, thought when the tin company said not to worry, it was time to worry. Jakob grew dizzy. One towering dark cloud flowed into another. Was he sick? No, only war and leaving could make him feel so bad. He flushed more with fear and determination.

In the movie in his head, he had been in an anonymous house with Pappie, fiercely fighting, with Albert as lookout. But it would be their own house shot up, destroyed, set on fire, gone, everyone scattered. The men would fight back against the Japanese like that. And, of course, the Vanderveers would be prepared as they always were. But when would it end? This is why the grown-ups said nothing—to not scare him. Yet they had no idea of his courageous determination.

Albert gulped tea and somberly lifted a teacup for Tina.

Sara tugged at her skirt. "Do you think Wim is reading any letters from us? When we all leave, how will he know our new address?"

"Don't you remember?" said Jakob scornfully. "We can't send anything, not even a telegram, because of the Germans. Wim is living with the enemy all around."

Sara had forgotten. Her face fell; she would cry.

He felt terrible. He'd been angry at Albert for talking to him like he was a child, not Sara. Albert eyed him over Sara's head as if saying, *Stop it with the scary talk.*

Quickly Jakob added, "Well, I think that someone in Nederland has our favorite books for him. He must still be in that nice boarding house he wrote us about, and they all take turns reading aloud. He takes his turn too, and wishes we could all do the story together. He knows that the Japanese are sneaking up on us and he's wishing he could fight."

95

"Do you think the Japanese are like *War of the Worlds*?" Sara scrunched her eyes.

"Well ..." Albert shrugged. "I don't think so. And I bet at Wim's boarding house, they read *The Jungle Book* too."

"So Wim can have his own wolf pack there, and we can have ours here."

"We are a wolf pack," replied Albert. They moved to the cushioned rattan chairs and talked about Wim all at once, as if their thoughts had been waiting to explode.

"Actually, you know," said Albert, "Opa and Oma must have traveled to get him. They're all okay, because they're together."

Sara turned Tina away from their talk, and hugged her close. "The nice Oma and Opa?" This meant Mammie's parents.

They all grinned. Their other Oma and Opa were strict, and Opa had cuffed Albert's ears hard just for coming to dinner a few minutes late. Albert templed his fingers together like their teacher at school. "I hear they have secret radios in Nederland. So it will make sense to him that we are evacuating to Java. Plus, after a few months we'll come right back to Billiton and wait for him. He'll know where to find us. Don't worry."

The older you were, the more you said don't worry, over and over again.

Sara stroked Tina's golden hair. "I miss him."

"I miss him too," replied Jakob, imagining Wim surrounded by Nazis shouting, *Zieg Heil!*

They kept talking about Wim but, except for the mention of Oma and Opa, all the details escaped their wondering. It was as if they each envisioned a dark cloud around him, which their imaginations couldn't penetrate. Behind that dark cloud, there was Wim, waiting longer than any of them, in a country already at war. They fell silent. Albert surprised them by speaking again, even though his head had sunk back into his botany book. "We could leave the island any day now. We must be prepared."

Sara arranged Tina's hair down her back. Jakob wondered if the hair fibers were mixed with real gold. Gold could be hammered infinitely thin. But no, probably Tina did not have real gold in her hair, and for their brotherly war preparations, Jakob had to trick Sara to go away. "Hey, would you get my popgun? It's by my bed."

Off she went; she loved to handle the popgun. Once it was in her hands, she knew she would have a chance to shoot the cork out on its long string.

Jakob said, "Joh, so we'll keep packing."

They spoke intensely about what to take, with Jakob insisting they could get knives from Adri, and Albert rolling his eyes.

† † †

At bedtime Min called them all like usual. Jakob hurried into his pajamas and they all went to say good night to Mammie and Pappie. They were in the living room, bent over Pappie's 1942 daybook, for next year. A little green ribbon dangled down, ready to keep their place. Pappie rubbed each of their heads, Mammie smiled. It felt good tonight to come up close.

Like Albert said, they had been planning. Up till now Jakob had focused on Mammie's shudders and Pappie's yelled commands. Cooperation was nice. Maybe Pappie would treat him like he had on board ship, pointing out longs lists to him, instead of seafaring routes. Jakob would help get everything organized. Organized — *geregeld*. That's what the grown-ups always said. Whenever you left or arrived anywhere, you were okay, once all was *geregeld*.

Falling asleep, Jakob thought of Albert. Not ready to hide, fight, or survive, impractical, inclined to haul along his heavy botany book. Although Albert could be very *geregeld* about finding plant samples, sketching, or labeling, he was

97

terribly unworldly. Grownups always treated Jakob like he was a disaster waiting to happen. Actually Albert was the disaster, for he would not be ready. Jakob would have to watch out for both of them.

He imagined Mammie and Pappie falling asleep, with a new, vague wondering. Mammie and Pappie loved each other, sought each other out, held hands, called each other *schatje*, liefje—treasure, loved one. They did whatever married people did, which stirred sharp, funny feelings in his belly. Did they take off their clothes? Was it like the dogs on the compound? How strange. How exciting.

† † †

Dawn came with first and second light as always, and for the first time Jakob opened his eyes at second light, late. Albert was the one out of bed first. Jakob stretched and pondered his dreams. Had he dreamed it, or did Pappie stand over him in the middle of the night, as Indian-quiet as he himself always wished to be? Pappie had hovered, peering down through his glasses. His pajama's stripes were silver and blue in the dark. Yes, Pappie must have been there. He must have stood over each of them, loving them all through the night.

† † †

I jump when the old-fashioned phone rings by my elbow. "Vanderveer reside—."

"It's me," says Cindy.

She's probably going to give me an earful for my shortness with Alby.

"Hey," she says, "how are you getting to the airport?"

"I called a taxi."

"The kids and I are going to go see Alby in the hospital. Why don't we drop you off at the airport on the way?"

Mama insists on briskly walking me and my suitcase out to Cindy, oblivious to Papa's need to move much slower.

They still look older, but holding their postures carefully, proud, determined. My heart pangs. Papa leans heavily on his cane and Mama sighs as I hug and kiss good-bye. Unexpectedly they do the European kisses with me, on each side of my face. Unaccustomed, I bump foreheads and collapse into the front seat.

"Oh, I missed you so much. Next time, a longer visit," I promise them.

Papa doesn't even warn me about getting to the airport on time. It's like all his energy is going to helping, which is something new — *or old*.

Cindy pulls out of the driveway and I look back at Mama and Papa, until they become waving dots on the driveway. I'm waving. I see the grandkids do it too, a habit from too many good-byes to the rest of the family in train stations and airports.

I confess to Cindy, "I think I was mean to Alby yesterday." Should I give her the details?

She pats my leg. "I know, I went to church this morning and prayed not to lose my temper with him. He can be such a force of nature, so driven. Obviously Dr. Ingstrom is right. He does need to stay put for a while instead of coming home. Don't be hard on yourself; he's not easy to talk to right now."

"Guess not," I say, amazed that she understands. "I say those prayers about not losing my temper too. I always failed at it when I was a teenager with Papa, and now with Alby."

She sighs. "Those theories and explanations are all he's got. He hopes he has a CEO and board who want to see him get help and come back."

"He's got us," Wade calls from the backseat.

"Oh sweetie, you're right. And family, that's the best."

I squeeze her hand and watch a tear run down her cheek. She's got to be tired of the kids being hurt.

As we near the airport, the skies open up, bringing the hardest day of rain yet. We can hardly see as cars and freeway blur around us. Houstonians are used to this; Cindy keeps a steady speed on the freeway. Wade sings along to the radio. Good, he must feel better.

Cindy's got the radio on an inspirational music station that's playing "Breathe" by Michael W. Smith, I breathe.

Traffic comes to a standstill. A car spun out ahead, blocking two lanes. Amazingly, no signs of a collision. I glance at the time on the dash, and resist saying we're running late. We start to ease along. Go, go, brake, brake, go, go. Fat raindrops fall, a rhythmic pit-a-pat—and I remember the last time I walked hand in hand with my brother, through our first neighborhood in Houston. Albert or Bertie, we called him then. Such an active, sensitive boy. This is who he still must be ... inside.

† † †

Houston, Texas
Spring 1970

It was raining of course. We were bored. Mama looked up from her card game with Corrie. "You two should put on your rain gear and go meet new kids."

Off we went down a busy suburban street, nothing like the village feeling of our time in Provo, Utah.

At each doorway, adults came to the door puzzled. Their eyes said, *why are you alone*? But we weren't alone, we had each other. Then we got to the fourth door down, Tommy's house as it turned out.

His mom came to the door. "Sure, we have kids for you to play with. Come on in to the kitchen." She looked like one of our teenaged babysitters in her cutoff shorts and neatly pressed blouse. We followed a great smell—cooking oil that simmered in an electric skillet, tiny drops of it spattering against the wallpaper in the kitchen. "Let me just pull out this fried chicken." She added to a platter heaped with layers of greasy paper towels.

Bertie looked at it wide-eyed. Fried chicken—his favorite.

"Tommy," she yelled, "visitors!"

Tommy came in as his mom put a steaming plate of drumsticks in the middle of the table for us. A little girl appeared, Corrie's age, long hair pulled back with a head band.

"This is my Tammy, kids. What did you say your names were?"

Tommy and Tammy, how cute.

"Liesbet and Albert. We're Dutch," I explained.

"Oh," their mom drawled. "We'll call you Lucy and Alby. Alby sounds like L. B., a real Texas name."

We nodded.

Lucy, not Liesbet. I felt broken and excited at the same time. A new city, a new name. I started to crunch on the chicken, wondering if I could lick my fingers. Looking up to see Tommy's mom still cooking, I saw a belt hanging in the wall, hooked over a nail. Tommy saw me look and blushed. I reached for Alby's hand under the table and squeezed his hand, prodded him to look.

"Delicious chicken," I said. I tried to smile the widest smile I could in Tommy's direction, to somehow make it okay. "Heh-heh," said Alby—L. B. on the short walk home. I knew what he meant.

"Poor Tommy," I replied. Houston, a whole new rougher place to be.

† † †

Sun is breaking though the clouds. We're moving fast again. I ask Cindy to turn off the radio and talk to the kids, hearing about their horses, the school, even what it's like to visit their Dad.

"Today we have a family therapy appointment," volunteers Marina.

I crane my neck to look at the kids. Their faces have lost the pinched, stressed look they had when we last came for a Thanksgiving visit. They look satisfied; something good is happening at *Feasta*.

Our family — Alby, Corrie, and I. No beatings with belts, an orderly home, dinner on the table every night at six, our stacks of books, our coziness. Yet always, I felt fear. Somehow it didn't bother Alby as much; he was sunnier than I. But I wondered all the time: When was the next *ruzie*? Who could survive Papa's rage or Mama's crying? Who was going to break?

Marina and Wade are singing along to the radio, which Cindy's turned back up. I'm too cautious to be satisfied with family therapy, promises, and hope. *I need you, Alby. And you're the only one who knows why I need you so much. You remember.* I never responded to what Alby *did* say that had nothing to do with his work. *You're a million miles away. You don't say what's on your heart.*

You're right. Let me tell you … That's what I should have said yesterday, but yesterdays don't come back.

Like a good Vanderveer by marriage, Cindy rushes me to my flight.

On time.

† † †

Daniel and Vincent stand in front of baggage claim, waving crazy arms to make me laugh.

I trip at the bottom of the escalator into Daniel's arms. "Whoa there."

"Wow Mom, watch out," Vincent says. "Family hug."

I'm tall, yet they both tower a head above me. I'm fortunate that public hugs don't bother Vincent at all. We walk out into the dry, cool Northern California air. As we hit the freeway, I try to ignore a sour smell and feel nauseous. Daniel must have spilled some milky coffee on the floorboard. I focus my eyes determinedly on the road and squeeze my wrist in a spot that chases off nausea, according to a guide on a whale-watching ship. It seems to work. "Amazing, how my time with Grandma and Grandpa went."

Vincent's suddenly deeper voice comes from the backseat. "So, how is Uncle Alby?"

"I only saw him one day. I actually talked more with your aunt and cousins."

"Mom, he's your brother. I thought that's why you went."

"We had our family appointment without him. He wasn't well enough yet for a whole emotional deal, I guess. Then I saw him alone and left."

"You're mad at him."

"Yeah, I guess." I sigh. I hate and love that Vincent reads me well.

"What about Opa?" asks Daniel.

I'm grateful for the topic change. "What Grandpa said blew me away. When he was a year older than you, Vincent, the concentration camps were finally liberated, but there was chaos. The survivors expected that since they were free, they would immediately be rescued by Allied soldiers, receive help, and return to their homes. Instead, there were no Allied soldiers arriving yet, and the Japanese were ordered to turn from being cruel captors to protectors. Liberation did not make their world safe; it ended up being called the *Bersiap* time. It was an empty freedom without safety. Imagine, the enemy, the Japanese were supposed to protect you."

"No wonder Grandpa never trusted anyone."

"Ja. Native Indonesians declared the country independent and began to fight the Dutch. The Japanese told the Dutch camp survivors, that in order to protect them, they should stay put in the camps. Grandpa, of course, didn't trust that."

"Of course not, Grandpa was too smart for that." Vincent sounds satisfied.

"Yeah, Grandpa longed to find his family, and he didn't believe they were safe. When he was just a weak and starving sixteen-year-old, he found a small resistance band and ended up fighting alongside Dutch and British soldiers."

Daniel looks over at me. "What? He found Allied soldiers there already?"

"Well," I continue, "there was some minor resistance, I thought, all during the war years." Daniel must have missed some of our words.

I see Vincent's straight Vanderveer-Lewis mouth in the visor mirror.

"Mom, why didn't they just fight back from the moment they were rounded up? You know, not at the end of the war, but at the beginning of the war? They had the Japanese outnumbered, right?"

Our exit comes up for home, and Daniel turns the car onto a bumpy country road. Calabria's farm fields gently lead us to the denser housing developments.

I'm fumbling in my bag, looking for a sour candy to suck on. "That's what Grandpa said he wanted: to fight the Japanese. All the kids lost faith in their fathers, lost their sense of heroes. Yet he knew why his pappie didn't fight. Imagine the brutality of the Japanese. From the moment of invasion, the Dutch witnessed others struck down, bleeding, even beheaded because they didn't immediately bow to the emperor-god in an L-posture."

"Oh." Vincent looks out the window, taking in the war, death. "But still, they could have overtaken them."

"They didn't have the modern weapons the Japanese did. And any place that the Dutch might actually win, there would be brutal reprisals in other areas. The Dutch civilians didn't stand a chance."

"Oh, so he couldn't fight then, and maybe he was glad to fight by the end. I'm gonna call Grandpa and ask him about it."

I yawn from exhaustion and almost say, *No. No way, he can't handle it.* But I stop myself. "Okay, why don't you?"

"Call him, Vincent," Daniel calls out loudly as if everyone in the car is hard of hearing like him. "We need to hear about the battles he fought in."

Daniel's tone is off, sarcastic. Does he resent me leaving after all? Papa often annoys Daniel too, with his many phone calls. We've had calls about passport renewals, where we invest our money, that it's time Daniel gets a secure salaried job and that we must move into a bigger house. Maybe listening to Papa has become a burden for Daniel, and all new to Vincent.

PART TWO

Each man carries within him the soul of a poet
who died young.
— Antoine de Saint-Exupery

CHAPTER 7

I leave early for work the next day, my AA sponsor Kemble's suggestion. "Honey," she said, "get to work early. Spend the first half hour alone in your office. You need to come back to yourself." It's wonderful to me that she talks in this motherly way, especially since with Mama my vague goal is to be closer to her ... one day. Both of us do the reveal, hide, reveal. We're more likely to talk about the rest of the family than ourselves.

Entering my office sanctuary, I wonder if my clients love this space as much as I do. The tiny Black Madonna is in her spot, glinting ebony and gold. A huge evergreen tree silhouettes my window. My marble Golden Bear, which I found at an art show, is settled by the clients' couch, blessing each appointment.

I wrap my hands around Black Madonna while listening to my messages. She always looks wise, being as ancient as she is, believed to be a melding of ancient myths of fertility and the mother of Christ. Next, I hold my glass bowl with black obsidian shards.

"Sis." Alby's voice.

I clench a rough shard into my fist.

"Hey, I'm sorry we didn't talk more." He pauses. "I hope you're okay; I miss you. Well, call me."

He never calls me at work, never had any of my numbers on speed dial or memorized like I do his. He must have gotten the phone number from Dr. Ingstrom. Why is it he only sounds like his gentle self when we're a thousand miles apart?

I can't call him back yet. Eight clients for my first day back—the back load from the days I missed. The last message is from Alicia's social worker, Italia, confirming they will keep their scheduled appointment today. I check my notes from her first appointment two weeks ago.

Being a teenager who is escorted by her social worker, I know she is likely to keep the appointment. County Child Welfare was under media fire for this one. Alicia and her twin brother survived torture for years by their guardian aunt. Child Welfare investigated the family during their early years, when they were in the care of their mentally ill mother, who died on the streets soon after they were taken. Once moved to the care of their aunt, another abuse report was made, yet they were left in her care. No more protection from Child Protective Services.

Why did Alicia's abuse go undetected for so long? Why did it take her brother Kristoff's death to bring her to safety? It amazes me that Alicia is talking to Social Services now, after being sent on to another dangerous home after the first report. Some captors have power and keep that power against all odds and institutions.

When the aunt couldn't hide Kristoff's death, an autopsy was performed. Burn marks, bruises, and scars showed the story of abuse. The police found a closet pole crusted with dried blood, electric cords, chains and shackles with a lock.

I'd like to weep over the appointment notes. No, no more crying at the office. I have to be ready to meet with Alicia. Papa's stories and Alby's unexpected voice on the answering machine have opened me up like a once-hidden passageway that can't be closed again.

One time I was in teen misery, but wasn't about to tell Mama everything. She held my hand and stroked my forehead, and I lowered my guard. I cried for everything that was broken and impossible: distances, boys, family words that couldn't be said, the certainty that I was ugly and awkward. But Alby and I had an ironclad rule: don't tell the parents your true problems or the problem just get worse.

So I depended on Mama's words, "Before Weltschmerz," she explained. It's a German word meaning 'world-pain,' when everything just hurts too much. When you're a teenager, you start to know this feeling."

When you're an adult, you know it more.

I get up to greet Alicia for her appointment. It's one of those moments when I think, can I do this? Many traumas do fit Papa's words—it's all too much. In the waiting room, Alicia huddles in the corner chair in dark sweatpants and a loose-fitting top, next to her social worker, Italia, who is wearing a tailored purple pantsuit. Italia displays long French-manicured acrylic nails and a short Afro, like you rarely see anymore. She rises up to greet me. "Hey, today can you and Alicia talk about school? She's doing great, and the judge wants her to have the chance to be back in school."

I stare at Italia. Back in school? Usually family court judges know not to rush the kids. "We'll see."

Alicia is bent over a book in her lap, long hair smoothed back with a series of colorful scrunchy bands, starting at the top of her head, and going down the nape of her neck. Her fingertips and jagged fingernails peek out of baggy sleeves. I know Alicia likes her foster mom, who is Latina like herself. I imagine them this morning. The foster mom smoothed back Alicia's hair after a big breakfast, went over her schedule for the day, and sent her out from a true home.

"Come on in, Alicia."

She looks up. "My name is Espewanza now." She lisps, having trouble with her *r*'s.

I smile, aware she will study all my responses. "A beautiful name. It means hope, right? Okay, you want to come in and get started?"

"Alone?" She turns to Italia.

"Alone, or I can come with you." Italia's earrings sparkle.

"Why don't you step into the office and then decide if you want Italia?" I offer.

Alicia peeks around the corner and sees it will be only the two of us in the office. She turns back to Italia. "Okay, you'll be right here?"

"The whole time," says Italia.

Good answer, no errands to run during our hour. Alicia/Esperanza needs security.

Last time, I had stuck with my personal rule of not inviting every disclosure in the first appointments. We established that I was sad that so much had happened to Alicia and hinted that she would recall some memories but not necessarily all of them. We talked about dissociation, how not remembering was nature's way of protecting her. Survivors have taught me how overwhelming disclosure is, about the flood of shame afterwards, the difficulty in returning for other appointments. Today and other days I will hear more.

We settle in. "Today we'll just talk," I explain. "No note taking for me."

She nods.

"How did you get your new name?"

"It's not new. I had it inside of me for yeahs. Every time she hit me, I thought, Espewanza."

"Did you ever meet anyone named Esperanza?"

"Yeah, on and off. It was always a cool name." She continues with her missing *r*'s, "Theah was this one little girl in thuhd grade. Her name was Espewanza."

"Tell me about her."

"She shared her lunch with me every day. She pretended we shared back and forth, but my lunch only had bread. The teacher never knew that was all I had. Half the time it had mold growing on it. Esperanza had these soft bread sandwiches, fresh every day. She always gave me half of hers. Well half of a half, I kept some for Kristoff." She raises her head proudly.

"Do you know where your friend Esperanza is now?"

She looks at me as if I'm an idiot. "No. That time my teacher saw bruises on my wrists and arms and said, 'Oh no,' she called the cops, and they came to the house. That was enough for us to move away. I didn't want to go back anyway. Esperanza and all the kids heard when Mrs. Ashton said, 'Oh no.'"

"What do you think Mrs. Ashton was thinking?"

"Well, she was this white lady who just thought we were lowlifes."

A white lady like me. "What else could 'Oh no' mean?"

"That it was just bad. Tía Isabelle says it is evil what was done to me. To not worry, to just spend time being safe now."

She's calling the foster mom "Aunt" — *Tía*. It's not good that the abuser was also her aunt. Not so good either that she is already giving up her name to be called Esperanza, unless in her mind she was never Alicia, the name the abuser called her. "Do all the kids at your foster home call your foster mom Tía?

"No, just me. She's so nice." Her eyes meet mine for the first time this hour.

"Could we make a deal that you just call her Isabelle or Miss Isabelle? If you call her Tía, it could be mixed up with so much pain from your other Tía."

"No, Tía. She is my good aunt." Her voice roughens, like a four-year-old pretending to be tough.

I study her. Did her eyes flicker, change, move back in her head? Is this her angry self? Such are the signs of Dissociative Identity Disorder — what used to be called Multiple Personality Disorder. "Okay, I am asking you, not telling you, because you're in charge here."

"Tía Rachel wasn't our real aunt; she was our mother's brother's wife. I always thought, how did she get us? Why did she even want us? When she moved us away after the police came, she found that place with the basement. So every day we planned how to escape." She flinches, then looks away.

Does she suffer even more because her brother's death led to her rescue?

"My brother didn't make it in that basement where she kept us. That horrible place, it's near my foster family's house."

The proximity she must live in gives me the chills. I'm tempted to ask if she saw her brother die, but I know that most of her story must wait for later. "Tía Rachel can't hurt you now. She's in jail."

She gives me another look like I'm an idiot, then her eyes crinkle, like maybe she imagines Tía Rachel in a basement jail. I say these obvious things because a lot of kids won't talk unless they're reminded the abuser is locked up. "I'm so sorry you lost Kristoff."

She picks at a ragged cuticle and stares at my shelves, for the first time showing curiosity about what's there.

Might as well jump in. The silence is good, but I sense now that she shouldn't be stuck with every lonely memory one more week. "Do you want to go ahead and tell me some of what it was like for you?"

She covers years of her life: locked into chains often, and beatings that happened over and over again. She relates how when she started to develop into a young woman, her Tía Rachel beat her more. "She called me names. She made Kristoff watch her beat me, and then she said she wouldn't feed me anymore, that it was not my time yet to be a woman. So Kristoff started keeping some of his food in his mouth, chewed but not swallowed. Later he would feed me. Like baby birds, he said."

I struggle with Alicia as if we are pacing ourselves on perilous mountain pathways together. There is a pace for healing: she needs to know I can hear it all; I need to know I'm not pushing her or faltering in my following along. I'm glad we have at least not discussed where Alicia was when

Kristoff died. From what I know so far, she would have been right there. Tía Rachel had them witness each other's abuse. That way she had a torturous economy of abuse — each blow was like two for the price of one.

I breathe deeply, determined to stay present for Alicia. She dissociates from the trauma, but it's not likely that she has alters — other personalities. She remembers so much right here and now, which is unusual.

Tingling begins in my hands and feet, and my stomach quivers with nausea. It wrenches me that the repeated abuse by a perpetrator who got away with murder left hurt and loneliness in Alicia's heart. She is infusing me with her sorrow, her pain and sense of abandonment.

I get a flash of me scared, lonely at my first HOW meeting, at last finding sobriety. Yuck, I'm feeling dizzy too, like that night. And what does it matter in the face of what Alicia survived? I rub the tingling out of my hands, keeping my eyes on Alicia, while her eyes are cast down.

To show my own sorrow and anger now is okay, but to cry an ocean because she was so all alone and bitterly hurt and lost the only one she ever loved … no. I take another breath, realizing Alicia didn't dissociate completely because she had Kristoff for comfort. This comforts me too and I can go on. The dizziness and nausea pass. I focus on when she talked about her love for Kristoff, and being fed by him, like a baby bird. Just like my Oma feeding Tineke Bevins, like a baby bird. "And how do you feel now when you remember it all?"

She growls again, "Lady, what feelings? I got skinnier because she didn't feed us. She fed us more again only for a little while, because our grandparents came to see us. We were so skinny I hoped they'd turn her in. She had told both of us she would kill the other one if we told about how she treated us. That one week, our rooms looked nice, we had enough to eat. Then they left and all the same started again." Her eyes pool with tears that don't spill. "I knew our house was nothing like other kids' houses. Our grandparents, they never did anything to help us except that one visit."

"And how do you feel now?"

"Nothing."

"I feel so sad, so angry that you suffered for so long and"—I take a deep breath—"that Kristoff died."

She studies me from the corners of her eyes while gazing at the shelves. Silence fills the room for long minutes. I'm the first to talk.

"Would you like to pick out some things?" I point to the collections of symbols.

She walks over to the shelves bent over, slowly pulling her hands out of her sleeves. Her fingers hover over the shards of black obsidian in the bowl. She takes some out, puts them back in. She crouches by the bottom shelf, cups her hands, and comes back.

"Can I see?" I wonder.

She shakes her head. Silence prevails. Her hands are wrapped tightly in her lap.

I feel nausea creeping in, I must be getting sick. Or is it the horror creeping around the room with us after all? I clench my armrest. Time is up. I hate to be the one to break the silence again. "You worked hard today, Esperanza," I say, and add to my own surprise, "I like your new name, Esperanza. Remember much of the past can stay behind here today. You're safe now."

She uncups her hands, walks slowly to the shelves hunched over, and I see what she puts back—the tiny baby doll. The baby, molded into its cradle, rocks gently and stops as she sets it down. She whispers, "Me too. Sad ... I'm sad."

Dizziness and cold sweat add to my nausea. "And we both know she can't hurt you now." I say this from my seat, desperately glad I don't have to get up.

When I hear the outer doors shut, I rush through the waiting room. I make it to the bathroom stall and vomit. It feels like fire coming up into my throat. Everything comes up—Esperanza-trauma, ignoring Alby, Alby ignoring me for so long. I stay on the floor, leaning against the icy toilet seat, just in case.

Icy like my first day of school in America, in Provo, Utah. All bundled up, we walked, Mama, little Alby-Bertie, and I. At the classroom door, Miss Holiday greeted us. I stared at her perfect makeup, pale skin, and dark hair, like Snow White out of a fairy tale. No cheerful elementary teacher in Holland looked remotely like her; instead, their regular skin glowed through. I strode in, trying to be brave, while Mama and Bertie hung back.

"I have to go to the lavatory." I had rehearsed the British-English words Mama taught me. Once settled at my desk, instincts told me the words would never work. Finally Miss Holiday marched us to the restroom before lunch and I settled in a cold toilet stall. Releasing my tense bladder, I had a small triumph. Only one thing would have been a true disaster—wetting myself on the first day. I stayed longer to hide, but worried about getting lost when I heard the last girl leave. I followed her and carried my lunch tray with strange food to the edge of a table. The children from class looked past me as if I were invisible. That night I watched Casper the Friendly Ghost, who had no friends. The daily TV, we never had in the Netherlands, became my friend. Often chatter surrounded me and I couldn't understand a word. Lonely.

My head numbing against the cold porcelain and pipes, I wonder if I can get up without vomiting again. I ponder Papa going away with his brother to the men's concentration camp. What happened? Papa, too, ended up alone, lonely, like me, and so much worse than I. Was he right there when his brother Albert died, and later when his own pappie died? Questions burn in me, and I flush with heat. I knew that he witnessed deaths, and knew death all too well. What would he have been like? What would his pounding fist on the table be like now, if he said it all decades ago? I'm still dizzy. Will I faint? No, but I vomit again, dry heaves rocking me over and over like a grim attacker until I'm done.

Esperanza-Hope, I muse, getting comfortable on the disgusting cool tile. The door opens and I scramble up, dark flashes in front of my eyes, waiting for the cubicle to stop spinning. When I can leave the stall, I feel strangely clear and solid. The rest of the day I am fine, pacing myself and nibbling on everything in my lunch box until it's all gone. It must have been a morning of too much sorrow and trauma. Probably Kemble will scold me for not calling her for emotional support, but I have no intention of calling right now. *Yes, it is all too much* — what Papa always said about the past.

† † †

Under the tree canopy portion of my journey home, sunlight flashes through, rhythmically, electrically. Gradually the chill that lingered all day is conquered by warmth, and my belly feels full. I could certainly afford to lose some calories when upchucking due to sickening abuse. Being in my forties is tough; hormones, anxiety, and depression struggles probably pushed me over the edge today. Esperanza had moments of better, or at least not so awful, with those brave-bird feedings from Kristoff. She hoped there'd be better times ahead eventually. I know there are eventually better times ahead for us Vanderveers. It's the eventually part I hate.

Papa has bookmarked the past now, with old events niched in time: before war and after war. I know about when he lost nearly everyone except Albert. I know more about the liberation which wasn't liberation — *Bersiap*. I understand better why he was always fierce. He would meet us kids on a battlefield of grades, and other places where none of us wanted his fierce control. His legacy to me — he was a fighter, and I am too. It doesn't matter if I call Alby back tonight or soon, but I will. I'll fight for his life until he fights for himself.

Nice to be in the driveway of my home. After this torturous day I'll embrace the comfort of our family night and avoid all phones.

† † †

A peaceful evening. I check out notes for my upcoming lecture to the dual diagnosis program for women with chemical dependency and mental health issues. My talk is on trauma resolution. PTSD — hard to treat. You have to be a good listener. I am grateful for the intro words I can start with. *PTSD is a normal reaction to abnormal situations — those we call traumatic.*

I go on a walk with Daniel. I check that Vincent has done his homework, and that it's in the correct school folder to turn in. Only eight o'clock and I'm lying back in bed, reading. After this draining day, I'm hoping I'll soon get a long's night sleep.

My cell phone startles me. The caller ID says Vanderveer. Must be Papa, and for the first time he's calling me on my cell instead of the house phone.

"Hello?"

"I want to tell you about another time before we left Billiton."

Vanderveers can be this abrupt. "Great, Papa. And how are you?"

"Having this memory so clearly reminds me that sad memories can bring up good ones too. You know, like when you and I talk about your Pake and Beppe?"

"Yes." This is one of the new conversations I have hoped for. Some of the eventually is here.

† † †

Jakob

Billiton Island
January 1942

Once a week the children joined Mammie and Pappie for dinner.

Albert handled his cutlery just right, from his side of the table. "I heard the Japanese are further in their attacks. All of North East Borneo has surrendered."

Mammie's hair fell in extra-silky waves this evening. "Well, we don't want you to worry — "

"Liesbet," Pappie interrupted, "they will know this soon enough. The Japanese invaded Tarakan two days ago. Seven hundred oil fields are at risk. You've looked at the maps with me and seen Tarakan, and its mother islands, Borneo and Celebes."

"Off the northeast coast of Borneo," Jakob said.

Ah, Pappie nodded. "Yes. With the Japanese so close, the Billiton Tin Company telegrammed us to remain fully prepared to evacuate." His hand clenched into a fist.

"And they're attacking the Philippines." Albert worriedly pulled a long end of tablecloth off his lap. Once, years ago, they were finishing dinner when he stood, jerking with him the cloth, which was wrapped around his legs and shattered most everything on the table. He still took caution.

"And Thailand too." Jakob tucked his part of the tablecloth away.

Pappie looked at them. *Oh, he will be angry.*

But no, he grinned and shook his head. "Apparently you boys have learned a lot, surely from the radio. Ja, I've seen you sneaking around. The Japanese, so many invasions. We now have ABDACAM, doing what they can: Australians, Britain, the Dutch, as they call us, Canada, and America. Families, air strips, harbors, manufacturing plants, plantations can all be protected."

"Ja," said Mammie. "Almost one and the same here, country and company."

Pappie gave Mammie a sharp look. "We keep being told by the company, 'Do not take too much.' That way no one panics or thinks we are in full retreat. The Japanese have taken each country much too easily. Surely all these allies can stop them. But the likes of China with all its vast land mass did not stop them either. So as the head mining engineer's family, you will make the appearance of taking little, but be well-prepared for anything. Are you worried, my liefje?" He turned to Sara.

She looked down and slowly shook her head.

Pappie sighed, then touched her cheek. "Everything will be alright, you will see. Women and children will be safe."

Jakob felt chills "What about our men?"

"Ja, my Jakob," Pappie said tiredly. "Although Thailand tried to be neutral, they had to surrender instead of facing Japanese invasion. Thus Thailand declared war against the Allies."

"The cowards of Thailand." Jakob's hand clenched into a fist like Pappie's.

"Or just practical," said Mammie.

"The British are the de facto cowards," growled Pappie. "The Dutch fought fiercely, but without concerted British resistance, the Japanese easily took British Borneo. Now you know why we did so little on New Year's Eve. British and Dutch forces were trapped in one small area, the Singkawang airfield. Less than a week ago, all of Borneo fell to the Japanese. Tonight we pray for Tarakan, a remaining Dutch island."

Praying. Surely everyone had prayed for China, the Philippines, Borneo, Celebes—and yet the Japanese won in every area. Jakob glanced at Mammie; her eyes dark with tears, as if she too wondered, *where is God?*

The boys conversed more than usual, each more expert than had been acceptable before. Sara left to go get Tina, then returned, snuggling her close. Kokkie had cleared all the dishes and left, with Min remaining for the evening.

Pappie made an announcement: "Before night falls, let's look at the sky together."

Albert raised his eyebrows at Jakob. *Why?*

They all filed silently out the front door, down the veranda steps and out to the hillside beyond.

"Look this way, towards Tarakan," Pappie instructed.

Min stood next to Sara who looked up at the stars hopefully as she held Tina in her arms. A cool breeze tickled Jakob's neck. The crescent moon smiled crookedly. The darkness was scattered with stars, the diamonds of the sky. Still, we saw a faint glow on the distant horizon.

"As I suspected," Pappie's loud voice erupted. "The British only sabotaged an airfield. But the Dutch are saboteurs extraordinaire; the oilfields —"

"Of Tarakan are burning," finished Mammie, coughing. "That poor beautiful island."

Papa directed, "Adri, close our windows." Rarely used glass window frames shrieked down, shutters were closed.

Adri returned. No one moved as if a great, evil storm had descended upon the Vanderveer home. The crescent moon was no longer visible. At first, Jakob breathed deeply. *It's just fire clouds.* He longed for the familiar scent of the nearby ocean, but was overcome by the acrid stench, like hot tar, invading his lungs. He covered his mouth in panic, imagining they would all suffocate.

Sara coughed. "What about the people there, and their homes. Are they okay?" "Yes, Liefje," Pappie assured her. "It's only the oil fields the Japanese want."

Jakob breathed tentatively through his shirtsleeve, determined to be brave. *Pappie's lying. Their houses couldn't be okay. The Japanese destroy everything.* "They are still fighting, trying to keep the oil fields."

"No, son," Pappie said, gently squeezing Jakob's shoulder. "Not keeping, destroying. Remember, we are sabotaging—burning our oil fields to prevent the Japanese from using our resources."

Jakob now understood the need to destroy what was theirs, so as not to feed the Japanese war machine. Like the monster Leviathan in the Bible, the Japanese roamed the Earth, gargantuan enough to defeat countries, blacken the moon, and cover the sky.

Jakob breathed through his sleeve. "Java and Sumatra have oil fields too." He hated his own words, the knowing.

"Yes," Pappie murmured next to him and Albert, so only they could hear. "They want our mines and oil fields and they mean to get them. But remember the Allied Forces, ABDACAM. We are protected."

They returned to the house to find the stench of burning oil had permeated every room of their living space. Pappie grumbled, double checking every window and shutter. Min placed baskets of crushed flowers in the rooms to minimize the stench.

Jakob got ready for bed and wandered in his pajamas to the kitchen. Gone were the days of uncertainty. Knowing was much worse. His neck prickled as he recalled the snakes of Pearl Harbor Day, ready to attack and feed on their prey. For the last month they'd lived in the shadow of danger. The sickening smell chased away his sense of adventure and battle. The Japanese were near, preparation was critical.

He sensed footsteps much like his own. Pappie appeared. "We will finish most of our planning, first thing in the morning. Soon we'll hear about evacuation plans. We must be ready."

"Ja, Pappie." He could have asked more questions, but decided against it. Back in his room with Albert, Jakob ran his fingers through a bowl of flower petals, leaning down to breathe in their scent. Jakob crawled into bed and with an ache in his throat; he asked Albert, "What's the most important thing for you to take?"

"My botany book, of course."

123

"But it's too heavy."

"I'm strong enough to carry it. What will you bring?"

"My compass," Jakob said with certainty. "It's light and necessary." He lay in bed thinking about Billiton and beyond, picturing in his mind's eye every island and region they had talked about at dinner. Far north, north, northeast—the Japanese had attacked from almost every direction. Jakob flexed and relaxed his muscles, one by one, to be sure he was ready for whatever tomorrow held in store. An order to evacuate to Java would mean hours of hiking with their only provisions in their packs. He could carry his own, Mammie's, Sara's, even Min's if she needed help.

While Min's crushed flowers made it easier to get through the night, they were also a reminder that Min would not be leaving with Jakob and his family. It was unimaginable that they would be separated.

† † †

At dawn Jakob woke up screaming, his hands flailing at the bed net and his head pounding.

"You had a nightmare," Albert said, trying to calm him.

To Jakob's shame, he had awakened with tears in his eyes. "I dreamt that the evacuation order didn't come in time, and our house burned to the ground." In Jakob's dream, his family had died, but all he said to Albert was, "I was all alone, I couldn't find you."

Albert shoved him affectionately. "Get up. We're all here Jakob. Pappie has left for work. The sky's still dark but come, its morning."

Jakob had slept so hard that for once he'd been the last one to wake up. He couldn't have fought the Japanese if they had come in the night. As piano music filled the house, he thought, *Mammie must be sad.*

Kokkie and Min greeted the boys. Sara was up too, feeding Tina and herself mango rice.

"Dag," Jakob croaked. He clutched his stomach to hold back the nausea.

Kokkie pointed to a bowl. "Chew on some ginger. All the old people are telling stories about how the sky was just as dark when Krakatoa erupted sixty years ago. Some were children then, others heard the story from their parents."

Jakob peered out at the dark day. This devastation was no volcano, but man-made. In his nightmare it was an omen of worse to come. "The trade winds blow from the northeast, where Tarakan is. The captain showed me when we came back from Nederland."

"Ja, me too." Albert saw Jakob's disappointed look. "Only once. You and Pappie looked at the navigation charts every day."

The stench lessened before sleep.

In the morning, the sky was awash in blue and gray watercolors. The island's lush green foliage was covered with flakes of toxic black soot, like dirty snow.

On the third day, the sky had cleared and the rains had washed away the soot.

† † †

"I forgot that some nightmares started in the war years," Papa says. "I suppose Mama told you about how I had nightmares for years after the war?"

"She did. How awful that must have been."

"You had nightmares too as a child, right after we moved to Utah. But perhaps you have forgotten."

I'm so touched that Papa remembers ... for a brief moment, everything stops.

"I can only recall one nightmare. It was very dark. Beppe and Pake were at home alone when their barn caught on fire. I thought there was nothing we could do, and ... "

"For weeks you had that nightmare," Papa says, "and you woke up screaming every time."

I feel tightness in my chest but try to let it go. *Papa has been through so much, worse than anything I've been through.* I'm determined to wait for a more perfect day when I'm not so exhausted so I can make sense of his nightmares and mine, and to understand what it all means in my life.

"Pappie, it must have been terrible, that darkness, the smell." I recall the reek of tar when the roof was repaired at my office. Without hesitation, I had canceled my appointments and evacuated my office for the day.

"Yes, terrible. It went on for days. Like a premonition of worse to come. I think it delayed our evacuation ferries too. The ocean currents and trade winds had cleared the air, but we could no longer escape the devastating reality of war. No way."

"No wonder you became such a worrier, Papa."

"The real worrying came later. I still thought we could fight off the Japanese and avoid being captured." A lively tone returned to his voice.

His words give me picture after picture: Papa's strong spirit when he was young, and some of the memories I always wanted to hear. I don't know how Albert died. One out of four died in some camps, but not usually young people. I think more than ever that Oom Albert and Alby sharing the same name burdened my brother and father. Trying to avoid telling his Alby how his namesake uncle died, I realize in a flash. How impossible to be open with us kids. Landmines everywhere.

"Thank you, Papa. I love you," I say. "No nightmares tonight, heh?"

"No nightmares tonight."

When I go to bed, expecting an easy, spent sleep, I lay awake with my own memories. Maybe I want Mama and Papa to search for my past too, when the timing is perfect of course. When Papa has said more.

My past has had too many hellos and good-byes, even name changes. When our world changed, so did our names.

126

In Nederland, I was Liesbet and Liesje for short, named after my Oma—a name to be proud of, considering her brave survival.

In Nederland, Albert was Bertie for short. He hung on to that name in Utah.

In Texas, with the fondness for letters as a name, Alby sounded like L. B. So Alby became L. B. Vanderveer. In Texas, no one bothered try to say Liesje anymore, and I became Lucy. Later, at my insistence, a final nickname, Luce.

We went through years of changes, and no American ever knew that our last name, Vanderveer, means "of the feather." How ironic, as feathers blow about with each new wind, impossible to navigate, landing where they must.

† † †

Jakob

Billiton Island
January 1942

When the ash and dark clouds had cleared, the children's rucksacks appeared in the *goedang* by the kitchen. There had been endless talk of packing, and they were doing more at last.

"We shall *regel* everything," Albert announced. "Let's bring the rucksacks to our room to organize them."

Jakob grinned. "Ja, *regelen.*"

Sara skipped back and forth from her room to theirs, carrying doll clothes and more. She rarely had the chance to be in the boys' room, and clearly she adored being with them. For such a little girl, her voice filled the house. "I will bring this … and this." She wanted to pack her favorite book, her favorite clothes, and Tina's doll carriage.

Eyeing the doll carriage, Jakob said, "That will never fit."

"It can fit with the luggage on the evacuation boat," Sara insisted. "Mammie said."

They took canteens from the family supply and fastened them on their packs. Even with the excitement of *regelen*, it was easy to fall asleep for *tidur siang*. Jakob was the first up from his nap, followed by Albert. They headed out to the veranda.

The Henry Ford scattered pebbles as it came to a swift stop in front of the garage. Normally, the men came home from work for *tidur siang*, their much-needed rest. There would be no rest for Pappie today. The car doors opened and slammed in the light rain.

"Hi, Pappie," the boys yelled.

Pappie nodded at the boys, hat in hand, his face red and his hair tousled as he ran past them. Seconds later, he disappeared into the living room, closing the door behind him.

Jakob saw Albert's face tighten and shared the anxiety of not knowing. The boys lingered on the dry veranda. Perhaps they could hear him through the living room window. His voice usually carried, but not today.

As they crept into the house they heard Pappie say, "Liesbet, hundreds on Tarakan were massacred. A barbaric reprisal by the Japanese against British and Dutch soldiers as well as civilians. They killed two hundred men to spread fear and stop us from sabotaging other oil fields."

They heard Mammie's voice but her words were indiscernible.

Pappie answered, "Ja, so cruel and sad."

Jakob and Albert looked at each other in silence, eyes wide with shock. Two hundred men killed in cold blood … what would happen next?

They remained in the hallway, ready to run off, just as Pappie raised his voice to Mammie. "We must be more prepared! When will you learn to handle servants? Nothing is done. They don't follow a single direction you give."

Albert signaled he was going to their room, maybe to pack some more.

Jakob went to the kitchen, hoping he might overhear more of his parents' discussion, riveted by Pappie's talk of war. Kokkie had already put away the morning's tea, which had been perfectly laid out. *Kokkie does listen to every word from Mammie. Does Pappie not know?*

Pappie's rant was over. Jakob came in and sat in the living room with Mammie. Mollie rubbed against his legs, then leapt up and settled on his lap.

Jakob noticed how Mammie's hands trembled and her face tightened. No one liked Pappie's yelling. She perched in front of their camphor chest.

When it came to Adri, Kokkie and Min, Jakob loved them all. They worked hard moving in this heavy chest, and in all their duties.

Mammie shook her head as if shaking off fire ants. The darkness of the living room enveloped her and she opened the shutters to let in the light. She moved deliberately, looking peaceful again, as if she refused to let Pappie's yelling rush her along.

"*Dag*, Mammie."

"*Dag*, Jakob." She smiled as she opened the camphor chest lid. Its scent filled the room. The strong smell told of importance and storage. Mammie's long fingers probed and maneuvered as she slid out the secret drawer. She did hurry in her own way, as if her fingers danced over piano keys. Her hands darted in and out of the special drawer.

Jakob wondered if Wim, Albert, or Sara knew what was stored inside the camphor chest, or if the secret was his alone.

Gemstones came out of their hiding place, which she dropped first in an envelope, then in the pocket of her housedress. Next, she opened her jewelry box, and a few rings and earrings went into another envelope and into her pocket. The rest—Mammie's gold bracelets, a locket, and loose jewels—went into the drawer. Then, her thumbs pushed the drawer back in.

Jakob had no idea how the drawer worked, and for once he felt no curiosity to find out. Mammie did a fine job, and she was the one to know all the drawer's secrets. In the main cavity of the chest, Mammie stacked loose pictures. Jakob reached over to hand her more. Mamie added one music book from her piano bench. The special silverware, bedded in a velvet-lined box, went in next, as well as the crystal Pappie bought her on the last Nederland trip. They each had a gift from the trip. Wim's gift must have been school, and oh yes, a special photo album, just for him.

Last, Mammie unfolded tissue paper and held up the family's baby christening gown, laying it on top like a treasured blanket, tucking in the edges. Watching Mammie take care of what they treasured left Jakob more peaceful. He had pushed the Japanese out of his mind, and now he could breathe easy.

Pappie yelled again. *"Liesje!"*

Jakob startled and Mollie jumped and dashed from the room. *Wouldn't Mammie rush right to Pappie?*

No, she lifted the christening gown again, rubbed the smocking against her cheek, and folded it back into the tissue paper. She reached for a few baby clothes, smiled, and folded them all in. The chest lid dropped with a whoosh. Her hands splayed out on the lid, as if she had just finished a piano piece. "There! All done."

"Mammie, you do a fine job," said Jakob.

She looked up and smiled radiantly. "Thank you, my sweet boy. Pappie knows it is best if there are valuables I pack without the servants. He's under so much pressure, especially after Tarakan." She stopped. Mammie wouldn't say the saboteurs had been killed.

Jakob's own hands trembled. Pappie would have to sabotage like the men on Tarakan.

She cleared her throat. "Servants have their temptations too. This way, only Pappie and I know what's in here."

"And me."

"Yes, now you know a secret. It is our precaution, Jakob. Pappie knows I cannot be in two places at once, though he would like me to be, so he yells." She stood and took a deep breath, "*Hier*, the chest is done," she yelled loud enough for Pappie's ears.

But he was already coming through the door. She whispered in Pappie's ear and he nodded.

If only Pappie wouldn't yell; at least he wasn't yelling now. *Baboe keeps an eye on us children; the garden is fine, Kokkie is fine. What is wrong? Well, as usual everything, according to Pappie, is at least a little off. In school we learned the First World War was the war to end all wars. What does that make this one?* His throat hurt again, wanting to speak up. If he said, "Pappie, Mammie, get the servants to do it all," trouble would follow.

Pappie whispered back in Mammie's ear, and she smiled. The packing *ruzie* had ended.

But inside Jakob's *ruzie* continued. War was all around.

CHAPTER 8

Daniel calls tonight's dining style "every man for himself." The three of us forage in the refrigerator for our own favorite frozen foods or leftovers, nuke them in the microwave, and then sit together at the dining room table.

Daniel's job took him all over today and he had lunch with a friend. Vincent got to study over at the new girl's house today, Tania. Wow, a name! Maybe soon I'll find out age, grade, hobbies — or even meet her.

I find myself being like Papa, telling with flat wooden words about Alicia becoming Esperanza — and the life she came from. Can't give the details, nor do I want to. My guys' caring eyes help me; they understand that I came home with other people's wounds, all tired out. Vincent's face is grave with compassion. I think of the sensitive little boy he was, always telling us everything, until girls started to break his heart.

Daniel's eyes light up when I say Esperanza's feeling better, and may be getting ready to go to school. He knows what it's like to have a childhood requiring an escape route. He understands. I haven't told him yet about me getting sick, but I intend to … later.

"Mom, your hair looks extra funny today," Vincent says. It's our running joke that I can be an absent-minded professor type, not bothering to brush my hair all day.

"Oh yeah?" I reach up to unclasp the barrette askew in my wavy hair. I find snarls around the barrette. "Oh wow, I can't get this undone."

"It's stuck?" Daniel grins.

"No, of course not. It just won't open."

He lunges over quickly, like he always does for something mechanical — even a barrette. "Oh, Luu-u-ce. Luu-ucie, this is another fine mess you got yourself into." He prods the barrette, pulls.

"Ow!"

"Your hair is all scrabbled around it. What all were you doing today?"

I lay my head down on the table. Vincent stares, this isn't exactly table manners. "I felt awful after that one appointment," I divulge. "Vomited and had to recover."

"Honey, you might actually be getting sick."

"I don't feel sick, just tired. It's a woman thing."

"Yeah, not really sick and your barrette isn't stuck. Hmmm, let me see …" He is switching into his problem-solving mode. "I can get that open." He strides out to the garage.

"Now you're in for it," Vincent says.

Sure enough, Daniel returns with pliers. "I can undo it with this."

I thrust my hands up to my head, going for comedy. "Aa-ack. No way."

"Wait, let me help Mom first," says Vincent.

"It'll be just a second," Daniel insists.

"Oh, no. I'll see what Vincent can do with a little patience."

We drag a chair into the guest bathroom. "Mom, it's really stuck," he reports.

"Okay, let me try it myself now." He wanders away, and I gently pull out strand after strand out of hair out until the barrette dangles. Even this small task wears me out. I grab manicure scissors and swiftly clip the remaining hair, throwing the barrette in the trash. I brush my hair out, but a tuft of hair sticks straight up. Great.

I find Daniel in the garage, where he is working on his truck speakers. He always has a project.

"Okay, barrette out."

He turns and laughs. "Oh honey, you did a great job by yourself. I can see you got it out. But you look like Vincent when he cut his own hair."

"Well, I did cut my own hair." I laugh so hard I get tears in my eyes. Walking back inside to a mirror, I see both an aging woman and a little girl mixed into one. I destroyed my hair. Oddly, I am kind of pleased. I worry so much about everything going wrong with everyone I love. When the only issue is hair, that's a good thing.

I go check on Vincent, and a wall of alternative rock music hits me outside the door to his room. I knock hard and barge in. I have to tap on his shoulder to get his attention. I yell above the music mayhem, "Turn off the noise." Click, silence. "Hey, how's your homework?"

He turns around. "Mom, you're a disaster. You should have let me finish helping."

"Yep, and your homework?"

"Right here." It's by my left foot, getting stomped on. Looks like algebra.

"And the rest? You haven't even added your name and the date, you know, maybe for identification purposes. Maybe so your grade will go up?"

He singsongs, "I'll add all that, I'll put it in my homework folder, I'll remember to turn it in." He has art supplies out, with a large project going, including his biggest sketchpad. As usual, everything else is stacked in disarray, just like me as a kid. He made bad grades last year, not due to lack of understanding, but lack of good old Dutch *regelen*.

Daniel's habit, on other the hand, is to have everything neatly labeled; most items are clean and hanging from hooks. He can always find his tools.

Both Vincent and I wander around with broken, missing stuff: my work bag with wire and duct tape handles, Vincent's backpack with the top handle torn off. Our towers of papers and folders, Daniel calls messes. But I know what's in my towers. Vincent — usually not, unless it's a permission slip for an interesting school field trip.

"Now Vincent! Fix that homework."

He snatches up the page, puts on the information, walks to his bed, grabs the homework pages, tucks them into his algebra book, and stuffs it all into his backpack.

"In the folder," I growl.

"Oh, it's at school."

"Okay." I sigh. "Bring your folder home tomorrow." It will turn out to be lost.

I watch him bend back over his art. "Hey Mom, wait a minute. It was great talking to Grandpa and hearing more about the fighting."

"Yeah? I didn't even know you had his cell number."

"You gave me his cell phone number to talk about that *Bersiap* time. Now he has mine too."

"You like to talk to him?"

"Oh yeah, he'll tell me anything I ask."

He must need a boy the same age as he was during World War II to tell it all to. "Doesn't that make you terribly sad?"

"No, because I already know how it ends. He survives. You worry too much, Mom. You wanted me to call him, remember?" He reaches for his sketchpad. "Want to see what I'm drawing?"

"Sure."

We move to his unmade bed, putting pillows at our backs. His room has a sweaty puppy dog smell, not too disgusting, mostly comprised of clothes that don't make it to the laundry. He flips back pages filled with sketches. "This is when they rested by an awesome waterfall, where they spent the first night out of the camps — Grandpa and his best friend, Matteus. They knew they'd have to be always moving and on guard again, watching out for the enemy, who were now the Indonesians."

I nod. The waterfall experience, I know. I remember fuzzily, it's another story Papa told us kids. How disquieting to realize I know. Another time Papa tried to tell, and I just didn't let it sink in. I call myself the sensitive sibling, but maybe I put up so many walls I became the coldest. Could I have gone to him on other nights and asked, *and then what happened next?*

Vincent's charcoal pencil has captured thin faces with large eyes. You can see they are hungry, frightened, and about to be embraced by rushing water, their first safety in four years. His sketches help me remember what Papa said about his best friend Matteus and he. They left the last camp quickly, just two boys taking off, foolish and brave.

"Well," I say, "your wonderful art is the best distraction of all. I'm so glad you and Grandpa are talking. He told me he fought before, but never the details like you're hearing."

Vincent's eyes look hurt. Why did I have to say *distraction* and belittle him? I'm jealous even of what Papa tells him. "Yeah," he replies casually. "I'm gonna make a whole book of drawings about Opa."

"Wow, you want to do that many?"

"Sure, he's like living history, and he was so brave. There are hardly any photos left in the world of that time." He must be researching too. "So drawings can help with the memories that should stay alive."

"That's awesome, honey."

"Yeah, it's better than the most exciting books I've read. Except for right now, I'm reading this great spy novel. The head spy uses a memory castle trick to remember all the secrets he can't record in writing. Everything has to be in his head. He imagines a mansion with rooms and different families of facts go in each room. He does that every day, until envisioning each room unloads all the information he has to keep in his brain instead of on paper."

"Memory castles, I like that," I say. "Your spy wants to remember. I think Grandpa wanted to forget."

"I know that, Mom. But I bet he put these memories away in different rooms, and now he's bringing each one out."

"Yeah, I see what you mean."

"Maybe he put them in his memory castle so he could bring them back out for sure. So they wouldn't really be lost."

Vincent is getting so bright. I have to agree with him. My eyes prick with tears because that's what I had always been afraid of, that memories — good and bad — could get lost forever. Now my own child states that memories can be put away and taken out when the time is right. I guess he believes what I've believed, that the past never ever truly disappears.

† † †

So Papa is using his cell for more than checking on my location when I'm flying in to Houston. He's tracking and connecting with Vincent. He's loved all his grandchildren. Yet when I was with him when the grandkids were younger, I was always on guard, ready to whisk them away. The grandkids chirped and shouted the ordinary noises of childhood. He would yell sharp words, and they would jump and shudder. Marina wandered back to him quickly each time, because she was with her grandpa frequently and knew his gentle side. Wade did the same later. They learned to do what I still do, to simply take Opa's barometer pressure reading and widen their circle around him. But Vincent continued to avoid him, preferring the comfort of Oma Nikki, Danny, and me.

So that was Papa's PTSD? What happened in the women's and children's camps when the children were noisy and distressed? The women weren't accustomed to soothing their own children — the baboes did that. In the camps they had to use every survival skill they had and keep children in line and safe from the Japanese. I've been on the internet, finding archival photos of living skeletons like those in the *Time Life* concentration camp pictures from my youth. Only these living skeletons are of POWs, civilian men, and women and children liberated in August 1945 from the *Jappen* kamp*s*. Many heard of the Japanese surrender days and weeks after the official capitulation. What was Pappie's freedom day? I don't even know. And if kids acted normally in the camps during their three years of imprisonment, did it lead to guards shouting—attacks?

My heart eases, and a lump forms in my throat. I go back to Vincent's room and tell him how touched I am, that he, the grandchild who developed a wary caution around Opa, can be close to him now.

† † †

Nighttime is like an antidote to all that hurts in the world—the Weltschmerz. Daniel and I come to bed with some kind of fire in us, which turns to long, slow lovemaking. I never think about the clock, or about another early morning the next day. I just sink into him again and again, and he into me.

Drifting to sleep afterward, I think of the mixed up memory castles in my family. Remembering just weeks ago crying about Beppe and Pake before leaving for Houston, I face my castle. I was close to Alby when we shared a memory castle. Ours was created to hide away behind the moat, to have our very own territory, and maybe never offer access to anyone. We both knew not to trouble our parents with our problems, or we'd end up in the midst of *ruzies*. Now Alby's castle has been off with him for a long time. I like to let my AA sponsor and others think mine's wide open. But I've always known I have rooms still shut, especially the one about losing Beppe and Pake when we immigrated.

Corrie and I, we have not given each other the space to be a comfort to each other for a long time, maybe not since the ultralight plane accident. Like me, she had her own circle of comfort, her own separate world. Mama and Papa's memory castles were separate yet again, but maybe not forever. If Dr.

Ingstrom helps us work out the past, what will happen? Our castles are as likely to explode as to come together. I can't imagine Alby ever being a comfort to all of us again. I remind myself, though, that this is what I try to convince others and my own family of all the time. You have to try. I have to try. *Willing to be willing to try. Willing to be willing to be willing to try.* That's what they told me long ago at my first HOW meeting, the place I got a toehold in my own recovery. I felt so scared the night of that first meeting and soon so energized that love could be around me again, not just in one friend or two, but in a fellowship of recovery. From one day to the next, my life changed.

† † †

Luce

Houston, Texas
Spring 1973

My feet lost the ground, falling, falling, my terrified body both too loose and too tight all the way down the bayou banks. A flash of eternity, like I floated in outer space and knew I'd burn up on reentry into the atmosphere. Finally hitting rough earth. My hip slammed into dirt and rocks, then my head. Everything darkened, blacker than the moonless night.

I came to, hearing Elaine crying, her hands on my head. "God, God. Luce, wake up! You are bleeding so bad."

"Do ... nuht ... tell my parents." My words slurred out of thick lips.

Elaine panted nearby. The rotten-egg smell of mud gagged me; we both lay curled up on gravel, my hand laying in a trickle of bayou water.

"You're crazy," she shrilled. "I'm going to get you out of here and call for help."

My nose flooded with an odd coppery-cotton smell — blood. "No, I'll be ... hohkay." I couldn't talk right and had to breathe through my mouth.

Elaine's face spun above me, tree branches spiraled, and the fragile planet we clung to whirled along. Mosquitoes stung me, while all over I felt a woozy aching, as though the heavy humid night sat on my chest. Elaine ducked under my shoulder, pulled me up, and my feet finally found the ground. On the long aching stumbling back to the car, her legs were my legs, as if this planet had weaker gravity than my old world.

"Do nuht call my parents," I moaned again when we bumped into her driveway, my head pounding.

Grimly she nodded, and together we pressed a wet towel to my nose and hurt head. Elaine helped me to sneak through the living room, which was as far as I could make it. I fell asleep that first night in a nest of old sheets and quilts. Her bed creaked each time she got up from her purple canopy bed to come check on me. She mumbled to herself about her mom's car. "Okay, I won't tell anyone," she breathed, still reeking of alcohol herself. "I remember now 'cause my mom's a nurse: head wounds bleed a lot. So it's just a cut. I'm going to try to stop freaking out now."

"Thatsh ... good, very good." Mama and Papa must never know. The room spun harder than the bayou, and my heart burst in my chest with fear. The first time she woke me, the room spun even harder. I slept intermittently only to have Elaine's olive-green Girl Scout flashlight pierce my eyes, along with her rambling worries.

"Stop, stop, eyesh are good." I pushed her away.

"I just remembered I have to check that your pupils are even. You'll be alright."

The spinning was better, I could sleep again.

Elaine groaned. "No, I have to tell Mom. Just let me wake her Luce, just in case."

"No. No way," I almost screamed, then I cried.

"Shush, shush, you'll wake everyone up."

"Yeah, dummy. Don't wake your mom." I giggled. "Shush, shush. Oh, laughing hurts. I promish ..." I close one eye and the spinning gets better. "I promise I'm okay and this will never happen again."

"This isn't funny," she whispered furiously, "and alright. Come sleep next to me." She switched to poking me all night long. "Checking you're still alive."

"Yes, I'm alive." It would be far worse than this endless night if Mama and Papa knew what I'd done. Upon each awakening my perception cleared, worse than death to disappoint them.

I woke up to broad daylight, and the smell of the spilled beer, that I didn't even like but drank anyway. It permeated my shirt, my hair. I dozed, next awakening to find blood had leaked onto Elaine's pillowcase. A hammer pounded inside my forehead as I lifted up to check the pillow underneath. Good, no blood stain went through. I checked the closet for a way to hide my bloody, matted hair. Elaine was probably busying herself cheerfully deflecting her parents. She'd be pretending we got home from an ordinary night. I would never make a mistake like this again. No more going to out of the way places when drinking.

Ah, a baseball cap. I got to the bathroom. No swollen nose, but brown stripes below my nostrils. I dabbed at my face, and rinsed the towel over and over in the tub. Soaking a comb in water, I pulled my hair back, and lowered the cap down cautiously. If any evidence were left in the bathroom, Elaine's mom would think I had my period. I steeled myself to enter the hallway. *Left foot, right foot.* I walked evenly to their sunny breakfast nook and murmured, "Hi" to Elaine's parents.

Elaine and her mom both had the popular silky straight hair I coveted. Elaine in her cutoffs and Mexican embroidered cotton shirt looked like she never had a daredevil day in her life. She coveted being a hippie, resisting her mom's insistence that she go out for cheerleading. Her mom had been a cheerleader, and then had kids and turned into our earth mother. Mrs. Rocca's laugh lines and round glasses made me imagine her being the cool mom. I used to think I could tell her anything, but not about last night. Elaine's dad sat in chinos with steaming coffee and the newspaper. I didn't think he ever got stressed or yelled like Papa.

I acutely felt my unshowered state. Convinced I looked peculiar, I had to get away from them.

"Let's hang out in the den," Elaine suggested, reading my mind.

Soon we lounged in the darkened family room, washing down cinnamon rolls with orange juice. We conferred, and Elaine went to ask if we could spend one more night together.

I had to avoid home at least one more night. Especially Papa, who had an uncanny ability to notice anything off. *Good, it's Easter vacation, no need to go home. My head hurts less. I pulled it off.*

"Come here," Elaine hissed after my quick call to Mama for permission. I followed her back to her room. "We're going to get you some help."

"You know this will never happen again," I protested, flinching as I bounced on her bed.

"You think?" She narrowed her eyes at me. "We're going to go to one of those HOW meetings and get you some help."

"Oh God, Elaine. That's so stupid. You go if you want to. Other than this weird accident, you get drunk a lot more than I do. Let's just go have some fun, you know, really just go to the movies." Maybe tonight, after the movies, we could get drunk, but less so of course. I could call someone else if I had to or hang out at the convenience store with a five-dollar bill, waiting for a stranger to buy me a Boone's Farm wine.

Her eyes blinked with hurt. "I know we're best friends, but half the time you come over here it's to get drunk because my mom's gone at work a lot. So don't tell me my problem's worse. Last night you made a deal with me that I would keep quiet. We are going to the meeting or I'll tell everything."

I wanted to argue, but protesting hurt my head. Instead, Elaine helped me maneuver my hurt legs over the tub edge and into the shower, while she lied to her parents about another movie. This made two movies we had to pretend to have seen. I twisted to a position to have the shower spray hurt less, fascinated by pink foam running down the drain. All the high-schoolers knew about HOW, the Honesty Openness and Willingness program, a place like AA but better. You go to get straight and sober, and supposedly it was fun.

Sliding into Elaine's mother's car, the vinyl stuck to my sweaty skin. Fear of the meeting hit. I imagined a crowd of counselors, some of them yelling at me for what I did. Well, I wouldn't tell them anything. I'd go this one time, fool Mama and Papa, and never get into trouble again.

Elaine checked the backseat. "Oh wow, I can't believe I didn't see this. I must have been so wasted too." She tosses me a bloody T-shirt from last night, a nasty abandoned one we had found on a picnic table by the car. Her mom would have spotted it right away. "We lucked out that Mom didn't need her car today." Elaine stuffed it under the front seat.

I swallowed my own nervous spit, which made my nose ache. My nose didn't look too bad; my head looked and felt much worse. We had stood somberly in front of Elaine's mirror, my upper forehead nothing but flaming red scrapes, a slow trickle of blood on my temple, ending at my ear. We carefully wrapped it, bunched up hair and all with a purple paisley scarf, before we left.

"Here, pulling out some tendrils, ah nice," Elaine said, trying to be funny like a crazy hairdresser.

"Hey," Mrs. Rocca called out to Elaine, as we were leaving, "nice to see someone wear that beautiful scarf your aunt gave you."

"Yeah," Elaine said brightly and we stifled nervous giggles. Nothing I would ordinarily ever wear, but a good disguise.

The car hummed along for ten minutes, then I recognized the large church fellowship hall as the place I went to for my church's junior high youth group, and left. Yes, I'd do the same tonight—leave.

I had felt the same icy sweat with the church youth group, and wished I could greet someone, yet felt relieved that no one said hello. I left and never came back, telling Mama my usual old story. I tried to make friends, but it was too hard. Moving all the time had taught me to easily know the truly impossible—feeling at home with new friends.

† † †

We slipped the bloody T-shirt into the trashcan by the door of the HOW meeting. We stepped inside and adrenalin assaulted me, my every step was shaky. The problem with going to this popular teen meeting, was that kids showed up sober. Everywhere teenagers hugged. Cute guys stood around hugging each other, hugging the girls more. Everyone looked like one of the cool stoner kids at school, except they didn't appear high. In the milling group everyone wore frayed blue jeans, halter tops for girls, polished leather hair clips, and surfer T-shirts for guys, not a paisley scarf-head was in sight, and no yelling counselors were to be found. I found myself plotting to fit in, imagining the halter top I would wear next time, the hair clip on clean, dry hair. These young people were like a good foreign country, not a bad one.

A girl greeter approached us. "Ready for the newcomer's meeting?"

"We're not new," I said swiftly, cutting Elaine off. I didn't want her to give us away. No matter where I went, I never owned up about being the new foreigner, I always pretended I already belonged. In such a large meeting this surfer-blonde gal in hip hugger jeans and a purple string-top would never know if we had been here before.

But she didn't give up. "Hey, I'm Devon, and I don't think I've seen you before, come on. Ay-ahnd, I do the newcomer's group."

My head cleared a little. I realized with dread that we did know each other before tonight. She was the scariest drug dealer at my first get-high parties. Devon, the person I believed most hated me then for being naïve, not knowing what booze, a joint, or anything was about. She'd roll her eyes like, *you're so lame*, and pass just-lit joints away from me. *Oh no, she's smiling weirdly. She recognizes me too.*

"Luce, we can go to the new people's meeting. Come on." Elaine gently tugged on my sleeve.

We were herded off. I see an older guy with a beard and a guy close to my age with a peeling sunburned nose, his sun-bleached dark hair turning amber. *Well, alright then.*

Devon told her story for openers. I tried to concentrate past my lingering headache. She ran away, she lived on the streets. She feels loved around all these huggy people. Her words started to crack me open, not just my aching head, but my heart. I wanted to stand up and warn her to not be so revealing. Sooner or later everyone would attack her. I wanted to be the next one to talk, I wanted to never talk. Her eyes settled on me, the second she stopped. "Luce, tell us why you came."

My throat convulsed. I wasn't used to anyone but Elaine remembering me or asking my name. Trembling, I missed the warm Scotch bottle hidden in the bushes at home, to drink before parties, so I could talk. The deep experience of foreignness dogged me. I decided to play it cool. "Well, last night I got so drunk I fell down at the bayou," I drawled, putting on a stronger Texan accent than I really owned. "No big deal. I'm okay. It's the only time I ever had a problem, so I don't know if I'll be back."

Elaine sniffled, then cried with big wrenching sobs. Two girls leaned in and hugged her. Everyone already liked her better than me. I noticed for the first time how pale Elaine was, with deep shadows under her eyes. In some ways she looked worse than I did. It must have been a real shock for her to pull me, a bloody mess, out of the ravine. A deep shame washed over me.

One of the girls said I love you to Elaine. I realized I loved her too. I fooled her parents, who are among the nicest mom and dad I knew, which made me feel awful. But I couldn't risk Mama and Papa finding out.

Devon moved next to Elaine and embraced her. "So how are you doing with all of this?"

"I had already started to wonder if I had a problem. I ended up driving us both away from my house last night, drunk, the road in double lines in front of me. We stopped at our old bayou hangout, all alone. I was just as drunk as Luce; I can't believe I got her up and out of there after she fell. It's a miracle that she's okay, except for that she thinks she can drink again." She glared at me.

Devon shot me a gentle look. "Well, when we first come here, everyone wants to get high and drunk again."

"Yeah, Elaine, I bet you can hardly wait to get high," I said. "Drinking isn't really your thing."

Everyone's eyes turned to me. Elaine's face was still wet with tears. It wasn't a cool thing to say. Up until today it was, but not here.

"Luce," Devon said, "if everything was really okay, would you talk to one of your best friends this way?"

The shame of hurting Elaine turned into a cold little knot in my gut. I nodded and my head pounded. "Yes … I mean no, I wouldn't be this mean." It was true; I really had to stop now.

Devon followed me when we rejoined the big group.

She's bound to tell me off. But instead, she hugged me tight and I held on to her, like maybe I wasn't going anywhere. "I guess I'm bad off. I could come back after all."

She pulled her head back. Her clear eyes, green eye shadow, and perfectly plucked eyebrows reminded me of the super-popular girls I hated, because I was sure they hated me. But she smiled. "It's not about if *you* were bad, it's about the consequences. You don't have to drink and get high again."

I turned away confused, my eyes blurry. I didn't expect the mean-girl drug dealer to be so nice. Others came up to me, all in a blur. Elaine was back at my side, and didn't look angry any more.

Warm hugs imprinted my skin like a trail leading to the North Sea Ocean of my Dutch childhood. You patiently hiked over one last dune, and there was the large expanse to greet you. The hugs are like touch I haven't had in years, like maybe I've never had, except from Beppe and Pake.

Everyone reassembled in the fellowship hall. I trembled, but no longer with fear. Over a hundred voices said the Our Father. We then headed to the parking lot. Trailing after Elaine made me think again about what a good friend she is. I hated to have to tell her I'm sorry. I despised apologizing. Was I really so horribly wrong? I put an arm around her since everyone was so huggy. Her hair smelled like leafy-green herbal shampoo. She squeezed me back.

"Hold up!" A counselor caught up with us at the parking lot. She had a special sobriety necklace with a white leather lace for her recovery triangle, rather than the brown everyone else had. I knew now that you have to get thirty days straight and sober to earn one of these, and a lot longer to be a counselor. "Hi, I'm Jayne. I wanted to talk to you. I'm glad you both came." She reached for my head. "May I?"

I jerked back. But then I let her gently unroll the scarf.

She nodded when she saw the wound. "So this why you're here. Good for you, it must have been hard to come tonight." Jayne's gaze shone luminously. I hated my own height, but she was taller, lithe, proud. She poked me softly in the collar bone. "You're courageous. You made it here."

††††

Courageous, I ponder sleepily. Courage, I forgot. The same courage it took to get past too many good-byes, the same courage it took to walk new neighborhoods with Alby and to help Corrie do the same. I can face these memory castles, and I can revisit openness about my own memories.

Within one year of starting HOW, I did my inventory steps, and had the opportunity to relate my whole life story. Devon was the one I read to, and she listened for a total of six hours, a record in twelve-step program inventory sharing, especially as I was only sixteen. In the months after she listened so well, I realized I no longer felt abandoned by God, that Devon had shown me that God was there all along. God was there when I cried myself to sleep, when I stopped sharing my own feelings, when I was lonely, when Albert and Papa almost died in the ultralight plane accident. Always there, like now.

I had wanted to tell Corrie and Alby that it feels as if we were all there in our parents' worst times, during World War II. Just like Mama and Papa we hate to lose things, and hate to wait in lines. We are harsh with ourselves over small mistakes, fret when we have to travel, panic over lost paperwork and act as if danger lurks in odd places—open communication. I would like my courage and faith to remind me that danger no longer lurks everywhere, and that I can one day be open, as Papa is open.

††††

Jakob

Billiton Island
February 1942

Waiting became worse and worse. Yet the grown-ups continued to talk of war, and preparations. The rain hissed, *it will be forever.* If war were inevitable like the adults said, Jakob wanted to get it over with, meet the monster, and defeat it. The children's rucksacks were back in their rooms, almost empty, because their most treasured items had to come back out. Jakob's compass was on his chest of drawers again, closed inside its case.

Sometimes he imagined all the compass directions the Japanese were coming from. He took sketch paper and made a map, color coded for the Dutch, British, French Indochina and the Japanese. There was too much red for the Empire of the Sun. Then he thought of the Americans, enraged over Pearl Harbor, coming to the rescue.

Some nights Jakob realized he was disappointed that nothing exciting had happened since Tarakan. Then he felt bad and said to God, *I can wait. It would be terrible if my wish for excitement was a prayer accidentally answered by you, oh God.* What if God had the Japanese attack, just after the family evacuated? All the men and Pappie would be killed for sabotaging the Billiton tin mine. The boring days were almost normal, everyone was still alive, and only Pappie's hours were different. He met often with the men of the Island, and they formed their plans. After that Pappie spoke of phase one, finally moving large valuables they could not take along.

Just as the morning changed from warm to hot, Pappie yelled outside. He'd been strangely quiet, now much louder again. It's how he handled servants; they would get everything in order for him. The chauffeur Adri lined up with an extra man, along with Kokkie and her family. Her two teenaged boys, wiry and strong, smiled broadly. It struck Jakob that much of the yelling from Blandas — whites — was ignored. They actually weren't as nervous of Pappie as he. Yet Pappie yelled still louder.

An oxen cart was ready, the only way to move heavy items. Pappie wanted it closer to the house. He was *regeling*, his face turned as red as his hair, sweat stripes down the back of his shirt. Adri moved quickly in front of Pappie along with the other helpers. Kokkie strolled out to Pappie. He wheeled his mouth open, then stopped. She stood in front of him, he inclined his head. He must be remembering to thank her. Kokkie signaled the men. Pappie yelled no more. *Kokkie's family will keep things safe for us.* These goods were going to Kokkie as a trusted friend.

Sara, Albert, and he collected with Mammie on the veranda, the place they went for fun, or to watch adventures like this. The men all marched into their home, Pappie following along. Out came the camphor chest, a chest of drawers, the living room sideboard, and some small chests carved out of teak. Then Mammie, Pappie, and the men hovered around the piano, which, after deliberation, was left behind and the rest loaded into an oxen cart.

"What about the General?" asked Sarah.

Pappie smiled about the family name for the General Electric refrigerator. "Well, we still need food. The General will have to guard the house."

Mammie had packed most everything that was important to go. *It will be up to us boys to guard the rest.*

The children ran after the cart as it pulled away into a soft rain. Off the cart went, with Kokkie and the helpers following along. The plan had been to move before afternoon monsoon rain. But the boys and men had tied oil cloths across the top. Oxen could transport in the rainy season, even over bogged-down roads.

Everyone else gathered on the veranda for tea — Mammie, Pappie, and the children — with Min serving. Jakob felt strangely empty; the first blank spots awaited them in the living room. Then he grinned broadly. It would be good to have it like this all the time. Pappie and Mammie joined with them for dinner more often, less yelling more talk.

Min did kitchen duty for dinner, and served them all fried eggs over heated *nasigoreng* rice, and kebab skewers with *pindasaus* — peanut sauce.

He adored the crisp *saté*-kebab roasted pork, charred lightly on the outside, tender on the inside, dipping everything in the *pindasaus*. He recalled yesterday. Pappie quietly sat by himself in the living room smoking a cigar. He spread out maps, and Jakob didn't dare approach him to ask questions. This would be a good time to ask. "Any day now, right?"

Pappie stretched back. "The Pacific British with their reliance on rank and class. They still don't know how to fight like desperate men ought to. Probably too busy waiting for orders or serving each other tea."

"Not fighting well, like in Borneo?" Albert had *pindasaus* on his chin.

"Even worse for us, for the world. They must defend Singapore, the bastion of safety for all of us."

Mammie's head snapped up, "The children. Should they?"

"Ja, they may as well know."

Jakob's neck prickled, he arranged a bite with egg, rice, and a dab of peanut sauce. When Pappie did let them know the worst, as if they were grown-ups, there was nothing left to say.

†††

The next day, visitors arrived at the harbor. The Henry Ford went to get Cousin Ankie, whom they called Tante — Aunt Ankie, and Mevrouw de Bakker and the rest. Soon excited voices called from the veranda. Jakob had his popgun out for his visiting friend, Matteus de Bakker, and

151

went to be with them. They children joined everyone before playing. Tante Ankie held her toddler, Johan, teenage Frederika talked seriously with Albert. Matteus and Riekie de Bakker sat with Jakob and Sara. All three women wore their hair loose. The breeze lifted tendrils around their faces.

Mammie spoke animatedly with Tante Ankie. With Ankie, Mammie's hands hovered and landed as deliberately as if pressing piano keys, not fluttering nervously here and there like around Pappie. Matteus handled the popgun, signaling thumbs-up for play.

Mevrouw de Bakker, pulled out her embroidery. "I'm making a grandfather clock cover." She was the kind of woman who listened quietly and then sometimes had a flood of words to add. Her needle flickered through the white background, adding delft blue to the royal-orange and green thread.

Tante Ankie held baby Johan, his shiny brown curls pressed underneath her chin. She always seemed to cuddle her kids more than any other mammie. Although, of course she had a baboe for help like the rest. Frederika too, had beautiful curls in Shirley Temple ringlets. Johan dropped his yellow stuffed bunny. Jakob stroked Johan's head and returned bunny to him with a big smacky kiss. Johan laughed and put bunny's ear contentedly in his mouth, then closed his eyes. "Such a sweet boy you are," whispered Tante Ankie to Jakob.

"Oh yes, at this one moment," said Mammie.

"Of course, he's sweet," said Tante Ankie.

Well, he didn't care if Mammie ruined the compliment. The best thing about having Tante Ankie was that she noticed him and that she brought her neighbor girl Freddie, along with the De Bakker *mammie* and her children, Matteus and Riekie, who were the same ages as he and Sara. Albert and Matteus had already settled nearby with books while the women talked. Riekie and Sara's happy voices chattered from the kitchen, surely helping Kokkie and the baboes. And

Freddie must be there too. Jakob pulled his own book into his lap.

Mammie pulled out the daybook she and Pappie had been making notes in, and read out everything that would have to go on the ferry boat with them: rucksacks and suitcases would be fine, light on clothes, heavy on provisions, take cash. The shocking defeat of Singapore had been the trigger; the evacuation order had come about.

Getting cash would be the difficulty, the women agreed, as the banks had been frozen in Nederland for a year already. The Java Island women would return home tomorrow, where their husbands would be awaiting their own orders. Tante Ankie's husband was in the *Koninglijk* Nederlands *Leger*—The Royal Dutch Army. All the civilian men had orders as well, so Matteus' pappie, too, would be told his directives.

Mammie pointed at Mevrouw de Bakker's embroidery. "Lovely. Well, we from Billiton are to appear lightly packed."

"Nonsense," said Tante Ankie, loudly, always the boldest. "We live in uncertain times. It is up to women to be prepared."

Mevrouw de Bakker put away her embroidery. "Of course we must do all we can, and I mean all we can."

Tante Ankie eased Johan into his baboe's arms. "What can the men say about it? Women are the strong gender. We bear babies, we persevere, and we ensure the family's survival. So right now, we'll finish packing you up today. We have hiking supplies we left here. That way Mevrouw de Bakker and I will be making a start too."

Dinner was fun with a children's table and a mammie's table. The boys giggled during prayer time, knowing none of their pappies were there to threaten to come over. Laughter rocketed around the room. Fifteen-year-old Freddie warned, "Hush now!"

Jakob stuck out his tongue and put his thumbs in his ears. "I'm an elephant, and I don't have to." Freddie's mouth squeezed into a line, while her shoulders shook. Then she had a laughing fit too.

Tante Ankie called mock-sternly from the grown-ups' table, "Stop."

Sarah turned red, trying to stop their giggles. Freddie patted her back as Johan babbled from his high chair and fed himself small balls of rice and bits of banana. Sara and Riekie had their napkins in their laps and tried to copy how Freddie used her knife and fork like a lady.

When they finished, all the children except Johan were called to help pack. Each Vanderveer child reassembled their rucksacks, adding mosquito netting and toothbrushes. Riekie and Sara helped each other. Extra clothing went into suitcases. Jakob ran to get his compass and reached deep into the familiar canvas of his rucksack, scratchy all the way down to the bottom inner pocket. There he safely tucked his compass and covered the pocket with everything else so it could never fall out.

Seeing this, Albert said, "I'll add my botany book at the last minute when we depart."

"And I'll add Tina," said Sara importantly. "Then we'll all have put in something from Pappie."

"Yes, we all have a way of thinking about Pappie," replied Jakob.

One family suitcase was left open on the dining room table, and Mammie, Tante, Mevrouw de Bakker, and Kokkie added tins of food, empty canteens, medicine, vitamin drops, and linens.

"Heh, we're done for now," announced Mammie.

"Put in the camping dishes and cups," said Tante Ankie.

"What? We are going to the mountains of Bandoeng, to a house."

"Still, it's up to ..."

"The women to think ahead," said Mammie. "We don't know what will happen with Japanese attack, or if we'll all have working kitchens or not."

Tante Ankie made room in the suitcase. "We must be prepared for anything, and the cooking pans also make good helmets for bombings."

Jakob stared at Tante Ankie admiringly. She was like an Amazon warrior—a strategist and fierce.

"More then," said Mammie decisively, and strode away with Min, returning with camping utensils, tin cups, pots, pans, rolled bandages, and iodine.

When they were done, Tante Ankie seated herself and Jakob settled on the floor, leaning back against her while she sometimes stroked his head. Mollie jumped over the open suitcase and her silver tail flicked away. Jakob froze, eyeing everything gathered near the front door. He would not be here when the Japanese invaded after all and worse, Mollie would be left behind.

He had secrets inside. He would miss Mollie, Min, Kokkie, and Adri terribly, more than Pappie. It was unimaginable to not visit the kampong, to not have Min take him by the hand when Pappie was furious, to not adventure with Indo boys, cook with Kokkie, or examine the Henry Ford with Adri. Not having Pappie along could be good. No one quelling his excitement, no one saying stop now, no one striking out when he had gotten out of hand. Even Wim's absence he half welcomed. Now he and Albert could show how brave they were. As for himself, being more alert than Albert, their family dreamer, he felt important. He held his breath as Mollie scampered back across the steps. Could he hide her? No—she had never been invited on an excursion before, so not this one either.

"Come on," Jakob called. Matteus, Albert and Jakob took turns roaming the house with the popgun, yelling, "Aha! Halt, you rotten Japanese," until Mammie and the baboes made them stop.

The boys and girls rooms were all full at night, extra mattresses raised on cots, as a precaution against an ant invasion. They chattered underneath extra clouds of mosquito netting. Evacuation to Java would be like this — everyone together.

The boys' room quieted, even though Jakob yearned to say more to Matteus. They needed to rest. Just as he felt the pull to sleep, he jerked awake. Where were the pappies, why were the women so determined to pack? The war-machine monster was near.

CHAPTER 9

Saturday morning Kemble is waiting for me at the coffee shop. I go for the perfect mix of cream and dark brew, toss change for the self-serve coffee at the end of the counter, and move towards her. Her familiar spiky-haired head is bent over her cell phone. She looks up with a wide smile and pulls out a chair.

Sitting down with Kemble for AA talk is nearly as familiar as reading church devotionals and meditation books in the morning, or hugging Vincent when he comes home from school. Her blue eyes are filled with her knowing of me, as she should, after twelve years as my AA sponsor. At least some people in the world are happy to stay sober, unlike Alby.

I'm always juggling a purse along with my journal, which I drop at my feet and pick up. I have more and more trouble holding onto things. "So I think I should call him."

"Well, hello to you too. Come on, hugs." She grabs me hard. I like solid hugs. "Call who? Do you think we could maybe talk a little about how you're doing and how Daniel and Vincent are?"

"One is sleeping in, the other is hiking."

"So Vincent is hiking while Daniel is sleeping in?"

"No silly, the other way around."

"Okay, so call who? God? Your brother? The state lottery?"

"Alby, of course." I feel a stress place between my shoulder blades tighten up.

"You act as if he spends all his time thinking about you, and wondering when you're going to call."

Laughter bubbles up. She does have a way of destressing me. "You mean he's not? His life is not all about me? Okay, okay. He left me a message at my office. So why shouldn't I call him back?"

She stacks her cell phone on top of an AA Big Book. "You need to stop this, this thinking your brother's recovery is all up to you. He's in treatment and maybe starting a sincere effort at sobriety like you always wanted him to. Luce, you just got back. So call him if you want to, but get on with the rest of your life too."

"Hmmm, the rest of my life." So I tell about looking up historical photos from the Netherlands East Indies on the internet: skeletal women, children, men. I wonder with her why Papa never told us. I worry that he did tell, when he screamed at one of us for not cleaning their plate at dinner, like when he dunked Corrie's reluctant head right into her spaghetti. And there were less brutal times when he said, *Hunger is so horrible, no one can ever understand it.* Maybe I didn't listen well to the few words he said, I tell Kemble. I know more now, and I'm gripped by Papa's life stories, not so much Alby's.

Kemble's smile lifts me as I speak. I'm not usually one for a rush of words, and for a long time she just listens without her usual quick comments. Finally, she puts her hand over mine. "Luce, something good is happening to you. I've never seen you look so happy, sort of radiant, and tired, all at the same time."

I wrap my hands around the steaming cup. I'm a serious type; people don't tell me a lot that I look happy, but I realize I am. "Yeah, all of the past is about unspeakable suffering. Yet, about Papa telling us, I'm happy. Like we're connected, like all those gaps, however wrenching and deep, mattered."

"Yeah. I think I get it, that you had this sort of barbed-wire bind growing up. You had only your family to understand, but they weren't talking. I've known you all these years, and you never told me this much."

"It's like people don't know what to ask where to start, and now I and we have a starting point." I clench my cup, my eyes fill with tears. "So thanks for listening," I choke out. "But Alby, he's still not listening to anyone. I have to call him."

Kemble touches my cheek near my eye. I flinch at her caring touch. "Luce, it's still not okay to cry? Go ahead and cry and hold on to some happiness, hanging out with Danny and Vincent here in Calabria." Her words on crying only make the vise in my throat tighten. I cry at Hallmark commercials, but not the past. "You can't fix Alby. And what about your own sobriety? I know you're not going to get drunk, but you've hardly been to an AA meeting. You must have been lonely with all of these thoughts in your head."

Yes, she knows me so well. "You know how weird I am. Sometimes I like being lonely."

"Control, control. When you're alone, you think you know what's going to happen. You're going to go to a meeting."

"Sure." I shrug. "Tomorrow's my home-group meeting, and the next day is Bible study at church. Kemble, I can be grateful and call Alby. He really wants me to call him."

"Oh, I'm not so sure about that. He left you a message at work. Haven't you ever played the game where you call someone at a time you know they won't be able to answer, only to be able to say, 'I called you'? That's what he's doing."

"You really think that?" I stretch my neck, which hurts. "I might as well call and get things done when I can. I am happier, but I'm so tired that it's now or never for most of the stuff I need to get done."

"You're happy and tired. You're there in your family past too, you know. Did any of them know what a big deal that was back then, when you sobered up?"

"Well, Alby was the only one who did, so of course he and I kept it secret. Corrie was too young; my parents didn't know I needed to be sober. I told them about the program I went to, but made it sound like a teen gathering with sobriety as an afterthought."

"Luce, do you know any teenagers who put themselves in an alcoholism recovery program?"

"When I worked in adolescent rehab, the kids who got their own help were always the ones who felt really neglected by their families," I say dully. I'm tired of her talking me into her viewpoint.

"So that tells you ..." She raises her eyebrows.

"Well, I wasn't neglected. My family was super close. Annoying for sure, but not neglectful. And yeah, I was in a lot of pain. But that was a long time ago. You know I've dealt with all of that."

She gives me the counselor look. "Of course you could be depressed; it might be physical ... or the travelling ... the past. Might be other family stuff. Luce, you were raised with high expectations. I could just see all of you not discussing your sobriety. Or later, with that plane accident, not talking, just to show each other you were all tough and got over it."

"The sobriety was no big deal; I didn't give them a chance. I was secretive, and later when Alby went to meetings, he was secretive too. But I know what you're saying."

"You know I'm saying that maybe they neglected to probe at your secrets, or notice that you might be depressed?"

"All of them," I mutter. "I thought you said I looked happy."

"You know you can be struggling with depression and happy sometimes. Your dad's past is exciting stuff."

Her words are eerie, like she's suggesting I'm seeking a sensational story from my dad.

"These family events, they bring you out of depression. Then it's natural that you would feel down after being with all of them."

"Yeah, and I've done that a million times: felt down, bounced back."

"So what are you learning about your parents' childhood?"

"Well, it was good until war took away everything and everybody for Papa, and almost everything for Mama."

Kemble's lifts her cup and looks at me intently. "I want you to think about how you thought you had to make up for that much loss."

"No, I didn't sit around and think that."

"You know their feelings, their moods."

I stare at the list of specialty coffees printed in colored chalk on the wall. "Okay I do remember that."

"Don't forget what it's like for us oldest kids," Kemble says. "We're both firstborns in our families."

Sometimes I love it that she happens to be therapist too; she can understand more. "Okay, I think what's bugging me the most is this: I keep wanting to call Alby because ..." I drain the last swallow, thump my cup down, and tell her what I didn't say to Vincent and Danny. Actually my secret reason for going ahead and encouraging Vincent to call his Opa. "I'm afraid my dad will wonder what's the use of telling his life story. He believes Alby's not really trying anyway. I notice he does talk to Vincent."

"So you think you'll change Alby so your dad will talk? Luce, maybe your dad's scared of the past. Maybe it's convenient for him to assume Alby's not sincere about recovery. Lots of us try to fix our parents, even going as far as tackling a whole war."

It sounds so simple to hear Kemble say it. I can't fight a whole war I can't control. I slump back, a wave of tiredness fighting for dominance with the caffeine high. "I'm not tackling all of World War Two. That's ridiculous. You don't get it." I'm frozen right back there — the thirteen-year-old too big to sit on laps, curious, shut out, not big enough for fully answered questions. "Kemble, I'm tired of this fatigue and depression when things are going good. It's time for me to 'let go and let God,' like I've heard in AA meetings since day one."

She rests her hand on mine. "I do get it. Your dad, your papa, is the one you want to be closer to. And that heavy tired feeling — will you go to the doctor? Remember you waited too long the last time to get out of a depression. Go see about what you need."

"Okay."

I try to ask Kemble about her husband's new job and her daughter's first year in college, and discover I can barely stay alert. "I think I'm ready for a nap," I say after awhile.

"Good." She smiles sunnily, assuming I'm going to take care of myself.

I let down in the car, sobbing. Kemble comes right out behind me; I thought she'd stay for awhile. I jerk my head around, not wanting to be caught letting all my fantasies of a different family matter so much. I wait until she pulls away and glance at my tired, teary eyes in the mirror. When I try to influence the family, I'm no different from Papa. I'll take a nap, make my Alby call, and do what Kemble suggests and get to the doctor. I'm feeling literally sick over the pain of the world, the Weltschmerz.

† † †

Might as well head for an afternoon nap. I lumber to bed, where I lift my legs up one at a time on my side, as if I'm Papa dealing with a painful hip, instead of an able-bodied woman resting on a Saturday afternoon. Kemble's right, I was worn down before I ever left for Houston. I must be struggling with the familiar depression that's always seeping into me, as if my insides are boggy ground that never quite dries to solid. But first, I stubbornly pick up the phone to call Alby's psych ward.

This forces me to get up one more time to look at my notes because I'm never going to get the hospital unit names right. It's not so much that Kemble said not to call; it's like she knew it would do no good for me to make the effort. But I can't fully rest until I try. I have a dead Opa, a deceased Oom-Uncle Albert, and I know nothing about how they affected my father, how he lost them, or why Dr. Ingstrom believes knowing more will help Alby.

"Hope Vista please, Alby Vanderveer," I say to

"He's now at New Vista. They have a shared line for all the patients." I hang up and stare at *New Vista* and the new number. I get it that the key word for the patients going on into rehab is replacing "hope," with "new."

So he made it to rehab after threatening to leave. Isn't that enough to know? I'm so tired, I'll rest first. Just as my blanket of weariness feels like friend instead of foe, lulling me to sleep, the phone rings. Against my *insinks*, I pick up.

"They're telling me I'm bipolar now."

"So I'm hearing all of this now from my idiot doc."

I flash on Dr. Ingstrom's kind face, think of her thoroughness. "Well, actually Alby —"

"I told her, 'Bipolar? That's where the research money is. The prototype my company is working on is beyond mood stabilizing; it's to help the central nervous system reboot itself. That way manic bipolar episodes happen further apart, or not at all.' Just because I've been lining up some great ideas and help for the other patients, she turns a new label on me. These docs and nurses, they don't like anyone challenging their godliness. Oh yeah, they have to be top of the heap. I'm giving out input on my nutrition to others and why I don't need medication. But the staff won't listen. They won't admit I know what I'm talking about."

It's like he has a talent for circular breathing. He just keeps going and going, motor-mouth at its worst.

"Bipolar disorder is the popular thing this decade. You know, previously manic-depression and hyperactivity were popular with the docs. Now they change manic-depression to bipolar disorder, and there you go. I know. My research firm is on to the break through medication for mood stabilizing. That's why the company wants me back so bad, and why the competition's after us."

"Alby, you gotta listen to them, and you're not listening to me." I want to kick my legs and scream to be free, to be done talking with Alby. Why did he even bother to call? Why did I feel that moment of hope and joy when he made the call? Why did I want to talk to him? I'm always thinking he is someone else, the Alby of long ago.

"There are these two kids here ... well, they're in their twenties and like their seventh year of trying to get a college degree. Spoiled brats really. Not like me, buckling down to science when Papa drilled me about making B's instead of A's. Always the high expectations. So after they saw me visiting with Cindy and the kids, I got them straightened out on family, love, how to stop using people. You know, like that saying from AA."

"Instead of using people, and loving things — Love people and use things," I say. "I do remember when we were both in recovery for a — "

"Yeah, that saying — to use things and love people, not use people and love things. Then I told them to use their tools, like their AA Big Book, which I'm studying on a daily basis, plus the nineteen thirties. AA history, that Oxford movement, Christian by the way, which started it all."

"Alby, don't make them think they have to be Christian for AA recovery."

"Oh, no worries. It's just the spiritual angle I told them to get. The second these kids noticed that their depression was totally gone my counselor Joe resented that. So he and Ingstrom think I'm in a manic phase of bipolar right now. If that were true, I never would have accomplished all I have

164

all these years, and I would have no job to return to. So I started to lead my own meeting for a bunch of the younger kids at six a.m. every day. Remember when we were both sober, you always slept late? But six a.m.? That was my best time."

"That's what I've been trying to tell you, your first sobriety was the best time in your life, not just a morning thing Alby."

"So now my counselor Joe and Dr. Ingstrom expect me to cancel out my morning meetings. Well, you know it's working if you get a bunch of kids to sign up for an early meeting."

"Alby, they probably can't sleep all night and they're awake anyway."

"When did you get so cynical? So you agree with them? I thought you'd be supportive." His voice breaks, like next he'll cry and I haven't heard or seen him cry in forever, not since the hospitalization from the accident, way before that better time in HOW meetings. "When I get out of here, I can get myself one of the most promising research meds if necessary, but full bipolar, me? No way. In here they should let my central nervous system heal from all the drugs, not label me."

So now he is admitting to all the drugs he did? And let me see what I know of mania: all-powerful, not sleeping, combative, and depressed. That means this conversation, like so many of our talks, won't really register with him. But I can't hang up. I'm too hooked in now. Plus I never give up. "So what else does Dr. Ingstrom say? And are you tying up the one patient line to call me?

"One of the kids has a cell phone and charger still. They're not very with it here with their searches. The kid and I only use this phone for good reasons. With Dr. Ingstrom, it's like the only word in her vocabulary is 'no.' She can't imagine having good reasons for private calls. I wish I had a creative-thinking doctor to work with. How did she ever make it through medical school? And she's not a psychiatrist of course. I talked to Shellie, head of the research department, just now. She said the prototype, which is a reworking of one of the atypical blood pressure medications by the way, is effective for bipolar and is working out just fine. The preliminary results are like patients truly rebooting moods."

"Alby, people aren't computers. Why do you keep saying rebooting? I can't get a word in edgewise; you're not listening to anyone. That's how a manic episode is. Pappie feels he can't talk to you anymore. I give up."

"Papa doesn't get it. I have to watch out for this one gal here, she's kind of a suit, says she came in to rehab from her political think-tank job. This funky little program is well recognized, by the way, all the way to Washington, DC. But I think that's just her cover story; she looks just like a woman I used to see at medical conferences. Obviously she's here to spy so her pharmaceutical company can see if I've still got what it takes."

He's paranoid too. The cloying, nasty feeling of always trying to change my brother breaks away. My heart crashes with worry. "Alby, I don't think anyone is spying on you. Please just focus on recovery."

"She's definitely with the competition. She's supposedly only here for detox, just one week. That's the perfect cover story. So there you go. A few days of spying, but I'll stay clear of her. And all she'll know is that I'm doing fine, don't belong here, and only need my release from the board to return."

"Alby, I love you." I tried, no progress.

"So I have a tape recorder too, because to just catch her voice in here is enough to discredit her."

"Okay, I think I understand. I'm going now."

"Okay, how's this for tomorrow's six a.m. meeting topic — rebooting recovery?"

"I gotta let you go now, Alby."

I gently cradle the phone down to the receiver. At the last moment I think I hear, "Luce I love you ..." Like Kemble and I were saying earlier, let go and let God.

When I close my eyes, instantly my heart stops pounding. I'm about asleep.

† † †

I'm in a kitchen. It is vaguely familiar but not my kitchen. Warm amber walls surround me along with older appliances like those I would find in an American farmhouse. Light radiates in from windows and a skylight.

I reach for a large woven basket filled with produce: the leafy fronds of just-pulled carrots, zucchini, tomatoes, lettuce. They are fresh from my garden outside and still covered with soil. I put a plug in the sink, slide my hands down the smooth ceramic side, and fill it to the brim with water, soaking veggies until the dark soil turns to mud.

I click the gas stove on and start to melt butter in a large pan on low heat. Meanwhile I set an enormous colander down into the sink, first putting in velvety carrots, dabbing off the dirt, giving them one more rinse. Each group of vegetables is carefully washed in turn, cradled in my hands, placed aside. I keep wondering about my rounded belly. It seems to be fat and bumps into the sink, cabinets, stove. I know it's okay to be fat; it is good to be healthy.

Chunks of beef sauté in the saucepan, and a stock pot simmers with water, ready to become soup. A beef bone and then the veggies I chopped are all added to the stock pot. I arrange lettuce on a platter and put it into the refrigerator. Alone in the kitchen, I am not lonely. Company is coming. I bring the soup and side dishes onto my large farmer's dinner table. I remember my company is arriving at the train station, and they are all from a concentration camp. Daniel is gone picking them up.

Everyone arrives, in clothes too loose for their skeletal frames. Oom Wim, Papa's older brother, and Tante Trudi silently sit across from me. I put Tante Sara, Papa's younger sister, next to me. Her face is beaming joy, because her husband, Oom Fiete is there too. Daniel and Vincent sit on my other side. Mama and Papa share the heads of the table. We all join hands and pray.

Like a child, I peek. Wim and Trudi stare straight ahead, the others close their eyes. *We are all here.* My belly is even bigger now that my emaciated concentration camp survivor family is here. My fatness sways forward as I stand to get the bread.

Tante Sara clutches my hand as I hurry off to serve us all. "You are pregnant," she says.

"Oh," I say. Oh.

† † †

Awakening, groggy, I write down the dream in my journal. Ah, the symbolism. I am on a *boerderij* — farm. And pregnant. Beyond symbolism, I wonder? No way.

I sit up in bed, finally refreshed; I know I can't be pregnant. First, there was Vincent when I was in my early thirties, then three miscarriages, then a time of birth control, then years after that with no precautions. We moved from sex with hope of conception to simply fun sex with no expectations and no conception. The not-trying-anymore was mandated by Daniel. Eventually, wasn't I glad? Too much hope and loss.

I finger the antique quilt on our bed, some dear one's tiny stitches and efforts, finally making it to us, and feel the soggy depression of lingering grief. I am forty-five years old, no period for three months, menopausal surely.

My shoulders tense and I relax my breathing. Depression hit hard the last time. Daniel tried to cheer me, to smile, but I just felt dull rage. "Are you taking your medication?" he would ask in a pseudo helpful way.

I wanted to yell like Papa would, *No, I would rather have a baby. I'd rather try again, see a specialist. To hell with medication.* I swallowed my screams, but Daniel knew my rage anyway.

For quite some time I turned away from him furiously, as shut down as I often was with my Houston family. He'd spoon behind me, tap my shoulder, and say, "Are you in there?" And I'd shake my head. I would visit my therapist, and in her eyes I could see she understood my hurt. I had to see her. Daniel would never understand, so he had to be punished. For the first time I was acting just like a Mammie-and-Pappie *ruzie*, but I didn't care. Bitterness wrapped and choked my heart.

One day Daniel reached for my hand on a mountain trail, and icy fury melted away between us. We lost our babies; I didn't really want to lose my Daniel too. At home we tentatively talked more about all that had happened. Daniel told me he just couldn't take the pain of double loss any more: no baby and worse for him as he wasn't carrying life—losing me. Lydia's yellow booties rested in our hands. I wrapped them in tissue, and put them in the drawer by my chair.

I cuddled Vincent more and felt the bitter layers of dense, dull wool wrapped around my heart release. Like the mystery of internal bleeding absorbed into the body, the worst of the pain disappeared.

† † †

I pat my fat little tummy; this dream leaves me wondering after all. It cannot be; this roundness is because I eat plenty of healthy foods like in my dream. I sneak in ice cream. Once a week I make *taart*—cake—smothered with whipped cream and fruit.

The numinous wonder of pregnancy resides amidst the reunion of my scattered family, finding the deep-seated roots of longing within me. Am I pregnant with the hope of the dream: reconciliation, love, and faith? Or is my deepest soulful self professing, *Oh yes, you are with child.*

Car doors slam outside, Vincent's car pool. He rushes in. "Hey, a bunch of us are going to the movies."

"I don't think so." I'm readying herbal tea. "Weekend homework first. Last week you said you'd finish and you still weren't done late Sunday night."

He stomps away. Soon his room is pounding with music. I check on him and he is lying on his back, doing nothing. "Okay, out to the dining room table, where you'll do some work. When's everyone meeting?"

"Five."

I glance at the clock. "It's four now. Show me some work, and I'll drop you off. You can drive." He's had his learner permit for one whole week now. Daniel took him for this test when I was gone. I missed a milestone. I miss way too much.

† † †

Monday, I'm free of work and all alone. I skip coffee, fix some weak black tea, and nibble on veggies, cheese, and fruit throughout the morning. Then I eat one large roast beef sandwich for lunch.

I shake off another afternoon nap, and soon I'm at the pharmacy. Ready to run in and out with what I need, I head for the family planning aisle. A cold glass cabinet, locked, is guarding the pregnancy test kits. I head for help and the clerk waves an enthusiastic hello. She's an ex-client enrolled in family therapy with me three years ago. I find a different clerk and whisper what I'm looking for.

"Personal aisle key," she calls out over the intercom. I swear it echoes.

I can see why tests have to be locked up, for nervous teenagers shoplifting to avoid public detection, but for nervous menopausal women? Surely no. I drive straight home.

My hand shakes as I balance the test wand on the sink. Which answer is good news, which bad news? I have no idea. Soon, a blurry pink plus sign looks up at me.

Warmth spreads in me as if I'm by a campfire, flames licking up the dried moss, twigs, until finally the logs take hold and burn. So I'm elated, yet I shove the wand back into the box, wrap it up with the plastic bag and shove it down into the bottom of the wastebasket like I have a secret.

So this is why I have been so tired. Does the plus mean a guarantee of life inside? Two of the miscarriages had been early, the last one, far later. For maybe four months now, I've been active, traveled, made love, no precautions at all, like the last pregnancy. Yet so far there's a baby; a baby who is still here.

She has been my companion for how long now? Yes, she, I sense. A sturdy one, like she's been in charge. Now that I know, I'm in charge; I'll protect her. Icy sweat hits, panic. No, no, no, not good for baby. Breathe, breathe. I wish I could make a call for reassurance. But if she and I remain a secret, somehow we are still safe. It's when you tell people that miscarriage happens.

Hot tears drip down my face as the dizzying panic leaves. I'm praying out loud. "Thank you, God. Thank you Mother Mary, help me." Peace settles in. I could call Kemble. No, wait.

A little like the dream, I head for the kitchen and start to cook. My heart pounds with excitement, not fear, as I chop veggies and meat for a stir-fry.

The garage door rumbles. Daniel's home early and bear-hugs me. We both know I don't care if he's dirty from work. "Mmmm, your turn to cook," he says. "Always better than my attempts."

"Not true, you're just saying that so I'll do all the work."

"No way." He laughs.

Like always, he goes to lie down for a pre-dinner nap. After half an hour, I tiptoe in from our garden; the bedroom's dark in dusk. I left everything ready in the kitchen, peanut oil, spices, the wok. His face rests; his jaw slack. As if he knows I'm staring at him willing him to awaken, his curled hand begins to open. I wrap his palm around a Peace rose, thorns removed by me. The Peace rose is a surprise champion of late fall, glowing and full with her pink, yellow, and orange hues. He slowly opens his eyes, face smooth, unguarded.

He lifts the blossom.

"Daniel, your forty-five-year-old wife is pregnant."

"What?" He squeezes my hand hard. "There's no way. Honey, I know you still want another baby, but ..."

"I took a pregnancy test. I'm pregnant, that's why I've been so tired."

He props up on one elbow, wide awake now. "Wow."

I go dig through the trash, pull out the twisted plastic bag, and find the wand. "Here, you can see for yourself."

"The pink plus. Come here, you." He pulls me next to him, cradles me in his arms in a way that feels like he's already careful with me.

What must he be thinking? He had been so adamant about no more pregnancy tries. Hope is back in me. Hope there's a baby's heartbeat inside me.

Daniel pulls back to look at me. "I'm so happy." His voice breaks. "Honey, I worry about you. How can we either raise another baby ... or face another miscarriage?"

"Oh, let's not worry." I squeeze him. "You know this pregnancy has to be pretty far along, by my calculations. I don't know either how we'll manage, but really, this baby will be fine."

Daniel's eyes darken; he isn't fooled by my cheeriness. "You know it's much easier for me to be happy over great news, than for you. Will you let yourself relax and enjoy, or will you do doom and gloom like Corrie says you do?"

On our dresser, a picture of five-year-old Vincent looks at us, swinging at the park. "I'll be happy, I promise. Shall we tell Vincent?"

"No. Doctor Simonian first, before you tell anyone, even Vincent."

I nod. We both know the risks of celebrating too soon.

He's out of bed. "Well, we have a miracle on our hands. And where's my dinner?"

†††

I know I can't tell Vincent yet, but I'm drawn to be near him. I sort of stalk him after dinner, knocking on his bedroom door several times.

"Mo-om, I'm talking to Tania."

"Okay, come see me when you're done."

Of course he forgets, but he comes out later to watch TV with Daniel, carrying his sketchpad and pencils.

"Can I see?" I ask.

There's more now, two skeletal young soldiers, their eyes sunken and their hands clutching weapons. So this is what happened to Papa. Vincent's sketch shows their fragile bodies, their faces lifted up; they want to fight. If Papa told enough of his story to help Vincent produce this, surely I shouldn't worry he will stop referring to his missing war years. "So you two are still talking, you and Opa?"

"Oh yeah, we have a routine. I read the problem to him. I hate algebra, but Grandpa likes it. Did you know that at first some of the teachers still secretly taught the boys while they were in the kamps?"

"No."

"Yes, they gave grades and certificates, everything. So after I read the problem, I hang up and we both solve it. I call Grandpa and he tells me where I went wrong. Now, I sometimes get it right the first time. He says I try to skip steps and not show my work. Then he tells me about when he was my age."

173

I have already told Vincent a million times to show his work in order to improve in algebra. I've asked Papa so many times to tell me about himself when he was young, and it's young Vincent he wants to talk to, not his yearning daughter. "So what's the latest?"

"Well, he finished telling me about most of the fighting during that *Bersiap* time, although I still have some questions about weapons, and how they got around. Now he's telling me about how hard it was to leave Billiton in the first place, what they did to prepare to evacuate, and what all happened just before the Japanese invaded."

Vincent tunes in to an American Ninja wannabe's strife on TV. I reflect on what I know so far. I always tell clients, "Don't worry about remembering more, and go with what you know now. When you respect what you do know, look for its gift, then the rest of our memories will emerge."

CHAPTER 10

Billiton Island
Late February 1942

Jakob's worry about Pappie and the others, and the war machine had soon been over. When Kokkie noticed the worry she said, "Storms make trees have deeper roots."

And Jakob felt wiser, because the men returned the day after Tante Ankie and the visitors left. Pappie sat on the veranda in the later afternoon, quietly smoking a cigar. He had deeper, quieter roots.

So it came as a shock when Pappie yelled after dinner, "Children, come here!" They hurried to the living room. What could be wrong? But he was only poised close to the gramophone, rubbing his hands together. "Ah, we will have a special family night." He ceremoniously eased a record out of its paper sleeve and balanced the edges across one hand, wiped it with a soft felt, and eased it on the little tower to play. He lowered the needle, just so. *Diamond needle, I'll never play with that. Or maybe one time before we are evacuated.*

Jakob and Sara settled on the couch where Mammie always sat. No one sat on the teak bench where Pappie and Wim used to sit. Albert settled near Mammie and Pappie. Jakob felt he must be the only one who saw Wim's empty spot everywhere.

"Under a Roof in Paris" began and Mammie smiled.

Pappie reached out his hand. "My dear?"

Mammie and Pappie started to swoop in little circles to the music. Horns introduced the song, violins carried the melody, umpahs of trombone and tuba carried the rhythm.

"Just a jug of wine and a loaf of bread," Pappie sang along, first in English then in Dutch. The last time he sang, "Just all of you," letting go of Mammie's hand so she swirled away.

It was like they really were far away on a roof in Paris. Oh no, under a roof in Paris, he remembered.

"Next," said Pappie. He signaled to Sara.

Both boys stood up for Mammie. She had on her nicest Chinese silk dress, jade green with gold brocade "frog" buttons to the neck, atop a long split skirt.

"The oldest first," she said, laughing. She held out her arms for Albert.

"One, two, three, one, two, three," sang Pappie with Sara. She stood on his shoes, craning her neck up at him, repeating his count.

Albert bobbed up and down next to Mammie like a stick, and then stepped on her foot.

"Oof, you will make a fine, smart husband one day, but you have two left feet."

"And for a future scientist, what does dancing matter?" Albert laughed.

"One day, you'll care," said Mammie. "You may be seated. Come on now, my Jakob."

Jakob reached out his arms, one hand to Mammie's waist, the other to her hand. He didn't have to count; each instrument gave him dips, told him how to move. It was like running a path in the rain, but slower.

"Ja, you can dance," smiled Mammie. They both hummed at first. "Let's see if you can twirl me."

Jakob stretched to the tips of his toes, turned Mammie, came back to her, one arm down and one arm up again. They moved in smaller and bigger circles.

"You, you will be a charmer as a husband."

He felt like Mammie's hero, the good dancer.

"Okay now." Pappie clapped. "We have a family announcement. Everyone, sit, sit." He picked up the needle on the gramophone.

Sara sat on Mammie's lap. Pappie stood. Albert and Jakob sat at Wim's spot after all. Crickets and frogs hummed their music now, surely louder than other nights.

Pappie rocked back and forth on his feet. "We have our evacuation order," he said. "We must all finish packing up our things to leave."

"Leave our house?" Jakob blurted out. So finally they had to go. He felt he could cry. He dug his fingernails into his palms, because Pappie had to see that he was brave.

"Yes, of course. Evacuate means to leave," Pappie said shortly. "One more load for Kokkie." He waved at the table in front of the boys, piled with more family photo albums.

Other photos, usually framed, lay spread out. Jakob craned his neck and saw the one with all four of them in the surf. Water glistened on their bodies, silver waves behind them. He remembered the day Pappie took the picture and how they all ran in and out of the surf over and over again. *Hold hands, run out, drop hands, spin, and run back*, Pappie had commanded. Wim acted like the photographer's assistant, calling, "Now. Drop, spin, turn." *A family dance for Pappie, this one in the water.*

Sara piped up. "We really have to leave our house?"

Pappie looked at her, and squeezed in next to her and Mammie. He lifted Sara to his lap. "Ja. The Company says take only a little, because we will come back of course. Of course we will also be careful and take as much as we can."

"Where will we go?" asked Sara.

"Well, first everyone has to get safely on the boat to Java. After that, it will be like a vacation. You'll be in the mountains of Bandoeng with our friends."

"Where will you be?" asked Albert. Jakob squinted through his eyelashes, viewing his brother as a blur. Albert could be alert when he tried—Pappie hadn't talked about leaving with them.

"I have to stay with the men of the island. I'll come to you later. We can't let the Japanese have the tin mine."

Jakob felt dizzy again. No Pappie? Evacuating without him was like spinning the globe and not knowing where to land. Bandoeng, vacation with friends was like a false promise of fun. Like not telling Wim he would be left behind in Nederland, he thought grimly.

"You all have important things to do. You will pack your rucksacks one last time. You will help each other, and most of all, you will help Mammie."

"But, what about ..." started Jakob.

"No more discussion. It is too late," said Pappie. He went around the room, flicking off each light.

Everyone trailed away as Jakob reached to pick up *The Jungle Book*. No more discussion, the family dance was over.

"You will be a big help to me, Jakob." Mammie startled Jakob; she was still in the room.

"*Welterusten*, Mammie." He said their usual good-night, with many what-abouts stuck in his head. What about boys staying to fight too, alongside the men? What about the trip itself? What about the Japanese? Would there be ships, airplanes? How many soldiers would there be?

"*Welterusten*, Jakob," Mammie replied. Rest well. The emotion in every syllable of her words told him she had the same questions. But Pappie was the one with all the answers. Or—Jakob felt a chill in his heart—maybe even Pappie didn't know.

† † †

Jakob stretched in the morning, remembering late night plans for a sailing morning with Albert. Oh no, Albert was up already. Did he make the mistake of asking Pappie for permission? The chance would be ruined with a refusal; it was much more certain to just go. They could take the native prows, canoes with an outrigger and a sail, out before asking.

"Hoi," Albert grabbed his own pillow and pummeled Jakob with it. "Pappie said we could go."

They would be paddling and sailing along the beach because Pappie's mood from last night had held. *Storms make trees have deeper roots.* Pappie sat at the breakfast table eating sticky rice, just like the children, dressed in old clothes for a rough work day. He smiled, and for once Jakob felt the warmth was as much for him as for Albert. They left home when Pappie did, each with their lunch wrapped in banana leaves.

Later, when the boys sank easily into *tidur siang*, Jakob felt as if he still bobbed up and down in the prow, with flashes of bright sunlight behind his eyelids. Dry crusts of ocean water remained on his skin, making him glad he had skipped midday *mandi*—washing off. He was still sailing on his ocean home and dug his toes into the bed as he had pressed his feet against the rough wood of the prow when wind gusts seized the sail. He wanted more—an infinity of time in his home, on his island, with his beaches. He hummed Baboe Min's *I'm the Captain* song and fell asleep.

†††

Jakob and Albert laid in turn on a dry part of the compound, to hover an ear just above the ground. They would hear Pappie's car arrive home just as Indian guides could hear a herd of buffaloes, or the singing of the rails from the Iron Horse. Cricket chirps dulled, signaling the hottest part of the day. They dressed the part of Indian guides, and Jakob's headdress feathers scratched his sweaty neck. Albert had a shirt and belt, each meant to be buckskin.

Jakob pulled up his ear for Albert's turn, midday hunger and languor setting in. This signaled the restful part of their day; lately Pappie sometimes didn't come home for midday meal and *tidur siang*. Hence, they spied for his return.

179

"I hear him, I hear the car," said Albert.

"Huh? No, you don't." But Jakob had noticed Albert's excitement while his ear was still down; he did seem to hear the rumblings in the earth. He had imagined himself as the sharp Indian scout. Together they watched the cloud of dust as the chauffeur quickly braked into the compound. Pappie and two familiar men got out.

"Hi, Pappie," they yelled.

He only nodded, his hat in one hand, his face red as he hurried into the house. He slammed the door. Jakob saw Albert's face tighten and knew his own did too. They retreated into the shade of the veranda. Pappie's voice always carried, so they could hear him easily. The boys changed course and crept into the house, each step soundless.

Pappie leaned back in his afternoon clothes on the veranda. Children's tea had been inside, for today. The company foreman Meneer de Meer, sat with him, his usual wide smile pulled down grim.

Meneer Westen sat quietly as always, his dark head nodding, blue eyes flashing whenever he looked up searchingly, which was his way. If volunteers were asked to help with wild boars or another fright, he and his men were always the first to call out, "Here!" Even though he owned a pepper plantation, with no mining equipment whatsoever, he would help. His daughter, Marijke, was the boldest runner and gymnast at school. Her little brothers adored her, and she laughingly led them to school each day.

Pappie and de Meer pointed to the map in front of them, their fingers tracing and jabbing. They threw out words, nodded, and eventually murmured quietly to Meneer Westen. As always, Pappie wanted to hear what Meneer Westen had to say. Jakob risked strolling nearby; he heard the words "mine sabotage" as he passed. He settled in a corner of the veranda, sitting on the sky-blue cushions.

"Jakob." Pappie's voice stretched to him. "Leave, this is men's talk."

He turned the corner slowly, heading for the garden, and afternoon rain started sheeting down. They might not hear him if he circled back with the constant whoosh of the rain. Albert went inside the house. Darn it, he could circle back successfully to hear the men. But if Pappie saw Jakob again, he would be in big trouble. The scent of damp earth rose up to him. Never mind, he'd go back inside to see if any tea cookies were left behind.

Kokkie welcomed him to the kitchen table, where he picked up the last cookie. Mollie jumped into his lap. Soon he might know some of what Pappie and the men talked about, and that they could all make their move to Jakob's hiding place. Since families had to leave, the saboteurs could go there.

"Shall I put the cookie tin away?" he asked Kokkie, thinking he could open it for one more butter cookie.

"Ja." She grinned.

In the *goedang*—kitchen storage—he saw Pappie's rucksack, stuffed full, fuller than any expedition. The men stayed for dinner. The children were allowed to visit for a bit.

"Meneer Westen," asked Jakob with his best politeness, "how's the family, Marijke, and everyone?"

"Ah, Jakob." Meneer Westen's face brightened. "They're all well. Marijke has been a great help to her mother. Like your family, they're ready."

When Jakob and Albert hovered in the hall after, they heard Meneer Westin's calm voice, soft and discreet. "We'll wait for you on the veranda."

They rushed to where they were supposed to be, their rooms to change for bed.

"Children," Mammie called out.

They all arrived in pajamas. Baboe Min's face always showed her feelings. Her mouth trembled with sadness, as she held Sara by the hand. Jakob wanted to make her laugh. Albert's face looked serious, expectant. So he made his own face somber, a true grown-up's frown.

Pappie said, "I am leaving tonight. You don't talk about my being gone from home if you are asked. It's important you know nothing about what we are doing. We men will leave the island after your evacuation."

"Pappie, will you need my old doll to keep you company?" asked Sara. "She is best friends with Tina, but she can keep you company so you won't be lonely."

"Oh, liefje." Pappie smile. "No doll can come with me. She might be in the way, as wonderful as she is. I have work to do, and will leave the island on a naval ship."

"Oh." Sara put her hand in Jakob's. He squeezed her damp hand. She had barely dried off from her mandi.

"Children, I expect your best behavior." Mammie's voice, which rarely sounded stern and was the reason Pappie thought she was bad with servants, was definite. In this moment Jakob would do anything she said.

"So ja, I will go," said Pappie. "Everyone be good. Listen to Mammie. Albert, you will be the man in the family. Jakob, behave, and watch that you use that smart mind of yours for good. Sara, you can be a big comfort to Mammie, and be her big helper. You all have to be ready on time for the boat evacuation."

Jakob's heart quickened. At last there was a reason that everything was packed.

Pappie stood up. Somehow Jakob had pictured him many times in a KNL uniform, although he was no soldier. He looked as strong as a soldier, having changed into hunting clothes with a knife fastened to his belt.

"Pappie," began Jakob.

"I will see you soon enough," said Pappie. "Don't worry."

Jakob swallowed, he had so much to say and ask. Albert swiveled his head to look at him. Their eyes connected, always those words, *don't worry.*

"Well, Pappie has to be on his way." Mammie clapped her hands.

Sara hugged Pappie; the boys shook hands and trailed him out to the veranda. Meneer de Meer and Meneer Westen's shook hands too, crushing Jakob's hand each time. He didn't flutter his hand after to help his tingling fingers, because men's handshakes were supposed to crush. Surely, besides sabotage, these three would fight the Japanese well. Meneer de Meer's idling car was nearby. His chauffeur appeared. The Henry Ford stood by, large trunk opened for Pappie's pack, where a rifle gleamed dully in the moonlight. Jakob rushed over to see if there wwas dynamite and more weapons, but the company chauffeur was already slamming the trunk shut.

"Bye, Pappie," shouted Jakob.

He didn't answer.

They stood with Mammie, waving, until the taillights converged into a single dancing firefly.

Adri checked the shutters and doors, like Pappie usually did. Jakob padded to his room in house slippers. His heart sank, Pappie was really gone. He would miss him after all. Albert could not defend them from attack like Pappie could. Why did Pappie have to sabotage the mine when surely they all needed protection too? He peered into the night. *For protection, this is why we evacuate.* No one would ask to see or use his special hiding place. They wouldn't even fight. With the moon's orb disappearing behind a cloud, the whole world felt almost as dark as the sky when Tarakan's oil fires blocked the stars.

† † †

Luce

Calabria, California
November, 2004

We had a lovely Thanksgiving dinner, after which Vincent was excused to go hang out with friends. Daniel rests and I journal.

> *Do all immigrants leave behind true names, with shreds of soul attached?*
> *Until finally, each name comes home desperately, like an abandoned child?*
> *On that day, we are whole. I live out every name.*

> *Liesbet after my* Oma.
> *Hanne after Beppe.*
> *Vanderveer, van der Veer. The feather is home.*
> *Lewis for my beloved Daniel.*
> *And what will Baby's name be?*

† † †

Amsterdam, Nederland
January 1964

The plane growled louder and louder after we left Amsterdam's Schiphol airport. Eventually it hummed and steadied. My seat scratched me right through my leotards and skirt. I sat next to Papa. Mammie and little Albert—Bertie—sat across the aisle.

When I smashed my nose against the icy window, scents of dust, fabric, and upholstery cleaner wafted up to me. Someone had been sick once in this plane; the cleaner smell had not made the sour odor disappear. My stomach heaved, oh how I hated to vomit.

So I pressed against Papa. His crisp shirt sleeve crackled against my cold ears. He smelled of aftershave, laundry detergent, bleach—better smells, but not pleasant enough to chase the sour scent away. I asked Papa for a raisin roll from the bag we had brought with us, and bit in. Lots of butter in my mouth, way more than we were ever served when visiting others, as Dutch families still economized all special treats. Our thick butter came from Beppe and Pake's farm. I bit in again. Papa ruffled my hair.

"All the people, trucks, and buildings, they become like tiny toys," I said. The last of the landmarks disappeared beneath us — windmills, cars, trucks, buildings.

"Ja, everything gets smaller," said Papa.

"Ja, and now they're gone." My stomach turned again. Beppe, Pake, and their farm, all gone. On the world globe, America was mostly green land on the opposite side from Nederland. Iran was brown. From Iran we used to fly up about once a year to Nederland's bright-green fields, not too far, the same side of the world. How would we get home now? Rain stopped coating the window, light broke through, silver ocean shone beneath. No dots, no people. "How long does it take to get to America, again?"

"Twelve hours, liefje." Papa wiped my face with the airplane napkin. This put a smear of butter across me, which chased the vomit smell.

"All day?"

He touched my buttery nose, smiling. "And into the night, but it won't get dark for a while because we are following the sun."

My vision blurred. We really would be gone. Mama murmured to Bertie. We were each dressed up; Papa in his best suit slacks, the jacket stowed away above us. Mama was in her best outfit, a bottle-green suit from Italy. I liked Mama's suit from Italy, and our time there. Beppe had strolled on the beach every day. Bertie had captured shoes from all of the dozing sunbathers. Every day before naptime, everyone came to get their shoes back. *Ah, the bambino*, they laughed. Mama smiled each time, *my bambino and bambina.*

Bertie chattered. I swallowed saliva, fighting not to be sick after all. A tear dropped on Mama's magazine. Papa's hand reached out to her. "This will be a good move."

She squeezed and squeezed Papa's hand and suddenly jerked her hand back, wiping her face.

"Why is Mama crying?" I asked Papa.

He looked at me and frowned. "Oh, you look like you don't feel well. Another bite of your roll." He sighed. "She's just tired."

"Oh, we can get her a pillow."

His face looked grim as he stared out my window, and he didn't push the stewardess button for a pillow. Mama knew that we would be too far away on that other side of the globe. Beppe and Pake must be sad. That's why Mama was crying.

Drops of water collected and rivuleted on the cold window, as if the plane windows were eyes, and cried too. I cried and pushed my forehead against the cold window so Papa wouldn't see and feel even worse. This time finding the dusty window smell helped my stomach not to churn. Little meals on trays came and went. Our stewardess brought Bertie and me KLM airlines flight pins and patches.

"*Mooi*—pretty," said Mama in her brightest voice, and held up the shiny pins and round embroidered emblems. "How nice to sew these on your clothes in Amerika." Her mouth didn't match her bright voice. Papa held out his hand; she gripped it again.

I shivered against the window. I would never sleep; I hated naptime everywhere we had ever lived. Hopefully there was no afternoon napping in *Amerika*.

But I did sleep. Papa's warm hand patted my back suddenly, "Hup, wake up, we aren't landing in New York, but Montreal. We can't fly all the way to Utah because of bad weather. The pilot says to lean forward."

I bent forward. The plane bounced on air; how could the sky have such big bumps during storms? The pilot's voice rattled over the speaker in Dutch and then the language I didn't know, English. "So it is night. We stopped following the sun?"

"Well, it is almost night ... and foggy. The pilot will land the plane just fine, but wants us all to brace ourselves." Papa's voice rang cheerful, with the giddy happiness he often had for a dangerous adventure which was bound to turn out alright. This was one of those times then, nothing to be feared.

Mama and Bertie sang the laundry-day song from home. "When Jonah was in the whale ..." The jolting was just like being swung inside a clean sheet by Mama and her friend, just a bounce onto the bed.

I stumbled off the plane at the Montreal airport. We had been traveling for ten hours, longer than any flight up to now, and we had further to go.

"KLM will put us in a hotel," Papa said.

My feet bumped into each other, not landing in the right spots, but stepping out at odd angles. Would we be by a beach, like the last flight to Italy? No, we walked along a large bank of dark windows by big buildings, still inside the airport. I trailed behind. Bertie held Mama's hand. Papa carried our shoulder bags, one old brown one, one new one for the trip, the straps crushing the back of his suit into wrinkles. I pretended we had arrived back at Schiphol airport. Soon I would hear Beppe's voice, *I will put you to bed now, liefje.*

Suddenly a force threw me to the ground. Reeling from the smack on my forehead, I realized I had run into a glass wall. On closer inspection I saw it was threaded with wires in order to be a visible barrier, only I never saw it.

"Oh, poor little Liesje," Mama said. She and Bertie ran to me. Papa's hands gently explored the bump rising on my forehead.

My lip bled from biting down with shock, a dull smell filled my nose—blood? I sniffed, yes, blood. "I'm sorry, I never saw the glass," I sobbed. In my exhaustion I apologized for being so wrong.

"*Stil maar*—hush now," said Papa. The shoulder bags bumped against me as he held me. I longed to be carried. Then he set me on my feet. "Come, Liesje, almost there."

† † †

I don't remember more of our move to America. My memory takes me straight from playing at Beppe *en* Pake's *boerderij* in Nederland to a flat cold tiled floor in the U.S.. Yet, what we don't remember, I have learned, is still memory. Missing memory is the threaded glass knocking us off our feet, scrambling to find footing again for the longest time.

CHAPTER 11

Luce

Calabria, California
December 1, 2004

Sharing the secret of Baby, Daniel and I have done a lot of hand holding these last few days. Each touch means the same as the Dutch *dag* — hello — also meaning: *I see you, there you are, I know you.*

Speaking of *knowing*, I find I *know* that Daniel never intended harm with his old announcement, *no more trying for a second child*. His *knowing* then was rooted in how broken we felt, our ability to heal was like a dried-out well, not a drop left. I secreted away anger and pain from his proclamation, yet had come to realize he was right. I spent the last nine years building my career, enjoying Vincent, and only crying on the relatively frequent anniversaries of either pregnancy or loss. Giving up on the ache of yearning for another child created an alternate universe. I lived in a universe where I valued my small family. On anniversaries of loss I dared visit the other world, grieving the family configuration of the four of us with two children. I'm used to alternate universes, I imagined the *boerderij* world with Beppe and Pake all the times I despaired over being a newly American child.

Today is my OB-GYN visit, a milestone to celebrate. I concentrate most particularly on positive thoughts, because I will not be able to treat my doom-and-gloom moods with any antidepressant medication. Dr. Simonian's nubby waiting room chairs are much like Dr. Ingstrom's — standard stock. Therapists rarely have these. We're too individualistic. My waiting room says, I hope, *welcome, something unique will happen here.*

I page through a parenting magazine and am suddenly, helplessly reminded of Dr. Simonian's kindness when I had to walk through this waiting room due to miscarriage number three.

† † †

We were at six-year-old Vincent's soccer game. The kids were still at the age where strategy gave way to swarming around the ball from one end of the field to the other like a fun-loving beehive. Every time Vincent or another kid shot away from the hive with the ball, the whole hoard followed.

Always, no warning. Sharp abdominal pain doubled me over, in the bleachers along the soccer field. I slowly straightened myself, afraid to alarm anyone.

Leaning against the distant pay phone, with Daniel's alert eyes on me, I was put straight through to Dr. Simonian. He arranged to meet me, alone, at the office, so Daniel could stay with Vincent. I waved at him across the field, and then turned towards the parking lot. My movements were code for; *we don't want to leave our son alone at a game, to come home with other parents.* At the car, I willed my body to hold on; this had to be a false alarm.

The emptiness of the medical offices felt like a scene from a science fiction movie. As if little of life had survived, leaving behind stark modern furniture, and an unpopulated world. Dr. Simonian greeted me and helped ease me up on the table. The pre-warmed sonogram paddle moved over my belly. No reassuring audio going thump, thump. No moving image on the screen.

"Dear, let's see if we can find the heartbeat."

Instead, we found the baby, a visual only. She lay curled, still as could be, large head, unformed body, the tiniest starfish hand reaching out. "Oh, oh no," I moaned.

"I am so sorry." His face was stricken, pale, as his warm hand rested on my wrist.

My hands clenched the exam table as if it were a chip of a raft atop a storming sea. I heard myself ask, "Can you see when she died?"

He rustled through my chart, not questioning my certainty that this lost baby was a girl. "Well, looking at when gestation started, and her size, I'd say about three weeks ago." He jerked my arm a bit to help me down, and I realized his anger — not at me, but at the grief. "I'm so sad for your loss."

"I was past the three months mark," I said. But Baby didn't get make it past the three months mark. I was supposed to have the guarantee of being in the safety zone.

He nodded. "Well then, how is the cramping?"

"Not too bad."

We changed to the surreal medical words used when plans have to be made about gestation and death. I could have outpatient surgery in the hospital for a D and C, or an office procedure. Hospital, I decided; I wanted to suffer as little as possible. I hated the cruelty of hope. Three weeks gone already, and all the while I *knew*, I just *knew* she was fine. At home I had the booties confidently given to me by Lydia; I had a picture of the previous sonogram. A mean voice said, *See, you can never count on anything*. She was gone, her little being gone.

No matter what I did now surgically, she was still gone. Anesthesia was the ticket for the aftermath. My eyes leaked before I left. Dr. Simonian handed me a tissue. I walked out with the number for outpatient surgery clenched in my hand.

On the way out of his empty waiting room, I stopped at the bulletin board by the door, scanning all the photos of mostly young families, and babies. Daniel and I had started and completed this game too late — I was too old. Although the doctors said there was no explanation for the miscarriages, I knew my hormones must be off-kilter, perimenopausal already.

I sobbed all the way back to the game and pulled over at the far edge of the soccer field to collect myself. Families walked toward me, with their kids dashing away and coming back. Daniel and Vincent were in the front of the pack, walking hand in hand. My throat choked; this was the only pregnancy for which we had told Vincent he would become a big brother.

I checked my face in the mirror, no sign of tears. I rolled the windows down for fresh hair. The cool breeze comforted me, until somewhere a baby cried. My chest ached; I searched for the source. A mommy cradled her newborn with one hand, heading for a bench to nurse. Her arms would be full. Mine would not.

Okay, okay, stop it, like Papa's declarations about the past. "Enough!" he would say. "Stop it."

† † †

Young baby-bump women surround me, some with a toddler in tow. I notice a woman with a huge rounded belly, reading her magazine. She smiles at me as though she's the only one in the room who assumes I might be pregnant, like she's wishing me luck.

I always did so much alone. A decade ago, I didn't grab a mom-friend to go to Dr. Simonian with me. The last miscarriage happened right before I asked Kemble to be my sponsor. She spent the years since telling me: "Don't live life as if you're all alone so much."

I wonder guiltily about having rescheduled Esperanza, among today's clients. My lecture on trauma resolution for a woman's outpatient mental health clinic was postponed, so I could be here. The clock ticks loudly.

My name is called and I'm shown a tiny room; I undress, crinkle the awkward paper covers around me, and wait. The door opens quickly, Dr. Simonian's smiling. "I think congratulations are in order?"

"Oh yes," I say. I want to go grab another older mom in the waiting room, to dance around. Light explodes in my chest. This is a miracle I can believe.

He grins. "When was your last period?"

"I really don't know. My periods are irregular. Could be three months." Not three months. No, no, I want it to be four, to know that Baby is alive and sticking around inside. I dig my fingernails into one hand so as not to cry. So quickly the miracle leaves my thoughts.

"Well, let's do a sonogram, and find out."

Relief washes over me. I remember the first time Daniel and I saw and heard baby Vincent's heartbeat, and the many other times we heard his heartbeat, always first, before the image, for all nine months.

I lay down. He must be in a hurry, no warmed-up sonogram paddle.

"Tha-thump, tha-thump, tha-thump." I laugh and cry.

"Nice heartbeat," says Dr. Simonian. "The heart looks healthy, which as you know is a good way to rule out Down's syndrome, and the fetus is well developed. My dear, you look like you are at about four months."

Four months echoes loudly to me. Dr. Simonian is a smiler, but never particularly enthusiastic. Yet he looks ready for both of us to cheer. *Four months!* I'm laughing and crying again and can't stop.

"Okay, office time," says Dr. Simonian. "Off the table. You change and I'll get your lab work ordered."

By the time we sit together in his office, I'm relieved the tears are gone. Whenever others are kind, I wait. I wait for the time when they'll say, *enough of the crying, no more now.* I vowed not to wear anyone out with my emotions since I was little.

Dr. Simonian's desk is the interior designer clear-glass kind, where he can't hide anything. The shelves behind him are stacked high with folders and a large ebony carved Madonna. She's reminiscent of my own, except for her size. I feel a burden dropping away I didn't know I was carrying. I am in the safety zone of pregnancy.

He looks pleased, reminding me of the Houston pediatrician we all had as kids. Like him, he is shorter than me, smiles all of the time, and wears sparkling-clean bifocals. His glasses never bear as much as a smudge. "How old are you now?"

"Forty-five."

"High risk." His tone deepens.

"So what else is new?"

"True, we'll take good care of you, and the good news is that the most risky stage is already behind you." He takes off his clean glasses to rub them again. "I know you and how you worry. You like something to focus on, and good nutrition always helps." He hands over a packet. "Here, prenatal vitamin samples ... and a healthy eating plan. Questions?"

"Any precautions for me?"

"Just no vigorous exercise and keep your stress level low. Not only do you have a high-risk pregnancy, you have a high-risk job. Obviously none of your clients have plans to attack you, but your work is stressful."

"What about airplane travel?" I ask.

He blinks, "You have travel planned?"

"Maybe," I say, thinking of Alby's ever-evolving craziness, and sitting with Papa to hear his stories. Why I would discuss any risk at all must confuse him, but I need to know."

He frowns and hands me a bag for the brochure and vitamins. "Well, if you take it easy, you can travel, but you do need to know what taking it easy means. If you feel any discomfort at all, or pain, you take precautions, such as slowing your activities. And get plenty of rest. You need to have a list of local specialists if you are going to be out of town. Technically you can fly, but you are better off staying close to familiar medical care."

"And my due date?"

"Well, we're working up to a beautiful day in late May, around the twenty-third. We'll see you every two weeks." His tone gets serious again. "I know you refused amnio with Vincent. With this pregnancy, you should consider it. We can give you an appointment with the genetics counselor, and then schedule the procedure."

"No, we're firm on that. It's too risky for the baby."

He gives me a puzzled look, his face flattening, like I'm disappointing him. "Here you ask about travel, but insist on no amnio. Fortunately, in our practice we have never had an amnio-related miscarriage."

I look away, hate that m-word. Say nothing.

He sighs. "Well, watch that travel."

† † †

Jakob

Billiton Island
February 1942

Early morning quiet, gently invaded by voices, mandi water splashed, breakfast smells. A bright morning of promised adventure, finally no nore waiting. Jakob found Mollie lying on a rug, then crouched down next to her. Her whiskers tickled. His fingers raked off shedding fur, while she purred and undulated, slinking in turn to rub furniture, the Persian rug, his side. Their canteens and camp goods rattled as Adri dropped them near the front door, and she sprang away. Suitcases snapped shut, thudding as each stacked up. Mollie didn't return, and time clipped along.

Sarah, Albert joined him around the kitchen table. Min touched each of their heads as she went around with a treat breakfast, pancakes. They took turns twirling the syrup ladle over their breakfast, mangoes and bacon fried in with the pancakes.

The hall clock had been packed up, no chimes on the half hour or hour. But Mammie came and pointed at her watch. Since it was eight thirty, they rushed to get to the ferries by nine. The Henry Ford chugged up the road to their house, with the company chauffeur behind the wheel. So it had not disappeared with Pappie. *Will we ever live in the highest house on the island again? Of course, in a matter of months we'll be home.*

The children all slid their hands over the warm hood, a hard good-bye this last ride. Would Pappie have to sabotage the Henry Ford? Would Henry be camouflaged and never found, until the day they returned? The chauffeur conferred with Mammie and told her that after the harbor drop-off he would drive Henry back to the factory.

Touring the empty echoes of their home, Jakob noted the naked spot on the highboy. Their gramophone, gone. He could not remember seeing it leave. Would there be music and a piano in their Bandoeng guest home?

"Hurry," Mammie called.

In moments they were in the car, bumping along, faster than usual. Were the Japanese so close? Too late for slow good-byes. Jakob's head rolled around, and sweat soon plastered him to the seat.

He thought about the time when the family, or actually Pappie, had left him behind. There he would be, with Min, Kokkie, and Adri—not such a terrible punishment. The servants took him to their kampong. The family returned with long stories of hot springs and volcanoes. He hadn't been able to join many of Pappie's geological discussions, and had to learn by peering at Pappie's photos of vapors rising from the ground. The reason for his punishments was hard to remember, just badness. What? Oh yes, running too fast in the house, dipping girls' braids in the ink wells at school, wandering away when the Boy Scout troop went hiking. No one understood he could find his own way; he had his compass.

With everyone gone, he and Adri had sculpted mud animals. Kokkie frowned, then laughed, reluctantly accepted a muddy cookie sheet for the oven. "Oh well, children must play."

The results—elephants, snakes, American Indians, lived secretly underneath the green canopies of Jakob's hideaways, until the rains dissolved them away back to mud.

No extra special good-bye to Min or Adri. When they were ill, Min had tended them all. With the measles, he woke up from a terrible dream where slow-moving volcano lava threatened to bury him. He fought to escape the unbearable fiery heat. He fought to open his stinging eyes, fought to hear singing. When his eyes opened, Min sang a song, as if he were her little boy. He was her little boy, he was sure.

"Oh, volcano," he moaned.

She had patted a cool wet sponge on his forehead. "No volcano, you are home in bed. Come now, we'll make you better."

She and Adri had each picked up corners of his sheet, and rocked him up out of bed, like a hammock. Out of the fire, and nestled in his sweaty sheet. As Adri and Min swayed with their song, Kokkie bustled. "There. Fresh dry sheets on the bed."

He came back to earth, and gentle hands rolled him from shivering damp to dry sheet. "You are weak yet." Baboe fed him little banana bites. "Now you will better." She wafted the white sheet around him like a cloud. "Rest."

There would be sickness on Java too, but no Min.

† † †

The car went over a bump. "Whoa." Jakob's head hit the car roof. "Mammie, quickly, let's go back. Just for a moment."

Her head bobbed as she dabbed her eyes with a handkerchief. "No, no turning back. We must be on time."

"But one more good-bye ... Min."

She turned around to him. "No baboe. You had days to say farewell." Her face was pinched and mean. Good-byes were over and done.

A deep pain spread between Jakob's shoulder blades, as if he had been sucker-punched by the worst bully at school, Wolfie. Such a coward, he always hit first from behind. Tears streamed down and he hid his face by turning to the window.

Sara knew, because his shoulders shook. She squeezed his hand. No more Min, no more Mollie. What if she became lost, away from her own home? Mollie would be alright. *But Min and Adri*, they disappeared when the Henry Ford was fully packed. "Ouch," called Sara in the next abrupt turn, squished between the boys.

The biggest ferry boat waited in the harbor, and the Henry Ford nosed forward all the way to the dock, easing into the chaos of cars and oxcarts. Albert and he jumped out and hovered close, elbow to elbow, each standing as tall as possible. Being big boys mattered more now.

The last time they had seen the big ferry, it was December 5, *Sinterklaas* Day. Sinterklaas and his white horse came to Billiton, bringing presents. Her smoke stack still gleamed, freshly painted red. The Sinterklaas ship had to be perfect. The excitement of Sinterklaas, Sara's birthday, and Pearl Harbor all happened in a row. Jakob dared not have fun at the harbor now. The invasion of Pearl Harbor, other lands, and islands happened while children everywhere were having fun. Silliness and fun had become connected with danger. Someone, somewhere must have been like a silly child, off guard, and then the Japanese attacked.

Women and children crowded on the ferry, few men in sight except for the crew. An uneasy feeling, as if they were being spied on, settled into Jakob's bones. Never had they boarded any ferry without someone's pappie or uncle along. *We are fatherless, just for a little while.*

The boys made their own way through all the women and children; the ferry was as sturdy as land when they jumped on board. They struggle around copious heavy suitcases and crates. Thus, no lightly packed traveling like all those instructions. Most important times, everybody breaks the rules. Ferrymen grumbled but let everything on board. Albert forged ahead to make space for them. Many mammies, already looking grim, had settled on benches. A woman with her hat ribbon tied firmly under her chin stared morosely at her feet, sitting next to dazed children. Of course, she had no baboe. Her little girl cried, "Where is my dolly?" The mammie looked up, turned and caressed her daughter's cheek, then switched to smiles and songs to set the tone for no more crying. She smiled at the boys, and made room.

"For five. I mean, no … four," said Albert. So he too, always counted Wim. Jakob went back and forth with Mammie, Zusje, and the luggage the chauffeur helped load on board. The four of them squeezed onto their portion of bench. Jakob wriggled out and wandered to the stern, checking the thick ropes fastened onto the large deck claws. Albert tugged on his sleeve, startling him. "Let's hurry back to get us completely settled."

How peculiar, Albert went from being a daydreamer to alert. Jakob wanted to say, *Shut your trap*, to be as rude as possible, to have each idea be his own, to receive no orders. But he looked at Albert's serious face, and knew he had to obey. No badness now. First, he could rush to the trees' edge one last time to pee. "I'll be right back."

"Jakob, what?"

"Nothing!" Jakob jogged along, and was almost to the shade of a pee spot, when he spotted bright-white, their Min in her finest pressed white blouse over a batik skirt. She stood weeping and waving to them all. Adri stood at her side.

Jakob ran up to them, breathless.

"Here." Adri handed him a little bundle. "The snake skins. One for you, one for Albert."

The Pearl Harbor Day snake skins. *"Terima kasih* — thank you, thank you!" Jakob held the skin, feeling its ridges and then Min's embrace. He breathed in her scent of fruitiness, steamed rice, spices.

Mammie and Albert called from the ferry.

"Go, go." Adri turned him firmly to face the ferry.

Deck hands yelled; he must be on the ferry on time. Jakob darted between the natives Indos settled with chickens and pigs in the stern. He jumped from bench to bench until he reached the bow. He pointed and waved, and they all turned to the dots of Adri and Baboe. In gratitude Mammie shouted, "Terima kasih!"

Ropes were cast off and they churned along. Ocean spray hit Jakob's face. Oh, he would definitely be a ship's captain one day if he didn't become an engineer like Pappie. They rounded the point that marked the change from choppy harbor water to ocean swells. His bladder hurt. Of course, he still had to pee. He looked at the horizon ahead, trying to fix his discomfort. No use, he curled into a ball of misery, knees pressed into his rib cage. He turned back to Billiton. Just beyond the harbor, the last sheltered inlet emerged. Gun-metal-gray boulders guarded one side, leaving only one way in and out.

Canoes and sailing prows dotted the glow of sand. The great boulders shadowed deep turquoise water. Skilled fishermen had to avoid their menace. If only he could skim past the boulders now, with his best friend Matteus, their prows rising up out of the water, while its seagull-wing outrigger hull skated the water. With brisk wind they could shoot over the waves.

Brave sailors like him clipped the sail just right. Albert and he had their last time in prows. But a Matteus adventure would have included competing for the highest lifts, like flying prows. One good thing, he would see Matteus on Java.

Bright morning sun silhouetted the last of the sheltered prows. Some had the delicate outriggers on each side, balancing out the sturdy middle. Soon the greater boulders blocked his view. His bladder burned and he smashed his knees harder into his chest. Everything tore away, everything looked smaller now: Adri, Min, prows, home, Billiton. They had really left. The hideous, awkward ferry, with its fresh paint, transported them along, like a dump truck of the sea, everyone crowded in—no ordinary vacation.

Jakob recalled how Mammie had played the piano in the house one last time, visited everything in the house one last time. He had petted Mollie one last time, sat on the veranda, shot his popgun, which had to be left behind. He helped Min pack the banana leaves wrapped around pork saté, *pindasaus*, and fruit—their lunch.

Jakob did not kick himself for lingering to say good-bye to Min and Adri one last time. But oh, how he wished he had peed; his bladder ached. Many people still struggled on board after him. He could have made the ferry on time after relieving himself, and now he felt fiery shame over his predicament. Yes, he should have controlled his own destiny. He would always control his own destiny now.

Swells subsided as Billiton's sun warmed his back. He could see Java's wavery strips of green widening: foliage, and rice paddies. Shades of peaked jade and ebony raised behind it all, Java's volcanic mountains. He'd rather have the shallow choppy water of their home harbor. He thought of leaping into the ocean, solving both the pee problem and the good-bye problem, except there might be sharks. No there wouldn't be sharks, just familiar warm water. For moments, he anticipated swimming all the way back to Billiton. Pappie said he showed promise to be the strongest swimmer in the family. After pulling himself panting onshore, he'd find Pappie, assist the sabotage, and they would escape together.

But none of that happened. Instead, he had to make a desperate maneuver, as far away as possible from everyone. Reaching the port side, he folded over the railing, purposely looking like a daredevil boy, too far away from his mammie to be stopped. He waited until a rogue wave broke against the hull. Instantly he peed himself with warm relief as salt water soaked him all over. He continued leaning over until the next breaking wave, then made a show of washing off his sweaty neck and back.

Settling back down with family, Albert stared at him as if he'd turned crazy. Mammie rolled her eyes. At least, he surprised himself with the thought; he had not been bad in a long time. War had chased out a lot of the bad. Sara sat in the middle of a stack of rucksacks next to Mammie. She looked happy. Like him, she loved the ocean. One last time, she turned her back to Billiton. Their island had become water-color brushstrokes of aquamarine greens and blues, dotted with gray.

Jakob blinked ocean water out of his eyes. He could make out all the landmarks. He went to sit with Sara and held hands with Mammie, being careful to not get her wet. Her hand squeezed his. "Oh, my boy."

"Oh, my mammie." Sometimes she didn't mind when he was crazy.

Java harbor loomed large. A chaos of uneven docks made with rounded poles appeared, and then the sturdier flat docs for huge vessels. He thought of the naval ships he had hoped to see; he saw none. Instead, brightly painted ships of the wealthier local merchants and fishermen bobbed nearby. This couldn't be an ordinary day.

They bumped the dock, alongside the other ferries, which must be from Tarakan, Celebes, and other islands. They had to stay put until other ferries disembarked, always waiting. Soon Pappie would be here too. All their friends were on Java, and Java was their fortress, protected by the naval alliance of the allies, their own KNL soldiers, and the airfields—concentrated here, powerful. The Japanese would conquer Billiton, but they would never get the large island of Java.

When they all stood, Mammie took a deep breath and looked at him strangely. He blushed hot from his chest to the top of his head. She could smell the pee after all.

† † †

Luce

Calabria, California
December 2, 2004

I sat in the car yesterday after the Dr. Simonian appointment, loving being four months pregnant. Savoring peace, not wishing to go anywhere. I played everything back in my mind, a new favorite memory to unwind like our old family movies. The doctor himself said that her heart looked good. I patted my belly and knew I would take no risks at all.

In the morning, words of joy swirled around inside and into my journal. *The past can never be replaced, yet the new still comes.*

I breathe into my favorite Scripture passages, Psalm 27, trying to memorize it. *One thing I ask from the LORD, this only do I seek: that I may dwell in the house of the Lord all the days of my life.*

I always turn to this psalm, because of being uprooted. Today's words illumine a new sense of home, as if extra roots grew out of me overnight. I will want only home. Baby is already home.

Anywhere—our house, the garden, the car, my office—can be home.

I change into sneakers and step out into early morning frost. Shuffling my feet along crystallized threads of ice on the patio pavement, I walk out with caution. I can't afford to slip on icy patches because I need to protect Baby, and I don't wish to repeat the long list of self-blame from the past: going cross-country skiing, taking a medication before I knew I was pregnant, running, making love.

The Japanese maple still holds some of its bright color, and I check daily for dull leaves spinning to death in the breeze. They fall and reveal bare bone limbs.

Each past baby, for me, was a boy or a girl, and each had a name in my heart: David, Xander and Sophia. Each was lost so early that I never knew why, being left only with the torture of wondering. Every pregnancy I felt less hope, struggling mightily to recover afterward. I wished to quit all grieving clients because their stories were too much for me. But instead, reluctant talks with friends, and reluctant prayer, shifted me to a greater presence with clients. I offered a hard-won prize, a fellow survivor of tough times, becoming a better counselor.

I come in from the chilly air, solid footing the whole way. With a happy sigh I settle into my easy chair and retrieve the yellow baby booties, caressing the paler yellow ribbon lace on each one. I delicately fluff each silky bow, just so. Perfect booties, back in the drawer. The lemon tree in our side yard scrabbles in every direction, rarely pruned. Some branches have brown leaves falling off, others shiny green leaves. A few lemons, grown large and ponderous, nestle beside a few blossoms gone brown. With Baby nestled at home in me, I feel like I'm living across the seasons of life all at once too: winter desolation, spring fertility, summer work, autumn harvest. No longer am I suspicious that I have the dreaded depression or some disease. I know I'm only tired because I'm growing Baby.

I am turning away new clients, and that worries me. What about our income? Daniel says not to fret, to enjoy my always-sleepy head, and rest. I flip open my raggedy book, *The Whys and Whats of Expecting*, which is as old as Vincent. At seventeen weeks Baby is becoming unique, her fingerprints are forming, and she has a survival skill: she can suck now. She's the age of awareness, as she hears sounds, sees light, and is the size of my hand. Any day now I could feel the first quivers of movement, recognition of being blessed.

Daniel and Vincent bang through the kitchen door with bags of groceries.

"Okay, Luce," says Daniel, tossing a bagel bag at Vincent, "we're going to spoil you with breakfast."

"Dad got me up early, and I don't know why we're spoiling you," groans Vincent. Today's the day to tell him.

"Son, don't spoil the spoiling," says Daniel.

Soon we are sitting with toasted bagels, bananas, oranges, and whipped cream cheese. Vincent leans back in his seat. His chair truly will break one day. Daniel says nothing, shakes his head, and gives me a look as if to say, *another one like this?*

"So," I say to Vincent, "I think you two are spoiling me, because you are going to become a big brother. We are expecting a baby."

Vincent smacks his chair down. "You mean we're like adopting from China or some place? That usually means a little girl, right?"

"Noo-o," says Daniel. "Your mom is pregnant; we are all going to have a baby."

Vincent turns red, he hardly ever blushes. "Oh, wow. That's awesome." He looks happy, and embarrassed.

"I guess teenagers really hate to think their parents still do it." I grin.

"Mo-om, don't make it worse by talking about it." Vincent claps his hands over his eyes as if to remove a horrid mental picture. "Okay, so when is the baby due?"

"In May."

Vincent rocks back on his chair. His grin disappears, and his chair thuds again. "What about going to the snow this winter? What about that I'm in high school and you'll both be old? This is so weird."

I don't know what to say; surprisingly neither does Daniel, who always tends to have the most answers for Vincent.

"It's an adjustment." Lame answer.

"Yeah," growls Vincent. "Our family never does the usual." He goes off to his room without a gesture of helping to clear the table.

I open my mouth about this, but Daniel shakes his head at me. Electric guitar music rips down the hall. I want to go infuse him with my sense of excitement and expectancy. He could be worrying. Was the last miscarriage a tragic memory of him?

I recall his hand prodding my belly, and his little voice asking, "Why did the baby stop growing?"

Vincent's guitar chords and notes sound better and better, no heavy metal for now. He's even singing. I'm tempted to go in, but then he would stop. Daniel sits and reads the paper, and I get out my journal.

December 2, 2004

> *Papa was evacuated from his home island as a boy and never, ever returned. I always wished I could have helped his pain. And although different, I ended up with shadows of the same pain.*
>
> *I feel like I, too, never returned to Holland. I went back at age eleven, again as a young adult, and so on, but it wasn't near enough, as time had shredded the roots*

between continents, and nothing was the same. So although I had learned to go through doors without smacking my head, and crossed oceans and borders again, for four years of childhood, ages seven through eleven, I was stuck.

Which is odd because four years is how long Papa was stuck in Japanese concentration camps. Everything repeats in our Vanderveer family.

At the beginning of the stuck years, in 1964, we found our way to Provo, Utah, where Mark Payne, Papa's citizenship sponsor, lived. By then, the juiciest part of my childhood was already gone. I became like a dry seed, split open, waiting for the tenderly prepared soil which never came, my own mud animals, made with servants in Iran, my long visits with Beppe and Pake on the boerderij went missing. We couldn't go back and forth anymore to Nederland for work sabbaticals, like when Papa was with the oil company in Iran. For a time, I cried, and then I absorbed all the tears, swallowed them down. The tears were always about missing Beppe and Pake, and feeling a stranger in a strange land. My Pake and Beppe's boerderij — farm memories both cheered me and saddened me. I have now lived my memories of them umpteen more years than I was side by side with them.

To Papa's citizenship sponsor, who knew us in Abadan, Iran, we were the family of a bright engineer. He was a guest in our Abadan home with French doors, a garden, servants, music. We were the family with a matched set of white-haired children, a girl and a boy, and Mama's good cooking to spare him hotel meals every night.

To Mrs. Payne in Salt Lake City, Utah, we were refugees. We were a family she was ministering to. Perhaps she thought we had slept on Dutch dirt floors before emigrating.

On our first day, after the bad night at Montreal's airport, we trudged tiredly into their vast Utah home with

*breathtaking views, split levels, and two rabbit-eared TVs.
I broke open dinner rolls for the first time at supper. Out
of the whole meal I ate only rolls, butter melting into
every bite. No matter how much Mama elbowed me, I
liked her cooking best, and left everything else — grayish
green beans, potatoes, and chicken — on my plate.*

After dinner we watched The Wizard of Oz *on TV.
Little Albert, who we called Bertie then, fell asleep. Even
when completely exhausted, I never was a child who could
drop off to sleep during daylight hours. I stayed awake as
dusk darkened the picture windows. Toto, Dorothy, and
the witch marched, sang, and flew all over. I didn't
understand a single word but shivered each time the
witch cackled.*

† † †

Salt Lake City, Utah
January 1964

The witch tried to snatch Toto away from Dorothy.
Dorothy cried, I cried; this *bioscoop* — movie — was too mean. I
touched the round lump on my forehead from my run-in
with the glass wall at the airport. My heart raced as I wished
with all my heart to step into the TV set, and protect Toto. I
had only watched TV a few times in Nederland, and was
fixated on the horror of Dorothy's dilemma.

I looked around to tell Mama I was scared, but she was
gone. Everything blurred: Kansas, witches flying around, the
flight from Schiphol Airport in Amsterdam to Utah.

Bertie slept deeper on the couch, curled into a ball. I heard
my own snuffling, crying as I walked the long hall to find
Mama. I found her with Mrs. Payne in a guest bedroom.
Mrs. Payne bent to show the bed, her hairdo never moving
as she nodded. I stopped crying, and longed to climb up on
the bedside chair and touch her hair. I needed to check out at
least one new thing here in America. Surely her chestnut-

brown hair would be as rough as a horse's mane. It would be like touching Pake's draft horse Kittie's mane, the first stiff part before it lay down warm and softer over her neck.

Mrs. Payne's voice went up and down loudly and cheerfully. Mama answered slowly, with the funny new English words. One word was bed, sounded out by Mama as *bet*, like we said. Good, bedtime soon.

Mrs. Payne laid a thin blanket, nothing like the thick wool of Nederland, on a twin bed for Mama and Papa. Where was the other bed? Mama's voice got thinner, duller. Mrs. Payne smiled, Mama did not.

Mama gave Mrs. Payne the same fiery-eyed glare she gave Tante Trudi, Oom Wim's wife, when we were in their big house in Holland. Mama's hand lingered on the one bed, the one blanket. Dutch Mamas and Papas slept on twin beds, closely pushed together. For guests, we always put cozy camping mattresses on the floor. Where were the Payne's camping mattresses?

I tugged on Mama's arm. "I'm scared of the film. They're hurting the little dog. It ran away."

She turned to me, her face looked dull. Papa appeared from wherever he had been, along with Mr. Payne. Mr. Payne, who had a shiny bald head, was the only one who looked happy. It no longer mattered if we were in Nederland, Iran, Utah; everything whirled together like Dorothy's tornado. Papa had his determined look that said he would make everything alright.

Papa and Mama spoke back and forth to Mrs. Payne. Mr. Payne had disappeared, that way he could stay happy. Mrs. Payne walked away, the back of her head shiny brown like the smooth chestnut heads I used to pick up in Dutch parks. Mama and I used the brown orbs for doll's heads. She was a doll's head, a mean one, maybe as mean as the witch.

Mama and Papa spoke to each other, in Dutch words the Paynes could not understand. "This is ridiculous. This room, this one bed," said Mama. "They have all these rooms, and they put us here?"

Papa answered, "We will have to make do, and make it right tomorrow. Surely they can do a little bit better by us. I know where the children are to sleep, down the stairs. I'll get them settled first, then you can come to say good night."

I held Papa's hand as we went to fetch Bertie. Papa carried the still sleeping Bertie. I followed them down to the dark basement, another whole room of furniture with soft thick carpet underfoot. Bertie was tucked into a sleeping bag on the floor. I was tucked next to him, in my own sleeping bag. Great sleeping bags. The Payne family was good after all. Mama came and kissed us good night. "It will be nice in the morning," she said in her too bright voice, which warned me it would not be nice at all.

My heart thudded with the click of the door at the top of the stairs. What if the witch came in here? Or maybe a terrible dark snake to devour us. There could be no such monsters, monsters aren't real. Eyes closed or open, the room emanated inky black. Mama and Papa were far away, Bertie breathed silently next to me. I thought of the lost little dog. I wished I had watched long enough to know if Toto was safe. At last, I curled in close to Bertie, which I usually never did, and his breathing lulled me to sleep.

If they were fully Americanized already, perhaps Mama and Papa would have casually asked for more blankets, or better sleeping arrangements. But as it was, the next day there were no cheerful voices. "Who do those people think we are? I will not stay another night in this house," Mama's voice barked in Dutch all the way down to the basement where I could hear. I didn't mind, I knew where Mama was. I grabbed Bertie's hand and we came up the stairs. I could see by the red spots on Mama's cheeks that she wanted her voice to go far. Bertie crawled into her lap, I snuggled her shoulder, and she quieted. But Mama had put her foot down.

We left that day.

† † †

Calabria, California
Late December 2004

I'm in the after-Christmas lull. Daniel hung new baby booties, purest white, on the tree. I almost wanted to snatch them down as bad luck, but he would notice. I gazed at the white longer, and knew I had to call Lydia.

I had acted as if Lydia had dropped off the planet when she moved away; this I tend to do with loss. It takes me a while to realize that people I lose are still living somewhere, that I can check in. I knew if I reached her, she'd call me honey, in that way that I tolerated from few people. I used to hear it too much as a little kid in Utah.

Being tired of phone calls, I wished I'd get her answering machine, so she'd call me. Always the mixed feelings, *Talk to me, don't talk to me*, as slippery as the ice outside on winter mornings. But she picked up right away.

"Oh honey, I'm so glad you called."

"Me too." We caught up on some news; I had the yellow Lydia booties in my lap. "Lydia, I'm pregnant and in my fourth month. The doctor says everything's fine."

"Yay, I could dance." I'd forgotten her enthusiasm. "Honey, that's the best thing that could happen for all of you."

"Really? But I'm so old now, and I worry. I've been here before, and lost the babies. Now Daniel has white booties on our Christmas tree, and I just want to take them down like they're a bad omen."

"Why don't you let them be Daniel's sign of his faith? Your guy, who doesn't like to go to church much, does this, and you want to take it down? It's great to have a sign of faith up on that tree, and it's not the booties that help or don't help this baby to be born, right?"

211

"Yeah, you're right. I feel so crazy."

"And you're not. You're just a brave woman who wants to have this baby, and is scared."

"I'm freaked out. My heart is pounding."

"It's all going to be okay."

We promised to keep talking and I felt calmer, as if I could have picked up the phone to call Beppe.

† † †

So I cherish the perfect symbol of loss and hope on our tree. I muse that what the two women, my grandmother, my elderly friend, have in common is the quality of home-spun love. Beppe knitted; Lydia crochets. Soon she'll send me a white crocheted blanket to put away with the new booties.

Vincent's Christmas present to Mama and Papa were his sketches, framed. Mama's gift was a sketch with an old-fashioned ice skater bent low, competing in the famous Dutch *elf-steeden tocht* — eleven provinces skating marathon. The long contest happens only on the years when winter cold is fierce enough to connect eleven provinces with iced-over canals. This is one of those years. He looked it all up on the internet.

My other favorite Christmas present is Cindy telling me that Dr. Ingstrom is a whiz and told Alby's board of directors to insist on more time in the hospital so he can strengthen his recovery.

I have learned so much from Papa's stories that my list of questions is longer. Before, I wouldn't have known where to begin. To be able to make a mental list of questions is so much more than the vacuum of sorrow I experienced before. Often, I hold my breath and get tense when we talk. Scenes of his rages play back in my mind, pop in with each catch of my breath, and leave. Papa's impatience, tight schedules, orders, hatred for unfinished food at dinner, the message to have perfect grades and a perfect life all ease. It all fades further back in my rearview mirror, helped by Baby growing inside.

All I could ask before was, "Tell me about the kamps." Now I can ask how the kids played in the kamps, how the mothers who were used to servants acted, and more.

I clear the last of the wrapping paper and boxes away, and start dinner. Shoved under the phone, I see the pad of paper with Alby's new number at the hospital. I could call; this is a tough time of year to be in rehab.

"Hello?" a Texan voice drawls, a fellow patient I assume. "Alby? I'll get him. Yo, Work-Boy!"

I hear Alby call out in the background. "Whatever happened to the confidentiality thing? Remember; say nothing about your fellow patients!"

Great, Work Boy? This is his reputation in rehab?

His tone is smooth the second he's on the phone. "Luce, I'm so glad you called."

"I really wanted to talk to you. How's it going?"

"Pretty good today. My head's clearer. I got more news about my liver, definite damage. We had a family therapy session with Cindy and the kids. Marina and Wade cried, particularly Wade. He doesn't feel safe with me; Marina's terrified she'll have to call nine one-one again." He pauses.

I exhale, not aware I was holding my breath—just like talking with Papa. "Wade feels safe knowing his dad is safe, by you staying there. You must have helped since he let himself cry so hard."

"Yeah. Maybe I'm helping him, but he's so sad and now I'm feeling it. I'm definitely not exactly father of the year."

He sounds so different. Oh, how we want to love and protect our children. "That's tough," I say gently. It's a relief to be able to just support Alby. I don't have to argue that addictions have scary consequences.

"Work is giving me one more week off, and then I'll be there for Cindy and the kids."

He just switched back to his usual self, Work-Boy indeed.

I swallow air. "What does Dr. Ingstrom say about that?"

"Well, she wants me to stay four more weeks." He imitates her accent. "*Den* you'll be truly retty to switch to outpatient. I concede you aren't bipolar; it took this long for your mind to clear. This is our actual start."

"Alby, you just told me you had major liver damage."

"But I just can't see that extra time. We're on the verge of a research breakthrough. Luce, I've been here a ridiculously long time. So I'll be discharged, and I won't use addictive drugs again," he adds.

"Yeah." I pause. "Do you know how many times you've said that?"

"Luce, what's wrong? You sound kind of odd."

I'm in my Christmas afterglow. What's wrong is you. You can't stick to your recovery more than a couple of nanoseconds. "Nothing," I say.

"Come on."

This is uncanny; Papa and Alby always do this, knowing something's different with me. I still haven't told anyone in Houston I'm pregnant, but it's like he knows. "Nothing's wrong," I repeat.

"So you think I should stay the extra month."

"Of course. That's what you need. You came into the hospital through the ER. You are lucky Cindy is still with you, that your kids are crying instead of acting out in other ways. You'll scare them more if you come home too quickly. You're a wreck, Alby."

"Gee, why don't you tell me what you really think," he says. We both laugh. "But seriously Luce, there's no way. Work's counting on me for a presentation on new bioengineering products to the board. I'm the only one who can speak everyday wordage along with fluent geek science. You know I've got the basic recovery idea again."

"You do?" I stroll to the Christmas tree and poke the baby booties with my fingertip. *Just remember Baby.*

"Sure. I just can't use drugs again forever, one day at a time," he chants.

"Alby, when we were teenagers, you knew being straight and sober was a whole way of life for both of us. Don't you remember that sense of fellowship, love, and spirituality from working the steps? You knew you were a wreck already way back then, abusing your pain pills to get high. You got happy in HOW recovery."

"I don't expect that whole happy-life thing anymore. I'm a wreck in a different way now. My wreckage hurts everyone else. I'm tired of my old ways, so never again. Most people don't get to be happy in this world. I'm going to watch out for my family and get back to work."

My brother the cynic sounds just like Mama and Papa at their worst, destroying optimism way before the crashing fall.

"You were, Alby. You wanted to be happy, and you were."

"Sis, I've been through the ultralight plane accident, the hospital, and physical rehab when I was a teen, my own relapses. I just want to get back to my family and, like they say in the program, 'do the next right thing.' I know myself. You don't."

"Gee, tell me what you really think," I reply, and he manages a feeble laugh. "Alby, it's because you've hurt a lot of people that you're supposed to stay long enough to get well."

"Luce, you never stop. Do you bug Vincent and Daniel this much? You know what's best for everyone. You don't want me to talk about leaving, but you only talk about others, nothing about yourself. And oh yeah, I love you too," he says in a nasty imitation of what teens at HOW sounded like at the end of meetings. We both plunk our phones down.

I slump down, hurt. The big, predictable dramatic hang-up.

215

Next I'm numb, a familiar situation which is better than hope, when dealing with Alby. He uses the word love like a dagger. He doesn't deserve Papa's constancy.

How is it that I rarely feel simple warm love with my extended family? I do love my family and they love me, but I don't feel loved in the relaxed manner my American friends do. Of course their loved ones have their share of dysfunction, but there's an easy American family thing that we don't have. Our relaxation seems to only come around music or books, which is great, but rarely in conversation or kidding around. No wonder I don't want to tell my Houston family about Baby. Our talk wouldn't be relaxed. Every moment that I ease into warm peace with Baby I want to keep, and not be hijacked into worry, stress, wondering. I can just hear all the comments now. *Luce, are you okay, are you being careful?*

Alby doesn't sound anything like the people in my AA meetings who are so done with getting wasted. I can tell he's going to make the whole work, drugs, hide-from-life machine of his existence go again. It's been so long since he's been happy he can't see simple joy when it's right there. I'm so done. I need to make certain I have a safe pregnancy. I've got a baby to protect.

I go back to fixing dinner. I'll stay in the security of this pregnancy. Yes, I'll keep my own strong sense of home, and drop all thoughts of traveling to Houston again.

My heart beats with the adventure of home life. I will be organizing—*regelen*—our new family for four. No wasting money on last-minute flights. I just reached the frequent flyer miles threshold from the last Houston trip, and Daniel and I will use those miles for fun travel. We'll vacation in either Europe or Hawaii, like an ordinary, happy couple.

I'm back to chopping veggies, hard, and I have a tough admission about my own childishness: I'm jealous of Alby. He's hurt and miserable, and still I'm jealous that Papa talks to him every day.

CHAPTER 12

We all have stories, I think of Alby's disgust with me. It's time to hear each story in a different way with no comparison, no bossing around by Papa and I, nor the rest of us. Mama, Beppe, and Pake seemed like the ones in our family who never changed, who provided the solid boerderij, always a sense of home.

Yes, we heard Mama's stories of the war years. As vivid as Papa's face freezing with questions about the kamps, was Mama's willingness to talk. Although her mem and heit, their nucleus of love survived, the fear threading her stories was as taught and cold as each unheated Dutch winter.

War destroyed everything for Mama, just as it did for Papa's family.

† † †

Nikki

Eenden Village, Nederland
April 1945

"It's like the Wild, Wild West, every man for himself." Papa—Heit—examined vestiges of everything they had hidden away.

In early morning light, well before any patrol might come by, Nikki stood by Heit's side. The earthy smell of unpaved ground, mixed with the soothing smell of straw, created a sense of no war, but every moment of alertness brought it back. They had few animals left to bed down with hay. Instead they hid the goods to barter: milk she would love to drink from a nearby boerderij, plus potatoes and carrots from their own garden.

Nikki tucked straw around the milk canister in one bale, and took care that no stray orange carrots glowed out from the other. Heit draped twine over the loosened bales, easily looping, tying, and tightening until they all looked identical.

They returned to Mama — Mem — in the house. Breakfast would be ready. Each dripped the last of the hot bacon grease over porridge. With no oatmeal for a year, it was made by soaking and cooking rough grains usually used to feed cattle. Mem meted out servings of the peach preserves from the cellar, and set down a pitcher of warm goat milk. Their cows were long gone. Heit would leave tonight.

Usually there was much to tell at breakfast, midday meal, and dinner. Heit excelled at story-telling: the news, gossip, and who was to be trusted on the black market, and who was not. Lately he left out some names on purpose, but they could guess which farmers charged children and mothers from the cities too much, who kindly looked the other way when desperate wanderers from the cities stole potatoes from the edges of fields, and who hoarded their food. Delicious or not, Nikki struggled to choke down the steaming goodness of food along with her dread.

Heit left at dusk and each night Nikki and Mem struggled with their dark home, the electricity disconnected by German command. If they thought the coast was clear, they used hidden knitting needles to tap into the electric meter, taking care to keep behind blackout curtains. Briefly they could read, and move around without tripping.

They spoke loudly during the day to fill the emptiness, and went for walks in thawing spring sun, knowing sun melted the canals and ditches for Heit and his smuggling. He had described his tactics, poling along on a short skiff at night, sleeping under the overhanging grasses during the day. No more trading during the day, like last fall, when they needed peat coal for cooking and heat. Now he would trade vegetables and milk for other foods, and linger on for peat coal if he could get it.

The worst was not knowing when he would return. Nikki slept in bed with Mem for warmth. Each morning they marked an old calendar, changed over to this year's days. Soon she counted fourteen long days, seven days longer than his last trip.

On the fifteenth day, Nikki went out to their chickens. She found two eggs and as her hand closed over the warm orbs, her heart stopped. Something was different. Each night she had prayed, trying to surrender her fear, trying to not make the sparks of dread worse in Mem's eyes by speaking of fear. But today she felt nothing in her prayers; the cord of caring between she and Heit had broken. She did not sense his nights and days, not a series of trades, not loading the skiff, readying to come home. He must not be coming back. At best, he'd been captured and sent to a labor camp, at worst dead. No one would be able to tell them. She and Mem would be left to grieve, wonder and starve.

On shaky legs she went inside as the late afternoon darkened, trying to restore her sense of Heit. Mem was quiet over their small dinner, heavy on warm goat milk, a little old bread, and some cheese.

The next day felt empty. When would they each start asking, *where is Heit? Is he okay?* Mem jerked a needle through a frayed jacket, pursing her lips. Oh yes, she worried, despaired even. A friendly, soft knock on the door and Nikki could go with her girlfriend, to play paper dolls. They cut up one of the last of the old magazines to create doll clothes. Nikkie snipped carefully and help up a find; her Mem doll had a fur coat now. The dolls settled around an enormous meal with fifteen of them around the table. Stew she and her friend agreed, stew was delicious.

Back home for early bedtime in the cold and dark, Mem served steaming hot tea, which she had bartered for by knitting socks. She told a cheery story, about her childhood family grocery business. She and her siblings had a system of lookouts to hide from their parents. The point was to escape from the endless work of their produce store.

Settling in bed, they were silent.

"Prayers, Mem?" asked Nikki.

"Of course. As Jesus taught us to, we say ..."

Our father, who art in heaven ... give us this day our daily bread. The familiar rote words comforted. The hot water bottle they took to bed spread heat.

"Daily bread, our daily needs will be met," murmured Mem. She didn't have to say that the daily need was for Heit to come home. Nikki touched a sore on her leg. Malnutrition. Mem carefully washed it daily by heating water with the bits of soap they had left, but it was slow to heal.

Exhaustion and hunger encouraged sleep. Mem's rigid body, full of dread, relaxed. Her slow breaths let Nikki sleep too. Dawn crept into the room and Nikki startled, a door scraped below.

Mem already sat bolt upright, holding the kitchen knife from under her pillow. Nikki jumped out of bed to go behind the door. They must defend themselves.

"Meine lievelingen," loud footsteps up the stairs.

"Heit, Heit," cried Nikki

"So brave, so courageous." Heit hugged Mem and she dropped the knife on the dresser. He reached for Nikki. He laughed. How could he think this was funny? Then they all laughed until they cried. Nikki felt enormous relief. Heit looked at the abscess on her leg. "Ah, it is getting better."

Yes it must be, if he said so. Heit brought hope, but he would have to leave again.

† † †

Jakob

Bandoeng, Java
February 1942

Jakob remembered Pappie's words like a promise, "We will evacuate to the cool hills of Bandoeng for safety."

The nearby garrison with friendly KNL soldiers, the largesse of the pristine city of Bandoeng, the Olympic size resort swimming pools, the splendid boulevards, and businesses all promised that Pappie's plan was good. The sometimes clear, sometimes misty views from their shared vacation home invited serenity: volcanic hills, the Great Lake, big plantations and terraced rice fields. They were far from the Japanese war machine.

Jakob imagined Pappie's arrival a hundred times, we will evacuate. There Pappie would be, visiting with the soldiers. Over days, his sense of ease melted as quickly as the ice cream ordered in the shops of Bandoeng because Pappie did not arrive. The Paris of the East had forced ease. Friendly soldiers became terse, and the peace of the hills became eerie. They listened to the radio, and in mid-February Palembang in Sumatra and its airfield fell to the Japanese.

Days later, the children returned from swimming to find KNL soldiers just leaving, but no Pappie or Oom Henri. Mammie said a hurried hello and went to the guest house piano, playing for the longest time since arrival. Every time Jakob passed by she was furiously working the pedals, music rising and surrendering over and over.

At tea on the veranda they all appeared in relaxed clothes, sarongs and white blouses for the women, play clothes for the children. But no one was relaxed.

Mammie clenched her napkin. "We have received word about Pappie and our friends from Billiton."

"They made it to Java," added Tante Ankie. "The Sloet van de Beele with many civilians and soldiers leaving

221

Billiton, suffered attack and sank almost immediately. All was in chaos. ABDACOM was involved, and it is now called the Battle of the Java Sea."

"But they made it to Java to fight?" asked Jakob.

Mammie's brown eyes widened. "To do whatever necessary."

"So when will we see Pappie?"

"We don't know, now we are at war and will make the best of things."

Only too soon, soldiers and refugees came in from Sumatra. The Japanese had overwhelmed the island with naval and air power, especially targeting air fields and Palembang.

The first time they heard planes, the boys filled with excitement, the KNL Air Force. But they were Japanese planes. Bombing missions were directed mostly to Bandoeng Airfield and the city itself. They dove into their hastily built air raid shelter during bombings, and carefully observed full blackouts at night.

Over days Tante Ankie and Mammie talked, in the stronger voices of women in charge, and then they announced, they would go back to Batavia, its harbor and Tante Ankie's house. They would leave forewarned, it seemed, by everyone.

"They say we are among the few families going towards danger," said Tante Ankie. "But danger is everywhere; we will travel while we can. Supposedly Bandoeng is the great stronghold. But my Henri would say Bandoeng itself is a target for the Japanese. So we may as well go to our home in Batavia, and be where we hope to see our men."

Organizing the move went quickly. Rumors had it that looting was out of control in the hills, with few men or authorities to stop the *rampok* rampage. They traveled in a neighbor's huge Daimler car, with his chauffeur to Batavia's harbor district, with a slow oxen cart carrying their extra goods. It would arrive many hours later.

It's not safe. No! The boys were refused a chance to ride on the oxen cart. Sara didn't dare complain of holding a crying Johan on her lap, as Tante Ankie and Mammie crowded into the front as well. They toured along the winding mountain roads. Their Indische chauffeur pretended relaxed talk each time they encountered locals, one hand lingering near a machete under his seat.

An hour into the trip, rumbling shadows filled the skies. "Our KNL returning," Jakob yelled.

The Daimler flew to the side of the road, as they surged out to huddle in the dirt. "Not ours. Japanese bombers and escorts!" Tante Ankie yelled.

Mammie shielded Sara. "The airfield. Oh, those poor men. So many planes overhead."

They scrambled up, riveted. Explosions sounded. A few lonely Dutch planes circled up to fight. Jakob held his breath, *please, please let them win.* Mechanical screams sounded as each KNL plane careened to the ground, exploding in fire and black smoke.

"Go, go!" ordered Mammie, pressing Sara and Johan into the car.

Jakob sickened with fevered despair. Between Bandoeng's military stronghold and the likely attack on Batavia's harbor, they journeyed between one hell and another.

† † †

Jakob's heart lightened walking into Tante Ankie and Oom Henri's house with the large garden in back. They had indeed escaped. Johan toddled around the back yard with his wagon and toys. Tante and Mammie sat on the porch nervously smoking their cigarettes.

"The oxen cart," called out Mammie, relieved.

"Even that, but here too of course, bombings, and all may be lost."

Jakob and Albert had pulled out their books, had their room arranged, and heard it all. Nowhere was safe anymore.

For a few days Tante and Mammie looked relaxed. But when the children tagged along to the *pasar* outdoor market, the usually smiling faces were guarded and serious. Each merchant asked either for more money, or items in trade.

"They don't believe the Dutch money will be good much longer," said Mammie.

Matteus and his mother lived nearby, and had invited another family into their home as well.

"Listen," Matteus said one night.

Jakob sorted through his marble bag. "What?"

Albert cocked his head. "I hear it now, looters,"

Jakob gulped his own spit; usually he was the best spy. So looters were here too? Mammie and Tante Ankie ran into the room. "We will hide everything, then everyone on the floor together. Strength in numbers."

Cupboards slammed shut, items were hidden in the kitchen goedang, and under the sliding leaf of the table. Mammie set items on top. "Okay, we'll leave out this broken clock, and a good tea set. Give them something to steal and we'll guard the rest."

Jakob positioned himself by the door with a hammer.

"Come here, they could turn that hammer against us!" Tante Ankie snapped. They gathered on the floor. "All I can think of to protect us is prayer," she added uncharacteristically.

They prayed, so useless. Jakob peeked. Albert and Matteus appeared to be seriously in prayer. The pulse in his ears roared in protest. *Perhaps prayer will help, but we must fight.*

The yelling swelled louder, and then stopped. Relief fell over Jakob and he wanted to cry, run, escape. He crawled into bed with Albert and Matteus as if into a nest high up in a tree, lined with fluffy feathers foraged from the ground — warm, safe. The boys whispered, figuring the danger had stopped only a block away. *So prayer saved us, this time.*

In the middle of the night, drunken yells, pounding, the sickening thud of nearby broken doors had everyone rolling out of the bed. Only Sara and Johan stayed asleep. Jakob brandished the hammer in front of Tante Ankie, she nodded. He leaned against the wall by the front door, balancing it in his hands. Albert stood on the other side of the door with a patjol. Tante Ankie, her baboe and Mammie guarded the back door with the shotgun, rolling pin, and a garbage can lid.

Crazed cries and whooping noises came closer. Then gunfire, a man's angry voice. Jakob and Albert clenched their weapons, ready to leap from either side of the door. Loud drunken voices came closer, another shotgun fire, then the attacks trailed away.

No one made a sound, until Mammie whispered, "Come, it is safe." They tiptoed their weapons to the dining room table, as if stealth could protect them all. The garbage lid clattered to the tile floor. Everyone jumped. Jakob hissed, "What a stupid thing to do. Who ..." He was ready to yell like Papa.

Tante Ankie rubbed his shoulder. "Thank goodness, we are safe now. Everyone relax. It's over. Done."

Her voice sounded shrill. So even brave Tante had been terrified.

† † †

Like all other changes, meals transformed too. Food, at first, became plain and still plentiful. With only one baboe to help them, and news that she might leave, the children helped bring in mangoes and bananas. Provisions, purchases and food storage were discussed much more. They were careful with rice, usually the great staple no one ran out of, and meat became rare. People's servants still came back from the market with food, but money bought less.

Mammie and Tante Ankie had their heads together talking. "We are doing well with making do, on the whole."

"The children need more milk and eggs."

"Well, now that is impossible."

Before the children automatically had enough milk and eggs.

Tante Ankie said, "Word is, that there's a man at the end of the street at midnight who will trade for milk. He will take fine linens and other items he thinks he will want after the war."

Mammie responded with determination. "But in the middle of the night, we can't risk it with those looters and rogue criminals; someone might overpower one of us if we tried."

Overpower; it was something awful that looters or wild men did do to women, to not just conquer but harm them. Jakob had a tightening feeling in his belly. Overpowering was like a snake striking too quickly, actually all too much like a man's snake, and it had something to do with mating, but it was bad. Not what they would want to have happen to Mammie, Tante Ankie, or Tante Ankie's baboe.

Just as in most playtimes, Jakob whispered to Albert about the black market, and put himself in the lead. Right before bedtime, with Mammie and Tante out on the veranda, he found the fine embroidered linen in the closet. He pulled out an embroidered tablecloth, and some pillowcases. As best he could he neatly restacked the rest, and counted. He knew if he bartered successfully at midnight, he would barter again.

Albert hissed as Jakob pretended to sleep, "Don't go, or let me go instead."

"I look darker and almost Indo, not so obvious like you. We don't want a bright blond head like yours doing the trading, plus you'll be too slow."

"I will not be slow, and I can wear a hat."

"Leave this up to me, and be my lookout with your hat pulled down. Tante Ankie said it was just at the end of the street. Stop worrying." Jakob willed himself to sleep and wake up at midnight, like the snake charmer's trick he read about in India. The charmer could go into sleep or a trance and then come to. He fell asleep in pajama top and shorts, to be on the ready.

The sky was dark with a half-moon when he awakened. Although the clock pendulums had been allowed to stop, so as not to alert looters of valuables; he was sure it was the middle of the night. He gently shook Albert awake. They crept out the back door and then around the front. Albert remembered to bring an empty rucksack to take back their goods.

"Okay, look out," Jakob whispered.

He was off without grabbing the rucksack, with the linens rolled tight under his arm. Padding along, he reached the end of the street. No one there, of course; he would have to go into the alley. Would Albert be able to see him? His underarms jolted into electric sweat, although he hadn't admitted it he knew the booming black market brought danger. He thought he heard a scuffle of feet; he sucked in air and his stomach clenched. But he went in that direction.

He saw a man's back moving away, and another Indo man with a shiny brown face and pitch-black hair, leaning back in moon shadow. Next to him, under a bush, was a box.

Jakob came up, greeted him as he would in the kampong back home, and called him headman. "My name—"

"No, no names, young sir. You will not know mine either. What do you want?"

Jakob thought he heard a rock drop behind him. He froze, stopped breathing, but nothing else happened. He whispered, "I will trade for milk and eggs."

The man faced the direction of the noise, and did not look alarmed. "Tonight, milk only. What do you have?"

"Embroidered pillowcases," said Jakob, hoping he could hide the linen table cloth for use later. He leaned back into shadow and pulled out only one case.

"Well, for one liter, I will need two pillowcases."

"For two cases, I will have three liters."

"Bah, two cases, one and a half liters."

"Two cases for two liters." Jakob acted just like baboe Min at the markets. "Or I could just walk away." He turned.

"Stop," the man hissed, bending for bottles.

"These are fine work," said Jakob as he handed the cases over, acting as the salesman of only the best.

"Health to your family." The man's teeth flashed in the dim light as he grinned. He looked curiously, eyes drawn to what else Jakob held. "Come again," he said, "two nights from now, I will have eggs. Be gone, *lekkas, lekkas*." Quickly.

Jakob checked the main street, thought he saw shadows. So he followed the alley around, then to the main street briefly, and scuttled quickly back to Albert, a bottle in each hand, so as not to create clinking. Matteus appeared beside him; he had followed them halfway, had known they were in the alley. Albert leaned into the shadow of the front door overhang, pale and grim.

Jakob grinned. "Piece of cake," he whispered, putting on a British accent.

"Be *voorzichtig* — careful — you bloke," said Albert half in Dutch, half in British English.

Bartering was like play battles: be alert, be ready, adapt, use your imagination. Their cash did them little good now, and he could keep this up. With a thrill, Jakob realized he was good at secret trades.

† † †

Jakob presented the milk to Mammie in the morning.

She shook her head. "Jakob, every day we hear warnings about being out at night. Anything could happen; you could easily be attacked or injured badly."

Jakob felt like he was a soldier a decade older. "Only the boys can do this, and we will be careful."

Albert kicked Jakob under the table. Tante Ankie shook her head, but said nothing.

Mammie glared at Tante, meted out portions of milk into each serving of morning rice, and added some small bits of the treasured brown sugar. Looking at its jeweled amber color, she sighed.

Mammie felt more defeated, Jakob realized, than when Pappie screamed his orders at home. So he must not tell Mammie when he would go again; then he could both relieve her of a sense of danger, and the worry about not enough food.

He did consult Tante Ankie on what to offer in trade. She would say to him from time to time, "This is what we can spare." He went out on his own. These nights sizzled with excitement, his heart pounded; his eyes flickered in every direction, not missing a single shadow, watcher, or trader. Soon enough, waking in the middle of the night became a habit. When everyone was asleep, he lay there with racing thoughts, making plans, anticipating smuggling. Sometimes his legs would cramp and he'd try not to moan out loud with the screaming pain. Must be lack of something. Food? On peaceful, lonely nights he could climb a tree and make out a quieted radio broadcast from nearby. He imagined wakeful neighbors, eager to get the first of the news, no matter when. That's how he heard one night that the Dutch had surrendered to the Japanese.

His heart raced. How could this be? The Japanese not only invaded, but conquered. Was Pappie safe and alive? *Rescued at sea, safe*, he remembered. A strange premonition of danger for all of them ran up his spine. He would hate the Japanese, already did hate them. The enemy was all the darkness in the world, the impenetrable vacuum of a moonless night, as bad as the night the Tarakan oil fields burned.

The Dutch could still *regel* it all. Even though the Japanese were victors now, they could still be conquered. The horrible Japanese must be transforming into their version of glorious victors, many red sashes, some samurai swords. He thought of the Governor-General van Starkenborgh's words of surrender. KNL men and dignitaries had to surrender their weapons, so the *regelen* would be hard. Tears flowed down his face that first night. No one knew yet.

The next morning they sat around their own radio. Matteus and Riekie were home with their mother, surely hearing the same news. "The Governor General and the KNL armed forces have surrendered. This is our last *bericht* — broadcast." The Wilhelmus national anthem played for the last time, and they all sang along, "My shield and reliance are you oh God ... Grant that I may remain brave, your servant for always, and defeat the tyranny which pierces my heart." Everyone wiped away tears.

Tante Ankie broke the silence, patting the radio, her face somber. "Very soon we'll have to hide this." The radio, their lifeline, would have to hide or go away.

CHAPTER 13

Luce

Calabria, California
December 31, 2004

Vincent's at an overnight youth group outing with church. Not much fun for the youth group leaders. Daniel and I laugh about how we'll go to the movies and get to sleep early, no staying up to greet the New Year for us.

Sure enough, we skip the movie, have a dinner of hearty soup, and sit companionably in our pools of light, reading. So like Mama and Papa, but not. We are our own people.

The phone rings.

We look at each other. Everyone we know is well trained to call us early in the evening, or use cell phones instead. Three rings in, nerves jangling, I pick up.

A light hearted, "*Dag, liefje.*"

"Mammie?" This is like saying Mommy, instead of Mom, I'm worried already.

Daniel stretches his arms, sighs. She's already greeting the New Year at midnight in Houston. Why would she call now?

I carefully mark and close my book. "How are you? This is unexpected ... Happy New Year's!" I'm affecting the cheery Vanderveer voice. "Hi Papa, are you on the phone too?"

"Well, liefje, Papa can't come to the phone, he has a *long onsteeking.*"

"A lung infection, you mean bronchitis? Is he asleep already?"

"No, it's pneumonia like what Alby had."

"What?" I'm disoriented. Then I remember.

"You know, our 1962 Nederland visit; we had to escape in the middle of the night from the raging fire at Beppe and Pake's house. You were four and Alby was one. Your health held as always, but Alby got pneumonia." Layers of sadness for Mama, generations of a family's life gone in one fire, and now worry about Papa.

Daniel has put his book down also, listening to my side of the conversation.

"So Papa is resting?"

"Well, supposedly he is. He was admitted to Southwest Houston Hospital. So if they don't bother him all night long, yes, he's resting."

I feel a thud inside, like a starship of dread dropping into its docking location, well established inside. "The hospital? Oh no. How is Papa?"

"He's weak and hoarse and receiving IV antibiotics. The first antibiotics they tried on him didn't work. No worry though. The doctor says he is expected to recover, but he'll remain weak for some time."

So it was all too much for him, the constant tension of Alby, death looming in the balance.

Mama's murmuring in my ear. "I wanted you to know now, since I knew you'd be awake. He's not relaxing the way the doctors tell him too."

"Of course not."

"He even had me call Dr. Ingstrom from his hospital room today."

"You must wish he'd stop worrying about Alby. Mama, do you need us to come?"

"Of course not. Cindy and the kids, along with Corrie and her new boyfriend, just left. We have plenty of help here. You just rest up; you looked weary and exhausted when you were here."

I thought I hid it from her. Being a mom myself, I should have known she'd notice. I worry she's desperate but her tone is quiet and measured.

"Remember that escape bag he used to pack? That's how I knew he worried when he went."

"What's an escape bag?"

"I thought you knew? Oh dear. He had it next to our library books, remember?"

"Oh yes." I fake my response. Something else I could have known or guessed, when I thought nothing came my way from Papa? *That's not for you!* The bag he whisked away, my hurt feelings and hurt lip.

"I know it's a bad sign he took it into the hospital. So I asked him to let me take it home, while he stays to get better. He was starting to relax before we all left visiting hours." She speaks freely as if taking away Papa's escape bag and trusting the medical establishment are both easy for her, which has never been her way. "They will find out what strain he has, and everything else they need to know so he can come home soon."

"Mama, I'm so glad you called." Daniel has come to sit on the floor and lean back against me, his solid back against my legs. "What can we do to help?"

"Like I said, we are fine. Corrie will call you tomorrow. Oh, and she says Alby seems much better."

"Well, he'd better be. I think the strain of visiting Alby all those times, brought Papa's immune system down. Who knows what horrible virus he was exposed to."

"Luce, stop it with blaming your brother." Now she does sound desperate, and it's my fault. "Here's what you can do. Do your best, to show your loving side to your brother."

"Ja, you're right. I'm so sorry. I love you Mama, and don't want to add to your worries."

I hang up and feel a huge lump swelling in my throat. I sounded like a six-year-old mad at her little brother. It chokes me to swallow this news that Papa *always* had an escape bag. I can guess why — if he ever had to be a starving prisoner again. Asthma breathing starts. I actually cough, which helps, and run my hands through Daniel's curly hair.

He leans back more and massages my feet. "So what is it?"

"Papa's in the hospital with pneumonia. And I'm a jerk about Alby, although I think the strain of visiting Alby so often did push Papa over the edge."

"Silly, this has nothing to do with Alby. Your father has always been prone to chest colds. You describe Alby as if he's a force of nature. But Jake's the original force of nature. He annoys you, when he push, push, pushes away at you, but you always forgive immediately. But Alby you always blame, or you find someone else to blame."

"Okay," I say with a dead voice. "I'll stop blaming." And I will. I must let go; my resentment is not just bitter, it attacks, popping into every new moment. Of course Alby didn't cause Papa's pneumonia. Daniel and I can send Papa flowers without my making all of this, yet another hospitalization, an emergency. Papa will be out soon. I wish we could touch the escape bag one more time, a time with simple understanding and love.

"We'll send flowers," says Daniel.

"Mind reader." I tell him about the escape bag, and about how the uprootedness of the past makes me try to fix everyone except myself. We agree that resenting my brother is my escape bag. Time to let it go. All this time Alby has stayed in recovery, while I have focused on his threats to leave. Like Papa, I know about escape.

†††

New Year's Day 2005 dawns early and fresh; I want to be brand new. I call Mama to fully apologize for blaming Alby in the midst of her worry. I enjoy our relaxed conversation, and knowing that Corrie is about to drive her back to the hospital for more news. I'm looking forward to telling Mama soon about Baby, and hearing her joy.

I ask Daniel to come out to Vincent's terrain with me, the college soccer field where he's been playing since age four. Even though the nearby hills have the best nature walks in town, I've avoided it all these years. Now we go here, I think, to celebrate peace; the field can't hurt me anymore. This is where the not-wanting-to-believe morphed into the yes-it-is-true—the last miscarriage. One weekend emergency visit to the OB-GYN, and hope disappeared.

That spring's bright light felt like a betrayal of a somber, dark loss.

Today's spring light streams all around and it's just the two of us, celebrating the benefits of no alcohol on New Year's Eve. We're the only ones here this early. Dust motes effervesce where currents of air meet sunbeams.

"Come to this bench," I ask. "This is where I waited for you and Vincent after I knew I was miscarrying."

"I remember."

"This is where a woman sat nursing her baby, and I knew I would never nurse a baby again."

"And now you will"

The empty soccer field stretches its hundred yards, impossibly radiant green because of all the weeks of rain mixed with breaks of light like this morning.

My cell phone rings. "It's Corrie."

"Go ahead and get it," Daniel sighs.

"Hi, Sis."

"Corrie?"

She's crying.

"I wanted you to hear it from me. Papa has more than pneumonia. Spots the doctor saw on his X-rays turned out to be cancer." Her words of explanation buzz into my ear. Details, specifics, don't absorb after that word *cancer*. I'm struggling to stay present, I have my own moments when

235

time starts to disappear, which I believe my family members don't know about.

"Oh, I'm sorry," I say, tingling with sweat, my heart in my throat. Will she realize how little I heard? "I'm spacey, tell me again."

"There's so much to take in," she says kindly. "It's so weird; I'm here on my patio telling you that its good if Papa has non-small cell lung cancer. That's the more treatable kind. She sighs. "But lung cancer is always serious. Those *kreteks*!"

"Kreteks?" Cigarettes. How did she come to learn this Indonesian word?

"Ever since Alby had to go to the ER, he snuck them, all gleeful about having a kretek now and again. He loves the word *kretek*. You know the doctors can't even tell us if the cancer's from exposure to cigarettes, there are so many factors."

"Factors? Will he give up smoking again?"

"I think he will, but you know how he is. He tries to change everyone, except himself."

I'm weeping, and try to pull myself together. "Honey," I say, like a calm Texas lady, "what should we do?"

"Well, we need to have hope. We need to take turns encouraging Mama and Papa; we need to learn about cancer … and treatments. I can do this, but I can't do it all alone. We'll get through this. He's always been ornery and tough, now he really needs us."

I long to explain that I'm even more sensitive than usual, and that I'm burning with worry about one life entering the world while another one leaves our world. But now is not the time to say I'm pregnant. I know Corrie's leaving Alby out of the helping-out equation and mostly Cindy too. They have their hands full with rehab. I feel closer to Corrie than I have in forever. "I could come out." *Am I really safe to travel?* "When is a good time for me to come?"

"Maybe in about a month. It's just that"—her tone changes—"everything is so explosive here. Mama is optimistic right now, but they're both going to get overwhelmed. You never know with Alby. Whatever treatment Papa needs, he shouldn't drive himself, and Mama doesn't drive on the freeways. So at some point, I can't do this alone."

My hand cups my belly; a chilly breeze lifts my hair. "Okay, Daniel and I will talk it over."

I tell Daniel on the car drive home. To him it's simple: I can't go. But I feel I have to go out to Houston again, with a tractor beam pulling infinitely more powerfully than the Starship Enterprise. I want to bring Papa moments full of love, many moments of ease, before it's too late.

††††

Jakob

Tjideng Neighborhood, Batavia
March 1942

The Japanese announced their presence in Batavia, not with a blaring cacophony of gunshots, or a majestic band, but with revving trucks spewing diesel fumes and shouting in the distance. No parade. Houses emptied through their dusty gardens as children, mothers, and a few old men headed to the nearby town square.

Mammie and Tante Ankie darted around the house first. Tante hid the remaining crystal, then pulled it out, then stowed it. Jakob hadn't seen her jump nervously from one thing to another before. Her hands were always so sure. "Look out the window, what is happening?"

"Everyone is going!" His chest surged with terror and excitement. They had waited so long, so this was the ending—for now. Before their Pappies came back to rescue them, of course.

237

Mammie and Tante Ankie each grabbed their youngest child by the hand. Sara and Johan were shushed and told not to wiggle.

Tante Ankie turned expectantly to her baboe. "Are you coming too?"

"There will be many of us glad to have the Japanese here," she said, "but not me. I will stay in the house. Better for all of us that way with the looters."

"Thank you," said Tante Ankie. Mammie nodded. Jakob felt his world turning cold in his gut. Until the war, every Indo he had known was kind and loving. When he was in trouble, they let him sneak into their kampong, or took him in, for a meal and rest. He had never thought that even one, let alone so many Indos, would be glad to have the Japanese here, and so angry at the Blandas, their bosses.

Mammie and Tante Ankie turned to the boys. "Stay near! We must stick together." Jakob dashed out front. "Stop, stay back," called Mammie and Tante Ankie.

Alby obeyed, but Jakob kept going. Mammie and Tante Ankie's voices pierced his ears. They sounded like shrill helpless women. Pappie had said to be the man of the family. Well, he had said *be the man* to Albert, but he was looking at Jakob too. Men had to be brave, resourceful, alert, and quick. He would not walk carefully behind, with frightened children.

Once in the town square, he pushed to the front of the throng of Blandas and Indos. He dripped sweat as all the heated bodies crowded in. Young Indo boys in the trees yelled, "The Japanese are almost here." Horror and excitement rushed into him, stretching upward for a look at the splendor of their uniforms. The surviving KNL would march in right behind, brave, even in defeat.

A few Japanese soldiers with bayonets jogged up first, pushing the crowds back. Behind them rows of soldiers, in what must have been old fatigues, approached. The bayonet men yelled words no one could comprehend. The noise of

238

invasion came in dull waves; first this loud roar of orders, more orders in the distance, then a hush that fell on the crowd. The yelling must have been a mandate for silence. The bayonet men turned their backs to the crowd and saluted.

Into the quiet lull, small men rounded the corner into the square, some on bicycles, many on foot. No horses. No sashes, no bright red to signify the Empire of the Sun. Most of the soldiers were shorter than Pappie. The red sun on the Japanese flag loomed, and an Indonesian flag too. The enemy arrived looking defeatable in their beige-green uniforms like sickly dusty moss. They appeared tired, not even proud, and no KNL were in sight. Jakob felt dizzy. Were all the soldiers shot?

Many looked harmless. Although they were ruled by Emperor Hirohito, whom they revered as a god, they themselves appeared ordinary, pulled out of fields and factories to fight. The next waves of men passed on bicycles, their rifles strapped on their backs. *With these now silent old men and boys next to me, we could grab their bicycles, knock them to the ground and gain the advantage.* He tensed his muscles, ready to grab and grasp. No one moved. More young men swaggered in, looking bolder now, under dull helmets. Most had rifles as tall as themselves and each weapon had a bayonet. A few had no weapons at all. The captured KNL must be nearby; many were Blandas, still more loyal Indos. The KNL would be thousands of soldiers, ready for uprising, and once they conquered they would look royal in their blue uniforms and sashes, rakish hats, and polished weapons.

With shuffles and screams, the Japanese assembled in the middle and edges of the square. Some soldiers screamed and struck out at old men and boys in the front. In shock, Jakob stepped back. How could they? The Dutch had surrendered; you do not strike out after the white flag.

They do not know the rules, or they do not care about the rules. Jakob locked himself in stillness for a moment, gazing out of the corners of his eyes. *I am on guard like stalked prey, and I am not a predator now. We are all the prey. I can count the many Blandas here. So many of us, why are we not attacking now? Well, because we surrendered.*

Other adolescent boys with rigid bodies, pressed in on him. His hands clenched in fists, some men and boys did the same, and then their hands went flat. Still, they need not surrender. If one fought, they could all fight, and win. The Japanese had not reckoned on the strength of civilians.

As if watching someone else, Jakob broke from his locked stillness. His arm crept down, picking up a rock. He could be fierce, fiercer than the beige-green Japanese shouters. Soon everyone would throw rocks; maybe many had hidden weapons nearby. The Japanese would never be able to see where the first throw came from, nor the first bullets, then all of them would drive them right back into the ocean and into the air.

He clutched the stone in the palm of his hand, looked for a target, and picked a soldier next to his bicycle. As he pulled back his arm, his elbow was wrenched from behind. "Drop it!"

He turned to see Meneer Zwanenburg, one of his previous teachers. His hands clamped Jakob's elbow and wrist. "Get behind me, now! You will kill us all. Jakob, what are you thinking!"

Jakob dropped the stone and switched spots with his teacher. Japs started to yell with fury and charged their area. Had they seen him, what had he done? His heart thudded like never before. How could he have thought to cause danger when the whole country had surrendered already? This was surely the worst thing he had ever done.

But the soldiers stopped and struck men in front of them, forcing all to bow correctly. Meneer Zwanenburg hissed, "We must." Everyone around them froze into low bows.

Hands flat against the legs, outside the knees, do not move about. A soldier hit a boy in the stomach with a rifle butt, so he fell to the ground, wobbled up, and forced himself into a deep bow. An older man had been hit in the mouth. He was spitting blood as he also bowed deep.

"*Keirei, keirei!*" It must mean bow.

Jakob studied all the boys and men. Tears stung his eyes. He hated what he had almost done, he hated tears of fury leaking down his face, and he hated the blood on the ground from the Opa-aged man bashed in the mouth. He hated the sturdy men nearby. Perhaps they were too old to fight as soldiers, but they could have fought here. He hated the moans, quickly silenced, of citizens hit in the stomach, the jaw, the nose, across the back, or battered to the ground.

"Keirei, keirei!" For moments the entire square turned to silence as, impossibly, more Japanese marched in, crowding the square.

Jakob peeked behind himself and saw through the motionless forest of legs that Mammie, Tante Ankie, Albert, Sara, even little Johan had all bent over, their hands sharply at their sides, just so, an instant harsh lesson. He should have stayed with them he knew in a rush. By being the man of the family, Pappie meant to protect, not to dash away like he had done.

Yells started up again. "Keirei, keirei. *Kiotsuke!*"

A Chinese boy he knew, who did math sums for his father's food stall, remained straight and proud. Just two days ago he had seen him when he helped Baboe go to market.

He would not bow. *Bow. Oh, please bow.* Jakob didn't want the boy to be beaten, but his smooth golden face never wavered. A blur of beige-green threw him to the ground, kicked him, and threw him back up like rabid dogs tossing up a hapless cat. Japanese hands forced the boy to bow, and a commander strode over. A blade flashed. Oh no, they would cut him? Worse? His head fell apart from him, the

241

body crumpled next to it. Horror hit. "Aah," he heard his own yell. Blood rushed to his head, he couldn't see, couldn't move.

Meneer Zwanenburg shook his shoulder. "Jakob, Jakob, protect yourself, stay down."

Women and children cried, "Nooo."

Another yell, a raised sword. This threat quieted the square like never before.

The Japs had enough weapons after all, and each man looked like a killer, hard faces, confused faces, farm-boy faces, all angry, snarling, showing off for each other. They were like a bad pack of wolf-dogs; more blood would spill. He wished he could check on Sara better, hoped she was safe, and bowed deeper. In his frozen fear he had been pushed into the midst of Meneer Zwanenburg's family: little boys of about six, four and two, and Mevrouw Zwanenburg. He had always wanted to visit more with her, a beautiful Indo woman with the nicest smile. The older boys copied and bowed like their father. Mevrouw Zwanenburg's mouth became a stoic line and she held her two-year-old awkwardly against herself. But she couldn't bow low and hold her toddler at the same time. A soldier spied her, the sun flashing on his glasses. He charged her way. Meneer Zwanenburg swiftly grabbed his youngest son, cradling him inside his elbow. Mevrouw Zwanenburg remained bent and bowed even lower. The soldier, his glasses just like Pappie's, turned back abruptly, a little cloud of dust where he was.

A box was brought to the middle of the square as a podium. "*Naore* — at ease!" Those in front of the throng were prodded to stand straight. The silent citizens raised up, the injured ones in the front swaying on their feet. Jakob was glad he could no longer see his Chinese friend's head, surely still laying there. *Ying Qian. His name is Ying, and I will never get to speak to him again, and he will never help his father again.*

He edged closer to Meneer Zwanenburg and squeezed his eyes tightly, so as to see a circle of light. For one last moment he imagined everyone dashing to pick up stones at the same time. It would never work, he understood now. If they did fight, it would be like the movies where the cowboys have the guns, and the Indians didn't. They would be the Indians, mowed down; they could not fight. Japanese announcements fired rapidly. They must be important, but no one understood. Jakob's heart raced faster and faster.

Opening his eyes he saw many Indos to the sides of the town square. Some looked terrified. Others smirked in a way completely unknown to him. They stood tall, faces pulled into flat, satisfied angles. He had thought of all Indos as cheerful, glad to serve. But these men were glad to see the Blandas brought low.

A man was jerked from the crowd who could translate Japanese words to Malaysian. He was shoved up to his own, lower platform. Haltingly at first, he translated. "Netherlands has lost in disgrace, and the proud Japanese are here to protect you. The Dutch language is now forbidden. You must speak Japanese or Malaysian only. The native Indos will be well treated. All Europeans must register. Everyone must bow for the Emperor. You will run on Japanese time, and use Japanese money. The year is 2602."

"Blandas will all stay where they are for their own protection; there will be no traveling. Also, for your own protection there will be curfews. You will be taken care of. No one is to fight and all are to pay homage to the Japanese flag. You will all be happy to see we bring your Indonesian flag to show we are saving Asia for Asians."

The Japanese flag, white with its violent red sun, was raised high. Jakob's ears rang with rage, seeing the flag in the sky. Another soldier flag bearer waved the red and white Indonesian flag.

The words went on. "Many Dutch men have allowed themselves to be captured with no honor, rather than dying in glory, as they should."

Jakob thought of the KNL's proud hats worn on jungle and field maneuvers, shot. They would all be bloody bodies and prisoners now, no sashes.

"Captured women and children are dishonorable as well, yet we will care for you."

The final yell went out. "Naore!" So this meant at ease and dismissal. Dully, Jakob followed Meneer Zwanenburg.

His teacher looked at him with huge caring eyes, and the crinkly white lines which didn't tan from years of squinting into bright sunlight. "You must be careful, ever vigilant. It's the only way to protect those you love."

Jakob nodded and turned his back to the square, achingly aware that the Chinese man from the market and the rest of the family must take away their beloved clever son, proud Ying Qian, in pieces. He made it home to find Mammie lying in bed.

He collapsed near her, his heart still pounding. She turned away, her face closed and angry. He had been wrong to dash away from her, but had he not been brave to run close to the enemy? He had hoped she would be as secretly proud of him as she had been with his trading. So horrid, to have Mammie upset with him. Nevertheless, next to her, he could calm himself. He sighed with relief when she spoke.

"I forbid you ... I forbid you to leave, trade, or break curfew. You will not get any of us, or yourself, wounded or killed. You must understand we are prisoners of the enemy now. No more running around in the middle of the night."

"You think there is no way we can get away and join the resistance?" Jakob asked, relieved she was talking.

Her eyes darted around with alarm. "Fight with Johan and Sara around? No one can fight now. They are here."

Jakob blushed bright red. What had he been thinking?

"We will wait for Pappie, and we will make do." Mammie's voice sounded dead. She reached out her hand.

So she wouldn't stay mad at him. "I am sorry, Mammie, for leaving all of you behind."

She patted his head; he held her other hand. He knew she wouldn't slap or spank him as Pappie would, but he wished she would. He wanted to be in trouble, then out of trouble. He had put everyone in danger. He pictured, unbidden, his Chinese friend's head rolling. Sick to his stomach, he wondered, what if Mammie had to see his own head rolling in the dirt? Jakob's heart felt as heavy as the weight of Meneer Zwanenburg's hand pressing him down to bow. That bow had kept him alive.

"Well, I'll get up." Mammie's feet hit the ground and she sounded more like her usual self. On the far side of the room, by the sideboard missing most of its dishes, Albert quietly arranged their belongings and rucksacks. Further along the hallway, Sara played house and dolls with Johan.

"Hoi!" Matteus came in with his wild yellow blond hair and curls. "Mammie and I have reloaded our rucksacks just in case. We barricaded all the doors except one. You know we are sharing with a Swiss family, who should be considered neutral by the Japanese. So maybe we'll be safer than some."

They joined Albert, and Jakob reached deep into his own rucksack for his compass. Closing his hand around the familiar roundness, he held it like a treasure. His stomach roiled with hunger. He was sick with terror and hunger. So far they always announced they had enough food to get by, but within an hour after meals, hunger crept up on him, gnawing away. He wished there was dinner to be had.

Oh, he smelled and heard Tante Ankie and Baboe beginning to cook vegetables and rice.

Tante Ankie called out to Baboe, "There's not enough," then stopped herself and switched to a cheerful voice, just like Mammie would. In her normal, louder voice. She said, "Ach, children, no worries, there will be enough and it will be delicious too."

Mammie cooked breakfast these days, Somehow she had not learned dinners from directing Kokkie, nor from Min.

On the best days she prepared boiled eggs and bread. On happy days they ate the same sweet rice Kokkie made for children's breakfast. On ordinary mornings they had thin soup, made up of the few leftovers from dinner. Jakob sat with Mammie instead of Kokkie in the mornings. There was no piano, so they hummed together, remembering the tunes. The hoped-for gramophone player, which they did own at first, had been traded for a week's worth of pork and chicken. Since meat could not keep one full week, they smoked half of it. Everyone helped, and Jakob wondered if they could call their smoked meat pemmican, like the food the American Indians made to get through the winter. It was hidden away in the back of an unlikely cupboard, in case of looters.

Tante Ankie's dinners smelled rich with spices and vegetables. Sharp red pepper sambal paste and sweet coconut scents filled the home. Tante Ankie sang a song, and Albert still fussed with their belongings. Jakob shifted himself to be face-to-face with his brother. He must have seen Meneer Zwanenburg stop him. Maybe Albert was as furious as Pappie would be. After all he was the man of the family now.

Albert jerked straps on a rucksack tight and stared him down. More heat flooded into Jakob's face. He had let everyone down.

But all Albert said was, "The Japs wanted to kill us."

Jakob helped jerk rucksacks up on their backs for practice. They never could remain furious with each other, and what did it matter? One friend was murdered, another's face smashed. "Yeah, they were hitting boys. The young boys were bleeding. They killed Ying Qian."

Albert raised his head. His eyes were red, his skin streaked with dirt and tears. "Ying Qian. I didn't know how he could be so brave, and so foolish. I saw Kees being carried away; he just didn't understand their words. His shoulder looked all twisted out of place, and his face was bloody."

Kees was older, almost Wim's age, a favorite of theirs. His father was in the KNL. They settled with Matteus on the floor. Their shoulders shook from stress, rattling the glass of the sideboard.

Jakob leaned away from the sideboard. "I'm so hungry."

"We are all hungry," Matteus said. "But for now we are trying not to think about food. Staying ready, come what may."

How could they not think of food? "Yes, I hope the hospital helps Kees. I hope they feed him well."

After noticing none of them shook anymore, Jakob said, "I miss just reaching for a banana whenever I want."

"We all have to be brave in quiet, hidden ways now," Albert said gravely.

Quiet, of course. Albert would be good at that. "And again, we're all hungry too, but it's no use complaining. It will just upset Mammie and Tante."

Jakob nodded and opened his hand. "Look, here is my compass."

The boys bent to study directions. "East, the way to the ocean," said Albert. "Some people got away to Australia."

Tante Ankie called out, "Hey, put all that away. You, Jakob, help your mammie set the table. Albert, finish with the heap of mess you boys created there. We have enough disorder with so many here. Sara, you can help scoop the rice."

"There is no heap we made!" Jakob hissed.

"And we don't have to argue with her. Let's just help, especially you," growled Albert.

Tante Ankie didn't order in the past; now she had to. Jakob knew his name was called first because he was the one the family most believed they had to jerk into good behavior. As he finished stuffing the compass back down in his pack, Tante came and grabbed his wrist hard.

"*Kom maar*—come with me. Girls, you set the table instead."

He stumbled behind Tante Ankie out to the small front garden. The deserted square usually crisscrossed with people, and their destinations this time of day. A cool breeze came up. Gone was the sweat of the hot square, the brutal orders. More than a dozen people must have been carried away wounded, and one brave, smart boy, dead.

He leaned against the garden wall. "Why were they the worst they could be? Why did they kill Ying?"

Tante waved him to her on the carved wooden bench, still gleaming, although no one had rubbed oil into it in some time. Teak was good wood for everything. "Jakob," she said his name in such a tender way. "The Japanese hate the Chinese the most; they already invaded and murdered many in China. They're greatly dangerous to Chinese people and they could treat us as badly."

"I saw his head rolling on the ground. He was so brave."

"And he was murdered for his foolish bravery." Tante Ankie reached to touch tears on his cheeks he didn't know he had. "You cannot be a hothead now in the name of bravery, only to die. Don't think it is good to be like your pappie now. Your pappie, although he is a hotheaded man, is wiser than you know. He would not shout near the Japanese, and he would never want you to be beaten or killed. It is hard that you know death now. Remember, anyone could die."

She snatched a handkerchief out of her apron pocket. "Families, friends, even whole kampong villages being maimed and massacred in retribution when people fight, or sabotage. That's what happened after the Dutch burned the Tarakan oil fields. I hope they do not go after that brave boy's family. You must think hard, with that bright mind of yours. Think well before every move. You have been our fierce trader, which I have not liked; I would rather be hungry and know you are in no danger. Now, like your Mammie said, you have to stop."

He met Tante Ankie's eyes. Johan had her beautiful curls. "I won't trade and I won't fight," he promised.

"Good." She linked her arm through his, pulling him up and toward the smell of food. Her tone changed. "The rest can't wait another second to eat."

Tante Ankie had sought him out, had appealed to him as an adult. Of course he would never trade again.

Many nights he vowed to stay home. Besides, either Mammie or Tante Ankie managed to be up late, keeping an eye out. They were not always watching to keep him from nighttime trading, but also standing guard. The enemy now had full power.

He missed the excitement of trading, the filling a need. Of course he would have to trade again. When he did, he would be even more careful and tell no one. But fight? No, he would never risk danger to his family again, only to himself.

† † †

Luce

Calabria, California
January 2005

I sit at dinner, spacing out, thinking about the first time Papa faced death, the town square along the harbor, all the drab soldiers who turned out to be so dangerous.

I think about another near death for Alby and Papa, the ultralight airplane accident.

Daniel waves a hand in front of my face. I flinch. "Earth to Luce. I do know that cancer is a big deal."

All I notice is that Daniel is upset with me. His hand is clenched, like he's going to pound on the table. "Lung cancer," I say in defense. "He could die."

"Oh Luce, this is not just about worry, worry, worry. You don't know that he's going to die, and you are bringing new life into the world. That news is how you will help him. Everyone will understand you need to stay home. Reach out to Jakob and Nikki from here."

"It's because I'm bringing new life into this world, and Dr. Simonian saying I have a healthy pregnancy, and bringing joy to Papa that I ought to go out again." I drum my fingers on our well worn table. We're fond of the crayon marks and so on. Somehow this is where we settle some of our biggest dilemmas. "Look, the state Victim Witness Fund checks finally came in. Six months of payments all at once. I think the signs are there for me to go. We can afford it." Inside I'm quivering, not so certain at all of the wisdom of going, yet certain I must.

Daniel groans. "Is it really okay with Dr. Simonian?"

He said travel was possible, be near a specialist. There's the Houston Medical Center there. "Yes."

He squints at me, his searching-my-soul look. "You're so determined."

"Yes," I admit.

We go for a walk, holding hands. I'll need to go soon. Unlike Daniel, I don't want anyone in Houston to immediately know I'm pregnant. I want to get to the bottom of helping Papa and Alby first.

"Luce" — he stops our walk — "I'm saying no. Stay so we can have the life we've always wanted."

I shrug my shoulders and shake my head. I will leave, again.

By the time we get home, Vincent has been dropped off by a youth group carpool. We tell him about Papa's cancer.

Instantly, he wants to call Houston. "Opa, you sound so hoarse. Mom told me you have cancer."

We hear grumbling noises.

"Oh, I didn't know you hadn't even talked to Mom yet. So, you feel pretty good? ... Yes, I'll get my algebra problem out."

Daniel taps my hand. "See how Jakob's fine for now? You have plenty of time to go."

I shake my head determinedly. "It's not going to be any easier after Baby is born. Papa probably won't be able to travel, and I won't want to visit with a newborn."

Daniel nods slowly. "You do have a point about timing."

Vincent's off the phone. "Timing, about what?"

"I think I should go visit," I say. "No more after this."

Vincent turns away quickly. "You tell me I'm impulsive." He sarcastically imitates, "Vincent, stop and think. Vincent, load up your homework folder. Vincent, stop and show your work. And this won't be the last trip. That's what you said the last time."

I feel queasy. I am impulsively jumping in to travel, but only because I have to. Even when Vincent shows me his results, and he solves an algebra problem correctly without Opa's help, I feel nauseous. I suspect this is not pregnancy related, but my own sharp worry about following my *insinks*, and going to Papa.

When I call Papa and Mama to ask questions and share my news, Daniel leaves the room.

† † †

Kemble is much more to the point when I dare to sit with her at Pine Street Coffee Shop, peppermint tea for both of us now. She adores espresso, but is always supportive of me, and I'm not about to have caffeine, artificial sweeteners, or anything unhealthy. I'm struck by how much I like her spiky hair, almost like the Peanuts' character Woodstock, except sophisticated. Funny, her short hair is a lot like Mama's.

I take a cautious sip of steaming hot tea, just knowing she's going to be shocked with my plan.

"Luce, I don't see why you would do this. You have worked so hard to let go of family stress, you tell me your most joyous news ever one week, and you reserve a flight to Houston again the next week? Cancel the ticket. Losing out on the money is better than the huge cost of going. Again."

"You make them sound like vipers."

"Having seen you come back from a bunch of trips upset, I'd say that's true." Kemble's mouth tightens.

She is tapping the AA daily meditation book, which rests between us. I feel as if my life is losing its moorings. I wish we were just reading a page together like usual, absorbing some wisdom. But I'm bumping around aimlessly, like no one's at the tiller and I'm bumping against the dock. I hate it that Kemble is upset with me.

I grit my teeth, and try to smile. "Daniel says it's okay; he knows something is drawing me there. This is different than before."

She thumps her tea mug down, and bores her eyes into mine. "Aargh, Luce, the dreaded 'this-time-it's-different' words? Are you listening to yourself? Daniel says it's okay? But he's not happy, right?"

"True."

"And you look exhausted, like you're not sleeping well. Honey, that's not good for the baby. I'm so sad about your dad, but clearly you have time to think this over. No one in your family out there has expressed this much concern about you, like usual. You tell me they don't respect your sobriety, other than that they think you can somehow fix Alby's willingness to stay in rehab. Yet you are going to go now? Don't do this."

Okay, breathe. Not what I usually have to say to myself around Kemble. I clench my hands on the table in front of me, and my knuckles turn white. She is making this trip so hard, and it's already all that I can do to muster up the energy to go. She has never told me flat out to not do something, and I hate going against her wishes, and let's face it — Daniel's wishes.

"I know it doesn't make any sense to you," I say evenly. "It makes sense to me. You don't get it. It's not about Alby this time, but about Papa. I want to be there for him, while I can. I'll never forgive myself if he takes a turn for the worse while I rest up, which I agree is a good idea, here in California."

"So you drop everything and go? Your Papa and his story are going to be around next week, the week after that, and the month after that. Just let Baby be your number-one priority."

I feel my eyes pricking with shame; I think of all the times in my dating days that I dropped everything to go out with a particular guy. The guys I dropped everything for always turned out to be the self-centered ones, the ones with no romance or generosity to offer. I hated to talk to my friends about how I struggled to choose well, struggled to believe a caring man would come my way. I feel like Kemble is saying I'm a loser for being ready to drop everything and go. Certainly she's saying that I have little faith in God's timing. The lack of faith I have to concede. The nervous voices inside me are back, and one says loudly, *it's all up to you*. This is a journey of love. I thump my cup down harder than I intend to. "I don't know why this is such a big deal to you. It would be a bigger deal for me not to go, to not see what happens with my dad."

Kemble sighs, eases her cup down. "Oh Luce." She carefully lifts the basket of tea leaves out of the glass pot in front of us, pours each of us more tea, and looks out the window. "I get tired of seeing you get hurt … and sacrifice yourself."

I see the softness in her eyes, but I feel spooked, like Papa will die if I don't go. I drain the tea in two long gulps, scalding the roof of my mouth. "Okay, gotta go. Vincent has a project he needs my help on."

"Okay then, see you soon." Her voice sounds wooden, which is unlike her. I wish I could explain to her that I have to be irrational, and I know Baby will be okay, and that's that.

Until now Kemble has been that one person who always understood everything about me. At least, I thought she did. I hate this lonely territory.

† † †

A few days later Kemble surprises me by volunteering to drive me to the airport. Vincent and Daniel send us off with smiles, no heavy air any more. Relief.

"Kemble, I know you're mad at me," I start.

"I said all I had to say. You made your tough, stubborn decision. I'm just choosing to help you along."

Ah, I breathe easy. No one's angry any more. I never worry about running late, all the way to the airport, even when an ambulance siren whoops. A Santa Clara County sheriff pulls us over near the airport terminal. Kemble charms him with her "I didn't know I was speeding" speech and smile.

Of course she gets off with a warning. Whenever I get pulled over, inevitably I'll get the ticket. Kemble and her charm don't.

† † †

Bumping my roller suitcase against my legs at check-in, I almost trip and fall. Kemble being so sweet was actually worse than her frustration. It's all me; she never asked me if I prayed for guidance, but I would have to admit no. I'm just going.

I will be home soon, I tell myself. This will be safe travel for me, Baby on board, more than four months pregnant. Double doors hum open as I casually stroll into the terminal. Eras of my life are different, but all airports are somewhat the same. Places of good-byes, leaving one world for

254

another, one family for another, one job for another, certainty for hope.

I plant myself at the gate, and recall the memory castle rooms Vincent talked about.

In my memory castle I've lost the boerderij living room, bereft and empty for my good-bye with Beppe and Pake. There is no key for the locked away cellar room of getting on the plane in Schiphol, Amsterdam's airport, at age six, no traces of good-bye to relatives and friends. There is arriving at Schiphol the summer I was eleven, with Tante Sara and Oom Fiete waiting for me, ready to welcome me "home." I know about the leave-taking when I was young, from Mama.

We said good-bye to Beppe and Pake at the boerderij. It must have been like many other mornings, a breakfast of hot buttermilk porridge with melting amber syrup pictures drawn on top, Beppe calling Bertie and me, "Liefjes."

I remember with a jolt, as I shove my suitcase along with my feet to get on the plane, the last walk on the boerderij with Pake. Like always, we started in the warm barn, steamy in the winter months of our leave-taking. We passed the few sturdy dairy cows, their body heat being all we needed. Then we walked out to the gray-white frozen canal our breath, forming tiny clouds in frigid air. There Beppe stood with us, and I asked who would feed the ducks in the spring, and she said she would.

Then Pake and I went out so very far away, perhaps only a hundred meters, to be surrounded by fields crusted with snow, long smooth lines marking the ditches between fields. Our feet found secure spots on the frozen rutted farm road. Then more good-byes tucked away forever. If we cried, I know why the rest of the memory is gone; I never would have wanted Beppe and Pake to be sad. As the oldest grandchild, I thought it was my job to bring them joy, as they brought me joy.

From Mama I know that Tante Sara, Oom Fiete, Oom Wim, Tante Trudi, and our best friends all came to Schiphol Airport to see us off. In the album I pulled out weeks ago, I looked for pictures and found a time I must have locked away in my own Memory Castle. A little boy sits on Mama's lap in silhouette, and a little girl, dressed in her warmest woolen coat, leans against the airport window, stretching one hand high. Beyond them are runways and planes. We had always flown back and forth to Iran, where Bertie-Albert was born. I put my whole life back in the photo, feeling my heart ache for little Liesbet-Luce. My young self had hope then, hope it was just one more trip, but it had turned into a one-way trip.

This trip, I hope, will close a circle of love and hope with Papa, Mama, and the rest of the family. Then I'll go home and complete my own circle of love.

PART THREE

One thing I ask from the LORD, this only do I seek: that I may dwell in the house of the LORD all the days of my life, to gaze on the beauty of the LORD and to seek him in his temple. For in the day of trouble he will keep me safe in his dwelling; he will hide me in the shelter of his sacred tent and set me high upon a rock.
—Psalm 27:4–5

CHAPTER 14

Tjideng neighborhood, Batavia
Late March 1942

Seeing Meneer Zwanenburg was a little bit like having a Pappie again. Jakob, Albert, and Matteus visited the Zwanenburg family every few days.

Today they walked there with satisfaction. Matteus's family and their Swiss friends had provided them all a substantial breakfast. Plenty of sticky rice and mango.

Matteus knocked on the door, and Mevrouw Zwanenburg peeked out of the door shaking. Jelle, the oldest boy at age six, held her hand as if he were holding her up.

"Oh, come on in. It's terrible. Jelle saw. We've been alone. The Kempetai seized Meneer Zwanenburg and others, in a night raid last night. Please"—she waved the boys in—"come in and play. The boys need you."

Jakob already knew about the Kempetai, the dreaded military police. Sometimes he had a terrible picture inside of Pappie in their clutches, screaming in pain. Everyone knew of the wails of agony coming from their headquarters, day and night. His back dripped with sweat already in the cool, shadowed home.

Just like Pappie on his good-mood days, they tried horsey rides with all the boys. The four-year-old giggled till he fell down. Jelle tensed his wiry legs around Jakob for his horsey ride. Although Jakob leaped wildly about on the floor, Jelle never laughed. Jakob tried a final wild bucking. No laughter. Jelle lay on the floor, panting, his little stomach heaving.

Jakob felt closer to Mevrouw Zwanenburg, sometimes she talked to them as if they were grownups, and now she needed them. "Can we say Tante Manda?"

She shrugged sadly yes and looked at her oldest Jelle, as if to say, *how can any of us laugh now?* "I'll try every day to visit him, and take a basket of food, vitamin drops, and so. But I hear they never let you see the prisoners. I'll have no way of knowing if he receives any of it."

The older boys froze gravely, their eyes locking. Did the little ones understand? The two-year-old, Benjamin, rolled them a ball. Albert rolled it back, sitting wide legged in the manner of children.

† † †

One time Albert, Jakob and Matteus visited together, and Tante Manda told them about yet another attempt to visit Meneer Zwanenburg. "Yesterday morning, a Japanese officer leered at me, talking through a translator, and told me I should give up. Soon the Japanese will ensure all of Asia is for Asians, he said, and I should no longer care for my Blanda husband. The worst is, I walked by there yesterday at dusk, what I heard was ..."

The little boys were in the room. Albert bounced the ball loudly.

"Oh." She stopped.

Jakob felt a strange calm, seeing the dull eyes of Jelle and four-year-old Samuel. Little Benjamin's cheeks flushed red. "Papa?"

"Papa will be home soon," Tante Manda said brightly.

"Come," Jakob said, "in the other room." He and Matteus could remove the little ones from pain, and he could peek around the corner and get their own report later. Odd, how often grown-ups talked to Albert.

Tante Manda softened her urgent voice. "The Kempetai, the military police, are feared the most, like barbarians. One Japanese officer, I know he must have been educated in

America. He said some English words, looked at me kindly for a moment, and said he'd do his best to pass along at least the vitamin drops. But he stopped immediately when a fellow police officer came in." She huddled on the couch and hugged a cushion to her.

Jakob pulled four year old Samuel on his lap, hoping for a giggle, but the little boy was quiet. Soon all three boys left, scuffing their sandals aimlessly along the road, hearing what Albert reported.

† † †

Tante Ankie called Jakob, Matteus and Albert the "Three Musketeers." Mevrouw de Bakker said the same, and usually when Matteus came over, his sister Riekie came to play with Sara.

Mammie spoke, with admiration, of Manda's daily visits to the Kempetai headquarters. "So sad, so brave and she never sees Meneer Zwanenburg."

With all the constant effort, Tante Manda still made delicious food for the boys when they came by. One day it was pisang goreng, the fried bananas like Kokkie made. The crisp bites of warm sweetness tasted and felt like home.

Another day she opened the door smiling, but with sad eyes. "He is home."

Jakob's heart surged as if he was spinning on the gymnastic bars at school. He often felt himself blush when he was near her, and he secretly enjoyed thinking of her as Manda, not Tante Manda.

One notorious rumor had been that no one came back from the Kempetai. He was elated to know Meneer Zwanenburg was home, and his heart lifted to see Manda happy. "So we can visit with him?"

"No, you must go, and hope and pray for your own pappie. This is not the time to come home soon."

"Our best wishes," called Matteus as they walked away. "Come on, boys. To my house."

Mevrouw de Bakker and the Swiss family greeted them. They didn't deliver the bad news to the grown-ups; perhaps they already knew.

Matteus had lived here before, so he had more than them at hand. "You can come help me finish my glider plane. I have the paints already."

They went to the garden shed work table and its balsa wood supply, where Jakob admired the small weights glued on just so. This way the plane would glide evenly, its longest flight possible. "Let's paint it royal blue and orange, like a Dutch-British flyer. Fantastic at a time like this."

"Horrible at a time like this, if we get caught by the Japanese." Matteus said.

Albert nodded.

Jakob flushed. Even slightly younger Matteus remembered nothing could have the Dutch royal colors, nor could they show the flag. "Oh, well then, camouflage will do."

They mixed colors to create jungle greens and drab browns. Matteus dabbed on the pain with fluid motions.

"Here, I'll add some detail." Albert held the tiniest paint brush, much like a pen tip, and dipped it in black. He delicately put on letters and numbers. "Look, it has each of our ages, and Java for where we are."

On the way home, Albert said, "What did they do? I can see him now, the nicest teacher ever."

"Ja, I wonder," was all that Jakob could say. *We are both thinking about the screaming. Wondering how terrible his wounds must be if he can't be seen yet.*

† † †

Mammie and Tante Ankie visited Mevrouw Zwanenburg.

Upon their return, they were too shaken to pretend the news was okay. Tante Ankie rattled spice jars together; Mammie busied herself sorting through their food supply.

Jakob felt leaden inside. "How is Meneer Zwanenburg?"

"Manda is caring for him. We brought them what we could."

"His hands," started Mammie.

Tante Ankie shook her head, and Mammie stopped.

What happened to his hands? In his mind he saw Ying Qian's head fall to the ground and the horrible flop of Meneer's hands as they, too, fell to the ground. What a horror, no hands to hold Manda, to ruffle his boys' hair. Oh, you couldn't even pee or poop properly. He felt ashamed of his thoughts, and pondered, *we must help.*

† † †

Houston, Texas
January 2005

Cindy has new wrinkles, and it's only been a month since I last saw her. They look like an extra tired smile, lines between her eyes, underneath her eyes, and a semicircle each side of her mouth.

"Happy belated New Year's," I say. "Where are the kids?" Now that I've stopped stumbling over my only carry-on bag, I'm enjoying wheeling around my only suitcase. I was determined not to lug along heavy baggage this trip.

"Hey, space cadet, it's the weekend. They're sleeping late, and Marina is old enough to be left in charge," she says. "Thankfully she's doing great and able to concentrate on her subjects again. Wade is excited about a new science project. Alby's advising him, and he kept it up all during the holiday break. I went out on a dawn ride today on Serenity. A great name for now, don't you think? Even the horses are happier now, because I'm riding again."

She's telling me they're better and that she's grateful.

"And how's my brother?"

"He told me this morning he's looking forward to seeing you because he's much better, and is sleeping okay. He's been there longer than most, five weeks. They'll release him any day now. Although they want him to stay three more weeks."

"You're looking tired," Cindy says when we bump down the dirt road to their property.

"Yep, the travel and all." We pass by their stable. The paths in back lead to open fields and scrubby woods. They bought well—neighbors on only one side, county land on the other. Later I will pet Serenity's velvet nose, to rediscover I can feed her a carrot without jerking my hand back in fear. I know I would love spending the day on this boerderij before our hospital visit, but it will have to wait until tomorrow. First a nap, then right to Alby. No rejecting him or running from him this time.

Cindy opens some mail and pulls out premade lasagna from the refrigerator for later.

"If you don't mind, I'll take a nap before we visit Alby."

"No problem, make yourself at home." She hums and grabs a stack of catalogues and magazines from the counter.

I love being around family who have fewer expectations than Mama and Papa have. I could just relax, but I'll call Dr. Ingstrom first. I reach for the phone, next to the vase of lavender and orchids, a touch from Cindy. I could never take the time to do such a considerate thing if I were in her crisis mode.

"You are in Houston?" Dr. Ingstrom sounds shocked. Perhaps she thinks I only travel at her request.

"Ja, I knew it would be a disaster for him to leave treatment early again. And have you heard about our father's cancer? "

"No." For once she has little to say, and I fill her in.

She's so quiet, without her usual alert comebacks. She must really care. It dawns on me I have a private line to reach her. Perhaps her cell? I ask about Albert.

"Well, the good news is, he's completely stable now. And for now he's cooperating with staying. I showed him a video of himself." Alby signed permission for Dr. Ingstrom to communicate with me. Sometimes I think he forgets about that.

"What did he see on the video?"

"Himself, paranoid, going on and on about the corporate spy."

"He didn't remember he had done that?"

"He didn't remember that the supposed spy was a twenty-something girl, fresh off the streets. He stopped constantly fighting for discharge and agreed to medication for his mood swings."

"Well, I'm doubly glad he's still there then. I'll come see him this evening."

"That would mean a lot to him." We hang up.

It would matter to him? Up until now I've been sure that addiction has taken over and the Alby I knew before is gone. In spite of his years of struggle I think of him as strong, a leader, a scientist. I know he is in terrible shape, and needs help. But has he needed me? Somehow I thought so; we all thought so, because we are family.

Folding into the dull need for a nap, I realize the sorrow I feel that Alby is agreeing to medication, a part of me was rooting for his constant fighting, his wish to go on mostly alone—AA fellowship, no meds. *He doesn't need me now*, repeats over and over in my head. I tell my clients, "Stop riding the ups and downs." I'll sleep, I'll visit. I'll tell Cindy that after tonight I'll transfer to Mama and Papa's, be their driver, help them out.

Tense pain in my shoulders and jaw scream at me. I think about how Alby has nearly dismantled his life as a bioresearcher, and all the fragments of his growing up and family life too. The fragments used to fit. He talked school science projects with Vincent when he was a middle schooler. He always got on the phone when I called. I haven't wanted to name how long it's been different. All the times I had called him and he didn't get on the phone or call back. He stopped reaching out to Vincent, and probably no longer responded to Wade's or Marina's projects either. Cindy was the one who held the shards and fragments, always her and the kids.

Small chilling moments with Alby are as bad as big times, like the invitations to those past rehab programs. Somehow small moments hurt more, like when he and I went for a walk Thanksgiving of 2003. Our families had gathered at his house. We hiked through the fields, scrub brush to our hips, then the woods. I spoke of a book making its way around the family, *The Horse Whisperer*. I was the only one who hadn't finished it.

"I'm rushing ahead to find out what happens with this wounded horse," I said.

"Yeah, it's such a great book. I loved every word. You're going to like the part whe-re—"

"Don't tell me and ruin it for me," I interrupted, jostling him, glad we were walking just the two of us. Bright sun seared jeweled rain drops off of leaves and branches, with tiny trails of ground fog clearing up.

"Yeah, you really will like ..." He went on and blurted out the ending, even though I asked him not to. Even though Vanderveers never do spoilers, because we're all such book lovers, he told me what happened next.

"Alby," I cried, "you ruined it for me!"

He shrugged. Maybe he couldn't track his thoughts, maybe he was too hyper, and maybe he couldn't keep up the rhythm of conversations anymore. Maybe he wanted to be mean in a small way. It was just one moment, but I got it— he really couldn't care less about what used to matter: a good story, togetherness, focusing on each other, the walks we made together, the walks we used to have as kids in new neighborhoods, the many repeated neighborhoods. He was too caught up in himself, or the drugs were too caught into him. Sayings at AA meetings: *First the man takes a drug, then the drug takes a drug. Finally, the drug takes the man.* I don't want the same to be true of Papa and cancer. Will he look just the same? I should have already changed my plans to stay with them.

†††

With a thick-headed feeling from my nap, I get in the car with Cindy, who then drops me off at the hospital, saying she'll give us some time alone first. It's good to be at the hospital first; afterwards I can focus on Papa.

I thought the fatigue of the first trimester was from growing the placenta, the baby's nest. In my fourth month I'm supposed to have renewed energy, not be tired like this. Maybe it's the older-mom thing. I wish I had already told Cindy of my pregnancy. She would have pulled out extra prenatal vitamins from somewhere, filled me in on how robust older mares can be, and been at my side right now.

I trace the route down familiar hallways, taking a detour for the new unit. I don't think I'll ever remember that the psych unit is Hope Vista and Alby's rehab unit now, New Vista.

This time Alby is in the common room, with the others. He stands and smiles, looking normal and solid, except for the dark circles around his eyes. I lean into him for a hug.

"Let's go out to the visiting atrium," Alby says.

We settle into wrought-iron benches with their plump pillows, which are not enough to soothe my aching back. The magnolia trees' waxy deep-green leaves droop in this January cold snap. Some old blooms collapse pale brown, edges of blossoms curling as if licked by flames. Dr. Ingstrom's office must be on the other side of the atrium, in the next hospital wing.

Alby plumps his own pillow, and then gets rid of a nearby ashtray contaminating whole patio with its rank smell. I notice all his considerate moments, simple times of caring, which have been so lacking. He settles into the other chair and his eyes crinkle. For a moment I see Pake's soulful look in his eyes. He drops his hands to his knees; his constant fidgeting is gone. "So how are you, Sis?"

"I feel good. Really wanted to talk to you, and not go off on you this time. Not be like Papa," I say slowly, remembering all the yelling when we were young. "I heard you had a lot of trouble." This is the closest I come to apologizing. Papa never apologized, just got nicer for awhile. I should get better at flat out saying I'm sorry.

A pained look crosses his face. "Trouble, huh? Everyone tells you everything, don't they?"

"Not everything." I try to look at him reassuringly.

"You know, I think they forget that people can hallucinate just from detox. I'm okay now. I don't really need this medicine they are pushing."

Just don't focus on work first, Alby. Think about who you are, the little boy who held my hand, the man who held Cindy's hand and then watched her or didn't even see, that she started to cover all family time while you were gone doing who-knows-what, but definitely up to no good. I speak carefully. "You know, about the medicine. Please stay on it. You've tried for years to stay sober." *Yes, he really did try, let the fury melt away.* "I'm here for you and Papa, away from Daniel, Vincent, and my work—again—because I don't want to see you lose everything you've worked so hard for. The hospital is a safe place to try medication."

"I don't know if my brain is working right. I don't feel like me on this mood stabilizer. And Papa, oh Luce, I'm so worried about Papa."

I spy a silhouette beyond the magnolias, Dr. Ingstrom in her office. I can see the ancient teapot on its sideboard domain near her. I dig my fingernails into my hands, eyes pricking with tears. We hold hands. "I really worry about him too, Alby. I just had to come and see each of you again. As aggravating as he always was to us. 'This is a B! Why isn't it an A?'"

Alby smiles. "'This A, why isn't it an A plus!' He's just so lovable. I always intend to be nice, then he fusses …"

"Then we get angry, then we just want to be nice again." I'm proud of myself for not pointing out to Alby that I can help right now, but he can't. And if he wants to do more, how hard could it be for Alby to just do whatever it takes, like I did when I got on the plane to come here? "And … you will be able to help Papa later. I've had to take meds for depression. I remember thinking I wasn't me anymore. It kinda evened me out too much, I thought. But eventually it turned out great. I know I could always go back on antidepressants when I need to."

"Yeah, but in your own field those experiences just make you a better therapist. In my field, when I take medication myself, I'm an impaired professional."

"Like you, I couldn't figure it out alone. You can't medicate yourself; I can't do therapy on myself."

"Papa can't do it by himself. He'll have to cooperate."

"Funny, he's always saying his hip hurts, looking for sympathy, but when you actually try to help him, he becomes Mr. Stubborn."

"You know I should be out of here, to help him."

"No, stay in to help yourself."

His face flattens.

"Sorry." I tap his leg. Why do I always forget he's in all kinds of pain and worry, and that it's not up to me to dictate what he ought to focus on and when? His hip was shattered much worse than Papa's in the accident. I wish my words weren't biting Alby with demands and resentments, but they are. I am making everything worse. "Really, soon you will be able to help him. And medication is hard, along with no pain medication. When I took antidepressants, I was a rehab treatment director, ten years ago—before private practice."

He looks up. "I didn't know." Good, he's not going to give up right this second, and neither am I.

He settles another pillow behind his head and leans way back in his chair.

I put my feet up, and can handle this lovely silence for maybe one minute.

"So what medication are you on?"

Alby looks away and drops his hands into his lap. He rattles off a name. "It's a new mood stabilizer, not a major tranquilizer, like the Thorazine shuffle or anything."

"Alby I know you're worried, your brain will be fine." I hold hands again. "Remember when it was just you and me as little kids, meeting all the kids in the new neighborhoods? Remember just me visiting just you in the nursing home after the accident? Remember how for over a year we were both straight and sober?"

He smiles his old expression for a moment, like the look he had when he used to win swim meets. He nods, gazing out beyond the patio. I know he's thinking of the sad times — in the hospital after the accident. I'm trying to cheer him up, but once you've been miserable in a hospital, they're not ever good places again.

At least we are in tune, like all three of us kids sitting in Corrie's room while she played her guitar, with Mama and Papa arguing heatedly in the living room. That's one thing I hope for this visit — to be in harmony, the three of us. To rally around Papa and Mama. I hope Alby remembers the good times too, the joy we had in being straight and sober. When I was sober we three siblings were in harmony, as we knew our parents couldn't be. It wasn't in them.

"I hear there are members of the president's cabinet who have had interventions and sobered up," Alby says casually.

He's trying. "Me too," I say. "I heard that around rehab. Alby, you really are a top professional, not quite presidential cabinet yet, but I know what you mean. You have an important job, and I never listened like I could have. I've just been so angry with you."

"Duh, really?' Alby smiles for a moment. "And I thought you didn't listen to me because you were jealous."

We both grin. Yes we were raised in a competitive family. Who had the best grade, who was the best at sports?

Alby's chair creaks as his gaze rivets beyond me, to the patient fellowship room. He grimaces as if he's in pain.

I twist around to see who he sees, a young guy just inside the patio doors. He hobbles by with a cane, thin as could be. He's like Alby, thirty years ago. When I turn back around, a shooting pain ricochets from my left hip to lower abdomen. The pain stops as I lean back. *Focus.* "It's good they're giving you one medicine at a time, it's a way to know what works," I gasp, as the pain returns. I go rigid, jamming my hands against the chair to try to lift up away from the ache, then collapse back.

"What's wrong?" Alby's hands grip my wrists.

"A digestion pain, I think." The acute stab of pain is gone, replaced by a dull cramping in my lower back. *Oh no.* "I don't feel so well. I don't want you to get sick. I'll just go." I try to stand up. Pain like a vise grabs my hips. I stop, pinned to my seat.

"You're sweating. Something's wrong."

"I should just leave; I feel sick." But I can't get up. I never had a pain like this with the other miscarriages. Is this what's happening, another miscarriage?

Alby's worried face is inches from mine. "Luce, you look like you could faint." He reaches out a hand to steady me. My heart starts to pound, terror sets in. I'm losing this baby because of my stupid travel. Kemble was right. Daniel and Vincent were right. Alby is okay, Papa is under medical care, but I'm not okay. I lean into Alby's arm, and wonder again if I can stand up. I have to fight this.

"Maybe your back is out. Too bad I don't have all the right pills for you anymore."

"Ha-ha. Ahh, not funny. Alby this is bad."

"I'll call the nurse." He's on his feet.

I call out in panic, "Tell her I'm pregnant."

His head swivels back and forth like a cartoon character. He opens his mouth, but then runs. "Nurse," he yells, "we have an emergency with my sister." Vanderveers are great in a crisis.

Another shooting pain wraps my hips and grinds me back against the hard part of the wrought-iron chair. I steel myself against the horrible sensation of losing Baby, waiting for the inevitable warm flow of blood, what an unfeeling nurse called the "products of conception" during the first miscarriage.

Immediately my favorite nurse, Endurance, is by my side. She speaks with her melodious Nigerian vowels. "What *ees* it?"

Alby hovers. "She's pregnant, and just traveled long distance to get here. She's all freaked out. Maybe she's in premature labor." Endurance's cool fingers check the pulse at my neck, while Alby growls, "So I suppose everybody except me knows?"

"No. Just Daniel, Vincent, and now you," I gasp.

"And you think I'm the idiot? Oh Luce, you should have stayed home."

Endurance glances at her watch, still counting pulses. "You be quiet now, Alby. No talk of *idioten*. She needs care. This is not about you." She positions herself next to me. "Okay, down on your side. Alby, hold her hand." They lower me to the ground, she runs for the desk.

"Code green, New Vista!" goes over the intercom.

I hold my breath, still terrified of the awful release of warmth between my legs. Nothing yet. Baby and I will hold on, we have to.

"Okay," says Alby, still hovering. "They'll get you some good care. I'll come with you."

Endurance is back with a wheelchair. "Well Albee-e and his *familee*, here we go. Now Luce, your brother is caring for you. Excellent you are right here at a hospital." They lift me from my side to my feet to a wheelchair as if I'm light. For the first time in years, Alby's body feels strong as he pulls my lower back securely into the chair. Patients hover around, including the skinny guy with the cane.

Other nurses wave them away, calling out, "Time for group."

"I thought there was nothing that could be done for a miscarriage," I moan.

"Miscarriage? Who says?" Endurance snaps up the foot supports of the wheel chair. "I'm going to wheel you right over to the ER and they'll check you out."

"Ow," I yell as the dull pain in my back stabs me in the belly.

"We're taking the gurney instead," announces Endurance, heading back to the nurse's station.

Except for the feeling of pressure, the pain recedes momentarily. Oh no, no, no, just like labor pains. "Calcium channel blockers," Alby mutters. "You need calcium channel blockers. Here's the gurney. Endurance, we got to tell the doc. She needs a pharmaceutical expert MD; tell him calcium channel blockers." They get me on the gurney. "I'm going with her."

"No," Endurance yells, as she and another nurse have me gliding down the hall and bumping through doors.

"I have to," Alby yells and jogs alongside us. At the next corner he's stopped by an orderly. One of the kids they don't want him to talk to anymore runs after him, and grabs his arm.

Alby's crying. "Calcium channel blockers. Calling Daniel," he yells.

"No." I groan as we bump through the next doors. "Don't call Daniel!"

"Too late, calling from the patient phone," he yells back.

Endurance frowns at me. "Daniel is your husband? Of course he'll call him."

I'm shoved into an ER examining room, and then carefully transferred to a bed, still on my side. And still no trickling of warm blood. No more labor pains as long as I lay very still. "I get to keep this bed for now, right? You won't move me anymore?"

"Yes."

"Thank God."

I hear Alby yelling. "I have to help her. Luce!"

My brother is finally coming to my rescue.

† † †

Tjideng neighborhood, Batavia
April 1942

Cries of "Piet … Isaac," and other names rang out along the road.

Sara ran outside first. "Pappies are coming back home, pappies are coming home!"

Jakob felt a warm ocean of relief. He hadn't realized he'd feel such joy and comfort at the thought of seeing Pappie. He had *good* stories about himself to tell Pappie. They all went out to peer along the road. Mammie and Tante Ankie held hands and had hints of smiles. How could they know if everyone would arrive home?

Some men arrived. Thin, their lined faces covered with streaks of dirt, hands empty of baggage, just a native-style wrapped bag here and there. Everyone stood in the streets waiting, and the boys lifted Sara to the fence. Jakob clenched his hands and trained his eyes to look for Pappie's flash of red hair. Matteus and Mevrouw de Bakker yelled three houses down. Meneer de Bakker spun out from the bedraggled rows and went to them.

Their little group waited and waited. Jakob's stomach rumbled, but they stayed. As long as they waited in front of the house, Pappie would come.

Tante Ankie sighed. "We can all go in. Your pappie is not yet here, nor is Henri. At least the others can tell us what became of them. I'm sure they're fine."

Jakob's stomach twisted. He imagined Pappie in rugged clothes, Oom Henri in his uniform, hidden in the jungle of Java. But the picture was fuzzy. Or they were captured, and he realized in all the weeks since the Japanese had marched in, they had never seen a soldier return yet.

Mammie touched him on the shoulder. "You can go back outside after lunch to be lookout if you like."

Jakob nodded, and he and Sara stayed until the hot sun chased them inside.

The next day they joined a few families on lookout. So different from yesterday's expectancy, no one calling out names. They took turns. No one. Jakob was glad of the exhaustion of late night trades; it took his mind off Pappie and Oom Henri.

Waking midmorning after such a trade, he heard Sara's excited voice from the veranda. "We'll wait for Pappie. Maybe one more hour and he'll be home."

Jakob went to join her. Sara and Tina rattled everyday teacups and saucers which made do as a doll tea set.

"Ja, soon," Jakob said to Tina, whose smile looked hopeful.

After what might have been one hour, Mammie called, "Oh *liefjes*, come here. Enough for today."

Jakob's heart felt wooden and dank, like driftwood sinking in water, too sodden to stay on top in the everyday world. They left the almost deserted street. Other families had given up hope.

After a week they hovered with Albert, in their dusty front garden all morning, darting down and away whenever they saw sign of the Japanese soldiers. "After tidur siang, we'll see what we can find out," said Albert. "Enough of waiting."

With a plan, it was easy to sleep. Sara stood ready to go with them.

"You can stay, look, and wait," said Albert.

"No! I can come with you."

"You and Tina are needed here, we won't be long."

"An hour?" Her set jaw showed determination. One hour, an eternity for a little girl, was the longest she could wait.

"An hour," said Jakob, relieved that Albert had a plan at last.

"Follow me." Albert loped along with his longest strides. The smell of pork saté with *pindasaus* made Jakob ache with hunger. They had no money, now that a few street foods were back.

They went to Meneer Zwanenburg's house. Manda greeted them. "No, Meneer Zwanenburg is still not having visitors, but tonight you will see him. He's starting to feel better."

They walked to the harbor to see the Japanese naval ship, reluctantly admitting it was huge, compared to the ABDACAM vessels. Jakob recalled Pappie saying the Japanese had modern-day ships, and ABDACAM ships were the best from World War I, but tragically behind the times.

Their explorations told them nothing. Jakob leaned against a dock railing. "Maybe Meneer Zwanenburg's hands were not cut off. Manda didn't look so sad anymore."

"His hands cut off? You and your imagination. No we would have heard something if he lost his hands. Tonight we'll finally know more."

Men came with their wives, to the De Bakker home. Matteus and Riekie sat on either side of Meneer de Bakker. They leaned in on each other, Jakob stepped away to hide tears. He wanted Pappie—now. He thought of the stupidity of prayer. He had prayed and now the only men not with their families were Oom Henri and Pappie.

De Bakker, always a stout man with a barrel chest, was the only man who still had a hint of a belly. His gaunt, strained face looked like a stranger's. He motioned to everyone, including the boys, rather than sending them away. "Your Pappie, Meneer Westen, and others were miraculously rescued after the battle of the Java Sea. Their ship, the Sloet van de Beele, was hit early on. They survived, first in the water, then secured the lifeboats. Oh, it was pure chaos, and a long story."

Meneer Zwanenburg sat with them; he indeed had hands after all, clutched under his armpits, his jaw set with pain. He shook, and held up his hands briefly. Deep red lines, some scabbed over, dented his wrists. "The Kempetai hung me up, their favorite form of torture. Arms behind you and overhead. Me, they did with wire because the Kempetai were so convinced I knew where rogue KNLers hid."

Meneer Westen patted him on the shoulder. "Good man, you survived."

Zwanenburg flinched. "And my shoulder dislocated. The worst is the pain in hands with circulation returning. But I will not complain. After all, through a miracle I'll never understand, the Japanese released me. So many were driven away in the middle of the night, no one knows where, probably never to be seen again." He stopped abruptly, glancing at the young people around them.

Meneer de Bakker went on. "So in February, we never saw Meneer Vanderveer on Java as expected. By the time the Japs rounded us up, we still had not seen him."

Meneer Westen, who had sat sandwiched between his wife and Marijke, stood up. Marijke smiled broadly, as did Jakob. He noticed she had gentle curves inside her blouse, and her calves looked so pretty. "When our ship, the *Sloet van de Beele*, suffered attack and sank almost immediately, we floated for hours. Eventually we made it to our scattered life boats. A lone Dutch pilot defied the confused Allied command. With no orders, he took it upon himself to rescue a few nuns. They were so stubborn those women; they had insisted upon being the last to leave the island. He returned again and again for men."

"Although your pappie and I were initially brought to safety, jubilantly grateful for a miracle, and kissed dry land as it was"—he pulled a wry face—"we still faced the Japanese. Although we had all changed into dry clothes, they could see from all his sores that Meneer Vanderveer had floated in the ocean. I am not as fair of skin, and didn't look as obvious. So, they grabbed us all and took us to the prison, but your pappie was shoved into the farthest cells."

Jakob thrilled to think of Pappie's courage, but his heart sank as he watched Mammie's pale composed face. Her right hand trilled imaginary piano keys, the other wrapped inside Tante Ankie's hand.

"And Henri?" asked Tante Ankie.

"We heard Henri and other KNLers were in the same part of the prison with Meneer Vanderveer. None of them betrayed him, although most of them knew he directed the sabotage of mining operations. Some KNL went to the Kempetai. Wim and Henri, we think—not. He was marked as a saboteur only, not as the top boss. Perhaps he'll be released soon.

"That any of us are alive thus far is lucky. Some POWs were immediately paraded in the backs of trucks, folded into pig cages, and taken out to sea to be dumped, helpless into the —"

"Enough, let's not add to worries even more," Mammie said, looking deliberately from him to the children playing in the next room. "Just what you last knew please."

Mammie is so brave. How terrible, tall Dutch men folded into pig cages.

"Those pig-caged soldiers were drowned in the harbor," Albert hissed into his ear. Jakob's stomach contracted as if he were punched. Involuntarily he gasped for air. What did that mean about all the other KNL soldiers?

Meneer Westen shook his head hard, like water had to leave his ears. "Ja, Ja." He steadied his own other hand by squeezing it against a bench. "So, at the end, they were left in the prison, and we made our way back to you. That's it."

His wet, usually handsome black eyes told a different story. Now, in the working of all his careful words, in the grayish pale behind his dark tan, he looked disturbed, a man on edge, who had seen horror, and expected more.

† † †

Jakob couldn't sleep, and Albert tossed and turned too. He heard Mammie and Tante Ankie's murmurs each time he closed his eyes. He was too far away to make out what they were saying, and too tired to get up and spy. His heart beat faster, like a wound up spring, every time he shifted under his mosquito netting. He imagined Pappie and Oom Henri in prison, staring down Japanese guards, proudly saying nothing. Then their hands hauled up behind them. He thought of Papa's glasses, broken. Maybe they'd been lost long ago in the ocean.

He saw Meneer Zwanenburg with two shadowy men, Kempetai, beating him. A thought brought him wide awake. If only Meneer Zwanenburg's hands were awful to see, perhaps Manda would have let them in. They hadn't seen some of the released men either, for days after they stumbled down the road. Most have been beaten, swollen, bruised. Meneer Westin's gaunt face had bruised black-eyes, out of which, fortunately, he could still see. *In boxing stories, a blow to the eyes can cause blindness.*

He saw Kees on the town square, struck down, only a confused boy, so hurt. Horrible pictures and sounds came to him. Pappie and Oom Henri screamed, and fought. A head rolled, a body fell, he could not look to see which one. They both had to survive, thus not true, only hideous imagination.

When he no longer heard Mammie and Tante Ankie, he got up, glad to trade. Lately, Matteus sometimes met him, sealing their friendship. Matteus would always adventure at night, or make up the best games during the day. They never tired of building models, playing marbles or any play.

Albert occasionally stood guard, making a bird noise if danger appeared. Glad for the moonlight shining in the kitchen window, he took the silver platter he'd had his eye on. He hesitated, no, it would bring much. With many natives feeling celebratory, protected by the Japanese, not accountable to the Dutch, he could trade well tonight. And he would be alone this particular night, a delicious thrill. Everyone was hungrier, all the time. This would be the best night yet.

He met his most familiar trader, in a dark alley the Japanese didn't patrol. On the way home, with so many things wrapped, he had to clutch eggs delicately. He heard a Japanese voice, and tried to run full speed. His wrapping job had to hold, because the voice turned to yelling and pounding feet running after him. He ran, skidded around a corner; still the running behind him. He dropped and scrambled through a low hole in thick bushes, which he knew from experience led into a vast garden. He muffled his loud breathing into the rice bag, glad the Japanese were not Indian-quiet. He waited endless minutes, in case they looped back around. Lying on his back, he felt a broken egg, coating his wrist in regret. Exploring the rest, he found only the one had cracked. He licked off gleaming ropes of yolk and white. No nutrition could be wasted.

He easily returned with all of the goods, and slipped them into the cabinet he had purposely left ajar. A whole row of goods lined up in the empty cupboard: pork, five eggs, milk, rice, sambal, spices, peanuts, dried coconut, all the result of reasonable risk. Although almost caught tonight, he liked working alone. Every decision only his, and no voice of reason, only the voice of yes — reasonable risk.

He eased in next to Albert's even breathing, quickly falling asleep. He twitched awake often, arms and legs jerking as if ready to leap and run. He had to run, because in his nightmare, the Japanese guards still chased him, and he had to run in endless circles away from their home, or they would all be hauled away to the Kempetai.

Mammie shook him awake, just as she woke up. Her eyes looked wild, her hair. "What have you done now? The silver platter — gone? We needed that in case of emergency. Right now our friends can still help us with cash money, even though no one can bank anymore. But that silver platter, Jakob, it would be to barter long after cash money's gone. Why don't you ever ask?"

"I'm sorry," he said, miserably, rubbing a fist into the wet sleep crust around one eye, his anger irrationally building. *Why didn't you tell me? Then I would know.*

Tante Ankie came in. "Liesbet, Liesbet, look how much he got." She squatted next to them, holding Johan.

"Ja-ak, Ja-ak, ob, ob." The little boy tried to say his name.

I wish I could get away from Mammie; she looks so disgusted with me. Albert sat up in bed next to him, shaking his head like a disappointed adult.

Tante grabbed Johan's hand away from Jakob's hair. "You made a mistake last night; I doubt you knew you could have traded for much more. That platter was silver, not silver plated."

Jakob's face flamed with regret. He saw the same man as usual from last night. They bargained briefly, instead of longer haggling, he had believed he was driving a great deal. But he knew it was no bargain; the man cheated him.

"Well, okay then." Mammie sighed. "What's done is done."

If only he wasn't so often the bad one, the foolish one.

Albert punched him softly in the arm. "Our families have more valuables, and lucky for you and them, you don't know where they are. You must listen now."

Jakob thought of the jewels Mammie had slipped into her apron pocket the day she filled the camphor chest. He had never wondered where they went. The tightening rope in his belly loosened, and he was glad he didn't know. No more blame. During morning mandi, he poured the dipper over himself again and again; he imagined Pappie's voice lecturing him. *"Why didn't you think? That's the problem with you, you just don't think. You act before you think. Away with you. Soon I'll come to your room, and we'll see about your punishment."*

No matter how bad the punishment, he wished Pappie could come to his room. It was horrible to try to be a man in charge. For the first time he wondered if it was horrible for Albert too. What a good brother, always trying to do the right and safe thing.

† † †

Perhaps to cheer him up, Albert suggested they see Meneer Zwanenburg. "Since we've now seen the worst, surely Tante Manda will let us in."

Indeed, Manda opened the door to them after they crossed the town square.

Meneer Zwanenburg sat on their teak couch with turquoise cushions. His oldest boy reached spoonfuls of *nasigoreng* rice up to his mouth. He shrugged, and smiled, a gleam in his eyes they hadn't seen when the men all talked about where they'd been. "Ja, I came home with these useless hands, and we hope and pray, no matter how bad the pain, that life will return."

Jakob's eyes stung with dread, his own wrists ached with sympathy pain.

"The pain is good; it means I am getting circulation back in my hands, meaning I will heal. My shoulders hurt less. Both were dislocated. In between being strung up, you might as well know, were the beatings." He turned to Jakob. "You especially should know about their torture. Manda says many Indos and Blandas know you trade at night, even with curfew, even with a crackdown on the black market. You are taking a huge risk."

Manda stared at Jakob and slowly shook her head.

"But why did they hurt you so?" asked Albert. "You weren't on the black market."

Meneer Zwanenburg looked them in the eyes. Jakob's stomach clenched with the terror Meneer Zwanenburg must have felt. *This is how it is to talk like a man, to hear the very worst.*

"A local native man betrayed me, claiming I knew the whereabouts of the few underground soldiers that survived and fought in the Bandoeng hills."

He looked away, moving the fingers on his left hand, and grimacing. "I'm tired and full of Mammie's good food now boys," he said to his sons, who wandered away.

Albert and Jakob stayed put. Manda gently lifted her husband's feet up on the bench, to ease him down on his side. She settled pillows around him.

"You boys," he mumbled, "you do not know the worst yet."

Manda patted his head.

Jakob tried to meet Meneer Zwanenburg's eyes. "There are soldiers in the Bandoeng area?"

Meneer Zwanenburg shrugged, his face pale, bony knees pressed together, telling them that every shift of his body meant being assaulted by pain. Methodically he reached out his lower hand towards a child's rubber ball and rolled it along the floor. "Ah, now I can settle. Better on my side."

"Come on, we must go now." Albert kicked Jakob.

"But I asked …"

Manda handed him a rubber ball. "Here an extra one for Sara."

Albert pulled him out the door. Once outside, he lectured, "Soldiers in Bandoeng? You ask the same question he was tortured for? Don't be so thoughtless."

The words stabbed hard. Jakob sputtered. "No, no, there were no Japanese in there, of course. I meant no harm; we need to know our fighting positions."

When Albert marched along, refusing to reply, Jakob gave up. Apparently he did interfere with Albert's task of keeping everyone safe and well.

He shook his head for the loss of valuable reconnaissance. *Albert stopped me and now we may never know about brave guerilla fighters in the jungle. I do know, having seen Meneer Zwanenburg's agony, that if he knew about hidden men, they are still secret now. He is a hero.*

It was as if Mammie and Tante Ankie heard or sensed that Jakob had been a bother. Not until days later were Jakob and Albert allowed to bring the Zwanenburg family a treat from their home. Mammie and Tante Ankie made cake, with hoarded sugar, rice ground into flour, and condensed milk. They added an extra can of condensed milk for the youngest boy. Manda opened the door silently, smiled briefly, thanked them, and said, "Wait, I'll send you back with a note." She left for a moment and they heard Meneer Zwanenburg's friendly, rumbly voice. Back at the door she smiled broadly, "Come on in, my husband wants to see you."

Meneer Zwanenburg had some color back in his face, and sat easily leaning back against the cushions. Manda sat with her beautiful posture, her feet tucked beneath her chair, and the boys settled nearby. Their teacher breathed with pain as he showed them he had some movement back in his hands. He flexed the thumb and forefinger on one hand, then the other, and finally laid his hands on his lap and pulled each up a centimeter at the wrist. "A little bit better every day. Remember, Jakob, I told you, watch your back. The Kempetai think nothing of picking up boys too. And sadly they don't need a reason, only a rumor, so you too Albert. You boys always want to know more. I might as well tell you, since boys are going to have to be tough too."

"The reason my shoulders hurt less is because the doctor came upon the night of my return and realigned my shoulders. That means he practically stood on me like the Japanese, but for a good reason, and he put my shoulders back in place. So terrible pain one more time for the relief I have now."

Neither said a word; finally Albert said, "We'll be careful."

"Ja," echoed Jakob.

"Oh Jakob." He moaned again, flexing at the wrists. "You are a doer. So your terrible pain for now is that there's so little to do—no fighting, no trading. You must listen to Albert's common sense."

The three little Zwanenburg boys all came into the room. Jakob and Albert sat on the floor with them, their legs in a star pattern, rolling a new ball back and forth. Funny how automatic it felt already, to play indoors, huddled together, nowhere near as fun as soccer. Manda must have made them this ball stuffed with kapok, the same stuffing put in pillows, mattresses, and life preservers.

Meneer Zwanenburg stretched with a moan.

Albert elbowed Jakob, the leave signal. He elbowed Albert back. *I won't leave.* He clenched his hands hotly; right now he could kick Albert, for being the boss, for embarrassing him.

Meneer Zwanenburg still noticed everything, just like all teachers. "No, no Albert, you can both stay. There is talk that all the Europeans will be locked up, men first, women and children later. That's why I told the two of you to be courageous. I will make sure that my Manda and the children will not have to go."

Manda got up and returned with a tray of balls of rice rolled in honey, and all five boys ate. Suddenly Albert elbowed Jakob again, and abruptly stopped. Jakob looked up from the warm deliciousness. Meneer and Mevrouw Zwanenburg weren't eating. This he could understand.

Hospitality, with plenty of food, had always been the islands tradition, but there was less to go around.

Manda forced a smile. "You are stopping? We have plenty for now, and more for later. Eat children." Only the young ones ate. She smiled at her husband. "If they come take you men to kamps, I do not want all our friends to disappear into kamps without us. We will go too, if women and children are called."

"Not called, rounded up. You must never go in to a closed neighborhood or camp. I will have to go first as a man and a Blanda. You and the children will all be Indische and exempt. You have no idea who will attack you in lockup. The Japs are cruel." He held his hands in front of him. "I wonder if we should separate already, so you won't be here when they come."

Manda stood and placed her hands lightly on his shoulders. He flinched. Dark bruises radiated away from his collar. He groaned and then relaxed into her.

Such a woman I would want, Jakob thought admiringly. "When they come again, we will fight. All you men you will fight."

Albert used his stern voice. "We can no longer fight. When will you ever learn?"

"In the open, that is," declared Jakob. "We can fight in secret, of course."

"Do not endanger all with such talk of hidden fighting. The cost is too high." Meneer Zwanenburg sighed.

Jakob squatted on the floor, getting ready to stand. Now he could tell for himself that it was time to leave. They cut across streets quickly to avoid Japanese military. They encountered one guard and automatically froze into the low bow to the road, knowing to avoid looking him in the face.

Albert's toes veered off of his sandals. He'd heard Mammie and Tante Ankie's worries. His brother was in a growth spurt, and they had no new shoes. His own sandals were so worn and soft they almost fell off, a risk for the next time he had to run.

The soldier cleared his throat. Nothing. After long moments they heard, *naore*, the Japanese at-ease command. They returned home agitated, Albert jerking the door open, each checking their rucksacks for emergency supplies. Albert cinched his pack with force and an umph.

Jakob sighed. *Strange, we are getting like grownups. Always so careful.*

Kamp Tjideng, Dutch Image Bank WWII

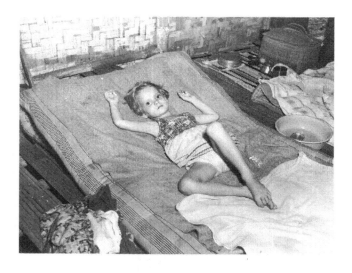

Kamp Makassar, Image Bank

Kamp Tjideng, Image Bank

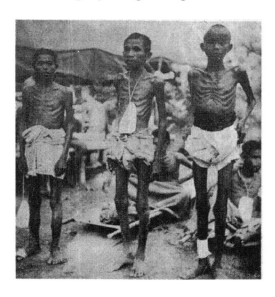

Java, Romushas—laborers intentionally worked to death

CHAPTER 15

Luce

Houston, Texas
January 2005

My brother finally came after me. Of course they stopped him from coming with me all the way to my ER room.

I've been examined, and I have a dreaded IV in. The needle in my hand hurt and burned going in, and feels odd, like a dangerous tug, every time I stir. But I need it for fluids or medication. My acute pain is mostly gone.

I wish I could relax. I try breathing, meditation, prayer—nothing helps. Forty-five minutes into my wondering and worrying, Alby's back, carrying AA books, a notebook, even a pillow, in case I need another one. He sits as if plugged into electricity, not fidgeting—just tense. There's a charge in the room, when he is the one helping me.

He makes me think of Papa, when he believed he could always protect Albert, when their names were called out, at Tjideng. Surely, that's all it was, both their names were up. But Papa believed he left earlier than other younger boys, to help Albert. I know about the need to believe in control. I want control now. I want to control Alby.

Ahhh, no pain for a while. Funny, Alby relaxes me. He appears to have nothing to say for a change. He plumps the pillow up underneath my IV hand, gets up and paces, sits again. Minutes tick by on the big black wall clock, as if the hospital wants everyone in crisis to know just how long they are waiting. Just as I feel relief, a stabbing pain launches down my left leg, completely random. "Ow, that was a bad one, but a good sign, I hope. No pattern, no true labor pains. The nurses keep telling me this, but I don't know."

With wide-eyed helpfulness Albert grabs the clipboard at the foot of the bed. "I see you have been refusing pain meds, even though there's little or no risk of harm to the baby. Gee, wide awake with pain-stress, good for you. Get that worried look off your face, and I'll tell you what Papa said about the beginning of the war, and how rapidly Tjideng changed."

I ease back into the pillows. So annoying, his attempts to order me around. He's giving me a taste of my own medicine: stay put, listen, and shut up. And he's right, I'll always listen to stories, so I nod. "Yes, I want to know. Tell me."

† † †

Jakob

Tjideng neighborhood
January 1943

Rumbling, an earthquake shook them out of bed. But no — trucks, harsh yelling, pounding feet, and banging on doors.

Jakob tangled in his mosquito net. "Are they attacking?"

"No, rounding up all the men, just like Meneer Zwanenburg said." Albert stood, half-dressed.

Within an hour they found Matteus and went to see Manda without permission. They had learned that women couldn't really stop boys, with no Pappie around for discipline. Matteus came out with shadows under his eyes. His pappie had said a careful loving good-bye, with notes for each of them. "My mammie says he's always so thoughtful. She tried not to cry. She didn't mind that I cried."

Tante Manda's dark eyes sunk back in too, no sparkle. "Come on in. Meneer Zwanenburg was ready with a rucksack; he knew what to have for emergency. The boys and I said our hurried good-byes. They went back to sleep of course. At least, the rumor is they all go to a kamp, no one to the Kempetai." She rubbed her shoulders and hands, as if she were Meneer. "The Japanese ran from house to house like a horrible snowball from our cold visit to Nederland three years ago. They roll up our men in larger and larger numbers."

That evening they gathered for dinner, invited by Mevrouw de Bakker via Matteus. Even though the four families had some fresh vegetables and even *pindasaus* with dinner, no one spoke much.

Sara put a spoonful of rice mixture in her mouth. "So they are all going to be with Pappie? And Pappie won't be back yet?"

"Don't talk with your mouth full!" Mammie's voice was unexpectedly loud. "Where did you hear that?"

"In the market with Tante Ankie."

Mammie shrugged unconvincingly. "Ja, they'll all be with our pappie and Oom Henri."

Jakob had still been waiting each day, fixing his eyes for red hair, and flashing round eye glasses. He looked up, when Albert kicked him under the table, and felt like one somber man across the table from another, no longer a boy. There was nothing they could do to bring Pappie home. He hung his head, but ate the delicious food. Hunger gnawed at him always, and he was growing taller.

† † †

On a tired evening the big orange sun hovered and sank. Sara ran in from the garden. "We will visit Pappie, we will visit Pappie!" she cried.

"Huh? No one gets to visit." Jakob's heart soared with exhausted joy, if only it could be so. He glanced sideways at Albert, whose face looked as bland as rice with no spices. It seemed that fewer *tjik-tjak* lizards ran up to the ceiling in the evening for insects. Even they must be suffering from less food.

Good news never materialized. Mammie and Tante Ankie bravely took turns bicycling to the bazaar for food. One week, Tante Ankie had returned with exciting news. The U.S. President Roosevelt had told the Japanese to get out of Java. Rumor had it that the Japanese had their evacuation plan set. The Japanese never evacuated of course, just more regulations, the switch to Japanese time, all Europeans were forced to pay fees and register, curfew was strictly enforced. Everyone was tense because beatings by the Japanese to boys and women could occur anytime. Sometimes friends they knew were beaten for forgetting to bow, sometimes they were just slapped. Sometimes Japanese officers viciously struck their own men down also, not always for a reason.

"Yoo-hoo!" Manda arrived with her boys.

It was true, she said. Jakob's folded arms fell down to his sides, as if he'd been carrying a weight he didn't know. Day by day they created a bag of food for themselves, and another bag with sulfa powder, first aid, *klamboe* mosquito netting and tins of food for Pappie. The trip was an exhausted blur of haggling for transportation, waiting, trudging.

When they reached the kamp, more than a thousand men lined up. Everyone could see their men through the fence with Japanese guards barking orders to a Malaysian translator. "You can view each other only. There will be no touching or public affection, as this is shameful and forbidden."

"They say all emotion is cowardly," Mammie said.

"There will also be no more than a few words or all will be severely punished!"

Mammie held Jakob's hand hard, and he squeezed Sara's. Albert was close to Tante Ankie, who clutched Johan's hand.

293

Everyone's safety required guarded silence, murmuring very few words beyond hello.

This must be easy for Albert, usually quiet anyway. But Albert had a pallor underneath his tanned skin; his shoulders hunched up. "We must be quiet," he whispered urgently to Jakob. And to Sara, "You cannot cry out 'Pappie, Pappie.' This is very important."

The mammies whispered, and moved Manda and her children up front, then Tante Ankie and Johan, then Mammie, Albert, Jakob, and Sara.

Jakob puzzled it out. The Japanese would treat Indische less harsh; therefore, Manda went first. Many native men were not being sent to the kamps, and only some Indos born of white and native parents. Tante Ankie appeared calm. Mammie plucked at the bow in Sara's hair, the buttons on her blouse, nervous but strong. She clutched the bag of supplies for Pappie, bread and fruit added to the bundle. The procession started in a long line along barbed wire, in full-on sun. In the distance a portion of the fence was shaded. Everything was a different world; by the enforced Japanese calendar, the year was now 2062. Ridiculous to be over a hundred years in the future, sweating during the hottest part of the day, usually rest time. Tidur siang had been permanently canceled by the Japanese.

Most of the men had no shirts, as if each were getting ready to swim. But no one had the soft, friendly bellies of men lounging by the pool. No man looked familiar. Pappie had to be in this line. Just as he wondered about Meneer Zwanenburg he saw him, as did his sons, who started to cry. Manda said in Malaysian, "Hush now."

Their crying turned to snuffling and then to whispering, "Hi, Pappie."

Meneer Zwanenburg and Manda each held up a hand as if they could close the yards of distance between them at the fence.

Meneer Zwanenburg's nose was crooked and swollen, with an angry red around his lips and chin. One ear was swollen too, and he held himself rigidly as if standing tall took effort. Yet, he looked at them easily; his eyes friendly, not dark and sunken like many men they'd already passed. His ribs stood out, and his thin arms looked like wiry ropes at the docks. His shorts had to be held on by a rope belt. Manda and the boys came close, murmuring, all holding up hands, without quite touching. Manda's hand moved to the height of his face, showing she wished she could touch the pain. She stumbled, and Mammie and Ankie steadied her. She and the boys stepped back and walked past, waving like a pleasant good-bye.

As usual when Jakob came closer to Meneer Zwanenburg, he felt the force of attraction, like their old classroom experiments with iron filings, paper, and magnets. He wished he could be pulled into his orbit, in a semicircle of energy like the iron fillings.

"*Dag*, Jakob."

"*Dag*, Meneer Zwanenburg. *Sterkte* — strength."

"*Sterkte*, Jakob," said Meneer.

Obviously Zwanenburg had been beaten. Jakob hoped Sara wouldn't notice, and felt a pang of sorrow. How could she not see? But Sara cried out, "Look!"

Only five men down, red hair and gold glasses flashed. Pappie! He looked peculiar, as if a foreign man pasted on his curly hair. He wore shorts and a tattered shirt, and his skin bumped with something — growths? No, they were all sores.

Jakob's breath caught, and he heard Sara do the same. Her face fell as she looked, "*Dag*, Pappie, liefs."

Mammie whispered in his ear, "Sores. They must be from the sun or his time floating in the Java Sea."

"*Dag*, Pappie!" Jakob added. Unlike most of the other men, Pappie had not turned teakwood brown from the sun. Proudly he thought of the medicated salve for Pappie, and food. He tried not to stare; some lesions had brown crusts, with yellow pus leaking. Albert, who didn't usually hold hands, reached for Jakob's hand and squeezed, and Jakob in turn squeezed Sara's hand.

Pappie nodded at Jakob, and said to the boys, "Sterkte." *Ja, we will be strong*. Then he smiled at Sara. "And where is Tina?"

"At home guarding our home," said Sara. She called every house they lived in, home.

Pappie managed a smiled. "Ja, home."

Mammie and the children lingered with Pappie, holding up their hands as if they could touch, ignoring grumbling from behind them.

Pappie said over and over, "*Dag*, be strong, I am well."

"My *lieveling*," said Mammie, her voice husky with her own strength and love. "Be strong, we will be well."

He was not well, as Jakob could see. This was worse than *don't worry, everything will be fine*. Pappie's fierce gaze through glasses with one lens, and strong posture showed *sterkte*.

Albert nudged him, as if to say we have never seen Pappie look frail.

Mammie scrunched, then widened her eyes so as not to cry. "Ja, we are well, we manage well. We have salve and food for you." Soon they had to move past him, and Jakob realized he knew most of the other thinner men too. He looked with different eyes at their own little group, also thinner and drawn down about the face with fatigue.

Ankie rushed ahead. Oom Henri stood with a makeshift crutch, his foot at an odd angle. But Tante Ankie smiled, and whispered, "Thank you, *lieve* God." Albert had overheard her whispering at night she wasn't sure if he was alive, and here he was "Everything is great," Oom Henri said.

Johan still looked dully around until the familiar voice registered. "Pappie, Pappie!"

A guard came closer. Tante swiftly held him in her arms. "Shush, my liefje." Johan wiggled and held up his arms for his Pappie.

They continued down the long line. Many men said to loved ones, "I love you, all is well, I am fine." Clearly the only words the Japanese would allow.

The women replied, *"Liefs, sterkte."* Many women replied, "Oh, I am glad you are fine. This will all be over soon." The words landed differently, *I love you, I'm so sad it's awful for you. Let's hope for the best.*

Behind them a woman said, "Soon the Americans will come."

"Still now!" another hissed loudly.

† † †

After the exhausted day of travel and seeing Pappie and all the men krachteloos—helpless to fight, Jakob was glad to go to sleep early. With blackout orders, no one stayed up late with lanterns. It was better to sleep than to feel hungry. His stomach was pretend full, but not for what his body craved—meat, eggs, vegetables, and more. Often they ate only endless rice. Jakob pictured Pappie's fierce look, and focused on plans. With the full moon casting light he practiced his own fierce look, glad no one would awaken to see and laugh.

Sometime his thoughts drifted and he imagined a Japanese soldier trying to attack Mammie. How would he save her? He'd take the blow. The Japanese would then ignore his mother, and take him to the Kempetai for torture. Which doctor would put his shoulders back after torture? Only female doctors were left now, the men were all locked up.

The full moon rose further and he could read by such light. He pulled the weight of *War of the Worlds* onto his chest, as a comforting presence on his loneliest day in this house full of people. His face ached with tears, and he cried, which turned to sobs which could wake Albert and everyone. So he buried his head in his pillow and longed for Pappie to be there to protect them, and Albert to fight. He reached for his compass under his pillow. He pinched himself hard. Why had he not taken it along to the line, a chance for Pappie and him to look at it one more time, together?

He finally slept, knowing that pappies were not always strong and that everyone only promised the Allies would come to defeat the Japanese and help them escape this new hell.

† † †

Luce

Houston, Texas
January 2005

Endurance arrives and kicks Alby out of the ER. One of the kids trails her. "Come on dude, they want you."

"But," says Alby, "we're waiting to talk to the doctor."

"She'll be fine," says Endurance. "I'm staying for now."

He leaves. New *Feasta*, has more influence than my fears are ready to believe. "Aren't you supposed to stay in New *Feasta*?" I say to Endurance like Mama, and Papa, for comic relief.

"New *Feasta*?" Endurance grins. "No, we made arrangements. They know I love the pregnant women, so I get to be with you. So how long have you been sober?"

"How did you know?"

"Well, you get that feeling, plus most crazy alkies keep coming to see their family even from far away, as if they can make their loved one sober."

"And I'm in Alanon too, where they tell us to let go and let God."

"And a fine job you are doing of letting go and letting God take care of you. Didn't anyone tell you to stay put when pregnant?"

"Yes," I say meekly.

A different nurse comes in and reports that I'm better than expected. The doctor will be by soon. Endurance squeezes my shoulder. "Okay, now is time for me to go back and do the daily check-in group. So I'm turning you over to God, like you should do with your brother."

More waiting. I finger the controls of the TV set, not interested in any program.

"Luce?"

"Alby? Won't they kick off your rehab unit for being AWOL?"

"Not if they didn't kick me out trying to start my own program with all the younger kids. Well, I see I made it back just in time. Cindy's here." I catch a glimpse of Cindy's long ponytail, Wade and Marina with her, clutching bags of books. Reminiscent of our family in the library and of kids too often in the hospital. I wave through the doors at the kids, adults only in the ER room. They drop their books, the doors close.

Cindy's warm, dry hands touch me in an examining manner. If I were a brood mare, I would want her to stay with me now, one hand on my neck, the other holding my shoulder and `withers, but in a barn like Pake and Beppe's.

Her touch brings tears, as if that's what the horrible ER clock was ticking away about. *Don't cry, wait, don't cry, wait, don't cry – or what?* "I have blown it so bad. This is what I always wanted, to have another baby. I thought it was safe to travel again. After all I already traveled once."

"You mean you were pregnant when you came to see us before?"

"I didn't know yet, but yes. I traveled pregnant then, and nothing went wrong. But this was tempting fate, to risk leaving home again, with all the miscarriages I've had." I turn with an *oof* of pain. "And I'm always thinking you're the idiot, Alby."

"Gee, thanks," he says.

Cindy laughs.

"I'm the bigger idiot."

"Settle down. You're fine, Luce," Cindy says. "We're just going to hang out with you, and then I'll check if the kids are actually doing their school reading."

Alby rests his hand on my shoulder. "Luce, Papa told me about the weeks after he and Albert left Tjideng."

"He told you?" Ow, another stab.

"Oh yeah. Hush, no complaining. Why should we make him tell each of us the same stories over and over again? Now just listen and mind me."

"Shouldn't you be in a group therapy or something? Ow. See Cindy, I'm losing the baby." Her eyes crinkle, there's something about her, I don't have to be strong, or cheery.

"No one has told us anything about losing the baby, only your pain, sweetie. Just relax."

"Try telling that to a Vanderveer." I laugh. "Ow, it hurts to laugh."

CHAPTER 16

Jakob and Albert

Kamp Tjideng
August1944

Only one boy spoke as the trucks belched diesel fumes and lurched away from mothers, sisters, and the few grandmothers still alive. Some kids cried; Wouter always chattered on through the night and now on the somber truck he did the same. "Well, I'll save my bit of food for later," he announced.

He was an *idioot* to refer to food. They all had the same from the kitchen mothers, a hard piece of bread and a lump of dark brown sugar. So Wouter, the fool, must have something extra. Although most boys were honorable, and lived by a code of never stealing, there were times they took food, especially now packed in with boys who didn't all know each other yet. Stupid Wouter. Such a baby, with no big brother or mammie to warn him how to be.

Jakob craned his neck to see Wouter's dull brown hair, his flushed cheeks, still talking. "And thirsty, I'm so thirsty."

"Shut your trap. We're all thirsty!" Jakob yelled, as if he were Pappie at the end of one of his worst work days back home.

Albert elbowed him. "He is younger than either of us, a baby."

"He's a cry baby and a blabber mouth," Jakob replied hotly. He focused on moving his legs wide for balance, then narrow to weave into the others, the press of bodies holding him up. Did the boys at the edges of the truck have truck

301

railing sized bruises on their sides from the pressure? How far was Tjiapit, their rumored destination? They rode on in the truck, crushed for hours. His hunger grew, like a vicious creature inside of him, as persistent as Wouter, never letting up. Hunger hurt. Most boys were silent, some held their teddy bears. How dumb to have one more thing to hold on to. He glanced at Wouter. He'd stopped chattering. His face was peaceful but his lips were moving. Praying maybe? He wasn't so bad after all when he could be relied upon to shut up.

Jakob felt the stirring of sadness for boys with bears and praying boys. He shook his head, willing himself to view only the road ahead. They had left Batavia and Tjideng kamp, and ignored the right fork in the road which passed the harbor. They careened left on the postal route road, cutting through jungle, and boys pressed in on him. They all knew the Japs would not stop for breaks. The sharp, hot smell of urine rose up from the truck bed, assaulting his nose. Albert and he had linked elbows, staying close, their bundled slings still pressed on. After hours, the truck slowed. They must be getting closer, and must be prepared for anything.

"Come on, joh," Jakob said in Albert's ear, and jostled them both to the truck's back. It would be useful to be the first to get off.

"Oof." Albert slumped for a long moment, as their hips were crushed to the edge and back.

"At least we can breathe and see," said Jakob. Yes, he would have to take charge, even of an older brother.

A breeze caressed his face and neck as he rocked up on his toes, ready for action. Another truck followed with a few guards, lounging on benches in the back. What if he and Albert could escape?

His compass from Pappie had been seized long ago in a raid by the guards. He had turned it in himself, when all valuables were to be turned in. Up to the last minute he successfully hid it away, until he heard the cries of a woman being beaten, then another. He stayed away; to see would have been too much to endure. He ran to put it on the pile, returned. Mammie put her hand on his neck. "Ja, *goede jongen*, but *droevig*—sad." Rumor spread that one woman had hidden a gold ring. She'd been pulled up by her arms for everyone to see her suffering. He had to look away from her face and her crying children. The other women were left bleeding in the dirt. Not until the guards turned away could friends help them up. Albert led him to the woman hanging up tortured by the taught cord on her arms. Mammie came.

"We must go, there's nothing we can do." Another woman took the weeping children. Mammie herself still had a ring hidden away; you had to take some risks.

† † †

If only he had his compass now. He checked the sturdier boys: perhaps they could run and join a troop of the resistance soldiers deep in the jungle. He himself had dark hair and was tanned and spoke Malaysian like Indos. He could pass for Indonesian. Matteus had blue eyes and blonde hair; therefore, he could only fight, not join the resistance, and he wasn't here. The de Bakker family had been called to a different kamp.

Albert's hair too was bright blond; how could he hide effectively? But they couldn't really run away. There were stories of everyone in the kamps being punished for one or two escapees, and of native Indonesians turning in escapees for money. He would not be the cause of anyone's punishment. Jakob crushed his eyes closed to take away the mind-picture of the beaten women he had seen, who transformed in his mind to Wouter, a boy stupid enough to cause other's beatings. Jakob worried about boys with their teddy bears or someone's pappie being killed for others' transgressions. He thought of Wolfie, gone in the transport with Siebe. Wolfie didn't care for others, only for himself.

The truck bumped the last twenty-five meters over deep ruts left from the mud of monsoon rains. Gedek and barbed wire surrounded all, three meters tall. The truck roared through the gate and guard towers. It would be almost six Dutch time, 4:30 Japanese time, dark soon. Guards swiftly pulled the gate shut, and Jakob realized with a shock he could not imagine the surroundings. He had never lived here; to him and Jakob this was prison, nothing more. Scarecrow men came up to the truck, many looking worse than the women they left behind. Cooler air soothed them, Albert's sharp shoulder blades relaxed. They'd arrived to Grogol, *we are the welcome wagon*, the men said. How would Mammie and Sara know where they went?

A few boys muttered, "Home sweet home." They and their mothers had come from Grogol to Tjideng, when it was a family kamp. Now it was a boys and men's kamp only. Japanese guards screamed and released the truck chains holding them in.

"Lean back!" Jakob called. He and Albert tightened their linked arms, but still fell forward, Albert on top of him. They both scrambled up, jumped off the truck, holding each other up. Their legs could hardly move. As best as they could, they ran to the front of the crowd of boys.

A freckled man with his spots forming into bigger patches due to constant sun, stood by a glaring light. "Welcome, boys. We have only water for you tonight, no food. Sorry, only a little, eh?"

"No sign of Pappie yet," whispered Jakob.

"The kamps are all over Java and Sumatra. If he is near, he will find us," said Albert.

Jakob had a funny feeling that if finding was to be done, it was up to him, but he said, "Yes, he will."

They soaked their Tjideng bread in the rations of water and ate slowly as always. Jakob's head pounded with nothing but the little water and the crust of bread. Before, Pappie always planned against heat stroke to prevent aching heads and exhaustion. He ordered salt tablets, water, fruit, and rest. Here, a great dry lump stuck in his throat; his head thundered. Where would he find Grogol's trickle of water to add to his cup, and swallow down his last morsel of food? Should he risk eating the sugar they had saved?

They were led to sleeping platforms in barracks, and put toward the middle. Of course they could not get the preferred spots at the edges with the less foul air.

They curled up and Albert breathed in, already in deep sleep. Albert had been much braver and alert than expected. Could his quick sleep each night be his escape? Certainly. One was always allowed to sleep, the rest of the time, they must be brave.

A full bright moon shone through the thatch roof. Torrents must pour on everyone during wet monsoon. Jakob moved his hand all around in the moonlight, outside of their *klamboe*. His wrist and fingers gleamed, skinny like the rest of him, whitish as if his bones showed right through. How would they guard their *klamboe* net during the day? Many of these men had nothing. Furthermore, how had his hand, his body, Albert and these thousands of others come into being? How had they come to be here, with the whole world at war, worse than the *War of the Worlds*? How would the guards treat the women and children left at Tjideng? Jakob shivered, moved towards his brother's warm and fell into the sleep of exhaustion.

At first light, Jakob stretched to feel hard planks and Albert's bony hips, just about as hard, next to him. Morning light spotted all around through the roof. It felt wrong to wake up here, never in his familiar bed. Hunger, horribly painful and wrongness ate away at him inside. He moaned much like when bully Wolfie snuck in not just one stomach punch, but on another day, a few more.

He shook off the pain and shoved his brother gently. Albert turned his head smiling. How could he smile here? "Our new home."

"Home? You're as crazy as Sara." Now his heart ached with missing her. All around them boys scurried up, a few with jokes, most with tired, dull faces. Some moaned as they stood up, not just hunger, but the same ache as his, awaking here.

Smoke from the cookhouse wafted in and greater hunger knotted his belly. He grabbed his pack and panic sliced through him; he had no spoon, nothing! In Tjideng, no utensils meant no food. He turned to Albert, who had gone to his bundle swiftly and brought out two food bowls and spoons. Jakob's breathing changed from gasps to slow breathing. Look what Albert had remembered. They made it through appel with all the familiar chaos of guards shoving, yelling, recounts. The Japs should be better counters; still, it was satisfying to think of them all as idiots.

Once they incorporated the new boys into the system, the cells of prisoners counted off quicker than Tjideng. Each cell leader reported to the Japanese. They stood in line and came back with their food, mostly tapioca, and a little rice, less than Tjideng. Meneer Krans, the kamp leader, greeted them. Jakob was assigned latrine corvée—duty—with just a few new boys. Why was he picked out so quickly for the worst job of all? Was it just being tall? Although he was thirteen months younger, he was centimeters taller than Albert. Still, they had made it this far as a team, and they could remain a team the whole war, hanging on until the Allies came, rescuing Sara and Mammie, with or without Pappie.

Albert had the familiar corvée of Tjideng: chopping up both elegant and plain teak furniture. There was no cured wood for fuel nearby, and they all needed a way to cook, the kamp kitchen as well as the Japanese kitchen.

Like Tjideng, the sewers overflowed into the street. Both the humming of insects and the vicious stench made Jakob feel sick. He tried breathing through his mouth. Except a fly flew in. He laughed and said to his bucket mate, "Hey, I don't want to swallow the flies, but maybe I need to. It's meat!"

The other boy laughed. "Yeah, anything for food. Have you tried lice yet?"

"Oh no, not yet. Really looking forward to that. But the smell of crushed lice, ugh."

"Ugh," the boy who appeared to be the leader noted. "We'll look for food anywhere we can get it." He had prominent ears, and a wide smile. Jakob could imagine him eating bugs and smiling all the while. "My name is Roland, you can call me Rollie." They were the same height, a good thing for carrying the buckets or barrels with a pole between them, shoulder to shoulder. In Tjideng the children received small extra rations for catching flies to turn in. The idea was to reduce the insects spreading infectious diseases, such as typhoid.

They worked with huge buckets, scooping up disgusting masses where they clogged the flow. Jakob, working barefoot, tried not to slip in the filth. He hoped he had no open sores to absorb infection. Be drawing a fresh air breath here and there, he found he could take measures to not vomit up the little breakfast inside. They hauled the buckets of human manure to wagons that went out to fertilize the fields. He recalled wrinkling his nose at the constant manure smell in the spring in the Dutch farmlands. Mammie used to say, *this is a good smell, you'll get used to it*. He would never get used to the human manure smell. Rollie, he and the other boys switched the burden of the buckets' pole for pulling and prodding the wagon along, as if they were oxen. Guards yelled and pounded the sides. All along the way as they heaved the wagon over ruts to the outskirts of the kamp, no boys had been beaten, yet. At the gate a brief breeze teased Jakob with freedom, he inhaled a fresh smell. Other prisoners took their wagon, and they returned to have the guarded gate shut again. For moments the yelling stopped.

Jakob felt dizzy that night, fatigue taking him over in the long queue. *There will be no heavier ration for heavier work, I suppose.* Day one already felt like an endless burden. Nevertheless, he had stood in line with Albert and received their soup and lump of tapioca. "Ah yum, a fish head." Jakob laughed.

"Yes, a delicacy. Maybe the server knew you had a tough corvée today."

"And you?" He still laughed, and forced a stop, hysterical laughter called attention.

Albert seemed not to notice. "A lot of lifting, not so bad."

"We have to tell our cell leader, Meneer Krans, to keep us together," said Jakob.

"Won't he immediately think we're complainers and troublemakers?"

"No, he'll think we're smart. We have to stick together. That's the way to survive. We can have our own *oranje boven* like the KNL, and get through the night."

The usual silence as Albert pretend-chewed. "You're right. Remember when Mammie stuck up for you? What the Japanese said?"

"I don't like to remember." But of course they both remembered anyway, the time in Kamp Tjideng the Japanese said Mammie had Samurai spirit for daring to protect Jakob. His shoulders clenched uneasily remembering. He had been playing a child's game running alongside a rolling bicycle tire hoop, sending it on its way around the corner … into a guard. For horrible moments, hauled into Commander Sonei's headquarters, he thought he would end up just like Meneer Zwanenburg. He was already hauled above the ground, his arms behind his back, when Mammie arrived.

In the most commanding tone Jakob had ever heard from her, she said, "I am disgusted with his disrespectful behavior. Give him to me to discipline, I will make him sorry," all the time bowing.

When Sonei said, "Naore," she hit Jakob on the hip hard with the stick he had used to spur the hoop on.

"Give him to me. I deal with his disrespect."

Amazing, that's when Sonei, he who randomly beat women and caused even the hospital patients to stand for appel half the night, said she had Samurai spirit. Jakob was quickly lowered, his shoulders cramping with terror, his shorts wet from the urine he released in terror. She pretend hit him all the way back to their crowded garage room.

Ordinarily she would have cried after, but they were all too dead inside with another terror evaded. They sat together after dinner line-up, in a daze.

It was Sara who said, "Bravo Mammie."

† † †

Luce

Houston, Texas
January 2005

Alone again in the eternities between ambulance sirens. Code Red announcements, rushed gurneys, voices, wondering when I will be seen. The wall clock clicks the seconds along with a louder ping for each minute.

I'm in acute care now, still right by the E.R. We have cubicles rather than real rooms. I call on my intercom; a voice says a doctor will come by.

I nod as if the voice could see me. I yearn to escape the time tyranny, and steel barbs of pain shoot me inside, coming and going. No rhyme or rhythm I hope, thus no labor pains.

Finally, shuffling footsteps, a doctor parts the curtains. He's somber, on the short side like Dr. Simonian, but his glasses are a smudged mess. He takes my pulse and brusquely, unconvincingly tells me everything's okay. "I'll send in the nurse-practitioner later." This is the loneliest I've ever been, and there's no one I can call.

"Yoo-hoo," echoes in the hall, signaling Mama and Papa's hilariously loud entry. This is their attempt at soft voices. Laughing, so much better than lonely.

Mama holds a bowl of fruit; Papa lugs an awkward bundle under his arm. He and his cane walk briskly along. He looks sharp, with his hair carefully combed back, like he used to for a day at the office. It's impossible to know he's very ill with cancer.

"Oh Liefje, why didn't you tell us?" asks Mama. I hope no reply and my big smile will carry us through. I used to hear it so often, *why didn't you tell us*? Usually as a teen, and my inside answer was, *you don't really want to know*. A very worn out excuse on my part by now.

Papa beams. "A baby, you are going to have a baby?"

It's one of the odd times their hopefulness brings out my worrier in contrast. I want to blurt out, *well, maybe. Don't count on everything turning out okay, not Baby, not cancer.* Their faces are broken open with hope, and I hate to attack rare unbridled Vanderveer joy. I won't spoil our happy-for-once-in-the-hospital mood, and respond enthusiastically. "Ja, what a surprise, heh? For Daniel and I too."

Papa bounces on his toes with excitement, awkward with his cane. "I called Daniel last night, right after he spoke to Alby. He's on his way as we speak. He knew you needed rest, so he decided not to call you."

"Oh, that's great," I say. Papa doesn't notice the divided feelings that hit me, relieved joy that Daniel will arrive soon, dread that he's too angry to talk to me, greater dread at what he'll find.

Mama peels an apple, the Dutch way with a paring knife, producing one long spiral. Papa adjusts the cubicle curtains so that we get a bit of outdoor light from a nearby window.

It still disturbs me that they look so happy; they should be warned. "I guess it's good Daniel's coming. A lot could still go wrong. I'll need him. And how are you, Papa?"

"Of course you'll need him, but not because you're worried. Stop it now," Mama says. "Dr. Ingstrom told us, when she asked us to come to that first family meeting, 'Sometimes you have to believe in miracles.' So believe in miracles, Liesbet."

She's serious using my given name, and Dr. Ingstrom said that? Amazingly, those words worked for Mama and Papa?

As if he can read my thoughts, Papa nods. He makes himself comfortable, no elaborate groans, or arranging his cane just right. He tucks it behind him. "Daughter, the greatest worries are behind us. You will know it for sure with more of Mama's and *mijn* stories of World War Two. You will know it when Daniel arrives. How am I? For now, no discussion of cancer treatment."

Of course we won't discuss. "Come on, Papa. At least tell me which lung cancer. I already know one kind is much worse than the other, and you don't want me to stress." *My trump card.*

"Okay, I have NSCLC. It means non-small cell lung cancer, which is the better kind. So enough then! And I'm in stage two, also good and treatable."

"But!"

Mama strokes my forehead with a wide, peaceful smile. "Really, liefje, enough. Look where you are, in the ER! That's where our focus will be."

What with their peaceful presence, I know I'll reflect on their shift in attitude for a long time. They practically force-feed me fruit, and I convince them to eat too. Papa's random coughs interrupt our conversations. I should never have written it off as only due to sneaking back to kreteks. I've been so focused on helping everyone my own way, that I am the obvious problem.

Like Alby, Mama looks at my medical chart at the foot of the bed. She was a midwife in Nederland and delivered over two hundred babies, a beloved career she couldn't practice in America. "Your blood pressure has been up. What are you so stressed about Liefje?"

"Nothing."

"Oh, we have all been in Alby's family appointments by now, and you tell me you have no feelings? No feeling of stress. Don't resent Alby." *Why don't I get to resent Alby, don't we all?* "Don't have any secrets of your own. Come on, liefje."

"I worry about Baby, is she's still a little life inside or..."

"Oh liefje, look what I brought."

She pulls out an odd shape. It looks a like a tool used to yell in the ear of a deaf person. But I recognize it. "Hmmm, from when our dog was pregnant when we were little?" Sure enough, we listened to tiny heartbeats.

"It's a pinard. And with all their expertise, doctors still don't know that a midwife's pinard can detect a fetal heartbeat before a stethoscope can."

Mama folds back my gown and covers expertly, to expose my belly and leans down with the cone-shaped pinard. The broad end goes on my belly, the narrow end on her ear. I'm glad her face is away from me, so I can't guess the results.

She stands, belly laughs, and kisses me wetly on the cheek. Yes, she is so happy. All I had to say indeed, instead of *travel*, was *I'm pregnant*. "We get to tell Alby no calcium blockers. Baby is fine."

"You must rest now." Papa glows, closing the curtains more gently than before.

"No-o-oh," I say in a childlike voice, bound to get results. "Just one story."

I see he does look weaker and gray, carefully leaning back on an uncomfortable chair, but I get my way. I feel a sharp pang of guilt, yet every story feeds me, eases me, especially now that I know Baby's Oma heard her heartbeat. We both look at Mama, she nods at Papa.

† † †

Jakob

Grogol
August 1944

Dawn. Hunger. Breakfast. *Meneer Krans, we have to see him, our corvées must be switched. Together we can explore the lay of the land here, and change the despicable sewage duty. I'll shake Albert to go queue up for food together.*

"The usual slop. Doesn't look any different from the sewage I messed with yesterday. Garbage goes in, garbage goes out."

"Don't talk so, Jakob. That's not good for anyone!" said Albert.

"What does it matter?"

Albert elbowed him hard and yelled right into his ear. "Watch your mouth!"

His ear rang with noise and hunger."Shut your trap!" He brought his foot down on top of Albert's, instantly sorry to see his pain. He hadn't kicked his brother since they were little boys.

The server shoved his face forward and snarled. "A fine one you are. Ja, I'll speak to Krans. We'll add you to kitchen duty and see you have no chance for extra pickings. You will only carry the hot barrels from the kitchen." Only a little bigger than Albert, and almost eye to eye with Jakob, the boy's eyes glared like obsidian shards.

Jakob's pulse thudded in his ears as he recognized Wolfie, from his Billiton bullying years. He surely ended up eating more scraps, with his kitchen duty, by the looks of him. He moved with more energy than others, and now he would have it out for them.

"See," hissed Albert. "You've attracted attention from that horrible Wolfgang. He is a wolf and you know it. He is going to hurt us. Such talk is bad, when all are suffering!"

Jakob closed his eyes, and then opened them wider. He wished fervently that Wolfie did not happen to recognize them. *I can't afford to add to Albert's woes, and Albert has no hard shell. I will no longer talk like this. My big mouth, now we need to find Meneer Krans before Wolfie does. His threat could be empty, just like his bullying words of old. But, caution first.*

"Don't be like the bitter old men who give up, gray before their time," Albert murmured. "No being sewn into burlap bags. At Tjideng they went into graves. Here they probably go into group graves."

Jakob tried to relax. Each time his eyes roamed about for Meneer Krans he tensed up again. Albert's talk of graves sounded like poetry, so strangely lovely it made his do's and don'ts make sense.

"Okay," said Jakob decisively. "I will find Meneer Krans. We will make different arrangements. *Alles regelen.*"

He made Albert laugh, with his Pappie imitation. "Yes," they said in unison, "we will make arrangements."

Outside, on a makeshift bench, the air was hotter. They did not continue to savor one hundred chews each of thin porridge mush; they knew they should go talk to Meneer Krans soon. Jakob crumbled the saved sugar he had wrapped in a banana leaf, into both of their bowls. They licked the leaf for every morsel.

Even tiny bits of food lift our spirits, thought Jakob, as they went in the right direction—away from Wolfie. His belly unknotted. Wolfie probably snarled at everyone; he was an unimportant bully. *What matters is having a better corvée, together.*

They saw Krans with another cell block leader. The man had a black eye, and swollen ear. Funny how nothing surprised anymore. If a block leader stood up for her people at Kamp Tjideng, she risked a beating. It must be the same here.

"Meneer Krans," said Albert. If Albert started a talk, then great determination was upon him.

"Ja," said Meneer Krans. Today they could see he appeared more skeletal than some, partly due to being well over two meters tall. His alert eyes flickered; he calmly pointed to places to hunker down and sit. He was still chewing his one hundred times, bowl in hand.

Albert spoke politely. "We are Albert Vanderveer and Jakob Vanderveer."

"Vanderveer? I have met your father."

"You have?" interrupted Jakob. "He is here?" For a moment he dreaded Pappie's fierceness, then a flood of joy bathed his heart. Somehow Pappie would have food, and salt tablets. He would make their bellies full, their heads clear. All would be well.

"No, no. Not at all boys. We were in that first horrid prison together."

"And how was Pappie?"

"Much better than here and now, we still had a visiting doctor, who brought in some medicinal cream for his skin lesions. Hungry like the rest of us, but those infections, they got better. You have a tough father."

When your pappie could be strict, then also, he could be tough. This is what it took to be a man.

"Thank you," said Albert. "You saw him alive and healing." They sat fully against the wall near Mr. Krans. Albert was always more accepting. No questions.

"How long ago then?" asked Jakob.

"Oh, not so long ago," said Meneer Krans.

But where was Pappie? And how long had he been well?

"Remember boys, there are near a quarter million POWs and civilians held prisoner."

Jakob breathed the morning air, already stale and sickening. Numbers were one thing, but no information? "So," he started, "about our corvée ..."

Meneer Krans smiled and leaned in to them. "And how do you want to earn your keep here, with all of us guests of the emperor?"

Jakob wanted to laugh. In spite of what Krans did not say; he had humor. Did he have children that he missed, or maybe even sons who were here? Albert was too slow to follow up on an advantage, so he said in a rush, "I have sewage duty and Albert is chopping furniture."

"We want to have the same corvée and watch out for each other," finished Albert.

"So then. You are very wise; I will have you both do sewage."

"What? Meneer, that is heavy, dirty work," protested Jakob.

Albert pulled on his shoulder, and said with a dead voice, "Yes, it is. So, well, you put us together."

"Really, Meneer Krans, there must be something else," said Jakob, not giving up. Pappie wouldn't have given up.

"This is for your own good. You will see."

They plodded along to corvée. Perhaps they each had the same dark, mean thoughts, not to be said out loud. *Where is Pappie? For you own good — the worst words adults said. Adults, so useless in the kamps, acting like they had authority. What does Meneer Krans know? This is all Jakob's fault, no surprise. Albert must take charge more, he's the older brother.*

Jakob decided to be cheery. "Guests of the emperor. We'll see what he means."

Boys waited for them. Another new one was Wouter, smiling. "Hoi."

Jakob grinned back. He couldn't help himself. Although annoying, Wouter could truly be cheery—like Sara. He hated to think of family; it hurt too much. *May she be well, she could be playing with Tina.*

316

"Hoi," said Rollie.

A few other boys stood around. In another world, the one with food, Rollie would have a lanky but strong build, maybe become a track star. He'd be the guy with long legs and wiry muscles, conquering hurdles. But instead he was bare-bones thin, and somehow had energy. "Okay — assigning new partners. We will be our own corvée crew, and we watch out for each other. So for now, Jakob, I'll pick you again. We're about the same height for the bucket brigade. You're my temporary addition as my partner is in hospital."

"Oh, sorry," said Jakob. Many did not come back from hospital.

"So, at least this is a good corvée." Rollie grinned and made croaking noises.

"What do you mean?" Wouter asked.

"Shh, not so loud; the guards will be right back. You will see. Not a word to anyone about what you learn. Always have a lookout at the end of the day, no matter where you are. Be on time always and ready to carry heavy buckets. We have to show we are a strong-boys' corvée, or lose this duty." He croaked again. "Do not think of more sewage, think of food."

Jakob didn't wish to question loudly as Wouter did. Hours went into clearing ditches, and carrying overflow buckets to the wagon going out to the farm fields. The smell rose eternally as they worked in pairs, Wouter and Albert together as one unit, Rollie and Jakob another, the other boys too. The guards had returned. One obvious advantage of sewage duty was that guards kept their distance due to the stench.

Rollie grunted during a quick pause. "Are you sick from the smell, and breathing by mouth? Come on now, let's swallow the flies."

"Just as delicious as yesterday." Jakob laughed until he bent over, tears flowing. He had to gasp to stop. Rollie laughed too. Their Indo guard, among those the Japanese had recruited, smiled too, and had not made a single effort to beat them for speaking in Dutch. When they slowed down however, he screamed. They ran from one part of a ditch to another, slipping in their bare feet near a deep channel. Jakob became terrified of sliding right in.

At the hottest part of the day, they stopped for a watery lunch: a few pieces of green and fish eyes. The worst was carrying the larger buckets on a pole between them again, after. The similar height was of extreme importance. Each shoulder already raw, all bone, as starvation had chiseled away any padding. He felt deeply bruised, even sliced into. Jakob hoped his skin had not been broken. Did Rollie have calloused shoulders?

Dullness set in at the end of the day. And then, they were dismissed. Following Rollie's signals they all lingered and casually circled around to a walled area of the ditches.

Rollie pointed. "Drop your buckets and poles here. This is a brief time, when we can hunt." The other boys left with purpose, one with a grin, another with a shrug. "You brothers can work together. Wouter you will be with me, no chattering."

"Ja," Wouter said rather loudly. Rollie grinned and punched him in the arm. Wouter nodded gravely, lips pressed shut, and followed him without a sound.

They were along a wall near the outer fencing, a dangerous place as the guards patrolled the area. Rollie pulled a small net down from the top of the wall. The boys were soundless, the frogs so loud, and numerous, sewage must be a feast. Jakob's neck prickled, worried an approaching guard's footsteps would not be heard. Rollie scooped twice, coming up each time with a full net. Hands flashing he grasped each frog by the legs and smashed them against the wall. Frog juice, oddly clear, splattered down. Then he netted and Wouter smashed frogs, grinning again. If one wiggled, he gave its neck a twist. The pair dropped their prey into their shorts. Wouter shivering, doing a dance, settling down. Rollie grinned and squeezed his arm.

Soon Rollie indicated through pantomime where to grab the other net, and how to keep lookout. Rollie and Wouter quickly disappeared. Other boys, nearby, soundlessly massacred their frogs.

Jakob looked, and saw no one. Albert had the net. Hundred of frogs remained, an endless food supply. "You watch, I'll scoop," whispered Albert.

Jakob reached for the net, shaking his head, but Albert scooped fluidly — six frogs already. He scooped again. Jakob saw the dull green of a guard coming their way in, and started a low whistle, their old signal for *Pappie's nearby*. Albert stretched the net up to its hiding place. They could not risk scooping again. They crowded together, low so as not to be seen and smashed frogs against the wall, dropping them into their shorts. Wet warm frogs felt like the misery of diarrhea, and worse, with their death wiggles. Albert wheeled as if to run, but Jakob grabbed him by the elbow. "Like smuggling, Albert. Walk; look like nothing is going on."

When they returned, Wouter and Rollie came to find them.

"This only works certain days," Rollie explained when they arrived. Four boys kept watch while the rest of them skewered frogs, roasting them over a fire. Wouter sat as if he would faint, and started to eat one raw.

"No," said Albert. "You'll get sick."

"He's right," said Rollie. "Wait."

Wouter already had a foot inside his mouth. He bit it off. "Oof," he said, chewing and gagging it down. He had the wild look some had before they screamed in the night or ran out of line, a look like Mammie when she first knew the boys had to leave Tjideng.

"Okay, Wouter. We'll roast the rest." Rollie put out his hand.

Wouter handed the frog over.

Two boys fanned a small fire, made of bricks on the outside, and twigs in between, roasting skewered frogs. No one came. Bits of fat dropped off. A couple of boys had spoons to catch the drippings, eventually passing the spoons down the line. Jakob yearned to poke out his fingers to catch the fat and lick it off, but he thought of Wouter, and knew he'd wait for more.

They ate their frog delicacies in turn, switching lookouts. Each bite nourishing, piping hot, smoky, a little like chicken. "Delicious," Jakob said. Many little bones, which they chewed and sucked out the marrow, burying the tiny remains. The bricks were moved with sticks by the wall, smoke darkened side down.

He strolled back to the huts and the food line, relieved at having nothing to hide. No late afternoon dizziness today. Wouter trailed them. They lined up for dinner. Meneer Krans stood ten men away. Albert went to him and returned. "I told him thank you."

"You spoke of frogs!" Jakob worried.

"Of course not!"

Neither stared at the soup ladle as hard. There was almost enough.

Wouter came back with them, settled back against a wall, and chewed his thin broth one hundred times. Albert hummed as he ate, something he hadn't done since Tante Ankie fixed their dinners. Wouter lowered his head. He brought his hands up to his throat, loud burps became retching.

Jakob patted him. "Take it easy."

Wouter shook his head violently, ran just a few feet away. "No, not here," said Jakob, who leapt up and ran close to him, whispering urgently. "You could make all of us sick, and what about suspicious Japanese?"

He hauled him to the closest sewage ditch. "Here, I'll hold you." Something like what Baboe had done for him before, but by the sink, bedroom chamber pot, or garden shed.

Wouter bent over again and again, soon on his hands and knees, till nothing more could come out. "Thank you. Oof, I feel so bad."

"You will be okay," said Jakob, trying to sound nice, like Baboe. "We will get you some food another day. Be patient."

Wouter nodded, clutching his stomach.

When they came back, Albert smiled at Jakob for his kindness.

"Certainly dysentery," sighed a nearby, very old man, who had not spoken before. Almost as tall as Meneer Krans, it looked like every movement pained him. His legs were swollen from beriberi.

He will die soon, thought Jakob, and he found guilty relief in not caring for this man. When gray-heads swelled up like this, they rarely survived.

"Bad news," said Albert loudly to indicate, *Let him think that*.

If everyone hunted frogs at the same time, the Japanese would find out. They were odd; it could be the food they forbade, it could be the little cooking fires forbidden outside the kitchen, it could be looking away too quickly or looking too long.

That night as Albert pierced sleep immediately as always, Jakob heard the usual camp chorus, but louder and manlier than Tjideng. Thousands of men-boys murmuring, coughing, moaning, crying out. Was Wouter near? Meneer Krans had been kind to them. Rollie had been kind to Wouter. In turn Jakob had been kind to Wouter, telling him everything would be alright.

We four maneuvered well, Wouter, Rollie, Albert, and I. Albert and I became a team. Every boy was carefully watching out for each other, like a wolf pack, Mowgli's wolf pack. This brought thoughts of his brother Wim in Nederland, making his chest

321

hurt. Kipling's *The Jungle Book* was the first book they read together, usually with Albert too. On special occasions Sara could be in the wolf pack too. The aching expanded until he imagined Wim careening away from Germans, with wolf-pack friends of his own. He had to be safe. At last, copying Albert's steady breathing, he pierced sleep himself.

CHAPTER 17

Luce

Houston, Texas
January 2005

I spent a full, relatively peaceful night, considering the hourly nurses' checks, and a not-so-great promise that I'll be transferred from the no-man's land called acute care to a standard hospital room today.

The breakfast tray arrives, which I ordered off of the cute menu-style hospital printout. I'm to think I'm being pampered, instead of, *Ugh, hospital food*. Lunch will be a cheeseburger with french fries and vegetables. Dinner will be Salisbury steak, something no patient can be tricked with, as it is slabs of protein found only in school or hospital cafeterias.

I eat my cereal and fruit and feel funny. Oh, oh, it's a flutter, what's known as quickening, Baby's first detectable kicks. So she is alive and we have everything we need. I could sing loudly. If it were wise I'd jump up and dance panoramically like Julie Andrews in *The Sound of Music*. I journal, I read the book Cindy brought me with concentration. Every breath says peace, hope.

† † †

"Fruit for you," comes a familiar voice.

Alby. He, too, has an elated glow as he walks in briskly, holding his Daily Reflections AA meditation book and a cafeteria bowl of grapes.

"Hello, Alby. Yum, but too late, look what Mama brought me yesterday, just like when we were little. When we were sick, it was always apples first, then bananas and oranges."

"Good, and I felt great last night. Endurance told me your pains had stopped, and I slept really, really well." He sighs dramatically. "I let go and let God."

"Oh, you let go, you really let go," I tease back.

So I do have the old Alby back. I love to make family happy — spent my whole childhood trying to make them happy. If I had known that he, too, would be this over-the-top thrilled for me and Baby, I would have filled him in as well. Then I would have stayed in Calabria, and I would be free of worry attacks.

Alby arranges grapes and orange sections on a plate for me, and then slices a banana. His hands shake a little; I guess it could be the new medication or prolonged detox, or — I remember with an involuntary pain jerk from my leg — central nervous system damage from all the substance abuse.

The same gruff doctor from yesterday comes by. I guess he's tired from seeing only acute care patients. "Well dear, you never had labor pains. The sonogram shows that you have PGP, pelvic girdle pain. In some older women especially, it's exacerbated by pregnancy. But, since you are at a high-risk age we need to stabilize you, reduce your pain, and lower your stress. I'll send a psychiatric social worker around to talk to you. Are you always this high stress? There are some pain medications you could take … "

"No," Alby and I say together.

He sits quietly, no wise cracks until the doctor leaves. "Ha-ha, welcome to my world. Psych eval, pain management." He rubs his hip.

"Does it ever stop hurting?"

"The hip? Never, but I sure experience it as less. It's just like they say, opiate pain meds skew your sense of pain."

The old Alby *is* back, a casual admission of opiate addiction. We both eat bits of fruit. He opens the meditation book. Like the best part of what we shared as teenagers, he starts to read. "When you seek first the Kingdom of God, all else will follow."

My second year in the Honesty Open-mindedness Willingness Program, Alby limped into the family car and came along to meetings. I was seventeen by then, he was sixteen. We laughed, we enjoyed everyone. As teens we did every crazy thing with these new friends except continue to get high and drunk.

It had taken six slow months for Alby to come home from the combination of hospital and nursing home rehabs. It took another confusing six months after that for him to admit to me he spent his days after school smoking marijuana and maximizing his pain-pill use.

I vaguely remember him copping to the drugs with me, and we never told our parents. Do they know now? I feel another small flurry. "Hey Alby, Baby just gave me a little bitty kick!" *The pinard heartbeat, two flutter kicks in one day. Thank you God.*

"Alright!" His face relaxes as we finish the meditation of the day, ending with, "Go into your day. Do your best to think God's thoughts after Him, and follow His will."

"For me, thinking God's thoughts after Him will be 'everything is okay with Baby.' What will you think?"

He raises his eyebrows. "Of course everything is okay with Baby." Then his face sinks back to his usual sad, dark shadows underneath his eyes, which flash dark blue and intense. With a jolt I remember Papa saying, *He could pass for Indo and escape the kamps, as long as he hid those eyes.*

"Are you worried about your work? What they might find out?" I surprise myself by being the one to bring up his job to put a happy spark back in his eyes.

He smiles slowly. "No, I don't worry. As far as confidentiality here works, what happens at New *Feasta* stays at New *Feasta*, and Dr. Ingstrom insists the board is holding my job for me. They want me back. With more than three medication patents to my name, I'm gold for them. I forget these things when I freak out. How about you, are you worrying big?"

"Oddly, no," I lie. After all, I'm relaxed now. "Your wife told me all about mares and baby colts and how everything turns out okay. I'm sure my little filly will be fine." I warm my belly with my hands.

"Yeah, Cindy can be spiritual. She has lots of patience left for you, Marina, Wade, and every horse on any ranch around for miles." He sighs. "But not for me."

"Should she still be patient with you?" I say sharply.

"No, Luce, she shouldn't. Our marriage is what I worry about now. You don't even know some of the things I've done, the conferences she hasn't been able to reach me at, wondering what I was up to. And I of course was up to no good."

"And she's still here for you."

"Yeah, and I still want her, if she can still love me."

"So you're stay—"

"Staying? Yes, I am." He turns to go.

"Wait!" I call. I can't be alone with my painful thoughts. I know Alby called Daniel, yet no calls, no nothing.

He spins around, surprised. For some reason I feel humbled, like I'm asking the greatest favor. "Tell me more of the stories from Papa I missed."

"Sure," he says, smiling gently, tugging at my heart strings again.

"Papa said once, 'Albert was not a fierce fighter like me.'"

"Ja," Alby says simply. "I think our uncle died in a fight, and Papa couldn't help him. Maybe he could save only one, himself."

† † †

Jakob

Kamp Grogol
September 1944

Once he talked to the old man who had beri-beri, it surprised Jakob how eager he was to see him at the end of the day. Smaken dragged himself to furniture chopping corvée each day, overseeing the boys who destroyed and stacked. He probably never fought anyone before, and also didn't try to best the Japanese now. Yet Jakob had to admit Meneer Smaken was fighting to talk, a brave battle of some sort, words between wheezes and gurgles of hunger edema going into his lungs.

"I hear you asked Meneer Krans to assign you together. You are good brothers." his voice went away with the wet coughing of his swollen body. He switched to whispering. "Good brothers to each other you are. Be sure to always stick together like you do."

Albert said, "Meneer Smaken, everyone says you must go to the hospital, get treatment for your hunger edema."

Meneer Smaken spoke up. "Yes, everyone has directed me. But no one comes back from that hospital alive."

"That is wrong. Some come back, you must give it a chance," said Jakob.

Smaken's rattly underwater breathing went on; it would keep them all awake tonight. He belonged in hospital. Should they make him go, carry him? He looked up at Albert's concerned face.

In spite of frog-hunting episodes, Albert looked weak, each movement slow, the whites of his eyes yellow, his hand shaking as he touched Smaken's swollen leg.

Right this moment Jakob would hate to make him help shoulder Meneer Smaken. *And who am I to say he cannot stay with us? And Albert always listens to these old men, even now.*

Later, Albert could sleep instantly. Jakob was left with Smaken's uneven gasps for air. Every time there was almost a rhythm to his breath, he rattled or hesitated. Jakob tried picturing Mollie purring at Kokkie's house, or Wim and Pappie. Wim was with the Dutch underground, smuggling radio parts, keeping the communication going. Pappie led the men in his kamp like Meneer Krans here. Soon the pictures jumbled together. His last image was of Meneer Smaken's pained smile as he said, "Good brothers."

In the morning as he and Albert got ready for sewer corvée, Smaken rasped, "Come here."

Jakob yearned to pretend he hadn't heard. They had to line up for food first, no time for a stubborn old man. But Albert was already by him, so he leaned down too.

Smaken held up his canteen to Jakob. "Here, you boys need this, with your corvée. When you do find decent water, you can use it."

"Here, pure water?" Jakob grinned.

"When I die, keep the canteen, and anything else that is mine. You boys will live to tell the story of this place."

"But you will not die," said Albert staunchly.

"No." He sighed and groaned, rolling to his side.

They agreed Albert would line up. Jakob held the canteen under a dripping spout, in turn with the others. The timing had to be right, so he could still join his brother in time for the front of the food line. No he thought, the old man will not die yet. He'll keep me awake again.

They made it through a day with no roasted frogs, but water to fill them, a small comfort.

Albert rushed back, Jakob following him. Smaken could have been moved to hospital, beaten for not being in hospital, or worse. Albert stood stock still when he reached the lump of humanity, which was Smaken.

Was he resting? Jakob bent down, lifting and lowering his wrist. "Still bendy, but cool to the touch. He is dead," he stated casually. But he did not feel casual. He thought the stupid, like Wouter, would die first. Or the bad like Wolfie and black market traders who kept too much food for themselves. But too often it was the good and the kind who died. Smaken had been truly concerned, passing along his canteen. Jakob shrugged his shoulders. *Well, he got to leave this hell.*

"His spirit is gone," said Albert.

"He gave up," said Jakob. "Some people fight to live. Meneer Smaken believed he would die, and decided to die the way he wanted to, like old Indians in America. Those old Indians left the teepee village to die. Smaken would have done so if he could."

"He looks peaceful, like an old Indian." Albert leaned down and closed the old man's eyes. "I'll go get a bag, and to tell Meneer Krans to send the wagon."

Jakob waited for moments, wishing he could hold his compass, his cowboy book, anything. Soon enough they sewed him loosely into the burlap bag. Handling his legs they felt only bone and swollen flesh; hunger edema water already releasing.

"Good-bye, Meneer Smaken," whispered Albert.

The wagon came, another corvée of boys who still had shreds of strength the men had lost. They helped heave and lift.

"He was a good man," Jakob surprised himself by saying. They stared after the boys hauling the bodies-wagon. It left a dark wavering stripe in the dust, life fluids released from the swelling of the dead. *Yes, he was good man, even if he put us in danger by staying out of appel this morning. We lied and said he was in hospital, and the Japs didn't check. Satisfaction, at least one danger is gone.*

Jakob and Albert hefted the bundle Smaken always kept close. It clunked towards Albert, oddly heavy. Unfastening the fabric, they found a photo of Meneer Smaken, his wife, and a boy close to their age. They looked just like Mammie and Pappie in their bright white tropical clothes, escaping the heat of the day on the veranda.

With their thorough record keeping, the Japanese would most likely inform Smaken's family. Albert pulled out shorts and a tattered shirt. "Good, we are completely out of fabric."

"Ja," said Jakob. He reached in for the rock, it rolled. He held up a tin can. Swiftly he snatched it close to his body. "Look!"

"What?" asked Albert.

"Here, condensed milk, a large can. It could have saved his life and now it's ours." In the end had it become more important to Smaken to possess the milk, than drink it for himself? Jakob's mouth watered; he was sure Albert's did too. They moved together to their own hidden gear. They transferred the milk carefully to the hole they had dug underneath their sleeping platform.

The next evening they visited the gravesite where ten bodies were buried. They brought their knife and fashioned crossed pieces of wood, carving it to read Adriaan Smaken, October 1944. They lingered after the few others left. "He was a kind man," said Albert.

Later that night, and every night thereafter, they sauntered outside, always finding a way to bring the can they had punctured in two spots, tap tapping it with their knife again and again to have the precious milk. Jakob excelled at distracting others at first with conversation, while Albert walked away with their treasure. Albert was no good at subterfuge. Each night they reunited by the roasted-frog wall. Jakob wondered if Albert, too, had Smaken's family photo behind his eyes, the good life once offered. Kokkie serving coconut milk with their breakfast, another full meal before *tidur siang*, then a light supper for when the Pappie came home; now light supper would be a feast.

After their milk ration sank in, they smuggled the can back, wrapped upright with Smaken's shirt.

In contrast to the temporary sweetness of evening times, getting up in the morning was an act of courage. The predictable and unpredictable kamp life chased away daydreams of food, leaving the terror of hunger pains, hard labor, and ubiquitous lice. The predictable unpredictable meant dead men found, a yelling man going crazy, thuds to silence him before the Japs came, and having to hold a bow in appel endlessly before *naore* was called. Yet Jakob woke easier. With the careful one swallow per night, Meneer Smaken's salvation continued for two weeks.

† † †

Luce

Houston, Texas
January 2005

The wheelchair sticks on turns, like getting the bad grocery cart at the supermarket. Wheels click-clack rhythmically as an aide takes me from the ICU version of an OB-GYN room to a shared room. Upgrade! I'm now low risk and in a safety zone of sorts. Every time the wheels jar me, pain stabs down both legs. I clench my knees together. *Breathe, breathe, gratitude, no IV jerking along with us.*

Only maternity and pediatric patients get the nice rooms like this one. The curtain between the beds glows peach like the in utero photos of a tiny amber fetus, in old *Life* magazines. I had them tacked up during pregnancy number three, to help me affirm a healthy outcome that never came. An easy chair graces each bedside. The hospital room's walls hold framed photographs of Texas nature scenes: bluebonnet wildflowers, an old weather vane, a barn, as if the decorator knew that with all the waiting and pain in OB-GYN, comforting images are needed. The double room has no roommate, what a relief.

I wonder if the other bed will be filled with a mom and brand-new baby just to torture me. I'd rather stare at the stark walls. By the time the other woman arrives to give birth, or to hold a healthy newborn, I might be saying good-bye to our baby, mourning her passing. I'm deliberating, since it's been over four hours since I last felt Baby. They'll try to reassure me, but there could be no explanation for on and off fluttering, and then today—nothing.

I'm dripping with sweat by the time the aide settles me in the by the window. Comfort eases in and I even have a gel pad underneath under the mattress pad. Someone got the word out about my level of distress. I often feel I deserve to suffer through this pain, which comes and goes like waves on a flat beach. Pain crashes, slows, and ebbs away. I breathe slowly some more, easing in, sweat evaporating under the air conditioning blasts. I hate these artificial hospital moments. No beach, no hills, no fresh air.

"Okay? How's the pain level?" asks the aide.

"Pretty bad, but lying still and stretching my back and legs out a bit does help. I know by now that when I'm arranged just right, the throbbing passes."

"Good. I'll see if the orthopedic MD is going to come by. It could take her awhile."

Just like that, perhaps due to a mention of waiting, a rushing of panic pulses in my ears with rapid heartbeats. I strive to pray, strive to ease my breaths, strive to still my thoughts, but they skitter away like the quick squeaks of footsteps striding along in the hallway. The aide neglected to arrange my few things. If I could hold my morning meditation book in my hands, I would feel at home and relax. Even my pen and journal would bring me back to myself. I have no words, no peace. I send breath deep into my womb to Baby; surely she is fine and will flutter kick again soon. Someone nears my room. Suddenly I know the cadence of those steps, Daniel!

He peeks around the corner of the door, grinning.

"Daniel, you're here!"

He scoops his arms around me tenderly, gently easing me up the bed and hugging all at once. One little pain, I tense.

"Pain, huh?"

No hiding from him. "Yes, but hardly any now. I'm sorry you had to come so far. The doctor says I never had labor pains."

"Yeah, Albert told me."

"And you kept talking to him and not to me?" I hold Daniel's hand in my favorite way—wrapped around his thumb and forefinger. His hands are far larger than mine. It makes me feel like his love always holds me. And just like that, the dizzying panic is gone.

He doesn't answer. Surely what Daniel is thinking, but not saying is, *you didn't have to stress yourself by going so far from home.* That's why he chose not to talk to me, I know. "So, why didn't you ever call me?"

"Luce, I could see you've been in a state of fear-filled red alert. I have a long list of frustrations too. I knew I had to be in front of you to say, what matters now is peace for all of us."

"Vincent?"

"He's fine."

So what constitutes Daniel's long list of frustrations? All the times we went along with family vacation plans to suit Alby's work schedule? The three times I traveled for his rehabs? All the times Papa gave us endless advice instead of just asking, *how's everything going?*

How many times have I wondered where Corrie is, apparently too driven by her marketing job to come visit in California? But I've been just as driven as Corrie. No one else I know would take a plane flight in the midst of a high-risk pregnancy. I hate it when my family members force results, especially Papa and Alby. Yet that's exactly what I've been doing, driving myself hard. I like to think of myself as a thoughtful, caring person, but I'm not. I never thought out this travel. If Baby is still okay, I don't deserve her to be okay. I don't deserve Baby, but she deserves to live. On top of it all, Daniel sees my stress and knows that I'm my own worst enemy.

God, you have said that Your love has nothing to do with being deserving. Please grant grace and let Baby live. Each flutter kick made me smile. But I've felt nothing after Alby's visit. I'll try for tenuous peace again. Surely Baby is just sleeping and will flutter kick soon. I groan.

"What is it?" asks Daniel.

I force a smile for Daniel. "Oh, just hoping this room stays empty and that I can finally sleep."

Daniel kisses and pats my forehead. "Let's rest then."

He lounges back and is immediately into one of his quick catnaps. I match his breathing and drift off to sleep.

We both open our eyes at the same time.

"I'm so sorry you had to come all this way." I check his face for response.

"So you've learned to apologize?" He smiles wanly. "Don't worry, I had to be with you, just as much as you had to be with Jake." He must tire of reassuring me.

"Okay, no more apologizing." I do my best attempt at brightness. "Tell me more then."

"Well, Vincent's been too quiet about term papers and schoolwork, so who knows what's going on."

"I know. He was supposed to do a research paper on Martin Luther King, to turn in right before the holiday. The rough draft was due at the end of his Christmas break."

"He was?"

"I told you before I left." I should have been there. I see Vincent the way he is when he has to switch from the pictures in his head to words. He'll give up. I always tell clients that teenagers need just as much attention as toddlers, and here I am far away, risking everything. I'd like to care for him as well as Pake and Beppe took care of the extra lamb which often ended up in Dutch farmhouses. In

Friesland, the farming province, whenever an ewe had twins, she chose one and rejected the other. I feel like I'm here with a chosen, lifeless lamb, while no one cares for the other. Farmers like Pake and Beppe took the rejected lamb into the farm house, for bottle feeding. This way the extra lamb would live.

I imagine Vincent's lost look. He'll be off with a sketchpad, which may become meaningless, if we never hear all of Grandpa's story. I ache to have our nightly talks, sometimes skipped now that he's older, sometimes amazing. I would tell him how precious he is. I have to be there to tell him that.

Daniel taps my hand. "Luce, you're spacing out on me already. He's supposed to track his own paper, do the necessary steps, and notice the deadlines. Pastor Sam told us he has to be responsible for himself some time."

I think of our Youth Pastor, way too relaxed and young. "But now? Like this?"

His face tightens. "Yes, now."

"Okay, yeah, I'll try not to worry and space out. How's your work?"

We're both avoiding talking about Baby. I know his concern is about me anyway, Dads are like that. But I can't imagine how I'll survive if I've lost her. He eases back. "Actually I have a lot of extra pick-up routes planned. Had to send Karl to sub for me the this whole week. He'll be on call, in case I need him next week. I'm sure glad he's semiretired and can do this." Lines of pale white around his eyes and mouth appear. If we were home, and he wasn't worried about me and Baby, he wouldn't be so drained, or miss even one day of work.

"My being here's got you worrying about money."

"Luce, you, Vincent, and Baby are my life. Money doesn't come into this right now." His voice catches. "We'll still have income while Karl finishes subbing. That's the point of having a sub." He looks out the window, a view of wall, ten feet away. It must be the back of the cafeteria, not a hint of landscaping. Some light green crabgrass vines straggle up faded red brick. "Most of the work I'll still do. It's just postponed, not lost." He grins wide, trying to cheer us both up. "We can go home soon. Your doctor says you have to have bed rest."

"Great, I'll just need a couple of weeks to shut everything down when I get home, before I go on full rest."

He jerks to his feet. "Luce, start calling clients today. You will be on bed rest when we get back!"

He's never yelled like this. It's worse than Papa's full-blown outbursts. My heart hammers fast. Do I feel Baby flutter after all? Now I can't tell. "Really, you're going to make me call today?"

He glares at me. "Yes, now. Let go of the money worries, we've always made it through, and we will again. Let go of your dad and mom's World War Two history. It will stay. Let go of Alby. He cared enough to call me, he's not so bad off."

"You're right. But the doctor hasn't said total bed rest, so you are jumping the gun. It takes two weeks notice, at minimum, to take a leave of absence from my practice."

"Don't twist the doctor's words, and don't you dare twist Dr. Simonian's words! He told me he was amazed you were traveling. Everything's an excuse for you. Even your Dad's cancer, what you really want is to hear his story! You're supposed to avoid anything stressful."

A new person strides in, I see her psych badge, the social worker! She spins right around. "I'll come back." Good Daniels didn't see who it was. Ironic that a social worker here to help me with stress, just escaped our stress.

"No one said I had to stay home," I say in a little voice.

Daniel goes right on, still loud. His face is red and he's clutching the sides of the easy chair. "Dr. Simonian told me! Luce you pride yourself on talking things through, but you've created as much chaos as your family does. No, you won't be working two weeks in the office first! What's wrong with you? I thought you got it how serious this is."

I'm dizzy. I don't feel Baby after all, and I sure don't want to tell Daniel she might be already gone. Must I keep remembering the soccer-field-day sonogram when our baby's heartbeat had already stopped? "Why are you attacking me? Your yelling is stressing me out. I heard the doctor and of course I'll be careful. We need to be practical about my income too, overhead for the office, all of that."

He turns away, speaking softly. "Luce, I'm not attacking you. It's hard enough worrying about money. You say Baby's well-being is everything, yet you take off across the country as if you can guarantee that she's okay. You don't feel like she is okay right now, do you?"

I can't answer, because he's hit too close to the truth. "That's why I said I'm sorry you had to come this far. I finally realized that I was taking chances I was never meant to take."

He sits back down in the chair. "You think you are such a spiritual person and all. You do your Bible study, go to AA meetings, and talk to Kemble. I spoke to Kemble too."

My heart sinks like I'm a bad kid. I should have told Kemble I'm in hospital. I bet she would have yelled at me for the first time ever too. Papa always yelled.

"Are you listening to her? Are you listening to God? Even now you say you'll be careful, but your plans will keep you busy as always. Isn't that what you say about Alby — that he always does what he was going to do anyway?"

Being compared to Alby is like a punch to the gut. "Yeah," I whisper.

He looks at me questioningly because he can't hear me, and arises to lean up against the bed.

"Yeah, I say that," I repeat. I get it that Daniel loves me, but thinks I'm insane — the AA kind of insane, Alby's kind of insane, where you don't do what's good for you. He thinks I'm just as bad as Alby, without the drugs as an excuse.

"What can I say?" I stare at Daniel, plucking at my blanket, wishing to hold on to him again.

"Then that's how it will be. We're both letting go, stepping up in faith," Daniel lowers his hands on either side of my head, shaking the bed accidentally.

"Ouch!"

"Sorry, hurt?" He kisses me gently, to my relief. "Stop worrying. Stop doing. Resistance is futile." He laughs. It's what the mind-control Borg machine-people say, a line from our favorite modern-stay *Star Trek*. Following the *Star Trek* tractor beam into war history was stupid. All it's done is get me in here agonizing over my senselessness.

"So, okay I can sleep here, and keep you company. The easy chair is designed for overnight visitors."

"I will rest, and rest better alone. You know how I am." The worry's too much; I need to be alone. If I have caused our fourth miscarriage, I don't deserve my beloved's company. It is worse to see his love for me now, when I'm in need of comfort, because the pressure behind my emotional dam will break. I'll sob and burden him with everything. "Thanks, darling, but please go home. Mama and Papa need you too, and you always rest well there."

He rolls his eyes. "Yep, with all the fuss that comes with it."

"You know how hard it is for anyone to sleep in a hospital, and you'll be snoring, and end up being one more noise in the OB-GYN unit keeping me awake."

He ducks his head and grins. His snoring reaches Vincent's room on the far side of our hallway at home. "Okay."

"Tomorrow they'll surely discharge me. You need some rest yourself."

"Yeah, we both must be exhausted. I hope you have made some work exit calls by the time I'm back in the morning."

I curl up small on my side, in no shape to make cancellation calls. Did I feel Baby flutter again? No, I was the one moving just now. Must be my imagination.

I lay for an hour, not able to rest, not ready to get up. Where is everybody? First I had too many visitors, and now I sent the one person I really need, away. When Cindy comes back, I'll ask to hear her stories, all about tiny creatures safely born. Funny how I've always needed stories. Is that part of why I am balking about closing my therapy office? I will miss client stories.

I would welcome a new roommate, even if she is glowing with a healthy pregnancy and about to pop. I would welcome Conflict Avoidant Social Worker, as long as she comes right now.

I scrabble for the journal and pen. With wiggling and pillow punching I find a way to write on my side. Ironically, my journal shows I was overjoyed three weeks ago, no entries about puzzling out the decision to travel. The writing looks like flowing love from a good mother, who would never risk Baby. I sigh and write.

† † †

January 6, 2005

Dear God,

I hate to write these words, but please take my despair. Has Baby died inside me, like the last miscarriage? When I saw a live Sophia for the last miscarriage, and then a no heartbeat the next month, I found a grief I could almost touch. For the first time an image of a baby who once lived, and then died. There is a chance that Baby is alive and fine. I must find peace and stop this terror. Oh please, please God, let everything be good.

I couldn't bear to have Daniel be here for another miscarriage. He came all this way for nothing. I can't even call Kemble. She told me not to come on this trip. She knew something horrible would happen. I think Kemble and Daniel were Your messengers, a clear, "No!" And I didn't listen.

Vincent was too little for the first and second miscarriages. He never knew what happened. With the third I told him. Now we'll have to tell him again. And he'll be upset, it will be so clear to him why — his mom's crazy carelessness. Why wasn't it clear to me? Why not till now when it's probably too late? Vincent always tells me I leave Calabria way too much to see the rest of the family. I always said no, not too much, but he's right.

And then there's what I can't talk about God, not remembering the goodbye with Beppe and Pake, nor my sweet Beppe's death. Not that I was there of course. Once or twice Mama said I was the one hurt the most by all our moves. True. I thought till now that they didn't want to hear what I had to say, but I realize finally there were gentle, clear enough invitations, which I never answered.

The weight of dusty old things I don't want to say, because I never did, like why I pretended to be nonchalant about Mama and Papa attending parents' HOW. It's the same old thing; I don't want to see their pain or guilt. I don't want to need anyone, and be hurt. They can need me instead. Ugh, I don't want to write another word. Please help, dear, loving God.

CHAPTER 18

Something must have pinged in the hallway to wake me; it's early, the window still dark. I'm sick and tired of hospitals wanting you to heal, but not letting you sleep. *I am lonely*. I stare at the blank brick wall, craning my neck see first light, and discover color at the base of the wall. Orange paintbrushes, wildflowers in winter time. I love wildflowers, planting themselves, unstoppable. I glance at the clock, and push the bed button to raise myself. I remember Daniel brought strawberries and eat hungrily, discarded tops turning the napkin pink. Whatever my worries, I can't fix them.

Lonely is familiar, lonely is reliable. Lonely is the home that I never had to give up, almost a good place to be, because nothing worse ever happens there, although little good happens either. I was so often alone growing up.

If I let Daniel know my loneliness, my truest fears, not the ones I want him to reassure me out of, as if that is his job, it would be this: I am so afraid that the reality beyond all my sturdy and tenuous faith is that I have lost Baby already. The shadows from my past grip me. I used to tell myself it was somewhat comforting to have a sonogram image of our last miscarriage, our baby already lost, no movement, no heartbeat, no insistent thump-thump. But now that is the picture I keep getting. How did I ever think a sonogram image comforted me only because it took away the dreadful uncertainty? So I knew when Baby Sophia passed away — so?

Am I facing the truth of losing Baby? Or am I like Papa saying the past hurts too much, therefore taking away only half-formed lessons. I try to make others learn important lessons, just like he does. But with no openness, no one else knows where the lessons came from.

You have to face the truth, is one of the half-formed lessons from Papa. The corollary is that the pain of hope is the enemy. A Vanderveer must believe the worst truth possible, no ugly hope ready to betray you. I'm not feeling Baby, and therefore the worst truth is—she is gone.

I sent Daniel away, with familiar Vanderveer words, *everything is fine*, and I miss him more than anyone.

I'm decapitating the last strawberry, when my new doctor strolls in and introduces himself, Doctor Jensen. He's in scrubs, adjusting his stethoscope. His nurse cheerily introduces herself too, MaryAnne.

They are both younger than me. Am I old enough to be their mom and Baby's mom? Maryanne is smiling. Good news?

Doc Jensen sits on the side of my bed. "Okay, let me fill you in."

"Is Baby okay?"

"We have every reason to believe your pregnancy is fine. As you know, to protect the fetus, we did a sonogram of your spine, rather than an X-ray. In diagnosing your severe pain, the team found that you have lumbar injuries around L-3 and L-4. These exacerbated your PGP syndrome—pelvic girdle pain. PGP pain can be far ranging, down your legs, in your abdomen, lower back, your pelvis. Because of pressure on nerves, any movement—even breathing—can make the pain seem rhythmic, just like labor pains. Your sensations mimicked contractions, but you were never in labor."

"But how could that be? I never had any spinal injuries."

"Many people don't know how their injuries happened. But they have them."

"So you really think my pregnancy is viable and healthy? Even with a history of miscarriages?" Oh, how I need my Daniel here.

"Yes." He smiles. He has a cute gap between his front teeth, and like everyone around me lately, he radiates reassurance.

I shift around, only a twinge of pain. "Okay, here's the deal. Most of yesterday and so far today, I don't feel any movement of Baby at all."

"You've been feeling movement already, and now you feel none?" MaryAnne's perfectly made-up eyes widen.

Doc Jensen flips through my chart. "Okay, checking how far along you are. I see, four months and a week, you would only occasionally feel a small movement."

"That's what I was telling you. I felt tiny flutter kicks three times, and then nothing."

Doc and nurse turn to each other. Both freckle-faced and scrubbed clean, they could be siblings. They nod deliberately, as if I need slow, remedial lessons on pregnancy.

Maryanne adjusts my lower back pillow and covers. "To feel any movement already is great. When movement goes undetected, that is not an emergency, just normal. You'll soon feel those flutters again."

"Not an emergency?" *Could I have that as a banner across my walls, one I take with me to California?*

Dr. Jensen puts his hand on my shoulder. "It looks like you're fine. Signs of life are all there, don't worry."

So young and they get how I feel. MaryAnne squeezes my wrist. "I'll stay to take your vital signs and get you more comfortable."

She leaves me feeling like the baby: swaddled, pillows under my lower back, a pillow underneath each arm. An incredible lightness, a piercing of joy hits me. Like Alby and I said yesterday, think God's thoughts after God. Stop fearing hope, fearing promises, fearing trust. *Baby and I are okay.*

If Alby's all negative again, which he will be, hitting bottom will have to take care of him. Bottom will kick him in the butt; the abyss will greet him; that is how it will have to be, because I can't do this anymore. I won't. I'm not going on any more real or imagined emergency room trips. That's how it is. I pat my belly; looking out at the wall, I can see more bright-orange Indian paintbrushes blooming and budding bluebonnets too. Alby will have to be okay. Because I won't let Bottom, the abyss, Weltschmerz get me. I think of Pappie. I will be gentle with him, he's the one who needs care now. How self-absorbed I've been.

I'm floating on clouds of pillows and joy, and doze into an early morning nap.

Refreshed, I walk around the hospital unit, per doctor's orders. Pain lessens with every step. Sliding back into bed, I love the lift of hope. Next challenge, I can go to the restroom on my own, and put on the pretty nightgown Mama brought me.

Returning to bed I see them: red spots on hospital-white sheets. I am bleeding. I check the hospital nightgown I discarded — more spots. Could no one see or tell me, on my happy walk? I struggle out of the pretty gown and jerk on another hospital gown, with its pathetic little ties, not caring that I knot it all up. The prism of light inside turns into shards of glass, cutting away. This is the start. I feebly battle for reassuring thoughts, telling myself I had some spotting in my first pregnancy and then delivered a wonderful son named Vincent. A steady still voice says, *all is well, and all will continue to be well*, and an abyss voice just like Mama's after the Alby and Pappie accident is louder. *All is lost, sink into loss.*

I call the nurse's station and report, my words feel surreal.

A new nurse arrives into the room, just as Daniel does. "I ran into Dr. Jensen."

"Of course."

New Nurse barges in. "So, let's see this spotting, honey. Here" — she turns to Daniel — "you can help her up."

Daniel's on his feet. "What?"

"I just called the nurse because I'm bleeding, just tiny spots, probably nothing. It happened with Vincent, remember?"

"I'll notify the doctor. Try not to worry, you two," nurse says kindly.

Daniel tucks me back into bed, gives me a look.

"I didn't want to fill you in yesterday; I hadn't felt Baby flutters for some time, not today either," I blurt out. "You looked so fatigued then; I thought it was okay just to chase you out and wait and see. Then Dr. Jensen told me everything's fine. Now more worry."

"And you think I didn't notice you chasing me out? But I was exhausted. Looks like you are living in a world of signs — pain, spotting, Baby's movement." His expression switches to concern, but not despair.

"I've been so stupid with this travel."

"You've taken chances. When I was mad at you yesterday I knew that Dr. Simonian never told you *not* to go. But he was shocked you asked."

"The worst was, I didn't listen to my own *insinks*." I try to chuckle. "Dr. Simonian did look shocked at the thought of me traveling. He even told me to figure out where high-risk OB-GYN resources were in Houston. Kemble advised me not to go. I never asked my deepest self, just this compulsion to come right back to here, to …"

"To be Jakob's cancer fighter, to fight for Alby too." Daniel frowns.

"To the fantasy I keep following. All the puzzle pieces would end up falling together here in Houston, I told myself, with a bonus of Baby being just fine."

"Here, come into this easy chair with me." My tense muscles release; he's not going to yell again. He pats the chair-bed.

"We'll break it and pay for that chair."

"We haven't broken an easy chair or couch yet. Come on, you, me, and Baby." He stretches out, and I ease onto his lap, with his hands on my belly. I feel his love can always wrap around me, safe, after all. He adds, "The funny thing is, I keep having this faith-filled feeling that Baby is just fine."

"Me too," I say. "Then I cancel it out with worry. And I keep panicking and then I panic about the panic, because that's not good for Baby." We both laugh, rocking the chair till it screeches. Yep, this one will break.

"Hush now, stop the freaking out. Isn't this what your journey with your dad is all about, being able to believe that sometimes everything is okay? Isn't that what his joy is about? Whatever his cancer brings, he told me, he'll be here for new life. If Vanderveers stop being stubborn loners, that's when peace is really restored."

"Uh, yeah."

Time passes, we laugh about old Vincent stories, like his running the bases in T-ball, his first introduction to baseball at age five, only to stop and chat with each opposing baseman. From laughter, we switch to calling him up, and he says everything is fine. *Of course his rough draft is done.*

A tall woman with long hippy-straight hair pulled back with a 1970s-style leather barrette arrives. "Hi, I'm Allison. Your doctor ordered a sonogram. This is a good time, yes?"

"Of course. We had no idea Dr. Jensen ordered one."

"Well, are your parents the ones with the accents?"

"Yes, what did they do now?"

"Well, I saw them half an hour ago at the nurse's station, and both of them insisted you must have a sonogram or you'd freak out."

"Of course they did." Daniel grins.

They do know me. Soon Allison has me flat on the bed, staring at the broad ceiling tiles, some pristine, one gouged as if an unhappy woman threw her dinner knife up there. Daniel crushes my hand as the wand goes on my belly. He relaxes when *woosh, woosh, woosh* fills the room.

"Okay, fetal heartbeat!" Alison crows.

I weep, Daniel weeps; we must each have suspected the worst.

"And now, here's your baby. I guess you're okay with knowing the gender? Her heart looks fine, umbilical cord, placenta, everything. There's no sign of labor or uterine distress. But look at these ligaments, that's your pelvic girdle pain."

"Wow," I say.

"Okay, just relax. Doc ordered a detailed vaginal sonogram too. That will give him an update on your aches and pains." She performs the vaginal sonogram and her face stays calm, a good thing. "I'll find your doctor and then he'll go over the results with you."

True to his nature, Daniel helps her wheel the cart out.

He puts his face right by mine. "Will you stop now? You are way worse than Jakob, who by the way had some great stuff to tell me last night."

"Yeah, I'll stop. Oh, she's so healthy and big," I say. Just like Papa's words for me my whole life.

He massages my temples. "Sleep honey, I'm off to the cafeteria."

I don't try to relax, I just do. First I'll write in my journal without the unwritten words between the lines all saying, *why did I, how could I?*

Dear God,

I hung out with new friends when You helped me get sober, and I told each of them about a different part of me. Always, I watched their eyes, to see if rejection was about to hit, like all the teasing I endured as the little foreign kid with an accent and different clothes. Rejection didn't happen, but still I persisted, never revealing more than little pieces. That is, not until the day I shared my whole life-inventory with Devin. Her eyes stayed kind, and it all came out. After that day the darkness of regularly losing all sense of you, God, then slowly returning to faith, was gone. I was still hiding from my family, but I knew you. I knew Your love was real.

I used to say there's no God, because I had lost Beppe and Pake, and my childhood friends. The American kids had friends, but not me. I didn't know what to do with all the loneliness and I couldn't escape it. No wonder as a teenager I loved alcohol. Oblivion became my drug of choice. After Devin listened to my story I realized that she, and therefore You, had walked through all the times I thought I was alone. And then, I knew you were there the whole time. I knew that when I said — I don't believe in you God, I was really saying — I hate you God, and you still loved me anyway.

Oh I feel loved now. All of this, this brick wall with flowers outside the window. Daniel, Mama, Papa, Albert, Corrie staying patient with me, when I lost patience with them, all of it feels like love. My amazement that Papa has been so strong. He's facing cancer, and all he wants is to know that Baby and I are okay. To lately not feel Your love, to go it alone with only fear, too much. Let the fear which has thrived in me all these years, be gone.

I've been feeling like Papa might have felt, trying to sleep as Tarakan oil fields burned and the sky went black. I'll never know why I, having suffered much less than Papa and Mama, have so often lived as if the world is dark. I don't have to compare my feelings with theirs anymore, shutting down because my own grief didn't matter. I don't even know where to start to tell my family more about my own life. But I will. And Baby is fine. She and I are glowing in Your gold love-light. I was never abandoned by You. I gave up on You, but You never gave up on me.

† † †

I wake up to Papa and Daniel singing one of my favorite songs from the 1970's, Bill Withers' "Lean on Me." Daniel knows the song because I used to tell him everything. Papa knows the lyrics because he went to parents' meetings at HOW. It's what we all sang at the end of meetings. Like Papa, I remember more of the good, as I reflect on my own past. Papa *did* show up for my tough times. It must have had something to do with his kamp years.

They look delighted with each other and me. Papa grins wider than he has in a long time. He forgot to insert his bridge that covers the hole of lost teeth, from when he fought for bread so long ago. He looks charming, as if childhood, old age, and every year in between, all blend today. I see all of who he is: the adventurous boy, the husband and father, the aging prison kamp survivor willing to let painful memories flood back.

I struggle up. "Ow!" My lower back and left leg go electric with pain.

Daniel rearranges the pillows behind me. "Say when."

The bed hums up. "When." I sigh.

My heart lifts with Papa's infectious smile. He plops into the chair next to me, throwing his cane against the wall. "I have news. Alby's home, I think he'll be just fine."

"What? He's not ready."

Daniel kisses me. "Why do you look so worried, now that you know Baby's fine? Alby will be fine too.

Papa laughs. "Luce, he's a grown man. If leaving makes him use drugs, he really didn't want recovery anyway, heh?"

"I guess not. You amaze me, no worry?"

Papa adds, "Of course a little, but he has changed. He's home with Cindy. She's smart as always. She told him he'd better check right into outpatient care. So no worries for you. 'Let go and let God,' as you always say."

"I talked to him last night," Daniel says. "He has one day at home, then tomorrow he's back at work. I bet keeping busy will actually help him."

349

He could have pain pills stashed away at home; he could be up to any number of things. Poor Papa, Cindy, Daniel. They are all deluded and dropping their worry too soon.

"So," Papa claps his hands together, "Mama's at home getting ready for you two. We are here to break you out of this chicken-outfit hospital. No Vanderveers in the hospital." I love his twisted Americanisms.

"We tried to check you out today," Daniel adds, "but the orthopedic doc wants to hold onto you at least one more night. You need more non-drug pain management." He settles into the large easy chair, leaning it way back.

Papa leans forward with his usual intensity, his cane barely catching him. "What can we do to make you feel better, liefje? I know my daughter; you are still worrying."

My friends other than Kemble think of me as peaceful, organized and scheduled. But Papa's right, I've not yet escaped the edgy fear whispering bad thoughts in my ear. "So, tell me a story," I say.

He grins and shakes his head. "Like when you were little?"

"No like what you left out when I was little. Alby told me some of what happened once you were in Grogol, tell me more.

"That's not a happy topic for Baby."

"How do you know? When I'm happy, Baby is happy. Knowing you better makes me happy. Also, I've known all along that after years of suffering you had a happy ending."

A disoriented look crosses Papa's face. "Happy? Oh liefje, you have no idea how long it takes for war to have a happy ending. The enemy surrenders, and nothing much changes, the enemy surrenders, and still everything is chaos. The enemy is defeated and still the death toll grows. Not everybody gets a happy ending. Albert did not survive, and my pappie died. It's too sad."

"Kamp life got even darker, as it always did." His voice breaks. "The only way I can begin to talk about Albert is the same way I did back then. By eventually telling my one adult friend, Meneer Bevins."

"So he was a good man?" I ask. I feel guilty. I'm asking Papa to say more about his teen years than I've been willing to tell him about mine. I take a deep breath, causing a twinge of pain down my left leg. I have to believe that like myself with Devin, that Papa wants to tell his story to us. But unlike me, not just for relief, but for a better world. The world said *never again* after World War II, but the horrific reality of killing fields, genocide and hellish camps never truly came to an end.

"Bevins, oh yes, a good man. But we couldn't help each other much, the Japs controlled everything. Life is backwards in war. The people who seemed good did bad things. There were many pious people, who I thought would remain good and focus on God. Most of them lost their faith. They were bitter, they argued. I felt the same. The Allies were our God. We kept counting off a new one hundred days, having faith that at the end of those one hundred days, or the next, the Allies would be our savior. Years passed. No God, no help. The supposed bad people often did good things — the good people bad, sneaky things. No one acted like you expected them to."

He rubs the bump on his nose, lifts his hand to the gap in his teeth. "Even though I fought early on over a crust of bread, I didn't fight another inmate again. Once I had that crust of bread in my stomach I knew that the other boy was not wrong but desperate like me. He and I, how-you-say, blew our fuses in the first craziness of starvation."

His fingers riff imaginary piano keys on his leg.

"*Tel maar*," I say. "Tell us," I translate for Daniel's benefit.

Papa shoots me a look. He knows I'm using Dutch words as a bridge between us. Where would I be without my childhood language? His preferred language, Bahasa Indonesian, I don't know. I wish I did. When Papa first called me about Albert, I thought he was zielig.

Untranslatable, the word means a sorrowful pity, with *ziel* (soul) as its root word. Now I see how quietly soulful Papa is — *zielig* in the strong sense.

Papa's distant eyes come back to me. "After Albert died, I tried harder to find my pappie. Meneer Krans, who watched out for Albert and me for a time, told us he had been with our father. This connection convinced me that surely Pappie might be nearby. I knew that some men came back from harsh forced labor on railroads or airfields. These men would reappear, almost worked to death, to the general kamps. So whenever possible, I looked for a way to leave."

"To escape?"

"Oh no, there was no escape, and if anyone did runaway successfully the Japs killed others in retribution. No. I just decided, when I could, I would maneuver myself to kamps and sub- kamps until I got to the one where my pappie was. I never thought I would have that opportunity, until the kamp where I met Bevins."

"No wonder you never give up on anything or anyone," I say proudly.

"Yes, no wonder." He says and flashes his rare shy smile. He hands me my ice water, with its bendy straw. "This you will always have enough of," he says, balancing easily on his cane. He is so much more *fightall* — vital — today, even with the cancer.

I drink deeply. I recall the cord of love from Oma's eyes to my papa and his brother when the Japanese made all older boys leave Tjideng. I understand, because I try to string cords of love between the past and present. Cords like diseased water to endless water now; no safety to our crescent shape Baby safe in my womb. Every cord comprising solid hope, because of the power of love.

"So you will tell?" I hand the pitcher back.

"Patience, more patience," he says sharply.

I clench the fingernails of the hand Papa can't see into my palm, stabbing away, holding my breath.

"Albert and I were lucky enough to survive together for a time, finding water and food. You know now how important simple things like a canteen were, and the rare sacrifice like Meneer Smaken and the milk. We did mourn his death."

A promise of more.

"So we knew him as an old man, probably all of forty actually, who gave up on his life. He was the one who thought our Wouter had dysentery because he suddenly became violently ill. He ended every talk with *don't take anyone, not me, not Wouter, nor each other to the kamp hospital. No one ever comes out alive.*"

I nod vigorously to show Papa I know about not going in and out of hospitals.

"Not true, but arguable. A lot of starving men and boys died there." His face collapses into sorrow.

My heart palpates in my throat. I don't want Papa to suffer now like he must have suffered then. Yet I hold my breath for more.

"Meneer Smaken cared about Albert and me." He sits back tiredly. "I'll never understand why so many good people died, Albert, my pappie."

"In heaven you will understand," I say.

Papa lifts dead eyes to me. Daniel subtly shakes his head. Instantly I want to take my words back. I feel ridiculous — bringing up the promise of heaven, like a child's Sunday school lesson. The peace I'm always wishing for emerged like a new soft creature in the room. Peace, I need to let her tender presence be.

"Heaven" — Papa surprises me with a small smile — "is a place we wait for. So, be patient with my story. At Grogol kamp I became sick with malaria. I went into the Grogol hospital delirious with fever, and did come out. Then Albert had to go into the hospital for a terrible situation. But just like Meneer Smaken predicted, he never left. It was all my fault."

"But Papa," I say, and reach out both hands to him, not caring about the pull of pain around my hips. *Not your fault that Albert was attacked*, I want to say.

"Jake, you were a kid," says Daniel.

Papa jerks to his feet and runs for the door.

Too much, too much. "No, don't go," I call.

Daniel heads out after him and Papa's already returning, coughing. He collapses back down next to me. "I can't run. I'm too old." Tears run down his face, which has turned to wood.

I caress his arm, "Ach, Papa, and too ill, no pushing yourself. You can stop now. Please stop."

"It's okay liefje, there has to be a reason to stop fighting the past. There is." He hobbles to the window, all the *fightall* gone, as unsteady as I have ever seen him. He plants both hands on the windowsill. I resist the urge to leap out of bed and help.

His voice changes, young, singsong, "What could I do Bevins? Be glad I had a canteen for survival, without a brother? Be glad I had the memory of Meneer Smaken leaving us his condensed milk, only for each of us to take turns in hospital? Smaken, in a burlap bag, yes, but Albert? Can you see it? Bevins, what could I do?"

Bevins? Daniel and I freeze.

Papa thumps his head on the window pane. "No one talked to me when Albert was gone, Bevins. They ignored me — I must have done something terrible for Albert to die in the hospital, after he took such good care of me. My enemy, Wolfie, a kamp smuggler stared at me with his nasty smirks. Mammie's ring was gone. So I knew I had lost it in a bad trade. Horrible Wolfie, not as skeletal as Smaken or Albert. He did his trades, got his food, oh ja, but did nothing to save Albert. Why did the Japanese not find out about his smuggling and beat him? Would it be awful if they beat Wolfie to death as an example?"

He snarls like an angry teenager. "That would be one death that would be good. Cain slew Abel, and never wanted it to be known. I killed Albert with my slow stupidity. I was the one who delayed him going into the hospital that most don't come out of. How can I ever explain? Especially when I can't remember, I can't remember." He punches himself in the arm.

Daniel and I stare at each other. What have I done to Papa?

Papa drops his cane. He turns and almost falls, Daniel's reflexes catch him, and pretty much carries him back to his chair.

"Oh, oh. Ja, it's you Daniel?"

"You should stop now, Papa," I say. No more, I finally get it that I know enough, he's done enough; we're done.

"No, I will not stop. Albert died and I will tell his story, only the memories are like a swirling monsoon, rain pelting from every side. I will tell you what I can."

My heart beats fast. Should I stop him? When Papa ended up in the psych hospital, when I was a teen, there was only me around to cope, the rest of the family out of the country. Will he have to go to the psych hospital now? How can he have psych treatment and cancer treatment at the same time? Dr. Ingstrom is the crazy one for having started all of this.

Papa goes on with a newscaster's voice, as if saying, *in recent developments …*

† † †

Jakob

Kamp Grogol
November 1944

Jakob usually fell asleep each night into a confusion of pictures flashing through. Ying Qian's head rolled in the dirt, Meneer Zwanenburg's beaten face grimaced as he stretched swollen hands. Pappie suffered in an endless line, skin sores oozing. Mammie and Sara left behind barbed wire. Meneer Smaken peaceful in death. Then he would force a switch to happier memories, the spray of ocean water, prows skimming along.

But now, waking or sleeping, a strange cotton-quiet descended on him in the dark around the groaning men. And only two pictures lived inside: Albert's face blurred, almost at peace, sunken cheeks, and bony skull. Albert's birdlike chest collapsed above his swollen stomach. The images lived inside and he could never return to the simple vision of the old Albert instead: round-cheeked, reading, playing.

The second horrifying picture snapped and then developed in the darkroom of his brain—Wolfie serving the food lineup. His arrogant smirk, the predator's look in his eyes, no greeting.

After days and weeks he no longer counted up, hunger blessed him with exhausted sleep each night, no pictures. Instead, thoughts came when stooping in the fields of his new corvée. *I killed Albert, and I would admit it, if only someone would talk to me. Like Meneer Smaken hoarding condensed milk, I needlessly brought death where it did not have to come calling. The minute I saw how bad off Albert was, and how he clenched his jaw in pain, I should have traded Mammie's ring.*

At night Pappie came into his dreams. He walked along thin, but confident, leading a corvée of men. Pappie's face lit up with recognition. "My boy, my fine boy," he cried.

Then he had to tell Pappie that Albert died, and Pappie raged. Sometimes in these dreams Pappie struck, leaving his ears ringing, but glad he had been punished as he deserved. Sometimes he woke up crying. The only one who cared about his tears was gone.

At least Smaken only did himself in.

One afternoon, news which was horrible to many, meant a means of escape for Jakob. At the end of corvée, he and Wouter's names were called, as among the two hundred prisoners called to transport to a new kamp. He couldn't stand the kind looks of the nicer men, or Wolfie's hard eyes, and a new kamp could mean finding Pappie.

In the morning they received extra crusts of the brown bread, by efforts of the kitchen crew. Wolfie slinked off to the side, but Jaapie, Wolfie's sidekick, handed the extra ration over with a special look, as if to say, *I am so sorry.*

Jakob deliberated about saving the bread, but decided to soak it and eat it immediately. He did not know where they would be next, but rumor was, stifling railroad cars. He already had his sling packed and with him; he checked the contents: Smaken's canteen full of water, a knife, and Smaken's extra shorts. He had not been able to bear removing Albert's shorts to use for himself. He would not see Albert, in burlap, naked.

He arrived close to the dirt-brown soccer field for appel. Wouter positioned himself at his elbow, his proud squinty eyes saying, *we will be partners.*

No more partners, ever. He glared at Wouter. Yet Wouter stuck like glue, as the Japanese yelled to hurry. "Lekkas, lekkas!" They marched to the railroad station. Wouter had a small pack, an old belt with a tin cup attached, surprisingly organized.

Indos manning the train, stood by strangely silent. These men were not hostile. They were herded into empty railroad cars. Jakob pulled away from Wouter, let him toughen up. *I will care now for Mammie, Sara, Wim, and Pappie. Let all others go to hell.*

Guards' blows smashed them all in, body against body. Jakob elbowed for a spot against the walls and near a door. Men and boys, crushed into each other, shoved into the walls, groaned. Jakob uttered not a sound, except to gasp for air, and turn his body sideways, bracing himself. When the doors shut, he twisted back around and found the little space he had strategized for himself. Nearby he heard Wouter's childish "Hoi, Jakob."

He swore all the swear words he knew. No one could tell him to be kind anymore. Other doors slammed shut, yet the train did not move. They were in full sun. "Water," some already said.

Jakob felt nausea rising painfully, as if a python were crushing him to swallow him whole. He grinned dizzily, how could he be a python's meal if he always needed food himself? He eased his canteen to his mouth centimeter by centimeter, not wanting others to know what he had. Water could keep him from retching up his miserly breakfast. A small boy crushed into his hip, his father on his other side. The boy's pappie told him a story, and gave him a sip of water from their canteen. A gangly older man leaned against the wall nearby, favoring one leg, occasionally groaning.

They stood for what must have been two hours, most gasping for air in the stifling heat—which increased minute by minute. Finally the engine started, jolting the cars "At last," someone yelled out. Jakob took a long time to raise his canteen and lower it again. Warm breezes occasionally hit through wall chinks and high windows. Spying buildings, he waved his hand up through a high window. No one knew who he was, but he let everyone know there were men in these cars.

They rocked along for hours. Men and boys took turns, sitting, standing, and leaning. Having a system made the unbearable almost bearable. Most could not get to the one bucket to relieve themselves. He had to release his own urine, the stench rose from all the others doing the same. He kept patting his canteen, the one thing to keep him alive.

They eventually jerked to a stop.

Voices called out, "We are here," Wouter's high pitched voice among the rest.

They were nowhere. The quick dark descended. The intense heat that coiled around them, choking them, abated some. Not a door opened. A man started to panic. "Let me out, let me out."

First gentle voices rippled through the truck, men using their mammie-baboe voices. "Calm now. There is nothing we can do."

The shrieker whimpered quietly, then went off again.

"Stop it now," voices commanded. Fists thudded; Shrieker was silenced.

A voice said, "We will not all panic. Again we take turns sitting and standing."

Jakob felt his canteen; only a third left. He let his mouth be dry, and thought of biting the inside of his cheek for blood to swallow his own moisture. Every thought was followed by dullness. He leaned against the wall. Suddenly he felt himself floating high. *If I die, no matter it is escape. I will see Albert, and I can tell him I am sorry.*

He lifted higher out of the heat, into the cool heavens, below floated linked railroad cars. He saw the tops of heads in all the cars, mostly motionless men and boys. Ah, they must be floating up too. A blanket of silent jeweled stars waited for him. Soon Albert would speak to him. No, not yet. Baboe whispered to him. "Rest, rest, oh my little boy."

"Rest, rest and live," came Mammie's voice. Live? He couldn't find her and drifted to diamond stars. Another screaming man below was silenced. No matter, so far away. Thud. Silence. Then a high-pitched scream.

It was the little boy screaming awake right by Jakob, pressing his bony hip into Jakob's bare feet. The boy's pappie leaned down to him. *"Hush, hush, all will be well."* Jakob felt everything again. Splinters and sweat added to the pee in his shorts. He wished *Hush, hush, all will be well* was meant for him too, and even more so — the truth.

The boy stopped his screeching, as diarrhea smell joined the sharp urine smell. The little body at his feet was hot—a sign of life. His pappie could keep him alive.

Jakob drifted back into a stupor, but no heavens opened up again. His bowels let loose. The train backed up for half an hour then chugged forward. He would arrive if they ever did arrive, sick and in his own filth. Maybe the Japanese were taking them to one of the ships to Burma, called hell ships, for slave labor on railroads. He heard Albert's voice clearly, the way he never did—commanding. His chest burst with relief, now they were both dead.

But Albert's command was, *Live, live.* Jakob would not be like Smaken, ready to die. He took a sip from his canteen and handed it to the tall man with the hurt leg, surprised by the croaking of his own voice. "Here, drink the last of this, but give me back my canteen." He would survive and need a canteen. The old man like Smaken, they could help each other.

The empty canteen was pressed back under his arms. He collapsed to the foul floor curled around the boy and escaped into heat, sleep, and dreams.

† † †

Everyone was on the ferry leaving him behind on Billiton, Pappie, Mammie, and Sara, waved madly, Wim stretching tall. Pappie glared sternly and mouthed, "You will not be on this trip." He had been bad.

He walked all alone to their house on the hill, finding it empty except for Mollie. His heart jumped up his throat. A king cobra hissed its low growl on the tiled floor. Mollie hissed back. It struck and took Mollie in its jaws, so he grabbed the snake behind its head to make it release.

But there were at least four cobras present. Mollie yowled desperately. He had to drop her and run to the grain sack in the goedang. He had to feed his hunger; he could smell the grain, imagined the food in the larder. But the shelves were

360

empty and a fat rat stood guard, chewing on kernels of rice and powder flour left beneath his feet. Jakob fell to his knees and shoved the grain in his mouth, soaked with rat urine. He didn't care; he was too hungry and ate the last handful of grain.

He remembered Mollie and returned to her lifeless body, and held her. He sobbed loudly, keening over and over, but there was no one to rescue him, there was no one left to love. He fell to the cold ground so he could wait for the snakes to kill him. He wished to feel their fangs, to die quickly. Suddenly he heard footsteps and whistling.

Albert came in, smiling. "Did you think I would leave you? Come." He held out a dripping wet canteen. "Come with me." He rocked violently. A python, huge and dark, had been under the table all along. Somehow they both got away from the python, already opening its jaws wide enough for a boy. Albert pulled him along, "Lekkas, lekkas. Come, come with me."

† † †

"Come." He heard Wouter's voice. "We're moving."

The train. They had not arrived of course, but they were on the move, cooler air circulated, so that the little boy next to him shivered in the warm muck. His fever must have broken. In his weakened dizziness, Jakob had dropped his canteen in the mire. He reached for it, feeling the boy who must be at least ten, old enough for men's kamps, but small of stature.

He struggled to his feet. His tall older friend said, "Here we go," pulling on Jakob's hand while the other clutched his canteen. The bundled sling rose with him, against all odds. Everyone moved weakly, some not, the dead.

Jakob's tongue cracked so dry he wondered how the older man had managed to speak. They had to be closer to the new kamp. He remembered dream-Albert, who looked like a radiant boy, well-fed, ready to take Jakob along on family vacation, to rescue him, to make sure he wasn't all alone.

He mumbled, wishing his dry lips could form words.

"What did you say?" asked the tall man right into his ear.

"I'm sorry," Jakob repeated.

"For what? You shared your water. You are a good boy. Maybe, because of you I am still alive."

"Thank you, and your name?"

"Smittey."

A *goede jongen* — good boy, if only Smittey knew how wrong he was. The train rocked to a stop.

"Lean back," men yelled. "Hup," and they prepared to *hup* — jump out. The doors burst open. Waiting for them were scarecrows, in the dark, one harsh light off to the side. They stood with one Jap guard, and scowling Heihos, the Korean forced-to-be soldiers. The guards backed off at their smell.

Many men stopped to help others make the leap as there were no steps. Wouter landed beside him, his face dirty and tear streaked.

"Wipe your face," croaked Jakob.

Wouter's eyes widened, he shook his head as if he doubted the vision of Jakob next to him, but he wiped his face with dirty hands. Together they started to walk a frail waddle walk, shorts sagging with filth.

Smittey placed each foot with care, trying to find his balance. The little boy stumbled next to his pappie. Jakob touched Wouter's shoulder. As Albert had done for him, so he would do for others.

† † †

Papa's sitting too still, like a boy desperately hiding. What can we say to despair?

Golden light illuminates the brick wall. Papa careens over to the window, forgetting to use his cane. He gazes out. I know his eyes are drawn to the blue bonnets and the orange paintbrushes, colors of the Dutch flag and royalty.

He turns towards us, sees I am patting my belly, and smiles like my papa is back in the room. He walks to us steadily, as if he's coming back from the precipice. Peaceful wisdom inside tells me to give up on words, and lay his warm hands where I feel a flutter kick after all. A kick he probably can't feel, yet his eyes widen with tears. Somehow we didn't have this moment of intimacy with my Vincent pregnancy. I feel many cords of love: Oma to Papa to me to Daniel to Vincent and now Baby.

I feel the shy intimacy of being unusually relaxed around Papa. He has told enough of his story; I finally see the ugly rusting rebar inside the concrete of the war years. We're trying to find life in and outside the ancient rusting rebar where the concrete always crumbles—such as the rusty heartbreak of anyone thinking protectiveness could work in war. I don't know just what happened to Albert, only that the brothers' plan to watch out for each other failed when Jakob went into the hospital. Albert suffered and died after that.

Without his brother and co-protector, Albert must have been felled by a terrible beating or illness. Young Jakob suffered because he couldn't protect him, by smuggling out Oma's ring for what—food, whatever … it didn't work. To know my papa saw Albert, his gentle bookish brother so hurt and then dying, tears me up inside. Yet knowing this is what I yearned for to be with Papa for such loss, comforts me.

"Let's rest," says Papa, "enough."

His command is not the usual shut down, but just right. It's enough.

Daniel shoves the easy chair close to my bed. "Here you two." He settles Papa in, and we hold hands companionably. When Papa sleeps, his face somber in rest, exhausted from cancer, I see his frailty, and know he feels better for the talk.

I rest back too, understanding where my family's need to be in control—and my own control—comes from. Gazing at the stark, ugly wall, with its stripe of darker shadow, I wonder what else Papa might tell us one day. He just said, *but not the right risk, not the right time.*

Papa opens his eyes, he was always a cat-nap guy, quick rests.

Daniel reaches over and hugs him. "Thank you." He has a way of delivering the words which need to be said.

"Thank you," I repeat. "I'm so sorry about Albert. Who is Bevins?"

Papa's silence lasts, as if he doesn't hear us. At last his shoulders shake, he's chuckling. "I'm being like Albert. He could be soo-o slow to answer. I heard you, I mourn many lives, and here we are with new life. Bevins is one of the main reasons I survived to meet your Mama, so you kids could even be here—as much of a pain in the ass as you are!"

Daniel cracks up laughing. They leave to check on my discharge time for the next day. Daniel carefully supports Papa, while both hum a Big Band tune, "Begin the Beguine."

I don't feel lonely at all, as I squirm to my side. Side sleeping is good for Baby. A nurse bustles in. "Don't check on me too often," I say. "I'm going to nap." By tomorrow morning I should be free, sprung out of this chicken-outfit-hospital, where none of us die, but everyone is eager to leave.

I bury my nose in clean sheet smells, light chlorine, traces of detergent. Baby must be on her side too, both of us cocooned in a safe, safe world. I love her; I love my amazing, wacky family. I even love Houston.

† † †

Luce

Houston, Texas
1967

I hated Houston, Mama did too. School, usually a sanctuary, whether in Nederland, Iran, or Utah, was hellish in Texas. An irritable teacher who often yelled and threatened, presided over a classroom in a building called a Temporary, with no insulation and no air conditioning. Worse the students spoke in a foreign Texan tongue, the translation for *Do you have a pin*, I learned was: *Do you have a pen?*

No matter how bad my days, I could always count on Mama's comfort. I would tell her much of what went wrong and what little went right. When she came into my room for good-night kisses was the best time to talk. "None of the kids like me."

"Surely some of them do?"

I thought of the kids, the twang, the voices, the rayon clothes so different from the cotton clothes from Mama's sewing machine. "No, none of them."

"Couldn't you invite someone over?"

"No, they don't like me."

"Could you —"

"No," I interrupted, for we had had this conversation before.

She patted my arm, her eyes dropping into tiredness. "It will get better." She left. We no longer said prayers, although we went to church most Sundays.

Our routine went on for weeks. Tough, tender, putting-her-foot-down-with-the-Paynes Mama remained my constant. Bertie, called Alby now, and Corrie had new beginnings in their first-grade and preschool classes. They would start school and stay in one new neighborhood. During those same school years I had lived in three countries, attending five schools. Daily I dragged myself to the hot classroom where all of us sat with our sheen of sweat.

Everything was flat in Houston. I missed the mountains and canyons of Utah. I grieved distinct seasons: my hot classroom gave way to an autumn of rain bringing wet footsteps into a damp classroom, with recess rained out. I yearned to bicycle for miles alone, wondering if I would ever make it back. In Utah, when I stepped off my bicycle, walking it around to the direction I just came from, I gazed at fields of green, and then a familiar neighborhood beyond. Those fields, except for their mountain background, reminded me of Holland. In the midst of lush green, I always made it back home

Papa picked Houston for the oil industry and engineering. Somehow I knew that the triumvirate of heat, humidity, and rain, was a version of home for him. But for me there was too much concrete and children with strange accents.

At recess, in dodge ball, I threw the ball just as hard as the boys. The girl, who asked to borrow *pins* instead of *pens*, ran up to me and yelled, "You talk crazy and you throw weird." She ran back to the girls playing hopscotch near the grass.

To make up for Houston's lack of country roads, I discovered the next closest thing—walking the ridges of the wooden fences behind all the houses. No one was ever in their backyard viewing my progress. For a long block, I spied dull-green crab grass invading the dark green grass, the good grass. Gray cement patios, just like ours, appeared in every yard. The fence ridges were so exposed to weather; they matched the concrete. Many times I told myself I edged along precariously for Alby; I'd be the scout that found the way. I'd invite him to come with me another time, but I kept it up alone.

When Houston winter came, my classroom went from suffocating hot to chilly. This cheered me, colder like Holland, although I still had no friends.

One night I squinted my eyes and Mama blurred into a glowy angel as she came through the door, beams of hallway light behind her. Resting on my bed, she stroked my forehead. "Good night, liefje." Her high rounded cheekbones gleamed. I widened my eyes; she smiled.

"Mama, I hate school."

She sighed, and her smile faded away. "Still?

"The kids are all so mean, and the teacher yells all the time. No one wants to be my friend."

She stroked my forehead. "Oh liefje, it will get better, just invite some kids over."

"That's so hard."

"I used to do it when I was little."

"But you always had lots of friends. It's easy for you. " I thought of Mama laughing when her girlfriends came over in Utah. Not lately, in our new home, but she always made friends again, no matter how much we moved.

"I miss friends too. It will get better, Luce-ee." She still sounded odd saying my Americanized name.

"No, it won't, and I miss Beppe and Pake. I wish I could see them, be on their farm," I said hotly. Tears flowed, running into my ears. A huge lump started in my chest and traveled up my throat to my mouth. This would be the big cry, the one that would break me wide open, and Mama would fix it with her love.

"You will see them again, but they won't be on the boerderij, farm."

"No boerderij anymore?" To not see Beppe and Pake again on their farm was unimaginable. Boerderij *was* home. "I have to see the boerderij one more time," I croaked.

"Well, we can't. They moved into an apartment. Pake now paints houses, and they are retired from the farm." She breathed her sad sigh. "Well, maybe the new people on the boerderij will let you visit there, when we can all manage to go."

"To not go inside and see my old room," I protested. "It won't be the same. Beppe and Pake won't be there."

Mama's mouth squashed into one thin line. She looked away, and turned back directing her fierce gaze at me. "Liesbet," she said, and dropped her hand from my forehead. "You will have to figure it out. Have the children over." Striding to the window, she jerked the curtains shut, returned and tucked in my sheets and blanket, shaking the bed firmly. "I miss Beppe and Pake too." Her voice broke. "Enough is enough. It is over, have the children come play, you will see."

I started to open my mouth, to tell her nothing helped, that at night, pain didn't leave. But she stood looking down at me. I realized my usual mama was gone. I couldn't tell her one more pain, or I would break her. She didn't fix me; I had to stop myself, because if she broke, I would break.

Somewhere inside she had had enough. Mama had held her *poot stevig* — had put her foot down with me.

"Good night," I whispered and turned away. The door closed, and more tears spilled out.

I huddled in the sheets, no longer cozy, but hot with misery. I kicked the covers off viciously, which took some doing as Mama had tucked me in tightly. I heard moaning. It was my own weeping. I buried my misery in the pillow and sobbed for Beppe and Pake, for all the schools I'd left behind, I wept for never ever sleeping in my boerderij attic room again, and for all the baby animals Pake and Beppe brought for me whenever I visited. Dry tears choked me for not getting to play with Dutch farm children. I would never sit with friends again on a generations-old desk, squiggles of ink stains around thick glass bottles. I cried for no golden light at night, no marching children on kilometers long walks with parents and teachers.

I sobbed for leaving Utah, just as I was ready to *invite the children over*, when living there. I cried for the blank faces at school now, the funny twang, the teacher who called out all of our grades in front of the whole class. Her voice cut if you were too low or too high. I cried because I couldn't talk to

Mama any more. She thought I couldn't fix my problems, that something was wrong with me. By not making friends I was proving that I was broken inside.

† † †

At midnight I awaken for awhile. I hear soft voices from the nursing station, a distant monitor pinging. I caress my baby bump and think of the child in me, and myself little Liesbet, who grew up to be the somewhat-tougher Luce.

How sad, to give up on friendship, to do anything for friends as I grew older. I refused to discuss friendships, Mama and Papa would have had no idea why. Baby will not have to move all the time. Like Vincent, she will have the one home town—Calabria.

CHAPTER 19

Jakob

Seventh Battalion Kamp, Tjimahi
December 1944

"*Lekkas, lekkas*—hurry!" yelled the Japanese guards. The same words. Stumbling men wedged between Wouter and him like a spring-monsoon log jam. He gripped Wouter's shoulder harder, but felt the boy ripped away. Wouter's head bobbed away in the river of men being marched down the railroad tracks. So much trouble with caring for others. If they didn't die, they disappeared.

He took everything in with the familiar numbness of hunger in his belly, a dry cracked feeling in his throat, and weakened legs from transport. The moonlit dark shapes of the men around suggested this was a vast compound, an army battalion; he heard men mumbling. He hoped they wouldn't have to march far. So he had arrived at Tjimahi, the Japanese randomly moving their prisoners. Over a year ago he had seen women and children arrive from this region to Tjideng, now he ended up here with men and boys.

The welcome prisoners stood silently before them in small cadres of men, huddled close for the chill in the air. To think this was their Bandoeng now, Guests of the Emperor vacation area, colder due to the altitude. Behind them was a field with a few naked trees at the edge. Like Grogol, all fruit and leaves believed edible had been stripped away. The guards faded away and the prisoners led them past a large gray field. One man was a leader; Jakob was beyond caring. The Japs always set up leadership; a very tough job for the leader, but well respected by the prisoners. There would also be leadership the Europeans set up, even more respected.

Jakob tripped, caught himself, and didn't worry about falling behind; Smittey did the same. He could be with the last now. "This was a soccer field, but for some reason we don't play anymore," a man said. Some of the newcomers laughed, others stumbled along in a painful walk, but somehow remained standing when they stopped. Smittey was among those who almost fell, Jakob against him, to prop him up.

To Jakob's surprise, Smittey whispered to him, "Thanks, friend. The Japs do have a strategy. You know how all the women and children are near the coast? That's in hopes the Allies won't attack those areas. That means we're winning the war, don't give up faith. The men are all inland, where they believe we skeletons are less likely to turn fierce and attack when the Allies attack. Of course they still don't care if we live or die; for them I believe the ultimate solution is for all of us to die of hunger."

Jakob nodded. Somehow the knowing was a gritty, yet reassuring account of what he'd suspected all along.

Their group separated into two barracks. He and Smittey were sent to the one for mostly men. The other set aside for mostly boys. "Boys Town," the soccer field voice announced; again a few laughed. Wouter still wasn't with their group.

They were much too late for dinner line up. But their greeters made sure they all had crusts of the usual rocklike bread. Last, they all queued for one dripping faucet. If he didn't need water, if he didn't have to rinse the sting of his own foulness out of his shorts, he would skip it. His fingers itched to tear off his soiled shorts. His heart pounded; he felt dizzy and leaned into Smittey for just a moment. All the entrapment of a day, or days, cooking in heat in the railroad car hit him. He wanted to scream on and on. He resisted the scream. He couldn't have it that the other men would knock him to the ground with their blows like they did to the crazy guys.

But how could he stay silent? He bit his tongue, drawing blood, sucking it down. His rage melted as they still stood in moonlight in the dark, an unexpected cool breeze lifted the sweaty hair at his nape, and the line moved. He glanced at the blurry figures behind him and ahead of him. *Not quite ready to go naked yet.* He grinned. *I can moan quietly to keep from screaming, swallow blood, and gabble like a crazy boy and no one will notice.*

Finally he dripped water into a dipper over and over, shaking his legs until most of the foulness slithered down like the sewage frogs. For a moment he closed his eyes, imagining he stood on the tiled floor at home, with an actual full dipper for mandi—rinsing bath. He filled his canteen and began to moisten and choke down the bread.

Next, they sat in a row outside the barrack. A man ran from inside to a large barrel, they caught the punchy smell of urine when the cover was lifted. The man fiddled with ragged shorts, relieved himself, walked back.

Smittey nudged him. "Doing his duty, they call it here. The kamp collects urine for yeast, the vitamin B, to prevent the worst of the beri-beri. They cook it into a form of bread, and more here have a chance to live."

"Ah, eating our own urine." They both shook with silent laughter. Smittey was a good man, who somehow kept finding energy after their endless ordeal.

One light bulb glowed faintly in their barrack as they entered. They faltered from shadow to shadow, light dappling three levels of sleeping platforms, the most levels yet.

He struggled up. His legs felt as awkward and wooden as the sleep platforms he had to climb. He wrapped his wet shorts around the foot of the platform, and pulled on Smaken's too-big shorts. Jakob shrugged his shoulders, glad he had been kind to Smittey, who lay next to him with the privilege of an edge. Smittey turned out to be the kind who knew all there was to know, now he had a friend again, against all odds.

† † †

Unlike the other moves, Jakob knew exactly where he was at morning light. A new kamp, the same reeking stale sweat, the peculiar odor of dead lice, and the murmur of voices grown louder. Reconnaissance time.

Going out to the do-your-duty piss-barrel, he saw the Jap-appointed man, who apparently was in charge of both barracks. Later he would ask him for farm corvée. Perhaps he would find snails, snakes, and frogs. Sometimes farming work meant extra rations.

As a young one, he had the chance to show he had the energy left for this corvée. To the pig farm he was assigned, without asking.

And so, familiar days in new surroundings began. Wherever Wouter was, he had no chance yet at the nearby pig farm, where the Dutch prisoner in charge kept an eye out so men could scavenge. The Japanese and Heihos relied on the farm first and foremost, getting the best. The garbage, twisted roots, dirt and such, went to the Guests of the Emperor.

† † †

From time to time he saw the familiar man again, the one who the Dutch and other Europeans turned to. He rarely stood alone for a moment, always sought out. His tall frame, relaxed but alert, didn't tense with the deep fear most displayed when guards approached. Although, he always bowed hastily. Might as well stay away from such an arrogant man, who imagined he was in charge while in captivity. Time and time again the highest toktoks, men used to being in charge, let all the young men and boys down, not fighting, not protecting them, only watching out for themselves. With few exceptions, the boys had to watch out for each other.

Each morning was an act of hopeless courage, each night he ate his extra ration earned for corvée in the fields — the stone-hard bread. Jakob moved in a stupor, thought in a stupor. He shared smuggled greens from corvée only with Smittey, who he learned was Dutch but had received his nickname from working on a British-Dutch plantation. Most left him alone, and kept to themselves. Jakob's voice dried out from rarely speaking. In the food lines he watched the careful ladles of food up ahead. Everyone insisted on equal portions. Sometimes in his mind the careful hands of the kitchen crew overlapped with Albert's careful hands, opening his botany book, sketching, and gathering plants. Only once had he thought of heaven, because of a vague recollection of what Albert said before he died. If there was a heaven Albert was sketching plants, saying all their names, and happy to be with the angels.

† † †

Farm corvée-ers soon lost their extra ration of brown bread, and meals no longer had bits of pig entrails or fish fins. Jakob sat on the edges of men telling food stories; they described as vividly as if each had been the family Kokkie. Talk covered every ingredient of rijsttafel, the cooking, the smells, the eating, the full belly.

Stupefaction settled in. Every cell of Jakob's body ached with hunger, days blurred together, with the courage necessary to get up in the morning still the worst moment. One dawn, he didn't fight to be up among the first, to see a pink sky. When a late-December night came he stood in the slow food line, and knew. *There is only enough to make me desperate for anything, to eat blades of grass, to swallow the gray tapioca starch, which is nothing. Smittey is quieter, an old man of forty or so who will die sooner than later. Am I ready to die?*

No! was the answer. A cool breeze snaked around him, directionless, nonsensical, and yet it continued. He flashed on the baby chicks he had seen at the farm, balls of scraggly fluff feathers. One hand had decided to cup gently, the other to kill and smuggle one out. But a baby chick was not a frog; let them mature for eggs or chicken dinner. *I am not a frog or baby chick, ready to die. The Japanese will not win. Not here, not now.*

He didn't want to die of starvation, craziness, or giving up like Smaken. Smittey said the war could be going well for the Allies. *No dying for me.* He forced himself to think of family again, he'd given up on family yearnings, because longing was a two-edged sword, it was a reason to live, and a daily pain as horrid as hunger pains.

But now he resolved to think about Pappie and chewed his grains of rice and thin broth one hundred times on. Somewhere in the world no one was starving, and the Allies won battles. If the war was going their way, the Japs would not be as now, harsher with food, thinner and grim themselves.

He went to sleep extra hollow from the lack of bread, and knowing something had to be done. His life must be about Pappie; Pappie must need him too, and of course he would find him. His heart lifted. Smittey moaned next to him. A dream and a hunger pang in his sleep? Here among over ten thousand men, Pappie might be close. He could see it, he could feel it.

As he fell asleep, he pretended he was with his corvée; mirages formed constantly down the dusty road, wavering images. The morning heat was already powerful enough so that from a distance the shimmering could be anything — a curve in the road, trees, men working, rescuing Allies, anything. Yet he knew to stare far ahead as his heart beat fast.

Shimmering brown smudges could be men. Yes, they came closer; groups even more skeletal than most, none had shoes, and most were close to naked. Now he could make out the eyes of those in the front. Most stared only feet ahead, or at the ground while a few glanced up with flashes of hope. A red-haired man in the back came to view, head bent down. Then, sensing something, he looked up. His flashing gaze went right to Jakob.

Jakob's heart leaped with joy.

"Jakob," the man cried. "That's my boy." No, he would not cry out, Pappie would never be foolish enough to cry out only to be beaten.

A silent scream went out between them, of joy, reunion, jubilation. The look was all the power either of them needed for the moment. A cord of love extended between them, just like with Mammie and Sara when the trucks came for the boys.

† † †

All his variations of seeing Pappie on the road felt so real. The plan he formed to end up together so right, that he woke up with a will to live daily.

One morning, the familiar man of the arrogant leadership, almost walked past him, in loose shorts tied with a rope. He stopped, "*Dag*. I think I know you."

Jakob tried to place the voice and peered into his face: the sunken cheeks, the twist to his jaw, the crooked nose like his own, and the look of a man who had been beaten. His eyes held the final clue—bright blue. "Meneer Bevins!" Siebe's father, one of the pappies who actually had serious talks with the boys back on Billiton.

Bevins smiled. "I've been looking for you, Jakob. Just say Bevins, a habit I picked up on from an American."

How could this be, discovering Meneer Bevins, a family friend, who knew his pappie, his family, right here. The one everyone sought out, had surprisingly—found him.

Bevins stared at him intently, like a mind reader. "Ja, what do you know? Out of ten thousand men we find each other. Smittey was talking about the Vanderveer boy from Billiton, and so I knew." The others parted for Bevins as they walked to the breakfast line, indeed the mark of a respected man.

"We must be in the same barracks?" asked Jakob.

"No, neighboring barracks, I think."

Looking into alert blue eyes reminded Jakob of their families gathering for fun. Even then, Bevins missed little. He once smoothly dove into the pool, to scoop up a little boy who had floundered into the deep end, before anyone else noticed.

Longing crossed Bevins' face. "You were with Siebe and Tineke in Tjideng?"

"Yes, let's get some of this garbage food, then talk." Jakob tried to sound jaded and bitter like a soldier, not like a boy. The first questions were always about family. When it was his turn to talk about Albert what would he say?

"And?" Bevins asked once they were shoulder to shoulder, properly in line.

"Your Tineke — Mevrouw Bevins — and Mammie, they helped each other when they could. It is just as hard as here, sometimes harder. Of course we had a bit more food then."

They both spun their empty bowls.

Bevins' bright eyes turned dusky blue, like ocean horizon. Jakob would not tell him how for a time, Mevrouw Bevins, almost gave up hope. Instead he would tell the rest of the truth, how kind she was, how brave.

"Siebe left before me, we didn't know which kamp. Mammie and your Tineke always encouraged each other, I'm sure they both watch out for Sara." His heart jumped. The mention of Sara meant he would have to talk about Albert.

"I pray for them and many others, by name every day — your family too, of course."

Praying? Jakob glanced at Bevins. Well, for foolish people who still prayed, there was plenty of time to do so, day after day, year after year. "That's all you can do."

"It is something." Bevins paused. "A lot."

"I suppose," said Jakob. They trudged along with the line, holding out their bowls at last for ladles of gruel. More tapioca again, a horrid starch to subsist on.

"Over here," said Bevins.

They went to the end of Bevins' barrack. Men cleared a spot for Jakob and him. "Knowing you have seen my wife and son. This is good." A tear ran down his cheek.

Bevins didn't worry about his tears. Jakob felt a spark of gladness, because he could tell Tjideng stories.

Over days, Jakob told of sewing, toy making, and carving. He described the Tjideng boys' invention of a play racing wagons, with bicycle tires as wheels. Make-believe meals were cooked and consumed in slow detail, pretending fullness from first course to last.

For a time they felt fortunate because they were closer to their mammies than in the days of servants. They learned about each other. Siebe Bevins' hands ran up and down painted pretend piano keys to practice. He taught Jakob notes and so he hoped to play with Mammie one day. Sara never let go of Tina, her doll, and bravely helped with all she could because so many tasks held urgency. She foraged for food, prepared meals, and learned to hide cooking fires.

As unbearably crowded as each room of Tjideng houses were, they found companionable times. They all learned to knit socks for the Japanese in order to earn money for food. It took several pairs of socks to earn a tiny amount.

Albert and Siebe learned to knit successfully; but he was hopeless. However, Jakob could make toys for the children out of bits of teak and wire, and the mothers paid him if they could. *When the Japanese punished me, and pulled me up by the arms and miraculously released me, Siebe was so nice. But I won't tell you bad stories, because that would lead to the bad story of what happened to Albert.*

Bevins' eyes sparkled. So he even told about Marijke, her delicate embroidery, which he still had with him in his sling, and how beautiful she was, even there. Bevins' eyes grew ever kinder, so he told about her abduction for "good care" by the Japanese, and return. How she hadn't talked for weeks, but held her mother's hand, then slowly came back to life.

He added there was one good Japanese, Ienega, also called Fat Nose by the Dutch.

Bevins explained the nicknames at Tjimahi for each guard, which they thought the Japs didn't understand. Certain code words *rood voor*—red in front!—to warn of approaching guards, had already been ruined however. A particular guard, fortunately not the cruelest, would approach and say *lood vool* without the *r* sounds and laugh. His nickname became Little Father, as he was shorter than most of the Japanese, and showed pictures of the children he missed at home. Of course he had been beaten senseless by an officer for kindness to prisoners, and now kept his distance.

At last Bevins asked, "Your mother, your sister, your father, your brother, and of course Wim in Holland? Tell me."

Jakob looked him square in his blue eyes. He felt an invitation, like a still pond to swim into; he could take a chance to say more. But he must choose his words carefully or Bevins would never speak to him again. A man who prayed would not want to be with a liar and a thoughtless boy. "Could you tell me first about Pappie, have you heard where he is?"

"Last time I saw your father, we were together. You saw us."

Of course, Bevins had been in that same long line. Jakob started to answer. "Mammie stayed brave as I said. We were separated from Tante Ankie and her family, as well as the de Bakker family, and we missed them terribly. Sara suddenly grew tall, but of course not out. How I wished I could have helped her." He wouldn't tell Bevins about the time he took a spoon of her food.

"Did they take Albert then, before you?"

Jakob turned away. "They took us; we *were* separated." The lie slipped out easily. After all they were separated — by death. Now there would be no more questions. Bevins would just think that they had left Tjideng at different times. "Oh, and of course while we were together, we all counted every hundred days that soon we would be liberated."

Bevins said, "Everyone says to believe in the Americans. I believe in any ally, including our own dear Lord. The rumor lately is that we will all be sent to Burma as slave labor. I hope it never comes to pass. In the meantime we can try to learn more about your pappie. So, let's have you move near me?"

Jakob hesitated. *Should he say, ja, to learn about Pappie and Albert?* "Yes," he said. He had to be near someone who reminded him of home. Bevins was kind as well as prying.

"Ja, I'm sure your family is fine," said Bevins, as they swiftly prepared to enter their respective barracks and line up for appel. "We will soon be liberated by the Americans."

† † †

Prickling lice woke Jakob one morning with a jolt. He hadn't thought of Pappie for days or looked for him. It felt funny, almost disloyal, to be like someone's son again. No words were said about Bevins being like a father to him, but they talked and stayed close, each on the sparse 30 centimeters width allowed for sleep.

Jakob learned mind tricks, which Bevins called a form of prayer, to survive. One was to breathe deeply while counting, pretending to be full. It often worked. He felt tinges of satisfaction. He never passed up the coolness of daybreak, while Bevins and most men would sleep a few minutes longer. He could stand in line to collect water for a small mandi—fill his lungs, and then his belly with a big breath of air, pretending to be full.

The light was soft outside. He ought to be grim; it did no good to feel even slightly happy. Smittey and he nodded from one barracks to the other. He suspected Smittey was glad he'd found a family friend. He continued breathing, ending the morning routine with the breakfast line. The food smell was meager; so it was good to fill his belly, and perhaps his soul, with air.

Bevins had slipped out of the barracks and was ahead, gesturing him over. So Bevins was still looking out for him, like an odd *welcome home*. Jakob could stand in front of him. Their bowls received thin gruel with a teaspoon of rice, and a few insect floaters no one minded, sustenance. They went to a wall together, squatting down. Jakob slowly took spoonfuls, eventually going for the rice, chewing many times as always.

He thought again how he had taken a spoonful from Sara, and how she had never told. As if he could pay Sara back, he lifted the next spoonful and silently held it over Bevins' bowl.

"*Nee*, no joh, but look over there."

Jakob turned to see Johan, maybe a twelve-year-old, recently arrived from the other kamps. He thought of him as Johan Two, as Johan-One was with Tante Ankie, and much younger. Jakob waved him over, and Johan Two came near, his face pinched and anxious, hunkered down with his bowl clutched in his hands.

"Here," said Jakob and dropped his last spoonful into Johan's bowl. He patted him on the back. Johan upended the spoonful into his mouth quickly, then began the slow chewing, closing his eyes.

Bevins disappeared for the rest of their routine, going off with Roelof de Witt, a kind man Pappie had admired when still on Billiton. He was an accountant, and capable of long math sums in his head. He could always translate the Japanese calendar day, into the true day in 1945.

Bevins' corvée was to watch the boys who chopped the last remnants of confiscated teak furniture into fire wood, not too harsh. Jakob no longer went to the Pig Farm, but a different farm, scrabbling in the dirt to till and harvest the vegetable garden. The farm labor started with being assigned the water run with Johan Two. He wished a taller, more evenly matched boy was available. They pulled heavy buckets four times between them, straps digging into their shoulders, each bent, Jakob more so than Johan. Instead of thinking, *what if this stupid younger boy makes us get a beating*? Jakob pulled as hard as he could, and noticed how hard Johan Two tried. He had spirit.

Late in the day they all walked briskly back after tilling and turning long rows of sun-baked soil in the vegetable garden. The quicker they returned, the better their place in the food line. Bevins was there, and Jakob smiled. For the first time since Albert's death, he felt that home in hell was still a semblance of home.

CHAPTER 20

Luce

Houston, Texas
January 2005

Mama greets Daniel, Papa, and me with a rich soup and dinner. I feel truly sprung from the cage of my anxiety, the hospital. Seems every generation of our family hates the hospital. Both leaves on the dinner table are pulled out and here is Corrie — all lit up next to Patrick, Alby, Cindy, Marina and Wade.

"If only Vincent were here," I whisper to Daniel.

"He's fine," hisses Daniel.

"I know, I just miss him," I reassure Daniel, but I think Vincent must be miserable, and doing nothing for school.

We sit down, and Mama says, "Now, nice calm talk. You all know Luce can't be stressed, she doesn't need one moment of extra pain."

Corrie and Alby grin. I try not to scrutinize Alby, but I notice none of us have wine glasses, and his pupils are neither pinned nor dilated. He sits without his usual restlessness; Wade leans into him, half on his lap. He's a striking eight-year-old boy: olive skin, blond streaks in light brown hair. He wears a T-shirt from his 4-H class. Marina sits next to me, and occasionally I reach over and hold her hand, pleased that she lets me.

"Oh yes," says Corrie, "none of our usual boisterousness."

Patrick's not fazed by our banter, and he looks like a present-day hippie, longish hair, neatly dressed, not my stereotype of a worship director at a conservative church. He talks about his daughter to Mama, who smiles, they enjoy the conversation.

"So were you able to get Luce a ticket home?" Alby asks. "She missed her flight. I understand it was my entirely fault," he smirks.

Silence from me. I blush, not able to either apologize or appreciate his gentle banter.

"Well?" Papa asks, this is the kind of thing he must know.

Daniel squeezes my leg under the table. "We have our tickets already. I was able to change Luce's to my date tomorrow, with a doctor's note. I was able to *organize* that." He knows how much Papa loves to get things organized.

"Speaking of quiet," I ask, "where are Sadie and Tutu?"

Wade speaks up excitedly. "Grandma and Grandpa gave Sadie to me and Tutu to Marina."

I grin at Cindy. "Wow, what a menagerie."

"It's great for us," she says, always a peacekeeper. "We get two house-trained dogs, and Grandma and Grandpa get some quiet."

"And soon we will adopt a kitten, or two kittens," Mama says.

Papa almost purrs, "Maybe Mollie Two, and the other kitten for Mama to name."

After dinner, Papa, Corrie and the men go to the electric keyboard in the back room. Cindy, Marina, and Mama go play three-handed "crazy bridge," and I curl on my side on the living room couch, ready to doze. Soon I'll be home, all is well. My eyes rest on the wall, a painting of the Rocky Mountains, and Papa's Indonesian shadow puppets, Wajongs. On a shelf large Indonesian carvings rest; their direction has been adjusted. Who did Papa get to go up on a ladder to realign it for good fortune? Probably Daniel; Papa would have insisted they do this for Baby, and Papa is much more "he who must be obeyed," than I am.

On the end table, a photograph of Alby and I still in Nederland shows us squeezed onto a little sled, bundled up in stiff woolen jackets, smiling as if no one had to say, *Smile, smile for the camera.* Another photo of us kids on a family camping trip in Utah shows Corrie's little toddler head poking out of the pup tent, our hands not so gently ruffling her hair.

All our homes string together. Mama and Papa's house is becoming like Beppe and Pake's boerderij for me, the home that is always there.

Mama, whispers, *"Ach, het schatje,"* as I drowse. She is thinking of me as ever so little, *schatje,* her precious little one, carrying another little one. Baby flutters again.

I check the Utah photos again, and remember that we all had special moments there, yet we left.

Papa has often told me how much he loved each adventure with Tom in Utah, they would see rattlesnakes, sometimes dying on the road from trucks driving over them on purpose, not allowed nowadays, I suppose. Sometimes they heard the rattle nearby that could make them scramble twenty yards away then laugh hysterically, once out of danger. At home I have an agate bracelet made with what they found, polished oval with smoky white threading across desert brown. I'll wear it all the time when I get home.

† † †

It's not until Mama wakes me up by stroking my hair that I know I've been asleep. Cindy and Marina have joined the singing in the back room. "What is it, liefje? *Ga maar.*" She's telling me to go ahead and talk. Did I shudder with a nightmare? When will I be like Papa and talk for her *ga maar*? I feel her soothing touch quell my fears.

Cindy, Marina, and Corrie join voices lilting to us in three-part harmony, the kind like family produces when always together. I shake my head as if I could escape the smoke tendrils of sorrow, dropping Mama's sweet hand from my forehead. What have I lost by living several states away?

The men's voices rumble in with perfect rhythm, rough notes. They've switched to "Oh Come, All Ye Faithful." All of the Vanderveers and in-laws like still singing Christmas songs on into January.

I struggle up. I'll go sing and avoid Mama's hurt look, she always wishes to hear more from me. Her eyes are crinkled, as she smiles, her short hair every which way. She must have napped also in her easy chair. "So?" she asks.

I don't recollect my dream as I rub my eyes — so I woke up crying. Mama holds my hand. My heart thunders. I went it alone growing up, after depending on Mama. Like usual I went it alone to come to Houston this second time. Just in the last few days I despaired, trying to hide, afraid we'd lost Baby. So I tell her.

"So …" I sit up, clutching her hand. "I've been afraid, and so sad. The doctors insist everything is fine now."

"I know." She nods vigorously, as if she's going to give me all her cheeriness.

"But I still worry."

She rolls her eyes. To my surprise we both giggle, the Vanderveer syndrome — worrying. To worry is to live, and even to love. Since I worry about Baby, I must love her, right?

"Oh Mama, with the last miscarriage, I was far enough along, so we told Vincent all about being a big brother. Then I still lost the baby, so cruel. So horrible that once miscarriage started, I instantly felt the change. You know that full feeling of pregnancy — gone. The next day Daniel and I woke up with this deep grief, and me cramping. We knew we wanted to tell Vincent immediately."

"Joy to the World" bursts out from the study and Papa's electric keyboard. No harmony, just loud.

"So there we were so tired and we sat with Vincent. My sweet Daniel, he wanted to believe that families grow in miraculous ways, fragile cell connecting to fragile cell, dividing, multiplying, and growing. But we didn't grow miraculously—again, and he looked defeated, so not like him. Vincent said in his high little-kid voice. 'We aren't having the baby anymore?' He pulled his favorite sky-blue sweatshirt around him. You know the one he wore forever?"

"Ja, the one he managed to wear for three years." Mama pats my belly reassuringly.

"Yep, that one. So I just said, 'No, honey.' And I hear back, 'Where did she go? She grows inside of you.' I explained she couldn't grow inside me anymore. I put his warm little hand in mine and told him, 'The baby came out and was too little, much too little, to live.'"

Mama caresses my hand.

"Vincent decided, 'Don't worry, Mommy. If she left, we can find her. I'll help.' Then Daniel had to say, 'Vincie, we can't find her. Our baby died. She died because she couldn't grow anymore.' Daniel cried, I was frozen."

Mama pulls my head on her shoulder, we rock.

"I pulled Vincie and his faded blue sweatshirt onto my lap. I told him, 'We are so sad, but you won't be having a baby sister or baby brother anymore. Our baby didn't just go away. We can't get her back and grow her again.' When he asked, 'She's in heaven?' I felt relieved. He understood. 'Yes,' I said."

"But I knew more had to be said." Daniel's voice is behind me, and he sits down on Mama's other side. "So I said, 'She's gone. She's in heaven, but we can't visit her there.' And Vincie wiped his eyes with his sleeve and said, "Oh, I know. She's with God, but I wanted to hold her."

"And Mama, I was so sad, and told Vincie, 'I'm so sorry; I wanted to hold her too.'"

I remember she can be quiet like this. All those nights in Houston, hot, ugly Houston when I told her I had no friends, and she murmured her ideas and then offered her silence for me to fall into. I'd forgotten.

She squeezes my hand. "Well, you are full of life now." Red blossoms on her round cheeks, a sign of determination. "This is a good time, and Vincent is getting his little sister. You know, we must keep talking this way, and also about Beppe, Pake, whatever you want. All of what we say, it does heal. This is a good time?" She lifts my chin gently.

"Yes," I nod. *I'm not ready to say more.*

Everyone's heading our way. The kids are the loudest. Wade's saying, "I guess pregnant mommies sleep a lot, huh, to grow the baby?"

"I'm awake Wade," I call.

Cindy calls out, "Of course you are. Keep resting honey. Let us pamper you one last time before you leave for California."

Tears well in my eyes. Everyone is kind, and soon I'll see my own Vincent.

They each lean down to hug me in turn, Papa's hug wavering in a way that makes me want to prop up his shakiness. He's doing way too much. I worry he'll collapse the second we leave. Cindy gives us a bag of airplane snacks. They quickly say their good-byes. When they're all gone, the house is in complete *stilte* — still. We each hold our books, in our pools of light from well-placed reading lamps. Daniel has been introduced to this habit long ago.

I lose track of the words I'm reading. My heart pounds, as I peer at Papa over my book-shield. I always have more questions for him. Can I disturb him? He looks so happy and I'm supposed to leave him that way. I tell myself to ask questions. To want to know is kind not mean. I reached an end point of talking with Mama, which we usually never do. We danced around our sorrows for years, which only created conversations we never finished. A mother can reassure a child forever, and it's the one time of exhaustion the child remembers, that creates a shard of glass in the heart saying, *see, you have no soft loving place to be.* I can believe

Vincent is safe now too, Mama and I are safe, and Baby of course.

† † †

Papa shivers a moment, pulling a throw over himself and setting his book to the side. He coughs mildly and clears his throat. "I don't mind talking about Bevins now because he helped me face what happened to Albert. What we could each do in our imaginations gave us the few moments of victory in the kamps.

"You know I did read that book by Viktor Frankl, where he told about the Nazi concentration camps. He described the moment of awareness, the knowing that the captors couldn't steal everything away from us. Our spirits, they couldn't rob. Most of us boys, and some of the adults, we still had courage, ingenuity, and imagination. You know about imagining rijsttafel, all the courses of an Indonesian meal. I could imagine being filled. I think you know that Bevins helped me with my spirit. Helped me to not lose my determination to keep a fine spirit, and … to live."

† † †

Jakob and Bevins

Tjimahi
April 1945

Bevins forced himself to farm corvée again. Numbers were down; hardly anyone was well enough to go. He insisted he could work and smuggle back a few greens to the kamp hospital. Laboring on pace with the rest, Bevins had a way of resting and breathing which renewed him for the next round. Was it a trick or prayer? Jakob wondered and watched.

Jakob still thought *home*, when walking back to the barracks with Bevins and the rest. His bare foot hit a sharp

389

rock and sliced his flesh, or so it felt. Was he cut between his toes?

"*Lekkas, lekkas,*" screamed a Heiho. He couldn't stop to look. Would the cut infect, become jungle rot and kill him? Bevins walked shoulder to shoulder with him. If he knew about Albert, he would not be so kind. Too kind, always.

Jakob drew a deep breath again, and found his pretend fullness shot; he was trembling. How could he hurt himself so carelessly? He always made mistakes.

Dust puffs appeared on the road far ahead. The mirage. His heart quickened. This could be the moment to see Pappie again. Bevins often said, "Among the thousands they move around, you never know who you will find." This could be a meeting, a moment like this. Green shimmered into brown, not just at the horizon, but on the road. Wavery figures turned from great dust puffs to long-legged storks, to beige people to a group of women trudging toward them. Oh the women's kamp. They stood straighter when they saw the men. They too carried rickety *patjols*—hoes—on their shoulder, and kept their silence.

An older teenaged girl walked in the front. She was long legged, and the curve of her calf flashed like an exquisite water-color brushstroke. Jakob felt the Marijke-kiss pang in his belly. So many women after seeing none; at least one hundred. Roelof de Witt always talked about Mevrouw de Witt, his Aartje. He would be so happy if she was in this group. He would have something to talk about tonight.

A woman with a long blonde braid, and a blouse made of a dish towel, turned their way. Roelof de Witt straightened. This would be Aartje? Aartje de Witt carefully turned her head their way several times. "*Dag*, Aartje," called de Witt softly. He had gone crazy, to talk like this. Jakob's heart froze while his legs still moved.

Aartje kept her head down, and then fluttered her arm briefly at her side as if the breeze lifted her hand, a tiny signal of powerful love.

"Silence, silence!" roared the Heiho and ran to Meneer de Witt. The women increased their pace, the beautiful girl tugging Aartje's arm.

Beater, as they called this Heiho, had already reached De Witt, snarling like a wild dog, his dusty ludicrous Japanese-issued pretend rifle brandished. The other guard, with a real rifle, bayonet glinting, stood by. Jakob and the men automatically stepped to the side, to try to defend their friend only meant a severe beating later. From his decimeters shorter stance, Beater swung his rifle butt up at De Witt's chin, then a seesaw stroke back again, smashing his mouth into a bloody circle, a tooth falling to the ground. De Witt staggered to stay on his feet.

Jakob held his breath. He knew now how Zwanenburg, Papa and now Meneer de Witte fought in the only way they could. The only way was to stay on your feet and survive, hands helpless at your sides. Hitting the ground could mean death — through kicks and stomping.

Beater smashed DeWitt's nose too. He reeled, and red spread over his entire face as he tried to bow. The guard hit him with his fist on the side of the head, then started kicking till he was forced to fall and roll into a ball on the ground, for a worse beating. The kicking went on and on, one sounded like a crack to his back. Finally Beater stopped, snarling words that must mean "bad ungrateful prisoner."

Jakob's breathing came in gasps. Thoughts rushed and rushed in his head. *If only he did nothing, if only he said nothing.*

Beater panted, too tired to do more, the signal they could help De Witt up now. *"Kom maar —* come on — Roelof," said one man and pulled him to his feet, wrapping Roelof's arm over his shoulder. The women were long gone. Jakob maneuvered under De Witt's other shoulder, talking in his mind. *De Witt, the idioot — stupid risks, near death.* Beater stared straight ahead for the remainder of the trudging march back to kamp, as if in a trance. They never let De Witt down to carry his own full weight, as one of his legs did not lower to the ground. Blood dripped red on his chest and his ear was swollen.

Will he be able to hear again in that ear? Jakob and the other man maneuvered him wordlessly all the way back to the barrack, hoping to take him to the hospital. If it had not been day's end, Roelof would have had to bake in the sun, bleeding, while the others worked. No prisoner was ever cared for by his mates during corvée. Corvée stopped for nothing.

They laid Roelof down in the barracks, after a discussion resulting in, no hospital after all. Bevins disappeared, and returned with a basin of water and fairly clean rags. He squatted down by De Witt and said, "Roelof, here I am."

Jakob left. He was done helping a man he barely knew from back home, who had taken a risk bound to lead to a beating. Squatting at the latrine ditch, Jakob cried. Why? He cared nothing for de Witt. He cried with no tears, heaving sobs and diarrhea. Little in, little out. Stupid! De Witt was stupid. Stupid to show his care for his wife, stupid to put her at risk, stupid to risk a beating. Such men were dangerous for them all. De Witt became Roelof in his head, dropping all boyhood respect. *No Meneer. Roelof, so stupid. Never, never be noticed. We boys all know this, why not a grown man? How many men here are useless, not fighting when it might help, yet stupidly speaking out? While all the time angry snake eyes watch. Pappie always said Albert had sense, and I have little sense, but Roelof has no sense at all.*

Roelof had one golden-brown eye when Jakob returned, the other eye swollen shut. Bevins gently turned to his good eye, whispering. Could he be stuck with caring for Roelof after all? Bevins obviously would do so. Ja, too kind.

Jakob nodded to the sleeping tiers and said to Bevins, "Shouldn't Roelof be in the hospital?" *I know more now than Roelof does. I'm a man.*

"And he would get such good care there." Bevins' eyes looked serious and tired, yet his mouth corners twitched. "And, if you say Roelof, his birth name, then you must still show respect," said Bevins, as if he could read Jakob's mind. "We will care for him here. The hospital has no more rations than we do. It is best we watch out for each other."

Jakob blurted, "Ja, but he never should have said a thing ... or moved. Who knows what they're doing to Aartje now?"

Bevins closed his eyes, as if he could sleep a long time, and opened them, sighing. "Let us hope that Japanese stupidity will mean that they don't know that she was the one he tried to communicate with; they didn't notice her. Or, even better, let's hope her group was with the rare guard with a heart." His mouth broadened to a genuine smile. "Or even a guard who knows he has a soul."

"Still Roelof was stupid. The one thing we can all do here is to use our heads."

"Jakob," said Bevins firmly. "Listen to me. Every bad thing that happens here is due to the cruelty of war and captivity thanks to the Japanese. You can use your head every moment and still be beaten. Do not be this hard on others or you will be this hard on yourself."

Jakob felt a chill. Anyone could be brought low. For a moment he entered the gray fog memory of Albert's last days. Had Albert been careful enough? Had he helped Albert enough? His stomach knotted as if he had to run for the latrine ditch again. With all else, he was quick and careful, but with his own brother, the answer must be no. He must be guarded with Bevins now, and hope that would make up for his stupidity. Nothing made up for a brother's life.

He nodded back at Bevins, a fog thickening inside, not knowing what to say.

Bevins touched him on the shoulder, shaking him mildly. "We have souls, yes? None of us should be caged like prisoners. Our only crime is that we were in the way. The quickest, most careful men get beaten within a centimeter of death."

For dinner, someone fed Roelof as if he was a child, lifting his head, and spooning soup into this mouth. Jakob muddled into sleep, feeling a shred of home next to Bevins, and the sad fog thickening for Roelof and Aartje. Each man or boy had to have at least one other. Roelof's other must be the one feeding him. Jakob's other had been Albert. More and more were dying.

Jakob had no other for himself here yet. Bevins would not be his other, watching out for him, because he showed care to everyone.

CHAPTER 21

Luce and Daniel

Houston, Texas
January 2005

We moved too much for all of our souls, soul tissue stretched thin by friends and family left behind.

I stretch with no pain, on my way to the neatly set breakfast table. I wish I would have talked with Mama more, about too many leave takings, my version and hers. I grit my teeth. *She is healthy and Papa may be dying. Priority — talk to Papa.* I settle in Dutch-style, with my own teapot of weak tea, and an array of breakfast meats and cheese. Daniel joins me, until Papa yells for both of us to come to the guest room. "Hey, let's pack you two up."

Daniel rolls his eyes. "Ah, the gentle call." He strolls away. Soon suitcases and snack bags are ready by the front door and I realize Papa never fussed once about leaving for the airport on time, only about being ready. Progress.

I'll miss this second home more than usual. Mama and Papa look rested, kicked back in reading chairs, relaxed. Peaceful silence is marred only by Papa's on and off cancer cough. I exhale, not realizing until this moment, how often I hold imagined dread. I feared Papa had lost every particle of joy he had this week. He believes holding his breath holds airplanes up in the air and prevents crash landings. I believe holding my breath will keep *ruzie* explosions from happening. But what I really need is to breathe and have conversations go beyond silence, *ruzie*, silence, *ruzie*.

I feel the urge to speak, just as Mama says, "Well, are you going to finish for us? What happened with Bevins?"

Papa lifts his cup. "Ah. Well, we had none of this … coffee in the *kampen* of course." He sets it down. "So more about Bevins? He struggled so with that almost-useless-patjol field work. He had been badly beaten early in the war, and had a limp. I would have done anything to ease it all for him, but couldn't."

He arranges his cane by his chair and faces the Utah Rocky Mountains painting. I ache for him. He's picturing Bevins.

"At first I told him I would rather learn the math I was missing, as some of the boys did, or to have real food, then to hear his strange teachings about breathing and such."

I laugh.

Papa chuckles. "He laughed too. But for a long time, after he was gone, I breathed like him." His knuckles turn white as he pulls the cane crossways in his lap, looking as if he wishes to break it.

"After he was gone? He died?"

"Another time."

"And it is good to remember him?"

"Ja." He breathes deeply. "Ja, I think it is good, and so I will tell you. And another time you'll tell me more about the moves when you were little?"

Mama gives me a knowing looks. "You are peas in a pot with Papa, holding back your own story."

"Ja, I will say more," I promise. If I must be *peas in a pot* with Papa, I wish I could be peace in a pot, much better.

"Good," says Papa. "For now, here is more from me. Prepare yourselves. Remember I always said I didn't want to hurt you with the worst."

† † †

Jakob and Bevins

Tjimahi
Days later, April 1945

No mirages, no possibilities, just more forced labor. Routes and fields alternated, but the stupor of sleep, try for food, work, try for food, sleep, never changed.

They walked a different route to the fields. Beater and another guard, a new Heiho, strode beside them, screaming occasionally for effect, "*Lekkas, lekkas!*" Guards tolerated more, that the men's pace only quickened for minutes and then returned to the same slow walk. Lethargy had become the stronger master. Jakob found that he was shaky, not just from hunger, but from nerves and days of wondering who might be beaten next. As always, Beater was at the back end, where his snake eyes could see. Jakob lifted his feed dully in the middle of the pack.

The line straggled out longer, a good time to release his nerves. He tried filling his lungs with a deep breath. No good, at least no guard could hear him now. He hissed to the old man next to him, probably Pappie's age, "A new route today. What will we see?"

The man flinched away. No talking.

Jakob's neck prickled, noticing too late that Beater had sidled up close. Never draw attention your way his insides screamed, not days ago by helping De Witt, not by whispering to another now.

Beater screamed unfamiliar Japanese words. It had to be a warning. Jakob walked as straight and swiftly as he could. Beater panted near him; he would be watched carefully now, no wrong moves or words. The building heat of the day didn't register as icy sweat ran down Jakob's back. *Keep walking. Beater will stop. If he must strike out, please don't let it be on the old man who jerked away. It's all my fault.*

Beater's panting continued. He yelled again. *He won't stop.* Energy raced through Jakob's body, as if every vein and artery turned voltaic, his hands twitched. *Don't look, don't look. He'll strike out.*

His feet stepped along, but didn't feel like they hit the ground. Except for low rations, sickness and death, nothing was predictable. Some days it didn't matter if they whispered, today it did; he'd simply picked the wrong day. Thoughts raced along. Why did he take such a chance? He knew better. Beater of course didn't know what Jakob had said. So far the new guard said nothing.

Beater's predatory panting dropped away. Jakob eased his breathing. Crisis gone? They approached a group from the local kampong village. Beater screamed again, louder, and swung his artificial rifle. He liked an audience. *Oh, for the new guard too, he's showing off.* The rifle butt hit Jakob square in the back. He gasped for air and hit the ground with white hot pain—broken back, bleeding kidneys? He clenched and released his fists, knowing he had to do three things quickly: leap up off the ground, appear to be badly hurt, which wouldn't be hard, and lower his head to show respect.

He swayed to his feet, ears throbbing with the rush of blood, rage, and hurt. The electricity inside would not let him bow. He met Beater's eyes, looking down into dark brown eyes, blood shot. He saw Beater could and would kill.

"Bow!" Beater yelled and swung for Jakob's ear. Beater's hand hit hard as a rock, wrapped as it was around the fake hardwood rifle.

He fell, blood in his mouth, his ear ringing. Jakob rose, keeping himself in a bow this time as Beater's blows and kicks connected to his shins, his ribs, his nose, and jaw. He swayed but kept his feet under him.

Jakob spun around on his feet with the next blow; out of the corner of his eyes he saw Beater's view of the villagers. They turned and backed away at seeing a starving young one so brutally beaten. Except for one man. He stood with hard eyes, bone-thin himself, probably glad the children of former masters had been brought low.

With his audience almost gone, Beater shook himself like nothing had happened, although he staggered with exertion. The guards stood still; the men stood still, but close. Jakob widened his legs, determined not to fall down.

"Marching on," Beater commanded.

The old man and Bevins moved in close to Jakob. They intended to be two trees on either side of him to keep him from falling. He stepped along with the rest, legs wooden. Each foot fall jarred into his aching ear. Blood ran down his face, his shoulder and arm. He bent to one side, from the sharp pain in his back. With his tongue he explored the blood and spongy soreness of his mouth. He drank his own blood gladly, energy.

As they reached a new field, Bevins murmured, "This is the pig farm again." To the old man he said, "Come, De Raaf," and motioned Jakob to stay between them. Beater no longer looked their way. Might he feel regret? No, just making a show of harsh aloofness, the fake samurai.

De Raaf whispered needlessly, "You must appear to be working or be hit again."

Jakob bent and stumbled up and down the rows. Bevins, De Raaf, and others helped by dropping clods of clay at his feet, as they, too, struggled up and down the pathetic furrows. Jakob tried to clear his mind, but every breath had the coppery smell of blood. He bent and picked for the appearance of labor, then straightened as much as his hurt back would allow. This was now the second time in the kamps that his nose had been shattered. The first time was by a Dutch boy fighting over food.

Bevins spoke casually as he passed him in a row. "Well, old man, now the girls will think you are very interesting after the war. That nose of yours will look like a curve on a road map. You'll be the handsome mysterious chap. Remember, you will heal."

Jakob heaved his sore leg onto a makeshift patjol—wood and a blunt knife lashed together. He mumbled around his thick tongue and loose tooth, "Ja, I'll look for you after the war, when we're all fat again. And why do you call me old man?"

Bevins chuckled. How Jakob liked to make him laugh, even now. He couldn't join the laughter; his side ached sharply with every breath.

"Ah, we don't have mirrors here, so you don't know. You have your first stripe of gray sprouting right in the middle of your forehead. Your gray streak is a lovely shade of pink right now, with all the blood."

They passed others a dozen more times, taking care that they never seemed to slow nor speed up when together. Jakob counted each pass, wishing they were laps in a swimming pool instead of dirt clods in hell. He stopped counting, grew dizzy, swayed more, stayed on his feet. The sun climbed in the sky. Feet, feet were all he could notice the rest of the morning. Finally the guard called a break, but only for water, not for food.

They sighed in moments of shade. Bevins dabbed at his face with extra water and a rag. "There, no more pink for you," he said.

Jakob took care to not answer. He could not cause Bevins to be targeted now. The yell came, *more work*. Everyone stumbled back in the heat. Only when the sun started to angle far down in the sky did they finally hear the call to stop: *"Yamero!"* Marching back to kamp, Jakob's aches turned from sharp stabs with every step and pulse to dull all over pain.

Jakob thought of Albert's scientific studies. What would he say of us? He'd say they were like amoebas, practicing the top rule of *tawanans*—prisoners: become an anonymous group. Do not be observed as anything but amoebas, or

400

individual *tawanans* would be targeted and beat again. Sweat dripped down his cheeks and back.

The latest rumor was that the Japanese planned to continue with deprivation and then transport them to Borneo to work in the mines. As he was now, he would never survive that.

† † †

Roelof de Witt returned to corvée, often grimacing from the effort to walk with a hitch on one side. He had to go to relieve Jakob, and in hope for seeing Aartje again.

The doctor had examined Jakob's swollen shut eye, declaring his eyeball intact, and that miraculously he had not broken bones other than some light fractures in his ribs, and only a mildly sprained his back. His greatest pain would be from the ribs, so he was given temporary corvée to help in the hospital, scraping pus out of men's sores with a metal spoon.

Jakob squinted with his good eye. Methodically he scraped men and boys used to the routine, some getting worse, a number improving. He flashed on a memory of Albert. He did wait too long and that's why his pain was so excruciating. Maggots were used here to eat out infection before spoon treatment. There was an organization to this kamp, embracing the macabre, the dark, and the unthinkable. Survival was linked to urine- and yeast-based bread, latrine sewage going to the fields, and the maggots.

Soon he faced an old man with the tainted sweet smell of gangrene. It had been Albert's smell before death, and he had been much too young to reek this way. His brother had been crazy to still visit Jakob for malaria, rather than asking for hospital help for himself.

He felt a fury for Albert; what an idiot to sacrifice his life so recklessly, when he still needed his brother. He collapsed back on his haunches, painfully, his side aching with the jolt.

The old man watched, few wrinkles on his face. So he was not so old, but someone's Pappie, someone who could be saved. Jakob struggled to squat again and started in, as the man closed his eyes, going as still as death. Jakob did his best Henk imitation, saying, "Okay, now almost done, then some rest and you'll heal." The man slowly moved his infected arm, nodded. Perhaps he had been one of the many hoping to escape into death, but finding he was still alive.

Jakob stood up dizzy, pain stabbing his sides, looking for the next patient. No, he could not do one more step. He walked to the doctor.

"I've been able to move enough that I know I can perform my regular corvée tomorrow. This work is the wrong kind of twisting for my ribs. Do you think I can go back to my barrack?"

The doctor stopped all he was doing. "Well, in spite of that beating, you are better off than some. Here, carry these bandages just in case. So you are telling me you are in too much pain to go on, and you will do farm corvée again tomorrow?" He shook his head over the irony. "Very well." It was unspoken that Jakob would take care to be unseen by a guard on the way back, or if need be, look purposeful.

† † †

He filled Bevins in as they finished a soup with more fish heads than usual, a feast. "I am well enough to return to corvée tomorrow. See, I can start to open the one eye, I can twist my back." He turned and moaned.

Bevins sounded stern. "Come with me." They went to one of the huts no one wanted to approach, where the Japanese would throw a man for days with no food, no water, usually pulling out his body at the end. They settled down on the shady side, their backs again the wall. "De Witt saw Aartje's crew again today; neither he nor she moved a muscle, of course. He has no regrets." Bevins knocked his empty bowl against the hut hard. "And you, you had to speak! You had to stand up without bowing? De Witt, I think, *had* to be reckless. The day came that he had to take the risk, because of the wonder of his Aartje. He only wishes he would have thought first—what if she were attacked."

"But she wasn't." Sweat drenched Jakob as if he labored in midday sun. His words sounded stupid. He was more stupid than Roelof. Men had cared for him, helped him, and covered corvée for him, all because he made the same mistake as Roelof and then skipped a bow they performed twenty times in a day.

"No, and you, you chose this crazy risk, first talking for no reason, then defying Beater. You knew it was too soon, you knew he would attack again."

"No." Jakob's face flushed with shame.

"You knew. Did you want to die?"

"No, I didn't want a beating, I didn't want to die," said Jakob hoarsely.

"So were you only going for bad pain? Your brother, you must miss him with the separation?"

Splinters dug into Jakob's back, a welcome distraction from his aching sides, and his twisted back. He slowly turned to Bevins, leaning against the same wall, seeing with his one open eye, the two deep-blue eyes looking back. No longer stern, his tone as warm as it had ever been.

His hands clenched his bowl with a deeper shame; he dug his battered spoon into the dirt. "We weren't separated. Like everything that happens in these kamps, it's much worse than that. He's dead."

Bevins nodded as if he had always known. "Tell me what happened." No one approached.

"Well, you see, I had been in hospital with malaria, and Albert took care of me, even managed to get me a little extra food. Finally I noticed as my fever broke that he was limping, and on the day I left, he went in, with a deeply infected sore on his leg."

PART FOUR

Everything can be taken from a man but one thing: the last
of the human freedoms — to choose one's attitude in any
given set of circumstances, to choose one's own way.
— Viktor Frankl

CHAPTER 22

Jakob

Kamp Grogol
November 1944

Jakob's empty, weak hands brushed at his sides all the way to the hospital. He had no custard for Albert. His brother had been amazingly resourceful, like Jakob had never known him to be. But Jakob had nothing to give.

Jakob had found nothing, nothing to make custard a boy could live on; sugar was one of their lifesavers and there was none to be found. Yes his hands felt weak, empty. Could an infection-fever break and disappear too, like malaria?

Blood pounded in his ears from the effort to get to Albert. The central soccer field was turned to dust, trampled by too many feet. The trees alongside the gedek were browner than ever, a few tantalized greener, just the other side of the *gedek*. When thousands of men were turned into slaves, they became locusts too when the Japs weren't looking. So little green left and no more food.

The dusty hospital building loomed ahead. The only good thing about coming closer was that everyone kept their distance: the new Korean guards—Heihos—as well as the Japanese. Infectious typhus, dysentery, and misery lurked inside.

Moans, like water buffalo lowing, came from the hospital veranda. So many voices. Had he sounded like that when he was ill? He hoped Albert slept today from exhaustion, as he had, an escape. Dusk merged immediately into dark. A compact silhouette crouched low in the silver moonlight—Henk.

One arm cradled Albert's hurt leg. Henk's other hand worked on his foot. "Ach, it's so deep," he said as Jakob walked up.

Albert lay rigid, a short wooden dowel clenched in each hand, his jaw straining and working around the belt clenched in his teeth. Muffled wails sounded through, "Wooh, aah." Henk tensed to hold the leg still, while working on him with his other arm. Jakob's hands curled into fists. He could shove Henk, save Albert.

But Henk's eyes locked onto Jakob. This was hospital care: no pain killers, no alcohol, and no medicine.

Jakob knew Henk well. When he had burned hot, and shook with chills, Henk sponge-bathed him for fever. Albert was being tortured. Henk worked on the bigger wound with a metal kitchen spoon, as bad a tool as the broken *patjols* scraping on dirt for the field workers. Jakob crouched down, as Henk went on cleaning the wound, scrapings clanging into a metal bowl. The foot wound was six centimeters long, spreading from the top of Albert's ankle up to his shin. Jakob realized there was a second wound, a horrid traveler–infection he had seen happen to others, up the shin a bit, one centimeter long.

The sweet-rot smell of gangrene rose as Jakob pried open Albert's right hand and put his own hand inside. Albert moaned and crunched his bones with his squeeze. Could Jakob's hurt take Albert's hurt away? Jakob leaned over and crooned Baboe's Malaysian words, "There, there, you will be alright. Henk is helping you."

He felt nausea rising, glanced at the spoon digging down to white. He went numb with horror. Henk had to dig down to the bone? So he counted seconds slowly in his mind, gritting his teeth through Malaysian counting, Dutch counting, but refusing Japanese counting. The spoon rasped over the wound, and Albert, moaned, "Raih, raih, awp." He must be begging no, *Nee, nee, stop.*

Over and over Henk swiped infected tissue into the bedpan bowl, then scraped again. Jakob glared at Henk. Still not done?

After seconds turned minutes, Albert's grip stopped smashing his hand, almost letting go. He would faint.

Henk clanged the spoon into the bowl at last. "Done. I've never seen anyone as brave as your brother. He will have a chance to heal. The maggots, my scraping leave healthy flesh to grow without infection."

Henk's jaw worked and relaxed as he tidied up the bowl and spoon, bundling them in filthy cloth. Then he reached to a neatly folded stack next to him and crooned to Albert, "I wish we had clean bandages for you. Ah, these which were disinfected in blazing sunlight, they will have to do." His hands flashed as he swiftly wrapped blood-brown bandages around Albert's ankle and leg, fastening each part with a tear in the bandage end, and a loose butterfly knot. "Even the bandages can hurt," he sighed. "Okay, now, I pull the belt out of your mouth. At ease."

Albert dropped his raised head, his leg and every rigid muscle back to the ground. He squeezed Jakob's hand.

Henk held up the belt. "Whoa, quite some teeth marks. Glad you have more teeth than your brother. Albert, I believe your little brother's trying to lose every tooth he has. Jakob arrived a fighter to Grogol, and here by my side, ready to punch me out for causing you pain while trying to heal you."

Jakob shrugged as Albert laughed feebly. "*Dag,* Jakob."

Henk patted the bandaged leg. "Cleaned in the sun, as fresh as the sun, may you heal."

Albert slept, but it was exhausted sleep. He glowed with fever. Jakob eased his hand away, and went into action. He waved over Henk, who sponged Albert's red face, his neck, wrists, ankles all his pulse points, and then started over, dripping water from the sponge into a cleaner bowl.

"Does he have malaria-fever also, like I did?" asked Jakob.

Henk gave Jakob a long look. "Malaria? Most likely not. Come with me." They went ten meters away. "Jakob, do not borrow tomorrow's troubles, each day has enough worries of its own."

"What?" *This is all Henk has to say?* "Does he have malaria-fever also, like I did?"

"The Bible," Henk said. "Each day's troubles are enough. God says he can take care of even the flowers of the field."

But the field is brown. Jakob looked away. Henk had become so stupid, quoting the Bible. *And also desperate, Albert could die.*

Henk touched his shoulder. "Malaria? I hope not, we think not. But it is bad; I do not say the worst around the patients. Each must believe they can heal. His entire leg is infected. You saw the red streaks?"

Jakob nodded.

"Those crimson stripes are a bad sign of spreading infection. We hope the gangrene is not yet going into the rest of his body or his heart. He should have come here much sooner. Doctor Maastricht hates to perform amputation on one so young, especially when the wound is already infected. Even for amputation, it is almost too late. The doctor has to decide quickly. Albert should have been in earlier."

Anguish flooded Jakob. He recalled the photos of World War I British veterans, one legged amputees standing all in a line, with spider-legged pointed crutches holding them up. "I tried; I told him he was limping when he visited me. You saw him too!" he added hotly.

"You young boys can be the stupidest and the smartest of all. Always tend to a sore immediately. You know that." Henk's eyes closed halfway. Henk, too, must yearn to collapse into sleep, drowning in his powerlessness to offer regular medical care. Getting a few extra food rations for working in hospital was not enough.

Jakob collected himself, tried his best to smile at Henk. "Thank you." He returned to his brother. He and Albert were the stupidest and smartest, this they had known. He ran his fingers over Albert's bandaged wound, feeling the large dent, the smaller dent. The sweating was gone; could the sponging already have made him cooler? Would Albert survive here? For moments he hated his own brother for not coming into hospital immediately.

Then he thought again of the delicious custard Albert had fashioned for him, the life-saving sugar. He had loved it, savored it. Custard memory filled him, like the cloying sugary, yeasty infection smell around him now. *No!*

"Henk," he yelled, feeling like his old self, a boy who didn't care if anyone told him to shut up. "What does he need, sulfa?"

Henk arrived, shaking his head, and bent down to whisper urgently. "Yes, he needs sulfa. We have nothing. You know that, and no more medication of any kind is to be found. Even the risk of trading through the gedek may not work now. There's no help to be had."

He could trade Mammie's ring. No trade, no chance. He supposed he could tell Henk his secret, but he wouldn't. His jaw clenched shut.

Henk had moved half a meter to the next man, and waved over a boy carrying soup bowls. Luckily Albert couldn't hear the next man's rattled slow breathing or see his grossly swollen legs and prostrate. Beriberi, malnutrition, and starvation. This one would not leave the hospital alive, just like Meneer Smaken always warned about.

Jakob carefully set the bowl to the side and shook Albert's shoulder. "You must eat, eat. You have an actual piece of fish, some green."

"Nothing, nothing," mumbled Albert, as Jakob raised a soup spoon. "It will all just come back out."

Henk overheard and called out, "But try again to eat. You must have your strength."

Jakob hoisted Albert up and leaned them back against the wall, with Albert's head resting against him. He recalled an old silliness in play, the steamship to Nederland, shipboard four years ago. Everyone roared. He saw Wim's laughing face, not knowing yet he would be left. For the children's talent show, a part of passenger entertainment nights, Albert reached up to pat Albert's hair or itch his nose like a deranged puppet.

Albert was so light, like a pet bird he had to be careful not to squeeze. "Here's the little birdie," he said as Albert took the first bite.

"Like Mammie feeding Mevrouw Bevins?" asked Albert.

"Oh ja. She did a good job." *Good, he's speaking. I must go quickly now.*

Albert did no extra chews, but took every bite. His body relaxed. His breathing became even He would sleep. Jakob eased them both flat to the ground, huddled on the mat together. Suddenly, Albert jackknifed up as if Jakob tossed him up, clutching his middle, then motioning desperately. Jakob grabbed the big bowl nearby.

"Ahhh." Albert vomited into the bedpan.

It all came right back out. Jakob eased Albert's bird bones straight again on the mat, then arranged him on his side, checking his breathing. He hadn't helped his brother at all. Dizzily he looked for Henk, then dully lifted the soup bowl and drank the last swallow for himself. At that moment Henk saw him. Well he shouldn't have given wrong orders.

Henk neither frowned nor smiled, but simply came over with a sponge. "Oof," he said as if in pain. Ever so gently he wiped Albert off. "I will give him some water soon. Rest can do him good too."

413

"Albert, I know what we will do. I will get you medicine," Jakob whispered.

"Um," Albert moaned half asleep.

"I will get your medicine."

Albert opened his eyes. "Just call on the angels."

"What angels, joh?" Henk had said to let him sleep; now he had awakened him.

"I saw them. They were Indische and Nederlander angels. They sang so loud." Albert radiated the heat of fever again.

"Okay, ja, angels. Hush," said Jakob. Albert had never said such a foolish thing at home. He tried Baboe's musical voice, in Malaysian again. "Soon, very soon, you will feel better."

Jakob nodded to sleep himself and jerked awake, bashing his head back against the veranda wall, with a dream-picture in his head of Meneer Smaken snarling. "I won't go into the hospital, because no one comes back out again."

They should have said to him, "All us young ones come back." But they had been kind that day, thus becoming heirs to the precious condensed milk.

He stood and rubbed the small bump rising on the back of his head. Time to trade Mammie's ring for sulfa and food. Still enough time to act tonight.

† † †

He returned to the barrack gasping for air from running. Although he still had time before curfew, he had much to do. It was time to trade. Should he go to the barbed wire wall of gedek himself after evading sleep, then trade in the middle of the night? His eyes pricked with a stab of longing. Pappie would know what to do if he were here. Use one of the smugglers? Wolfgang—Wolfie—it would have be. He had no time to learn the ropes; he'd have to rely on Wolfie.

Jakob had to still his breathing, to clear his mind. Funny how lonely he could be, as if he was stuck on rough coral on a snorkeling dive, unable to come up, no one noticing, beyond rescue. *Be calm like Albert would be. You can spare a few moments to sort things out, but only a few.*

He absently captured lice from his own body and the mattress, eating some for the joke-of-protein. The prickling, the constant irritation, forced him to focus his mind and consider how best to trade Mammie's ring.

Wolfie was the one who could bring in almost anything. He didn't like Jakob, but he did like gold. Did it matter that on Billiton, Wolfie, two grades older, not deemed bright enough by his family to send to high school in Nederland bullied everyone, and that Jakob had found a way to wreak revenge? After a week of sore shoulders from sucker punches on the way home from school, Jakob had organized the younger kids to attack Wolfie as a group. On a signal, Matteus, he and younger kids had turned on Wolfie, fist swinging at him, crowing that they would get him, and get him good. Albert said no, he would not act like a bully himself, but the attack was a great success, Wolfie ran away like a coward, and everybody knew.

No matter, decided Jakob. Smugglers have no friends, only associates. Wolfie never looked you straight in the eyes unless he knew he had one up on you, and he always had a system, a way to make things go. Word was that he had never yet failed a deal at the *gedek*.

His sense of time told him it must be half an hour before curfew. *Lekkas, lekkas* for real. He trotted away and found Wolfie in the neighboring barrack, a nearby light bulb brighter than most. The naked bulb cast dark shadows all around. Wolfie restlessly sat cross-legged, leaning this way and that, sharpening his knife with leather and a whetstone. He looked up with *hello, you* in his eyes, but no particular malice.

Jakob had no choice but to hope that Wolfie was not a snake, or if a snake, a clever one. Jaapie, Wolfie's comrade who worked in the kitchen also, sat next to him. What with

415

the kitchen corvée and their smuggling, these two were less skeletal than most.

Jakob sauntered up, trying for a casual voice. "Wolfie, I must speak with you, alone."

"Oh, you can speak in front of Jaapie." Jaapie looked up and grinned with missing teeth. They must have been knocked out in a fight, like his own. Jaapie's eyes widened as his hand snuck up to his teeth and surprised Jakob with a nod, that said yes, *I know.*

Wolfie laid down his sharpening tools. His hand rested on a tin next to him. That must be where they kept some of their extra food. "Out with it then. What do you want?" Wolfie's gray-white teeth glowed in the light, the tin at his side the same color.

Jakob's chest tightened and he risked a steady look at Jaapie, although Wolfie was clearly the boss. He had to be sure only these two snakes heard him. "Okay, Albert is in hospital, I must trade for sulfa." All casualness left him. A guy like Wolfie, it would be smarter to feed him information a scrap at a time, not let him see how hungry, how starving you were for help. But he had to act and act now, and he had to have it all, overnight.

Wolfie's dark eyes flickered everywhere: to him, the food box, his knife. "Albert, huh? Everyone's trying to keep out of the hospital or get out. Well join us for a minute, sit down."

Jakob sat close on the empty slats near them.

Wolfie slanted his knife along his forearm, shaving off body hair to show its sharpness. "And don't you mean quinine, not sulfa? They all have malaria."

"No, he has an infection. You must trade tonight."

Wolfie rolled his eyes. "Of course you think I will trade tonight. What do you have to trade?"

"A ring," Jakob said even more softly and distinctly than before.

Wolfie stared him right in the eyes. "I will have to see it."

"Yes." He left and strolled across the yard aimlessly, yet hurriedly. He had maybe fifteen minutes before curfew. He quickened as he rounded the corner of his barrack. Would Wolfie steal the ring, could he trust anyone? No, this duo would never cheat and end up as two snakes without food. Wolfie thought he had him, but he had Wolfie in turn.

He pretended for precious moments, to rest on his sleep tier, and noted no one else nearby yet. When he was sure, his hand crept to the hole. He and Albert had made it in turns, each night softly sawing into this beam, with the knife they left Tjideng with. His finger poked into a fabric pouch, then into the ring, and brought it out to the dull light.

He had not examined it all these months: Mammie's wedding ring, with her and Pappie's initials on the inside of the band. He bent down, slipped it on his toe as if he were scratching an itch, and covered it with dirt in case he was stopped.

He made quick time back to Wolfie's barracks as he could let others think he was returning to his own barrack for curfew. He could do this deal with the Wolf-snake. Like Henk said, hardly anyone had anything left to trade.

When near, he bent over and coughed, palmed the ring, and handed it over.

Strange how Wolfie's hands shone clean as he ran his pinkie finger through the ring, and checked it low, by the light, where no one could see. "So, yes, it is gold," he yawned. "But no stone. This will not bring much."

"You know no one has gold or a watch or anything anymore!" Jakob hissed with hot rage. This was a game, like Kokkie at the market saying, *bah, these vegetables are no good* to get a reduced price. Only this game was deadly. He had to bargain, he had to control himself. Desperation rose inside. He thought for second of Albert's visible and invisible angels of so long ago.

His poor feverish brother. He turned terror into a growl. "Look, you will have to make it work; you know you

417

haven't had anything like this for a while. You will trade it for sulfa and eggs. You will trade it tonight."

Wolfie's eyes flickered to the ring, then to Jaapie. "Eggs too? Okay, tonight it will be."

His strong tone had helped; he had Wolf-snake's respect for now. Jaapie gave him the smallest of nods.

He made it back to his own sleeping platform at the last minute, with all the moaning and murmuring of men settled in. As others quieted again, he poked the hidden hole, no ring. Everything connecting him with Mammie gone, he scrunched his eyes tight. In the resulting flash of light he imagined Mammie and Sara. They nodded their approval. *Call on the angels*. He sensed Mammie and Sara were alive, thus not angels, but that golden light when he scrunched his eyes again. Gold ring, gold light, gold angels. Finally, all could go well.

CHAPTER 23

Papa looks exhausted, and he's coughing. "Remember you are still on antibiotics," says Mama and comes over with a glass and pills. He shakes his head. "You have to finish them all," Mama says sternly.

He closes his eyes and is fast asleep.

"You two go outside too while the morning sun is still so nice," commands Mama. A morning can switch quickly to nasty weather here.

I feel like saying no, everyone is so bossy. Daniel drags me outside.

"Look." He points to the flower beds.

"Hummingbird in January?" The blurry grey flits around a few flowers, and the red feeder. "Wow, there's so little out here in bloom, and yet it finds the one wildflower ..."

"Indian paintbrush," we say together.

"Jinx. I'm glad for this fragile bird."

"Looks pretty tough to me." He squeezes me.

"Ow, Ow, Ow."

"Oh, toughen up, old hummingbird. And no working for you when you get home."

"Just enough to say good-bye to clients," I say.

We hold hands and turn to the hummingbird's next darting blur.

"Look." Daniel lift-turns me gently. I turn; make a sneakered dance step, spinning on one foot. The hummingbird floats by a vibrant yellow mustard flower I couldn't see before, a weed.

Papa comes outside carefully, with his cane. He coughs.

"Let's take you inside," I say.

"No, I must finish, because all did not go easy or well with Albert and I."

He rests on a lounge chair, grabbing the rare breeze here in Houston, muggy even in the cool seasons. His eyelids close for a long blink, the way old people do when they think hard. What must he be recalling; he's silhouetted in the chair facing the one live oak that ever increasingly shades the fence and house. Its large roots cause difficulty. In my Japanese maple tree moments in our own garden, I do the same, looking for peace in a tree which grows well. He must feel in good company with his sturdy live oak, as I do with the maple.

† † †

Jakob and Bevins

Kamp Tjimahi
April 1945

Jakob's throat constricted, he would say no more. Because Bevins would say it now, *Jakob, you idioot. You should have traded right away. You had to see it was a long shot to stop infection, as the Americans say. The only thing to do was act decisively, at the first sign of infection.*

Instead he had traded at the last and worst sign of infection.

He was glad they were side by side, and that he couldn't read Bevin's every expression, and more glad of the quiet.

Men lined up for latrines, for water.

Clucking chickens tantalized them from the other side of nearby gedek. Bevins' silence and bony shoulder pressing on his, reassured him to say more. "Strange that he perished just a couple of months ago, because it seems like forever, with so many dying."

He felt Bevins nod.

"The next day was horrible, I woke to silence, an eerie stillness in kamp, one of those days when you can tell something is going to go wrong."

Bevins sighed, and Jakob felt he could spill it all, and hope for understanding. He pressed the stabbing pain of his hurt back against the rough planks. He could tell it all.

† † †

Jakob

November 1944
Grogol

Jakob's inner clock woke him at the edge of dawn. He padded along behind the barracks, heading to the outhouses, which bordered the gedek where it joined thick jungle. His entire spine, hips to neck, tingled. There were no distant sounds, no bird calls, giving the eerie feeling that nature herself feared the day. Where was the nearest Jap patrol? He remembered when Mammie could still get dysentery medicine to save them. His palms itched to hold a cure. Henk said no one could access medication anymore, but somehow he had to. If he had traded when the kamps were still almost open, he would own a supply of quinine and sulfa now. It was just as Pappie always said, that he didn't think. His heart pounded so that he tried to tell himself that of course the trade had occurred in the middle of the night. He would help just in time, as Albert was clinging to life. Stay wise, stay careful.

Returning, he saw Wolfie and Jaapie in the food line. Matteus stood nearby and to his surprise shot him a special "I have your back" look. He could sense his friend holding his breath, willing this all to go well. Wolfie waved him over with a hand. Jakob stood endless seconds next to Jaapie, who slumped where he stood. Wolfie's eyes as always flickered about. The comfort of Matteus brought shreds of solace. He had arrived by walking transport, finding Jakob in the hospital, and Albert caretaking.

Jakob asked Wolfie in code, "So what do you have for corvée assignment today?"

Wolfie looked ahead, expressionless. "I have the same corvée."

Jakob's heart pounded. He wanted to make sure he understood. "The same, nothing has changed?"

"Nothing. Tonight corvée will change. You just got back from the gedek; you saw for yourself, we saw you. Everyone was being watched."

"But ..." His throat held a lump worse than the driest rock-hard brown bread. "But you must." Matteus bumped him to signal, *Quiet down*.

Wolfie shrugged and turned away.

Matteus murmured, "Albert, how is he?" You couldn't have secrets most times, and especially not with one of your mates.

"The infection is worse," Jakob answered.

"Ja, I know. Maybe tonight they will get what he needs?" Matteus whispered. He did indeed know. Albert's grim situation had made the rounds.

The day's corvée brutalized Jakob, each step like lifting an anvil, each movement useless except that a day of corvée pushed time along. The ground had hardened, after the wet monsoon rains to cement-like dirt, as hard as Jakob's despair. They rarely ate what little they did grow. Some went to the Japs. In one kamp, he had heard the commander turned wild pigs loose on vegetables right at harvest. Whenever prisoners were a hundred meters from the guards, they did pick some greens, under the pretense of breaking up dirt balls with their hands. One hand would tuck the greens away, right by the privates. Already cooking, thought Jakob with the slightest flash of humor.

Jakob had his hand on a clod with green, when Matteus alerted him. "Careful! *Rood voor*," the code for Japs coming.

On the next laps, far from the guard, Matteus tried to distract him. "Lood vool, ha ha," like the one friendly guard, imitating the Dutch warning, with none of the *r*s that rolled off of Dutch men's tongues.

"Lood vool," said Jakob feebly back, as the other boys laughed, sharing the joke. *Live, Albert, live!* Was Dr. Maastricht even now amputating his foot or leg? No anesthetic and how was he to survive the surgery or labor again for the Japs? Why did God send Jakob a vision of medicine coming in, only to wake up with nothing and more worry?

By the end of the day, constant hunger became a gift. In a hunger trance, Jakob sleepwalked through the work; the sun burned away and finally began to sink. He couldn't remember walking back with the rest, but found himself in the food line, and there his feet froze. At best he would get a fish head, garbage still reeking, the broth barely a flavor. Unbidden, he had a quiet picture of Albert in his head. Was he healing, dying, or dead? He had to go now.

Without soup, without one hundred chews, he left, feeling his feet pull to the veranda. Matheus looked at him, his eyes asking if he should go along. No, he motioned, cupping his hands, signaling to get him his soup. Everyone respected his need to be alone. His heart pounded as he got closer to the familiar moans.

He could not go further, yet no force could keep him away either. His legs trembled as his jaw tightened. Tears had left him for a year now; he could feel a stone of loss stirring in chest, yearning to break up and sob. He had thought he was a good brother to Albert, being the one who noticed everything, who planned and became practical. Yet Albert had been forced to stop day-dreaming into his botany and science books and sketches, and become the practical big brother watching out for him. Each of them thought of every necessary thing, usually.

Jakob punched himself with his right arm on the left shoulder—not much pain—and punched again. Perhaps he had ruined everything. Painfully punching meager arm muscle into bone erased the sobs bubbling up. He found Dr. Maastricht on the veranda right away. The lines in his face looked like he was starved for sleep.

In a hushed tone, Jakob spoke. Albert must still be alive if Dr. Maastricht lingered to talk to him. He explained he had no sulfa yet, leaving out for now the hope for an egg. Everyone would try to take it if they knew.

Maastricht put a hand on his shoulder, the painful one from being hauled up in Tjideng, and squeezed. He motioned Jakob to sit with him against a wall. "I will speak to you as a man. No one has been able to get sulfa now. He is weak; survival will be tough with infection. Go see your brother. The will to live, that is how you can help him now."

Jakob went to what he thought of as the *Broers'*—brothers'—Vanderveer hospital room, the hard packed dirt of the veranda. Albert lay curled up and shrunk, sweating and breathing rapidly. The red streaks on his leg reached his thigh now.

He thudded down, and Albert babbled. "Pappie, I will get it for you. Mammie help me." Albert too always thought of Pappie and searched for him, and of Mammie and Sara left behind.

He touched Albert's wrist, and circled his hand around it, pulling the loop of his hand right up his arm. So thin, wasted away to bones. How did he live, how do any of them live? "Pappie, I have it now," Albert said, jerking his other hand around. Jakob examined Albert's left foot. A sore had grown from the bottom of his foot to the top. A new sore glistened on his shin.

Albert had no inkling yet that Jakob was here, willing him to live. Dr. Maastricht returned, squatting down next to them.

"Will you have to amputate?" Jakob asked.

"He is too weak. We need to have his body fight off the infection for awhile; we can't cut it all out anymore."

They both lowered their heads to hear Albert's softer and softer words. "Sara, I'll play with you, I promise."

Maastricht's mouth grimaced into a smile, Albert must be happy in this dream.

Henk came by and left Albert soup.

"I'll wake him for food?"

"No. Guard the food, let him rest, feed him when he awakens on his own."

Jakob sat, praying, *please, please*, and then stopped. God gave him last night's image of Wolfie trading medicine, but it was false. What could he do? Would he and Matteus beat Wolfie for cheating or for lateness? God, fighting, revenge, all hopeless.

He startled as Albert spoke in his usual voice. "Remember our baptism?"

Jakob leaned over. "Ja, I remember."

"That is when the angels came. It was such a beautiful day. I was six and you were five. Wim had been baptized when he was a baby. For some reason our baptism was delayed and we were baptized along with baby Sara."

"Ja, if we were in Holland, we would have been baptized as babies, but on Billiton the *dominee* — pastor — spent most of his time on Java."

"I'm glad I was baptized on Billiton and not in Nederland," said Albert.

"Because Billiton is home?"

"Because I wasn't a baby, because I remember. I looked up at the ceiling of the church when Dominee Veld dropped the holy water on me. The rafters and beams opened up. Angels sang there. Remember?"

"There were no angels."

Albert clutched his hand. "You didn't see them."

Jakob's hand sweated with Albert's fever. "No."

"Ja, I thought this before, that I was the only one. So I never told you. Jakob, through the roof, the sky was bright blue, and the angels glowed when they sang."

He looked down at Albert's earnest face. He mustn't say it, *Joh, you are in hunger delusions, fever delusions.*

"I wasn't hungry then, don't worry, and it isn't the hunger now," said Albert. His voice grew faint again. "And don't worry so. I see your face. I will get better."

"Ja, because I will get you medicine."

"No one has medicine anymore," Albert said with soft finality. "You didn't see the angels that day, but still you remember what a good day our baptism was?"

"Oh Ja, a good day. Pappie was happy and Sara had just started to crawl. Okay, soup time," Jakob announced.

Albert had no interest in lifting spoonfuls himself. Jakob fanned his fever, and started to lift a spoonful. "Henk will be here in a moment."

Albert struggled up the wall a bit, closed his eyes, and swallowed each spoonful of soup. "See you in the morning," Jakob said with conviction, and walked away with his heart pounding out of his chest. Would he? Would he get medicine? Henk was arriving, carrying his bowl and sponge for fever. Albert had to be okay.

Leaving, he felt surges of power; maybe last night's vision of help was for tonight. He would go light a fire under Wolfie as the Americans would say. He strode straight all the way back to Wolfie, who scowled when he saw him. A night passed and this cheater had not traded! Jaapie lay centimeters away, his back to Jakob.

"And! What now? Are you going to let him die!" yelled Jakob.

Jaapie sat up, alarm on his face, and a strange expression—grief? Was it possible he cared?

Wolfie glanced up casually. "I let no one die and I don't make anyone sick or starve in this hellhole. Now stop your yelling before we have *rood voor* and I cancel your trade! Go, leave us."

Jakob's heart pounded as if it would never beat normally again. He would be cheated. Albert would die. He went and waited in line for a trickle of water for mandi. As he weaved on his feet, he felt dizzy, worse from having missed his meager dinner. He turned at the sound of feet padding quickly behind him.

Jaapie gasped for air, bent over, clutching his knees, signaling him to listen. "Listen, they have never patrolled carefully more than two days in a row. Last night was already the second night. Some of the Japs themselves trade and don't want to be caught either, it should work tonight. Have hope. Tomorrow morning you have the medicine."

He thanked Jaapie, gap tooth to gap tooth, and crept forward in line. Cool water dripped over him. Cool water Albert needed, but surely Henk was with him. Let his fever leave, let him not get cold, because chills and shaking could be even worse than the heat. Getting back to the barrack he went to his tier. Matteus silently handed him a bowl of cold soup.

"Your deliciousness."

"Thank you," he whispered.

Matteus smiled.

His heart finally stopped pounding, or perhaps he had a quiet, starving heart that couldn't pound anymore.

CHAPTER 24

Luce
Calabria, California
Late January 2005

Driving back from the airport in Daniel's old Volvo station wagon, our suitcases stowed with tools in the back, the familiar grasslands of home blur by. We take turns playing air guitar to Journey's "Don't Stop Believing," with Daniel on the short riffs due to driving. My spirits lift, I have needed to be home, to say this is home. Blobs of white decorate a golf course in the distant, and I cry out. "I see it. *I* see it. Look — deer!"

Daniel laughs. "Good for you."

The first to see wildlife, and I feel relief from the pain which still hits every time I sit.

I reflect back on our plane flight home. The worst part was being held captive in the airplane seat. Before we left, what I liked to call the *Hope Eternal* unit, we met with Dr. Jensen one more time and the nervous social worker who I had finally had a great talk with. She had me gratefully being the patient, breathing with her, doing relaxation imagery with her. They explained to us that extended sitting would compress my spinal column and temporarily worsen the PGV, pelvic girdle pain. Within half an hour from takeoff, the pain hit, and I was trapped for the next three hours. I thought I'd help myself by going and stretching at the back of the plane. But my efforts became an *oh, what's the use* — a real one. Nothing worked.

Being within minutes of home, on the other hand, is like easy street. We will pick Vincent up at his friends' home.

Vincent's been to Sunday youth group with his friend Jason. In a crisp striped shirt borrowed from his friend, and a matching T-shirt underneath, he looks older. Most would think, with his height that he's all done with high school. If only he'll finish okay, with none of the usual surprises of low grades, mixed with high grades, mixed with missing theme papers.

We gather around our dining room table with steaming Dutch hot chocolate, made the slow way with heated milk and a rich chocolate paste of hot water, cocoa powder, and brown sugar.

Vincent cups his hands around his favorite red mug, and I wonder if he's to tell us of disaster. His voice is light and cheerful. "The theme paper's fine. What did Grandpa say this time? Now that everybody knows we're having a baby, what do they think?"

"Wow, you're cheerful," says Daniel. "So Grandma and Grandpa are totally excited and they made everyone tip toe around your mom. *Be careful not to upset herrr.*" He imitates a Dutch accent.

"And your theme paper?" I ask.

Vincent pulls my laptop over. "Ho-kay, Mom. See this e-mail? This is where I sent my English teacher the paper as an attached document. That was sent one whole day before the rough draft was due."

"Don't you have a printed copy to show us?" I ask.

He rolls his eyes. "Mom, this is how the teacher prefers it. I sent it on Jason's computer. I got a week to finish the final draft."

Later, even though it's the weekend, Daniel calls Dr. Simonian, who calls us back. I'm to take an extra week off to rest, and then two weeks on a spread-out schedule to see clients and announce my medical leave.

"Okay, dear one," Doc says at the end. "I'm so glad you're alright, and that you picked a good place to have those pains."

"Yes," I sigh and hang up, watching Daniel on the other extension, studying his new bossy expression. His eyes bore into mine, like it's an effort for him to be tough about time off, and I melt inside. Sleep inducing milky hot cocoa is catching up with me, and he cares deeply. For now I have no argument, and pat Baby in my belly, like the little miracle she is, and convince myself that none of my clients would miss me for one more week before I returned. Once Daniel sees how well I do, I can always stretch out the weeks of work left.

In the morning, I close up boxes of Christmas decorations, taking care not to shove or stack.

I admit, as I plop down in the corduroy easy chair, that I can't imagine how I could have worked today. Handling the white Christmas tree booties alongside the yellow booties, I'm also lulled to sleep, angling my head back just as the phone rings.

Papa. "*Dag*. You forgot to call us and say you got home okay." His tone is animated rather than accusatory. So he's not the possibly devastated, tired man we left.

"Today I was scheduled to speak to Wade's elementary class some more. Do you know they wanted to know how you brush your teeth in a prison camp? And so much more." He chuckles. "Teaching them, it was nice, to let those innocent kids know as best I could what happened. Who said that saying: 'That which does not kill you makes you stronger'? Oh yes, Friedrich Nietzsche. Mama and I have a new book of quotes in the house. He also said, 'A casual stroll through the lunatic asylum proves that faith does not prove a thing.'"

I've been vowing to be more open, and just blurt out my thoughts. "And remember Papa, I visited you in the mental hospital."

"Oh you. 'Lighten up,' as Albert says. I am not there now. I thought you wanted to hear more about Bevins."

"Of course." I close both pairs of booties in the drawer next to me, pinching my fingers, sucking my fingers for the sharp pain.

"What's wrong?"

"Nothing, just stretching." He doesn't miss much. "Go on."

"It must have been about April '45, a time I now know that deaths increased exponentially in all the kamps. We could tell at Tjimahi. Many men turned inward, yet Bevins still focused on me and others. We stood in line in the evening, one day after I told him about smuggling too late. All day words and pictures had pushed in on me and I felt only tense surprise that he would still be with me and my horrible secret. So I asked him, 'Bevins, what do you do with your secrets?'

"First he laughed; no one had secrets in the kamp. Then he gravely said, 'We will go back to the same spot.' Off we went to the same punishment hut. 'Let us talk of our memories of Albert,' he said gently. He made a little speech about me being reunited with Wim in Nederland, how lovely Albert had been, always with his botany book, how great we three boys had been, sailing prows along the beach."

"We sat again by that desolate punishment hut. It was if the ones who suffered there said, 'Go on, go on, and tell the rest.'"

† † †

Jakob

Kamp Grogol
November 1944

Jakob recoiled as he turned to Albert at dawn; he was gone. Of course, Albert was still in the hospital. He slid to

431

the ground, nothing could be slow today. He had to help. Matteus stirred nearby, still asleep.

As he escaped the barracks, birds called. A good sign: no extra patrols then. He maneuvered close to the gedek, and forced himself to stroll normally. Birds called on, a breeze soothed his neck. He turned and wished he could shake Wolfie down in front of everyone, and then run as the wind to Albert, but he couldn't appear that frantic.

Matteus must have awoken to go straight to the food line, already near Wolfie and Jaapie. Without words, Matteus knew the strategy. Jakob needed to cut in and be close to the other two, who huddled their heads together. On everyone's scarecrow ragged shorts, pockets were long torn off. Even smugglers had little to wear, but they must have the urgent supplies tucked away.

Jakob eased next to them. For once he was in the right place at the right time. Wolfie bumped against Jakob and palmed a small cloth into his hand. His fingers closed around the bumps of a small packet—medicine, and the distinct smoothness of a miracle—an egg. Just like that, in a moment, he had what Albert needed.

He had to leave food line in a horrible slow dance as if casually departing from macabre dance floor. First he dragged his feet like the rest, and then hurried. Watery broth trembled in his hands, ready to slosh out.

Away from everyone, he ducked inside a dark barrack and swallowed it down, no careful chewing. A man, his chopped white hair sticking straight up, every rib visible, stared up at him from a low platform. Their eyes locked. Surely this one must be of the Smaken ilk, refusing the hospital, about to die. White Hair raised his hand and lowered it, not to reach for the soup, but like a blessing, as if he was saying, *Someone has to get soup. So take, go and stay alive.* Jakob nodded at him and licked the soup bowl clean.

Albert is almost dead. Doctor Maastricht says he is close to the end. "I must run."

White Hair smiled, his teeth large in his skull-like face. Jakob trotted away as fast as he could. He had only so many minutes to tend to Albert and return for appel. Meters blurred by, at last the *foetbal* field. Pain seared his stomach as he bent and gasped for air. He licked a few grains of rice clinging to his bowl and went on. He felt strong enough to race now, strong enough to do anything for Albert, but he couldn't all-out run and risk crushing the egg.

When he closed in on the hospital veranda he felt dizzy. Albert lay very still. He approached slowly searching for signs of life, and crouched next to him. Oh good, his chest rose and fell. His breathing today was rattly, hunger edema near his lungs. He needed the egg and medicine desperately.

Something fell on Albert, his own tears, long suppressed. No time for heart, emotion, spirit. Squatting, he unwrapped the egg first. The way it rolled in his hands, it felt like it could be already hard-boiled, *ja, must be*. So he could have raced the whole way. Stupid, stupid for not investigating and gaining extra minutes to save his brother's life.

Jakob's hands shook as he slipped out pills from a triangle of paper. He noticed Henk and waved him over. Did the man ever sleep?

Henk dried his hands on a soiled towel at his waist. "Hoi. What have you there, young Jakob?"

Jakob reached up to hand him the pills.

Henk dropped his exhausted mask for the first time since they had met. "Ja, we can give him one now. I'll make sure he gets more later."

Jakob touched Albert's cheek, his throat, still feverish. His foot and body gave off a stronger rotten-fruit smell of infection. He worried the odor would make him vomit before he could help.

Albert slowly opened his eyes. "Ah, *broer*, there you are. Everything hurts. I'm sorry, again no corvée with you today."

"Oh you, so lazy." Jakob tried to smile. "Well, here's your medicine."

Albert opened parched lips. "Better than pudding."

So he knew Jakob's worries about wanting to be the good brother who mixed bread and sugar for custard.

"Okay, medicine," crooned Henk, putting the pill on the back of Albert's tongue.

Together they coaxed water down his throat. Jakob wished he could lie next to his brother and take away the radiating heat of fever. All day he'd do every ragged, labored breath with him, more heroic than breaking up a row of baked solid soil in midday sun. *Breathe, in, out, in, out. Please, please live. Live for me, live for yourself. Tell the angels you have to live.*

Henk stood up. "Don't miss appel. We'll take good care of him."

The cord of love between he and Albert had grown every day since they had to leave Sara and Mammie. The cord told him to stay, but he had to pry himself away as he slowly rose to his feet. "You'll be better now." He left. Nothing to do but to rush in the wrong direction, for another day of labor.

† † †

How had he made it back to morning appel? His eyes blurred with tears, then cracked open, drying. Swaying in his usual place, each leg weighed down with the burden of not being with Albert.

All around, were guard screams of "*Tenko*," for appel. Then prisoners calling in turn, "*Ichi, ni*—one, two ..." and more only to hear, "Start again! He peered at dusty boots around the edges of the mostly shoeless men. He hated every Japanese, the Korean Heihos, the Indonesian hire-ons.

Usually he resisted letting rage build, so as not to rob his own alertness and survival. But today his anger steamed and flowed like active volcanoes he had seen with Pappie and the rest of the family when out trekking. His fury burned, and then turned to clear ice. He must fuel Albert's survival. Ice and fire boiled inside. *The damned Japanese, eternally damned Japanese.* They never had to suffer death. Although their officers beat them, none died. The worst ones should die.

Finally they pulled out of appel, one group at a time. They trudge-marched the two kilometers to cracked, dry fields. Every day was the same, breaking up hard clods of dirt, carrying heavy watering cans from one end to the other, of each sorry furrow.

He had to make it through this one day and then back to Albert's side. For one bright moment he saw his brother's sweet smile, heard his words: *Sorry I can't work.* His own reply: *Oh, you slacker.*

God's medicine for Albert had been late. Still he whispered, *Lieve Heer*, Dear God, because of Albert's faith, a test run of prayer. "*Lieve Heer*, keep Albert alive." Hope lifted him; Albert's angels were caring for him.

By mid-afternoon he hated the sun too. He, like many prisoners, hoped to never see the Japanese white flag with its red sun again. Today's sun tediously traversed from hottest noon to low, but not coloring the sky. The order came to return. Matteus fell into step behind him as they arrived back at the gate. "Go to him," he whispered urgently.

First with plodding steps and then running all the way he rushed back to the hospital. His bare, dusty feet flashed below him, free of sores. *God, hurt me instead; save him.* His hard as leather feet still needed occasional relief in the shade. After each moment of cool, he hurried. *I deserve no relief from scalding feet. Always the difficult one, Pappie said. I traded at the wrong time. Nights earlier, since we already knew that infections don't get better; then no Jap guard would have stopped Wolfie from the trade. Wolfie, a cowardly bully to the end, I should have known.* He punched himself in the arm as before, matching each blow with words from Pappie: *always the difficult, the bad one*.

Out of breath, he neared the hospital veranda. *Henk is at our spot, hurry*. Once he was shoulder to shoulder with him it was as if their nurse had a vow of silence. Henk met Jakob's eyes, shook his head, and left them.

Panic wrenched Jakob's chest. Albert was already dead. His touched his beloved brother. No movement. Albert's stomach, swollen like the rest of him, rose and fell suddenly. He was alive, but infection and hunger edema were slowly killing him.

Jakob settled on the ground as he had longed to do all day. "Hey, *broer*. Oh, you're much better," he lied.

Albert gasped, breathing out of rhythm, like a battle rampaged inside of him. Was he free from pain, or did the streaks of infection on his leg, and his edema make him throb with every breath? Albert fought against the body fluids of starvation. Even his neck was now swollen. The breathing battle hitched on each inhale, finished, paused, finished, shuddered, and paused too long.

"No, joh," Jakob commanded. He lay alongside Albert, and transferred his will to him. "Breathe."

Albert fluttered his eyes open, and then shut. "*Dag*, Jakob. Such a fine *broer*. I'm better."

Jakob smiled and squeezed Albert's wrist. Puffy, not bony as always. "Ja, you are better."

They continued to breathe. Albert opened his eyes again, staring. He must be seeing his angels, the ones Jakob had never seen. *Go away, angels, you can't have him; you can only save him*, Jakob thought, anguish searing up through him. Their breathing, with all its jerks and stops, went on. Jakob tried to lead Albert's breaths to give him the rhythm of life. *Don't give up, don't give up*. He could keep this up long enough so the medicine had its chance to heal.

Where was Henk, so they could get the nighttime dose of sulfa? *Breathe, breathe*. All the usual noises surrounded them, but he focused only on Albert's lungs, each gurgle, and each choke. One more stop, a long stop. Should he resuscitate him like the lifeguard who saved a child at the Billiton swimming pool? He rose to do so and exhaled each time he pressed Albert's chest to exhale. Albert's diaphragm muscles fluttered deep beneath his swollen stomach. *If you exhale, then you can inhale. Come on, Albert, breathe. Don't drown in a pool of your own fluids.*

He waved one arm wildly for Henk. Next he sought the pulse at Albert's neck; surely he was fighting to breathe. Oh, he was strong; he had the Vanderveer stubbornness, and medicine.

He continued with compressions just like the lifeguard, he knew what to do. Albert's frozen face eased; oh, it was helping. He could soothe his *broer* by lying next to him again, quieter than he had ever been. He felt a funny peace, *as quiet as anyone ever wanted me to be, as patient. Please God, please.* He squeezed his eyes so tight golden light burst behind his eyelids. Did one of Albert's angels appear?

He opened his eyes, of course not. Yet he felt Albert's chest, shallow breaths. How could he know for sure? Albert was here in this swollen body. He prodded the puffiness of his leg, moved Albert's head onto his shoulder. Bit by bit Albert's fever diminished, his temperature was getting better. God — the *Heere* — *was good.*

The six o'clock sun vacated the sky. As fleeting dusk settled on them both, and darkness hit, he realized Albert's fever had broken. Their doctor on Billiton always said, *when the fever breaks, the patient will heal.* At last, the medicine turned the course of the infection.

A long moonshine-shadow arrived. Henk squatted down, clasping his hands in front of him like a prayer. He pressed his fingers into Albert's eyes, and gently smoothed his brow with his other hand. "Be at peace, young one."

"He's better?" Jakob's heart thundered.

Please, Heere, please no. Henk's warm hand fell on Jakob's shoulder. "He is in a much, much better place. You keep the rest of the sulfa in a safe place." He wrapped Jakob's fingers around the bumps in their white paper. "This will still save lives," he whispered. "Albert would want that."

"But he's not dead."

Henk shook his head and walked away.

Then lice did what they did with the dead. They swarmed away. Moonlight glimmered in dismal gray patches through the thatched overhang on the lice evacuating, on Albert's smooth face, his grotesque belly. He still reeked of rotten-sweet gangrene. Thousands of men here and not one who mattered. He rubbed Albert's bony hip, and the first edema wetness released, warm as shore side ocean.

If the Allies finally came now, those are the words he would have to say.

My broer? Oh, he is dead.

"Nooo," he heard someone yelling. The noise never stopped here, it went on and on. An exhausted Henk arrived and shook him.

"Still now, still." Henk soothed. The wailing was his own voice. He had seen little children die, older people, but this was Albert. His wet skeleton of a body would go in piles of other bodies, leaking life-force onto wagon slats, leaving a trail of wet for the few mourners who followed.

Henk rocked him, he had to be quiet. Screams stuck in his throat, his stomach heaved as if he might vomit, of course there was nothing to release. He couldn't be the one to bring guards running. "Okay, Okay," he whispered.

Henk left.

He hit himself on the arm, then in the stomach. He thought of Mammie, who had only been angry with him a handful of times, now furious, desolate. He waited too long to trade. He hoisted himself up against the wall, his legs gladly pinned under Albert. More moisture released. Water ran off the mat, the last of life, the smell like childbirths in crowded Tjideng, except there, beyond all reason usually a live baby entered a miserable world. He and Albert only one year apart, one a smart scientist with no dancing rhythm, one who didn't deserve to live. He hoisted them up the wall once more. A splinter dug into his back.

† † †

Jakob collapsed his back against the scorching hot splinters of the punishment hut wall.

Bevins murmured, "Here, lean in," and maneuvered Jacob against his own shoulder. Jakob ached for the recent horrific beating, for all the rough walls like this one, leading nowhere, for always waiting for something or someone who might already be dead. He shuddered as if in death throes of despair. He tasted the rough bread pudding Albert brought him in hell. His parched mouth watered for sweetness and he coughed.

"There, there," Bevins murmured sweet words, and Jakob moaned, knowing right away the animal noises he heard were his. He punched himself in the arm and cried, everything broke inside. Bevins gripped his hand to his side, "No more hurting yourself Jakob, no more." He wept for the endless moments he believed that Albert still breathed. He felt his brother's body, no longer him and the worst-sweet smell ever — gangrene. He followed the wagon with slats carrying Albert's body away and the empty barracks-spot by his side. His sobs left him hollowed out for everything he lost — Marijke, Pappie's compass gift, surely all of Mammie and Sara's trust. Bevins wrapped his arm around him, no words.

Gathering men kept away out of respect. Jakob knew Bevins cared for all he had lost, every moment, every person, everything.

Bevins shifted his weight. "You will live to tell the story."

† † †

439

My mouth's dry now, I'm hoarse. "Oh, Papa."

"Yes, losing Albert was terrible, and there were other terrible times ahead. But in hell I met an angel after all, Bevins. I wished Albert could have met him. Although of course Albert knew Bevins from before, but not like I did."

"Papa, this is what I always wanted, to help each other out of pain, to understand."

"My tragedies?"

"That you would tell me, tell us." I take a deep breath. "There's so much I didn't tell you either. I always thought …" My eyes fill with tears.

Somehow he knows I'm weeping. "What, Liefje?" he says with infinite tenderness.

"I always thought we would tough it out together, like you said was so great with those Vietnam vets."

"Well first, you are not so tough, and I'm glad you're not. I never wanted you as world weary as all us boys who survived the kamps. And if you want to talk more, you'll have to talk to me like those vets did. Tell your own war stories. The vets, you and I, we earned the right to talk the hard way. So why hold back any more?"

CHAPTER 25

Talk to me like they did ... we've earned the right to talk, niggles away at me as my last week of work approaches.

Also pulling on me is guilt about telling each client that it is their last day. Geez, I mean, last appointment—that's all. These are not the good-bye standards for psychotherapy, but they are excusable for bad health. I waffle again. Am I really that severely in need of rest? Yes, I am.

Vincent's already in bed and I know it's Daniel's late night. I'm not doing such a great job of resting, due to this feeling, so I check Vincent's homework. It is indeed all done, and the haunting *you don't know everything* feeling lingers. I go to my laptop and click into the internet Calabria High School-Connect program. First I see tonight's homework is the correct assignment, and warm relaxation drifts in. Now I can sleep. Over and over recently I think how I live the furthest away from Papa and my worry habit is the most like him. Next my mouse wanders over to the grades page, and instantly I wish I hadn't clicked, all Ds and Fs. The dark pit between my stomach and heart awakens. The only thing he's *not* lying about is today's homework assignment. I go back and check more of his English assignments, a zero for a rough draft on his paper, the one he somehow proved to us he submitted.

I fear for Vincent. He lies too expertly, and I have no idea what other secrets he may be keeping. What could make him give up like this? He went to such great lengths to pretend everything is okay. So he's smart enough to show me an attached-sent document but not wise enough to submit a real theme paper to the teacher. I feel dizzy and check other

441

English assignments: zeroes. Much of this would be removed or changed if Vincent crisis is not included.

I always thought Vincent would be open, not guarded, a great school accomplisher. We didn't raise him with the pressure Papa raised especially us two older kids with: *A's are supposed to be A plusses. A grade of B or lower is unacceptable.* Alby eventually followed an accepted career in biology, psychotherapy was not acceptable, and I should have had a doctorate by now, not a master's. The only reasons I can think of to hide, are the same ones I had: parents offering up high pressure, booze and drugs getting in the way. If I haven't pressured him too much, have I neglected him too much? Wide awake now, I think of how I like to lull myself into sleep nightly thinking all guardedness on my son's part has been the caginess of a typical teenager.

I close the laptop. Ordinarily I would fly right into my frustration with Vincent, and wake him up with angry satisfaction. But I promised Daniel to stay calm and partner with him. I expect him home any moment; unfortunately it's late and he'll be exhausted. So I force myself to breathe deeply and survey my orderly kitchen. Glass canisters on the counter display their contents and spices in the cabinet are alphabetically arranged, due to my lessened work load.

So it all fits. Vincent's being in bed exactly on schedule is another too-good action, to try to deflect parental suspicion. I fix a pot of tea for Daniel and wander off to bed; Vincent's Opa-Jakob sketchpad is left out. Detail and degrees of silvery shading bring life into each image. He has used charcoal pencils, smudgers, everything to expand his art. What talent. I remember Papa talking about his brother Albert always drawing. Vincent clearly has the same talent and devotion.

On the last page is a whisper of a lanky sixteen-year-old boy, with Papa's features extrapolated into youth. Jakob is dangling his hands, which are shaded darker, bloody from fighting. A machete lies on the ground. His expression appears desolate and triumphant at the same time. Young Jakob must have wanted to fight to protect those he loved. He would have yearned to return to Billiton, which he never did. I have many of Papa's memory-pictures, memory castle rooms inside now. He must never have wiped out his last images of leaving. He never saw Baboe, Kokkie, or his home's peaceful shores again. So he had to fight. But something about the months after the war snags at my own memories. What is it? My talk with Tante Sara—I had called as Papa said to do.

When Oom Fiete, Tante Sara's husband, was still alive, they visited us in America. We all kept busy on excursions, the way Dutch people tend to do. Tante Sara and Papa sat together and laughed everywhere they went. He always said the Netherlands wasn't home for him, and time with Sara brought him to his "real" home. Papa visited Nederland only for business trips and when Oma died. Some of her jewels, successfully hidden away during the war years, came to him. Papa, Oom Wim, and Tante Sara had a circuitous path for their rescued treasures and memories. The journey for four kids gleaming wet at the ocean's edge twisted away from expecting to remain in paradise with servants, pets, secure jobs, and retirement. Instead they were spilled out on new shores scattered all over the globe, still looking for home.

I'm surprised Daniel isn't home yet. I guess he didn't want to call and risk waking me up.

So, from Tante Sara I learned that Papa was one of the first to arrive at Tjideng in search of family. He arrived alone. They had a joyous reunion, not as wooden as some, whose family members came back brittle, like empty sea shells looking for a spirit, but too hurt to allow the spirit of love back in. Papa, Oma, Sara must have all had a sturdy spirit inside. Part of their joy was Papa's surprising trip, coming to them among the first family members to arrive.

443

The research I do on the internet describes the Bersiap fighting between Dutch and Indonesians fighting for independence. New brutalities caused many deaths. But Papa told us they fought for weeks, right after the Japanese capitulation. They were crushed when their commander said he could no longer have teen soldiers, only adults. It was time to be young again, to return to life, to look for family.

I page back through the sketchbook. On another page, young Jakob has a machete, and a battered canteen dangles on his rucksack. *The one Smaken gave Albert and him.* Longing is clear in his eyes. Longing for everything he can't have: strong men to fight with, a safe world. Dutch civilians and Indos were attacked by Indonesians. Trains were attacked. Men recently released from kamps were captured and put in the same jail where they had been tortured at the beginning of the war; some were executed before others were freed.

My pulse quickens, as I recall more of the details from Tante Sara. So maybe the timeline doesn't fit. Next to young Jakob, the other — young Matteus — is preparing to walk away also, shoulders slumped. They must get about the business of survival. I know by now that there is so much beautiful and ugly truth, but this brings me no peace. I can't sleep. I listen for the sounds of Daniel coming home.

† † †

He arrives. "Oh, you're up."

"Yes, just for you." But if not for Vincent, I would be asleep.

"Okay, what is it?" Daniel tiredly rubs his eyes.

I pull the Dutch tea cozy off the pot of chamomile tea, and pour into turquoise tea cups. I tell him about Vincent's horrible grades, his extraordinary art, and my uneasy heart over Papa's World War II battle timeline.

"Honey, Vincent is one thing. We'll get to the bottom of it. Your Papa? If Jakob made it up, out of desperation, you said with liberation they still weren't free, and there were no allied soldiers there yet. Chaos ruled, the war ramped up again, everyone had false hope."

Daniel sips his tea serenely. His assumption conflicts me. My therapist training and my own instincts say, *Believe everything a survivor of trauma says. The worst thing anyone can do is to not believe a story of what happened.* "Really? A false memory?"

His large hands wrap the entire tea cup. "I know, honey. Isn't it just plain simple those memories get twisted? I remember holding a toy saw as a kid, and trying to escape my backyard by sawing through the fence. That way I would escape my parents' yelling and hitting, their disappearances and coming back. It was very true to me, but did I escape with my toy saw? No. Did I believe for a while I did? Yes. Jakob needed to fight even more than I needed to escape my backyard, so he believed he did."

"But ..."

"Maybe Tante Sara's the one who remembers it wrong. Maybe pretending helped Jake forget the terror of Albert's death and his father's death. Maybe that created space for something else. You know maybe he borrowed stories from all the Vietnam vets you told me he was with during his psych hospitalization."

The psychiatric unit. I remember visiting Papa all alone after summer Girl Scout camp. I was picked up from camp by the neighbors instead of Papa, because the rest of the family was in Nederland. *Another family chapter we never discussed.*

"Don't we need to know the truth?" I ask.

Daniel shrugs. This is far from a calamity for him. "He may have fought, just not as many days and for as long as he believes. Or he didn't fight, yet fought in a different way every day to survive."

I sigh. "Okay, I'm ready to change professions. Papa's memories, client memories, they're all supposed to be true. After Baby's birth, I shall drive a truck like you. I'll make good money. I can stop occasionally to nurse her, and be home by six each night."

He smiles. "Then we'll have to find you short-haul routes, with no lifting. We'll get to work on your commercial driver's license when she's one month old."

"Fine, it's a deal. And what about Vincent?"

"He's got a lot of 'splaining to do," Daniel says, back to his Ricky Ricardo imitation. "But first we rest up."

Usually we're independent sleepers, each on an island within our king-size bed. Tonight we spoon; anything's possible, I think. That's the point of all the wondering, anything's possible.

† † †

Early in the morning, before Vincent is up, Daniel and I talk about how to handle his low grades, and worse—his lying.

"One bit at a time, right?" Daniel says. "Call his school counselor. Get the update on every single class. We'll take it from there."

I'm left in a too-quiet house, calling the counselor and receiving an e-mail later in the morning with the whole update. I take a deep breath and print out three copies. The news is grim. He's missed classes. His only solidly passing grade is a C in Art. His other classes are Ds skidding to Fs and solid Fs. I feel desolate as I find a seat outdoors by the Japanese maple tree. A cool breeze stirs my hair. There's a lot of the semester left. Light is reflecting off of diamond dew droplets on foliage, reminding me to not make such a drama.

That night Daniel serves the stew I fixed in the slow cooker. Copies of Vincent's grades are at each of our place settings.

He sees it, and gets up to walk away.

"Sit down," growls Daniel.

Slowly Vincent lowers to his chair.

"How did this happen? What the hell is going on with you?" I ask, not exactly with the kindness Daniel and I discussed. Sounding like Papa again.

"You mean what's wrong with all of us?" Vincent throws back, crumpling his copy of grades. "All anyone cares about is Baby."

I get a sinking feeling. My hip stabs me with pain. I'll never make this up to my son. "Vincie, I'm sorry."

Daniel waves his hands in front of me, like he's erasing my words. "What are you apologizing for! Come on, drop the garbage. What's going on, really?"

"Nothing's wrong. I'm just in a family of liars, that's all. You're always gone driving truck. Mom's hanging out all dreamy here at the house. Even though she's finally home from Houston, it's like she's not here at all."

"You think your mom and I have been lying to you?"

"No, Grandpa. Every time I talk to him it's a different story. Sometimes there are some British soldiers he fought with, sometimes only Dutch. While you were gone, he told me he jumped out of a plane with a parachute and a mortar strapped to his knee. Later he said he needed the mortar, so the parachute would open properly because he was so lightweight due to starvation. That's a pretty wild story. How stupid of me, to buy that. Why did it take me so long to figure it out? He wasn't fighting at all."

"Why does it upset you this much whether Grandpa fought or not?" asks Daniel quietly. Where Daniel is calm, I'm finding my heart pounding. Papa was telling us true stories while telling Vincent fabrications, impossible things. It's him I should be asking, *why would you do such a thing?*

Vincent's shaking next to us and grabs his sketchpad, which I left on the edge of the table last night. "Well, I was so proud of him, and I thought if he could to that, do conquer his starvation and fight, that I could conquer my ..." He stops abruptly.

"What?"

He clenches his mouth, as if to bite back words. Pages lie splayed out on the table. They are torn out like casualties of his disappointment with Grandpa. A bony young soldier looks up from a smudged and root beer-stained page. The boy's body looks young, his eyes ancient. Up until now, this sketchbook was the only belonging Vincent carefully arranged each day, alongside a carousel of charcoal pencils. My hands shake as I tap and straighten the sketchpad, flattening every page. I can never handle an angry family member well.

If Vincent's given up on Grandpa, I worry what else he's given up on. Prayer and instinct tell me Baby is going to be okay, but Vincent? He could be hiding more bad grades, he could be trying drugs, and he could be pining away over a girlfriend we don't even know about. Or, he could just be wondering who his heroes are, no one left who's a truth teller, a truly brave person. I feel like a coward. What kind of mother am I that I don't get the story out of him?

He stands to leave, knocking a glass down on the table, which Daniel's hand and his grab at the same time, righting it before it spills. Then Vincent swiftly attacks the sketch pad, ripping out fists full of pages.

"Oh no," I say, grabbing some back and holding them. "No. This is beautiful work."

Vincent's face is hard like I've never seen it, like he really doesn't care, and this sensitive boy of mine always cares. "It doesn't matter, Mom. Well, maybe to you. It's all you care about."

"Son," Daniel says calmly, apparently not suffering with parental guilt. "Consider this. Being brave and fighting is exactly what Grandpa did. He stayed determined and fought to stay alive in the *Bersiap* craziness."

Vincent looks no softer with his dad's gentle persuasive words. "Why would that matter? He was no real fighter."

"Think about it, Vincie," I say, and he glares at me. "He had to travel in *Bersiap* craziness. Each moment took gargantuan effort, just to survive."

"Okay, I guess I get that. But to lie to me ..." He tries to grab the sketchpad again.

I snatch it back to my lap, tucking in a sharp wire poking out of the jagged, wounded spiral.

"Why do you care so much about sketches of something that never happened, and leave to find out more?" Vincent yells at me. "You didn't even care about Baby. You almost killed her!"

I freeze, and find I can't talk.

"Jakob's doing his best to tell the truth," says Daniel. "Let's hear your truth. Why does it matter so much to you and your mom to hear the whole story? Why is this a big deal to all of us?"

I'm glad Daniel includes himself in the *big deal*. I release clenched hands, but still protect the sketchpad.

"He doesn't even love me enough to tell me the truth. Remember when he shoved my face into my plate when I was little, for not eating? I don't care if he remembered starving; I wouldn't treat my grandkid that way. He's a horrible Opa." He pounds his fist. "And, there's something wrong with me. Every semester I start school knowing I'll make great grades, and that I'll stick with it. Then pretty soon I'm way behind and lying. I thought if Grandpa could be so brave when he was my age, and never give up." His eyes widen, like he gets the point—*never give up*. "Then I could be brave all semester and never give up, but he was lying."

"And you are lying," says Daniel.

"Yeah," replies Vincent.

"I used to do that too, Vincent," I say. *Because of drinking. What else are you up to?* "Let's get you some help."

"What do you want, Vincent?" asks Daniel.

"To make great grades next school year."

449

"You have time left this school year," Daniel chuckles. "Let's work on that."

"I'm already flunking."

"You've got time. Tomorrow you and I will visit your counselor."

"No, Dad, please. That would be the worst!" Vincent leaps up, knocking his chair down. "You're treating me like a baby."

"Tomorrow we will go and you will show me your homework tonight," Daniel says, unyielding.

"That's so stupid," Vincent yells again, running to his room and slamming the door.

Daniel notices me literally wringing my hands as I squeeze the sketchpad into a bookcase to hide it from harm. Yelling makes me feel like catastrophe is brewing. "Hey, you rest like you're supposed to tomorrow. I got this."

"I can rest *and* handle this," I say.

"Nope. Rest for you, truth for Vincent. My job."

A coil of tension uncurls inside. Vincent had a fleeting look of relief before he ran. He knows his dad will follow through. As I slowly clear dishes off the table I feel the old yearning I can't name. I wanted Papa, with no missing time, with none of us held hostage to the past. I yearned for Mama, to feel the ease many girls have with their mother. I bang my knuckles when reaching for the garbage can, blood wells up. Stop. The tension inside uncoils completely. I have no idea what I'm going to do with myself, waiting, waiting. I do know I will be there for Vincent, and all of my family.

Daniel comes and taps my shoulder, kisses my sore knuckles. "Come to bed. We have some stuff to say I didn't want to discuss in front of Vincent."

In bed, Daniel arranges the body pillow in front of me so that I align my spine and face him. We rub each other's tired shoulders, and I fear what he will say.

"Okay, so Vincent is right, it is like you are often gone, and when you're not gone, you're still preoccupied. All those times in the past for Alby's rehabs. He and I thought you had that out of your system. You know once would have been enough. Then you started all over again, saying you 'have' to go because of Jake's cancer, when all he cares about is giving you what you need. I'm watching Vincent, honey, and thinking that it takes a crisis to get you to stay home."

The fear grows. *Not true*, I want to say, *this is the only place I ever want to be.* "I can see how it looks that way," I croak out. "Yet I've never wanted to leave."

"You have, you have left, and I think there's a chance now that you've finally come home. Therapists say, right, that kids act out to fix their parents?"

"Yuck," I moan. "I'm so sorry." The s-word I rarely say, sorry. I feel such regret. Twice in a month now, Daniel has tried to turn my head back to our child and child-to-be, creating a peaceful home. Even though I think that's where I am at—home—that's now how I act. "I'm sorry," I repeat and Baby starts to kick. The irony of pregnancy; if I am moving, she is rocked to sleep. When I lie down, she wakes up. I find the hard spot that must be her head, and put Daniel's warm hand there.

"It's okay. We're already okay. Believe it, huh?"

I nod. Baby's shenanigans stop. I hope Vincie's shenanigans stop too. Daniel's already in the even breathing of sleep. I breathe his rhythm, and hope it's true. *We're already okay.*

† † †

Vincent is much calmer once his dad and counselor exchange daily reports from his teachers.

For me, hobbling around is my new life. Driving increases the shooting pains in my hips and back. I tolerate it for quick outings, but then it worsens after my first day back at the office. I ask friends to drive me in and pick me up, or sometimes Daniel. He of course calls it "Driving Miss Lucie." I call it pain.

What is it like for my clients to watch me grimace when I move to rearrange my hips or legs? This is not the most effective way to provide counseling. So I'm okay with the decision to see each client only once before shutting the office doors. My office will be sublet to an experienced clinical supervisor from the local trauma clinic who wants the opportunity to add private clients, and a young children's therapist. She has already brought in bins of toys; Babar the Elephant peeks out.

Most everything personal in the office will be gone. Both the supervisor and the new therapist like the arrangements on the Black Madonna shelf: crystals, obelisks of obsidian, sand-hewn beach glass, pebbles, symbols of all world religions, not just the Christian faith which brings me solace.

I can follow clients' life-threads even in the midst of pain. I swear that some white-hot spasms make me focus better. In between appointments I sweat, as my heart beats fast with the ache. I can do nothing but breathe slowly to dissipate the white-hot moments in time. Then I'm with the next client, ready to focus.

When stretched out on the office couch, like now, the pain melts away. I'm doing my most important job, letting Baby grow. I have a secret name now for her, based on Papa's first memory story with Dr. Ingstrom. I cannot tell anyone. As much as I pray more peacefully day by day and, consider a quote from Thessalonians: "Give thanks in all circumstances." I have my superstitions. I will not utter Baby's name out loud. No, not superstitious. I'll channel the power of ancient naming myths, where a child's truest name wasn't spoken until they grew into it.

Gene, the patient who never misses a session, except the day Dr. Ingstrom first called, is in the waiting room.

He first came to see me with a driving-under-the-influence video from the police. He had been pulled out of his car for erratic driving, ranted about how he could drive better than anyone, could easily pass any field sobriety test, and offered to do perfect cartwheels to prove it. Surprisingly, the breathalyzer showed he wasn't drunk. He was manic-behind-the-wheel. Two years later he is doing well with the right medication, a less stressful job, and his wife and children's understanding.

He surrendered his childhood story week by week to me, life with a terrified mother and a brutal father. One day Gene's dad grabbed him and his brother, harnessed them to their farm plow, and whipped them like mules, roaring, "Mush, go!"

Somehow they went on. He's doing fine. The brother, who *is* alcoholic, came to join us for appointments. They traded stories as barbaric as the human-mule one, supported each other, discussed how school years were a happy escape—no surprise one became a school principal, and the other a college counselor. After receiving Gene's love and support, George became willing to go through rehab and stayed sober.

Today it strikes me that the worst acts of cruelty follow unspeakable patterns. In the war years Papa, too, labored like a beast of burden—an ox. He and other boys were beaten to force them against the makeshift harnesses that made field and road wagons go. I see it, the same kind of wagon as I sat on with Pake, on Dutch country roads. How Papa must have liked to join Pake on the wagon seat, gently rocking behind Kittie, reminded that the slave labor days were gone.

I hold Black Madonna, the symbolic carrier of motherhood, despair, joy, and miracles. Healing comes to me when others have told me their stories; somehow it healed some of my family wounds. A circle of deepest meaning happens when sharing the ebb of pain and joy with clients and friends. It's that circle that I've craved my whole life with Papa, like both of us having sat with Pake on the farm wagon behind a horse named Kittie. I have glimmers of meaning, like today, and Papa's been telling me he wishes for more glimmers of me. Vincent said the same, *you were always gone.*

I turn Madonna's face to me. She began life on my shelf as just one of a set of sand play items from a catalogue. She became precious to me and she reads my mind, talks and even nods. *Yes, it is okay to heal, to be a wounded healer.* I hope God is pleased. Somewhere in the edginess of the terror regarding leaving my office behind, I hear a yes to all of life, this life inside of me, and do my own breathing. Another glimmer, Papa and Bevins inspired breathing came to me long ago, even though I only heard the story this year. Decades of the fear Papa leaked out informed me well. Fear of waiting, fear of surrender, fear of being unprepared, fear of loving only to lose who you love.

Hope hurts, I know that well. In my jagged circle with Papa, I have fragile, new hope. The therapy room is still perfectly arranged, and flooded with light. I place Madonna back on the shelf, collect myself, and open the door to Gene.

Receding hair surrounds his face like a dark halo, and his lips curving into the grin he never had the first year of coming here. I waste no time in telling him about my long leave for a healthy pregnancy. He then settles as usual, a pillow behind him, a pillow under his elbow, his supports and shields.

"So you need less stress," he says. We both get the irony, him repeating the same words I often said.

"Yes, I need less stress. I'm not sure when I'll start appointments again. I can give you a referral so you don't have to stop counseling."

"I am ready to stop."

"Isn't this early on? You have done a lot of healing, but you don't have a support network outside your family yet."

"I'm ready. You know how you're always telling me to go to the twelve-step meeting for family members of alcoholics?"

"You mean Alanon?"

"Yes, I'll go. I'm ready."

"I can find you a schedule." I reach over to the basket of pamphlets next to me.

"I have it, I looked it up."

"Good for you." I feel motherly to this man who is ten years older than me. "What do you think will help you about Alanon and encountering others who grew up in alcoholic families?"

"All those gaps, a chance to meet a bunch of people with mostly empty and hurt spots." Tears run down his cheek. He's never wept like this before. Usually he punches a pillow, his voice coming out swallowed and vomited up, saying he hates the ache of sorrow. "I'm ready to be with people who understand having holes in their lives. I want to know what it's like to meet others raised by a drunk who beat them instead of loving, and hit them instead of teaching."

Tears pool in my own eyes. I love the moment a client leaves the assumption of a vast loneliness. A burden, which only they carry, becomes shared.

Do I tell him yet about the gaps in my own life? This could be our last appointment ever. I don't, because his eyes are riveted to the tears running down my own cheek. Tears tell the story for him.

I shift to pragmatic words. "Sounds good. Are you going to call the Alanon office to see about a support person to go with you?"

"No. I have one; George is ready to go too."

We talk more; he likes the idea of graduating from weekly therapy appointments. His wife will go along for the first meeting too.

Gene glows as we say good-bye. I force myself to not give him the name of Samuel, the psychologist-clinical supervisor who will sublet here; because that's my way of saying, *you're amazing. You're so big and healthy.*

Other days go on like this. I am less necessary; clients and families are ready to move on. Alby is still home with Cindy and the kids, no relapse so far that I know of. Corrie sounds more peaceful. She suggests we take turns calling each other every week "for our new closeness." Papa wants to hear how I feel, applauds my leaving the office, but hasn't shared any stories lately.

Kemble comes to see me. We check the Japanese maple together, the crazy lemon tree which has small green lemons and flower buds. I don't go to church most Sundays. My body bids me: rest, rest, rest. My weekly Bible study comes to me. I've learned. The less stoic me cries with them all the time, and this is good.

After a Sunday nap, I admit to myself I go to church less because of my never-filled baby booties memory. That way there are fewer reminders of the times I felt betrayed by hope.

Daniel and Vincent attend church less than I do, so my friends don't bug me. I don't tell Kemble about this need to avoid happiness at church on sunny winter days. I don't tell Daniel either.

I do tell God and the Japanese maple. I'm settled in the Adirondack chair, fortified with outdoor pillows for my back. The last of the fire colored leaves quiver and fall. One by one they surrender and spiral down. When a red leaf lands in my lap, I recall the spots of blood at Hope Something OB-GYN. The little leaf, splayed like an infant's hand rests in my hand and I am overcome by joy. I determine to keep some of my worries to myself. Listing fears too often, only multiplies them to a carpet of worry like the fallen leaves before me.

† † †

The next day, none of my clients tell me that it will be rough without me; most don't want referrals, perhaps they are in the realm of transference. They are being the "good" family members who don't wish to guilt me for leaving. Such insights don't bring joy like the little red leaf did. I'm always picking up a batch of worries again and as a result don't sleep well at night. Tomorrow is the last day at my office. I'm ready for the finality of locking the door behind me for what could be years. Baby will be safe, and now I will wait only for her.

In the evening Vincent and Daniel help out. First they clear away the dinner dishes, then settle: one studying, one doing bills. They have school covered. The phone rings, and I know who it is. Vanderveers, especially Papa, do not interrupt meals. We all have the knack of waiting for dinner to end before calling, usually at seven.

Vincent gets on the phone briefly, flipping a pencil over and over with one hand as if he's bored. "Ja, I'm fine. Here's Mom again."

"Hello, liefje," Papa says brightly, as if Vincent's clipped tone has no impact on him. "I want to report, Alby is just fine. No more worry about him relapsing. None of that. Your mama is so relaxed."

Vincent's walking away, his door slams. Daniel follows him, studying is not done.

He is more relaxed than I am. "Papa," I venture. "I've been reading about the forced 'comfort women.' Is that what happened to Marijke?"

He sighs. "Ja, her innocence wrenched away from her, they raped her. She never talked about it, and in her honor I don't tell more of her story either. I hope that somewhere she is well."

"I think she is." I feel the indescribable horror of World War II, the assault of a lovely young girl who likes gymnastics, and young Jakob who still cares for her. There's pain, as well as joy. I see the lovely embroidery she made as if it survived, right here with the nearby booties. Loud voices come from Vincent's room. I hope he's okay.

"Papa, when Albert died, was he just gone? Or did you do a memorial?"

"Actually, ja. Many cared about Albert. The body wagon made its rounds all the time then; he became one of the few who still had a funeral of sorts."

† † †

Jakob

Kamp Grogol
late November, 1944

Men and boys spiraled in a slow line to the mostly unmarked graves. Wary eyes flickered about, always on the alert.

A Korean-*heiho* guard, who they'd nicknamed Spitsspeler, after the attack position in soccer, walked nearby. Even today, he could earn his nickname, looking for a chance to beat a man to the ground, and kick his head as if it were a soccer ball—*foetbal*. Jakob tasted acid from his barren stomach. Even now, the terror of Spitsspeler, never a full reprieve.

Spitsspeler strolled placidly however, and followed their small group. All their ragged feet circled inward to the open graves, filled with bodies sewn into burlap bags. Some men leaned in to hold each other up: Matteus, unknown men, White Hair, who was nothing but ribs and on the edge of his own death. Spitsspeler raised his hands, everyone tensed for escape. But he signaled his hands slowly like a cross, and pointed to himself. *Of course, missionaries, even in Korea. Eerie that Albert had gently pursued God, his angels, the Holy Spirit, and now Spitsspeler, here.* Jakob shook his head, dizzy. One day full of evil, the next guarding them as they grieved.

Dr. Maastricht, a few boys and a prisoner with a battered but polished violin came forward. He tucked the instrument under his chin, one string hung uselessly, snapped. Impossibly, "Jesu, Joy of Man's Desiring" began. His fingers strained, working with the strings he had. Pure notes trembled to heaven, and Spitsspeler bowed his head. Astonishment rushed through him as the melody went on and on. Each part a little different, straining for freedom and shelter. Spitsspeler murmured Korean words and made the sign of the cross on his chest. Jakob tapped his own chest, felt his aching heart, yearning to be free and floating up with the music. Matteus moved shoulder to shoulder, and Jakob's eyes ached with unshed tears. This particular burlap bag was Albert, who could not hear this music he loved. Albert would have said, *See one good guard,* and would have leaned against Jakob for comfort. *No, I see one evil guard on one good day.*

The violinist played the final note and lowered his instrument. A gentle breeze touched Jakob's neck, a touch of heaven. At least Albert no longer suffered. Doctor Maastricht stood apart. One skeleton-white hand clenched around the other hand. Finally Dr. Maastricht, gave Spitsspeler a look, and addressed them. "Heavenly Father, they go to a better place. Feed them at last, take them home, give them comfort."

Jakob floated up with the words, below was a circle of burlap bags, a circle of men's heads, and useless words. The violinist started again. Jakob felt Matteus' arm around his shoulder. *I can never go home again without my Albert. My only comfort, he is in the better place. I hope he is with his angels.*

† † †

Vincent trudges back to the kitchen table with Daniel. Soon his pencil is flashing over his least favorite subject, algebra.

Papa coughs and I wonder about his chemo treatment. "For many days after that, I foraged behind the Jap soldiers' mess hall, looking through the garbage. Soon Spitsspeler discovered me. I froze in place, bowing, and backed up step by step. He could have hit me again to save face with the Japanese officer beside him, but didn't. Unbelievably the officer looked bored, barely glanced my way. The next day I went again and found the garbage barrel richer than usual: fish heads, rotting vegetation, rice with maggots—all life sustaining. I ate. He left garbage out for me almost every day. It made me a little stronger. I lived a bit better on the outside, but was dead on the inside."

"Yes, I know about feeling dead," I say shyly. "That's how I felt after the last miscarriage, and—"

"Now you know everything is well with you and your baby," he finishes for me. "Me too. Now I know, our Alby is well. I think I finally figured out you're all of you grown up."

"So tell me about the chemo."

"Well the chemo infusion room is surprisingly nice, kind of reminds me of how you kids describe A.A. Then I go home, and vomit. Never you mind. It's all for the good, and it makes it easy to sleep at night." He sighs. "I wish I could sleep during the day. My body's exhausted, but my thoughts race away. So off I go."

We say good night.

I go over and rest my hand on Vincent's shoulder, and unlike lately he doesn't shrug away. "You know," he says, "doing my schoolwork is not so bad."

"My talk with Grandpa was nice."

"Well, that's good." He's warming up to Grandpa again.

CHAPTER 26

On the last day of office time, I awake in dull pain, twisted up around the special body pillow meant to soothe my hips and back. I've reached an ending as well as beginning. Kitchen water's running, our steam kettle whistles, and news blares on the TV. The hallway bathroom door rattles as Vincent gets up. My nice small home, like Beppe and Pake's boerderij, letting me know where everyone is.

Daniel brings me a steaming cup of tea in bed, and kisses me good-bye. Vincent starts his annoying too-long shower. I lift out of bed, knowing I won't be moving quickly, nor driving. Moving around, the pelvic girdle spasms attack my hips and abdomen. I breathe to get through it, as if I were in labor. *Ah, but I'm not, all is well.*

I plant myself in the living room, waiting for Vincent. He appears, shaking water off his head like a wet puppy. "What, Mom!" These days he often treats me like I'm irritating interruption to his *real* life—that of adolescence.

"My last appointments are after you finish school. Please come straight home later and drive me."

"Why me?" he sneers. "You've got everybody driving you around."

"Honey, I'm in pain," I gasp.

"So take your pain medication and don't go." He jerks a notebook into his backpack and drinks milk—his only breakfast.

"You'll come home. You'll drive." My fist hits the side table. Channeling Papa.

"Okay, whatever," he yells, slamming the door. I won by being the loudest. Although I feel defeated; I have no idea why he's so angry.

† † †

Vincent drives along in the bright sunlight, like, *what argument*? He chauffeurs with the conscientious care of a boy who still has his learner's permit, and is sorry he yelled. He's like Papa and I when I was a teenager. I recall he always yelled at me first, or did he? After yelling, Papa never apologized, and stubbornly neither did I.

My knees quiver with anxiety at each intersection. Vincent doesn't turn his head back and forth the way I want him to. I can't do the imaginary brake, like Moms do, because leg movements hurt the most. He starts easing into gradual stops, uses his turn signals, and continues to drive well. Confidently, he turns the radio up loud.

"No please!" My pain makes me too loud, again.

He clicks the radio off, no argument. "Will you miss your clients, Mom?"

"Actually I will. I get to be home more with you and Dad. It's exciting that Baby is growing and safe, but I'll miss helping people."

"All of my friends' parents are out working, and you're coming home. Weird."

"Yeah," I groan. I scooted the passenger seat back as far as it will go, my lower back is cradled in pillows and my legs are elevated on a sofa cushion from the living room. Electric shock agony hits, and my legs shoot straight in front of me as I breathe slowly like I would for painful labor. Thank goodness I don't have to worry about real labor. In May I'll have another C-section, as I did with Vincent, less pain but a tough recovery. "A pain spasm just hit," I explain.

"Duh, Mom. The doctor gave you pain medication. Take it!"

"You know I don't take any risks with Baby."

462

"So you're going to be like this all the time?"

"Silence. Please." He has a point. I could take pain meds sparingly, per Dr. Simonian, but I know I won't. I am either too narcotic avoidant, health oriented, stubborn or, I've come to realize—self-punishing. Even with Vincent's caution, it feels like he hits every bump. In the parking lot, Vincent leaps out, and heads for my waiting room door with the keys.

I fumble for the car door latch, and then begin to lift one foot out. The resulting twist to my back makes me want to scream.

Vincent is back. "Wow, Mom, you are slow. Okay, here we go." I tense up, expecting him to jerk on my legs and back. Instead, his tone and cadence are like Daniel's. "Everything is okay." He finishes easing my other leg out of the car, grasps me by the shoulders, and steadily tugs me until I am sitting sideways, ready to exit the car.

"Okay, duck your head." He grasps my wrists, and draws me out and up. "Let's get you in there." My other baby is growing up. Last night he actually checked the answers on his algebra, and redid one of his problems.

Once I'm settled in my office chair with its footstool, I feel fine.

Vincent exits for a nearby coffee shop, promising to do more homework. One of my last appointments is Esperanza. She had to be scheduled at an odd time, so I could see everyone on my shortened schedule. So today I'll meet her foster parent for the first, and probably last, time.

Esperanza wears a tank top. Her unzipped hoodie sweatshirt fits, her collar bones glow like rounded nubs of wings and she no longer hides an emaciated body. The biggest change is—her eyes are seeking mine. A smiling woman, with a little girl clutching her hand, accompanies her.

"This is my tia—aunt," says Esperanza, her voice louder than usual. She is proud.

"Yes," I say, and have no more worries about Esperanza's adjustment from an abusive Tia to a helpful Tia. Rather than trying to block off old pain, Esperanza is ready to relax into a better life. Possibly more ready than I am.

As we settle in for our appointment, I give her a note full of counseling referrals; she will need them for sure. I rearrange my legs, and a whimper of pain escapes.

Esperanza's eyes widen. "Pain, huh?"

I want to deny it. But she misses nothing. Survivors of great trauma are like that, noticers, and lying would only violate her trust. "Yes, I have some back pain from the pregnancy, but no worries, it passed already." *Almost true.*

Esperanza's clear brown eyes look wise, as if she knows all. "I hope you feel better, and that you have a wonderful baby. Your baby is so lucky." She smiles the widest grin I've seen from her. "And I don't need the referral list. I'm going to fly solo as my new Tia says. I can make friends, do church, and be in gratitude. Tia and I make gratitude lists every night."

"Oh?" I want to talk her out of flying solo, but the next wave of agony burns at my left hip. I wiggle, believing I'm undetected, until I see Esperanza's eyes narrow.

We underscore her gratitude, revisiting the house of terror she came from. She folds up the referral list after all, in case of an emergency appointment. The r lisp in her speech has smoothed itself out; she has come a long way, far enough that no one would guess the suffering she came from, unless she tells you her story.

"This was a good day you picked for us to meet," Esperanza says, her face somber.

"Today's a special day?"

She nods, and strolls to the cradle-baby figure, which I had left out on the shelf, just for her. She brings it back in the palm of her hand, along with an amethyst crystal. "Today is the anniversary of when Kristoff died, and my freedom started. My old Tia thought I didn't notice the date that horrible day; she never wanted us to know what day it was. But I checked an old newspaper then, and got pretty close, and double-checked with Italia, my social worker, when I was freed."

I nod. Esperanza got out of a dungeon, out of her own concentration camp. "And you are thinking?"

She slides down to the ground by the couch, clutching the baby crib and amethyst together. "I hated having to feel him go cold. But at least I was there at his end of life, he knew I loved him. His last words were 'fight for your happiness.'"

I shiver, the same words Tante Sara said to me during our phone call this year. I slide to the ground too, pain-free, reaching out a hand. Esperanza drops the amethyst in my hand, holding on to the baby.

I weep. I'm done thinking clients will freak when their counselor cries. My gift now is to be the embodiment of fragile and strong. She is doing all the hard work of grieving, all I have to do is to be here, a loving witness again. Hereness and hearing, is what I needed more of from my own parents. "Kristoff gave you a lot when he said to fight for your happiness."

"Yes," says Esperanza. She beams, proud once again. How she must have hungered to have more than moldy bread and beatings in her world. "You know he fought her that day, like he wanted to risk his own death. I did too. Either of us would have died for the other. And then finally, when Kristoff was gone, the ambulance people and the hospital staff figured everything out. Bad Tia had cleaned me up, handed me some clean clothes, offered me a meal, and threatened me to stay quiet. But the investigators could tell, even though she had me sitting on the upstairs couch like that's where I lived. They took me away from her. I got to see the police haul her off." She cackles with satisfaction. "We weren't lost from the world anymore."

"Yes."

I was lost from the world for a time, falling and falling. None of my family knew. No wonder they puzzled about my sudden teen involvement with HOW.

She rubs the baby crib against her cheek. "Tia is helping me with a scrapbook; it shows the newspaper articles about the people who came into our world. Strangers grieved Kristoff's death—good people. They gave their money to be sure he could rest in peace, and I would have a grave to visit." She cups her hands. "Tia Isabelle says all babies are perfect. To me this baby, except that there should be two, are as perfect as Kristoff and I were. I have asked Tia to get a foster baby, but she says it breaks her heart too much to say good-bye. So instead of a baby in the house, I'll think of Kristoff watching me from heaven."

"That he is," I say simply.

I have yet to hear Esperanza blame herself, the way most survivors of trauma do. The power of a brother—they were each other's witnesses to the monster.

Esperanza stands and helps lift me up at the end, slow and steady from the floor. Still no pain. Seems every client is leaving me with a gift. Gene's gift was the reminder that family connections heal and Esperanza's gift is to underscore we have to fight for our happiness, to rise up from hard places no matter what, to expect pain to leave.

We walk out early because clearly we're done. Esperanza, Tia Isabelle, and I say our good-byes. I sit in the comfort of my office waiting for Vincent. There will be no mistaking him when gets to the waiting room door. He is not one for stealth.

Kristoff's in heaven, watching not just Esperanza on her drive home, but also me. I think of my uncle, Oom Albert, somewhat of a dreamer like me, seeing angels, watching from heaven. He would have been my peaceful uncle. Papa's rages always terrified me. I shiver again recalling red dripping down the wall in our home in Utah. A traffic ticket, led to yelling at Mama, breakage and red dripping down the wall like blood. I remember Mama cleaning it up, while Alby and I peeked in. Down the hall, Baby Corrie fussed her way into sleep, with Papa's murmuring, "I'm sorry, I'm sorry," to the kid who didn't know what was wrong. One of the few sorrys I ever heard him say. They went right back to their arguments after that night. Maybe the *ruzie* never quite stopped until the grandkids came along, because they cemented their bond of *ruzie* that night.

How Papa must have wanted Albert's angels to be useful and save them both. I wish angels could have saved our other babies. An angel must have saved Baby, when I didn't even know her, and kept watch when I recklessly flew to Houston again.

The door slams open, and Vincent holds out his homework.

"Whoa, so noisy, what if I was still with a client? We'll look at that homework after you get me home." We settle into the car. "You are so big and healthy," I say, and pat him.

He gives me the same odd look I must have given Papa, all the times he said the same to me. Papa patted me, because at every age I became he could affirm I was big and healthy, not starving like Sara, Oma, and Wim in Holland. Not dying like Albert and Opa.

† † †

Halfway home, relief hits. Relief to drop the brave front when working through pain. Relief to not feel divided between clients and peacefully growing baby. I just said good-bye to fifteen years of showing up for clients. I'm trying for courage and faith, but I fear I'll never be back. In appointments, I'm like an ocean kayak rising and falling between the waves of trauma which are strangely natural to me. I groan, just as Vincent can't avoid a pothole. We're both jolted, and I whimper. *Oh yeah, glad to be going home.*

"Mom, you really should take your medication."

"I told you it's bad for Baby."

"But what does the doctor say?"

"That there can be some exceptions." Maybe he'll grow up to be a therapist. "So all your homework is done, and I'll see its correct when I check it?"

"Everything except Algebra Two. I'll visit Tutor Time at school tomorrow."

"Okay." I have never known Vincent to act so independently and resourcefully in high school. I guess the time I had to be away with Daniel's help was good after all.

† † †

Mama calls often, as does Papa. "I hated to end with my clients." I tell him bits and pieces about Gene and Esperanza, feeling the rare satisfaction of knowing I helped. "Each one had closure," I add.

"So you often help people give up their guilt, heh?" Papa asks. "You know Bevins did that for me. I remember my wonder that he still sought me out after he knew everything."

† † †

Jakob and Bevins

Kamp Tjimahi
April 1945

Bevins turned to him, his mouth corners curved up ever so slightly, as if the talk were not about the most horrible brother ever—Jakob.

"So you thought it was entirely your fault, arriving too late with the sulfa?"

Jakob nodded, spent, doubting he could speak one more time. Bevin's gentle gaze disturbed him.

"Ach, we all feel enormous pain for this mass torture. In a world war so enormous, it is beyond us. We thought we would fight, save our women and children. You thought you would fight for your brother. We all have this terrible ache of being krachteloos — powerless."

"Ja," Jakob risked, feeling as if his jaw and vocal cords had turned to rusted iron. "But you know it's still me who should have traded for medicine sooner."

"That's in the past, and you still have your precious supply." Bevins put a hand on his shoulder.

"How could you know that I still have the sulfa?"

"How could you not? Each of us must hoard any advantage here. It will save another life, maybe your own. You wish you could control horror and death, you blame yourself. I do the same, I think of how I should have prepared Siebe and Mevrouw Bevins, but no one can prepare another for this. This kamp, Kamp Tjiapit, and all the rest are hell on earth."

"I would gladly have Albert, alive. But I was much too selfish, stupid and slow."

"There are places we shouldn't have to go, things we shouldn't have to do, decisions we shouldn't make. You were brave the whole time, not too late, the whole time."

"But Albert brought me ..."

"I remember. Kamp pudding? And if you had found him some, he still would not have lived. Let it go."

"But ..."

"I saw you give young Johan one extra spoonful. You now know, that one spoonful of food helps him to live, not because it is solid food, which of course it is not, but because that one spoonful is a huge ladle of caring. I want you to feel how much God cares for you, and to know that you are not a bad boy."

A bird called as they walked back together. The silence invaded Jakob's heart. No angels to see, yet he could feel it this half hour before dusk, God's love. Bevins grabbed his hand, shaking some. He and Albert had been sad together, and loved together. Not a bad boy. "I thought I felt nothing of faith. Albert saw angels, but not me."

"Jakob, everything you tell me is about God's work in you: finding and hiding a knife while in Tjideng to take with you, readying to help Albert not leave Tjideng alone, like Siebe, even the decision to trade for medicine. It was selflessness, you and Albert sacrificing for each other. Selflessness is our finest hour. One day you will be free and home. This is the furthest we will ever be from our true home with God, in this hell on earth. Let's go get our evening water." He dropped Jakob's hand. "And here is one more important thought. Most likely the sulfa, even earlier, could not have saved Albert. Please Jakob, let it go."

Jakob felt a squeeze of panic about not rushing for water, then a flood of peace. Bevins would save him a place in line. Nothing could be more horrible than the body wagon coming for Albert, yet God loved them. Bevins said he was selfless — one of two good brothers who tried all to keep each other alive.

He took a turn next to Bevins, almost at the end of the water line with his cup and canteen. Miraculously, the steady drip worked just as it had for every other inmate.

Leaving with wet canteens, moonlight illuminated planes on Bevins' face, almost as if he were the radiant angel. Hoarsely he said, "Remember these words, from Matteus, tenth chapter: 'Whatever town or village you enter, search for some worthy person there and stay at his house till you leave. As you enter the home give it your greeting. If the home deserves, let your peace rest on it; if it does not, let your peace return to you.' I may not live until the end of the war to go home, Jakob. Each of us is the worthy person in the Scripture. Do not let them break your spirit. Take your spirit with you. You will always know worthy people. The enemy can starve you, they can take your home, but they can never take your home inside. They can never take away the breath with which you breathe in God's love."

That night, he focused on Bevins' breathing. He wondered about faith in Christ, and that Christ, too, suffered. He sensed Jesus' spirit, right there. He did not need to open his eyes. If he did, he would see him bleeding, starving, and loving them all. Before, he would only have wished Jesus to lead an army. *He comes not with an army, but comes to our suffering.* He shivered as he recalled having the same thought of Jesus as his comforter at Albert's graveside, but pushing it away with the horror of death. Now he would not pull away. *So Jesus, never, never leaves us alone.*

He drifted into his first prayer since Albert's death. He prayed for Bevins to live, and find Siebe and Tineke Bevins. He prayed for his own family to come together: six minus one.

† † †

Although eerie dark still fell each night at Fifth Battalion Tjiapit, Jakob's lonely thoughts at night were no longer as deafening as all the men's moans and groans.

Ten thousand men spread over various barracks, battalions and nearby kamps. One of them held Wouter. Only rarely now, did Jakob think of the barrack or sub-camp which could hold Pappie. His instinct told him not likely. Somehow, they would be reunited. How, he wasn't sure. He wondered how Pappie would greet him. There was the matter of how Pappie would react to hearing of Albert's death. He pushed the thought away. There was the matter of the compass stolen away so early on, and he pictured their hands on charts and maps on the slow ship home. Then Pappie ruffled his hair, took him to the ship's bridge. A good memory, it became his fall asleep thought each night.

Sometimes hundred of scarecrow men and boys arrived from faraway kamps. They knew by now what the Japanese strategy must be: men's kamps inland in mountainous regions where they would not turn and fight in case of Allied attack. The other strategy: women and children near harbors and the coast, no risk for fighting, and if detected, a shield to avoid attack. Somewhat of a shield, as no white cross for POWs or civilian prisoners was ever painted on kamp roofs or the transport ships known as Hell Ships. Even with additional arrivals, their numbers decreased every day. So many bodies went on the wagon, up to twenty a day; most burial ritual was lost.

Last night, as he always did, Bevins read out loud from his Bible: "Deuteronomy thirty-two, verse four. 'He is the rock, his works are perfect, and all his ways are just. A faithful God who does no wrong, upright and just is he." Bevins stood upright, did not bow in the barracks.

He always read in a soft clear voice, which carried easily to a small circle of men. Automatically another circle of men beyond them formed, appearing to talk, but actually serving as a sound screen. They were the lookout for *rood voor*, Japs, protection against having a hidden bible, and hidden words. Next the whole routine reversed, and Bevins repeated his words.

† † †

During morning appel, even ill prisoners had to stand now. Counting went on and on, starting over and over as if the mud sent the tally off again and again. Bent over for hours, Jakob knew the same pain, which burned up and down his limbs was worse for others. He focused on Bevin's words: *I may not survive the war.*

He craved to help Bevins, as fervently as craving pure water instead of brackish sludge. He could be the stronger, the helper. To that end he had bumped Bevins one day, and helped bear his weight. Jakob stiffened anytime dry or squelching boots came near, and Bevins understood to stand on his own then — pointed hands toward his ankles.

Bevins said, "Jakob, you have that good solid touch. You are my rock." A new hope grew in Jakob. When he saw Pappie's familiar red head again, Pappie would also say, "You, you are a help to me. A rock."

Nights, Bevins often read a psalm: "For those times we are lifted up, Psalm forty. 'He lifted me out of the slimy pit, out of the mud and mire. He set me on a rock and gave me a firm place to stand.'" Then he assigned Jakob a turn reading from the Bible. "The best chapter of all," he said, "Romans eight says 'Nothing can separate us from the love of God.'"

Jakob's heart pounded, it had been so long since he had read, much less out loud. He still had doubts about all that Bevins read, though he wouldn't hurt him by saying so. This *I will do for you, for I know that you believe.* Pappie had read the Bible out loud, Sundays only.

He began, reading, "Nothing can," and then again, "nothing can." And he had to stop. He felt warmth, as though Albert was alive, like not being separated from heaven, like everything being okay one day. In the closer circle of men, the ones who listened, emaciated men, stared at him, a few smiling like they had lost their minds. He couldn't risk losing his own mind. With as much respect as he could, he slowly handed the reading back to Bevins, and collapsed on a sleeping platform, shaking. Nearby, the listeners rested, only a few looking at him oddly. Some carved on bits of wood, and all waited to hear Bevins finish the interrupted reading. A small distance away, some men covered the sound of reading with discussion.

Jakob thought of regular life. He missed studying Juffrouw in front of the class, teaching his class, her calves curving with every graceful step. He missed Marijke's fruity kiss, the look of her when she bent to pick up her little brother. He wished he could see Aartje de Witt's companion, with the swooping curve in her calves, however bony she might be. Now these men had no women's curves to see for over a year. Jakob reflected back on the reading. *I am not losing my mind. It is true, nothing can separate you from the love of God, even if others spit out words about you, even if you grunt in the night with other men, where everyone can hear, even if your new friend Bevins knows you stole food from Sara, and that you*

473

failed to save your brother's life. But the existence of God rings true. Just as rumors of Europe's near freedom had reached them, God would have to send the Allies to the Pacific too.

He felt warm again, nothing can separate us from God's love. His heart pounded without fear, and he felt Albert's love near. He closed his eyes, with no wish to open them, as he sense angels all around. No need to see them. *Do not fear,* angels always said. They could be liberated soon. *Oh lieve Heere, God, make it soon.*

† † †

They were back to brutal sunny days that turned the mud into cement. Men's bare feet burned on the hot baked dirt on the asphalt for all of appel. Unbearable, yet they had to bear it. Recently, Jakob's few clothes loosened, and Bevins hobbled often to the latrines. Some mornings he was too weak to get up before diarrhea hit. Jakob cleaned him, with rags turning brown and bloody. Like the hospital staff, he rinsed the brown rags and left them to dry in the sun. Such mornings his heart beat with alarm, and love. He thought of Mammie carrying Sara to the toilets nightly, caring for her when she had dysentery, then having to do the same for him and Albert. Such vivid thoughts of Sara and Mammie brought longing and love. He hung up rags on barrack platforms, thinking, *and they love me too.*

Even the only treasure he had left, sulfa, would not help for amoebic dysentery, said Dr. Akker, the Tjimahi doctor, who looked as haggard as Dr. Maastricht. He and the men, always so inventive, tried remedies, such as having Bevins consume much of the last salt, while drinking as much water as could be gathered. The treatment only left him moaning in pain.

Dr. Akker took to coming by, joking about home visits. "You know you are supposed to be in hospital." He hunkered down and pressed on Bevin's abdomen. "I am worried you will have a twisted intestine soon, yet another danger. Take as much water as you can." He trudged away, shoulders permanently slumped, taking a moment to sit by a makeshift table, with his head in his hands. The next time Jakob looked up, he was gone.

One of their group was always in line at the dripping faucet for Bevins' water. Although he still spoke to them all, mentioned Bible quotations and joked about the foul drinking water being like piss, he fell silent more often—the hunger stupor.

He looked away when Jakob cleaned him in the mornings. *What will become of Bevins, and then me?* Jakob rinsed and hung up foul rags and wondered about a good God. *He does no wrong, upright and just is he ...* Would a just, good God let Bevins slowly waste away, and have Albert die? Jakob's puzzling darkened with his own trance of exhaustion. He made himself think of the courage of Bevins, Roelof, and the others. He had faith in Bevins' morning routine of leaning on him for appel. He counted each day of surviving appel, and not losing Bevins to the hospital veranda, as good.

The morning came that Jakob woke up next to Bevins in a wet pool of overpowering odor. The shitty foul smell of rotten fruit and fish guts emanated from Bevins. Even as his stomach roiled with Bevins' waste, Jakob lingered only a moment. He waved Roelof de Witt over and together they supported Bevins for a quick drip—mandi—from the faucet, and then had him drink water.

"It will just come back out," Bevins sighed.

"And you know you must have water, and some of this delicious morning gruel, um ... tapioca starch," said Roelof.

Bevins managed a chuckle. They made it to appel after gruel. The leaning routine could start. Bevins weighed nothing now. Roelof edged over a bit to help. Jakob exhaled in relief and inhaled, just as boots scuffed to a stop in front of him.

Too late, he stirred Bevins to stand alone. The guard blurred into motion from his full height, only a little higher than the inmates' bent backs. His fist came down in a mighty blow to Bevin's head. Bevins crumpled down with a small oof.

Stand, stand. You must stand. Never give up.

The guard, with his flat country face, a bit like Fat Nose's, snarled. He hit again, well-muscled arms smashing down. A distant commander's voice rang out. Country Boy brought down the butt of his gun in the middle of Bevins' back. For a moment Bevins' arms strained on either side of his white head in a feeble pushup, his elbows wavering up. Country Boy kicked Bevins in the head with his hard boots. No more moves. Another loud call cried out from the commander. Country Boy's face went blank, confused, and he stepped away. Jakob's face was a fire of pain, wishing to scream, to kick out. The mud of weeks ago would have been better. It was as if Bevins hit cement.

Jakob strove to cast out his terror; Bevins lay motionless. He must not know yet that he could safely get up. Jakob, Roelof, and all the rest stayed bent. Country Boy backed off more. The commander strode over, his face grave. He must not have intended for Bevins to be punished. *Perhaps he sees Bevins, the rare man with Samurai spirit.* The commander grabbed Country Boy's weapon and struck him in the ear with the butt. Stunned, the young man swayed on his feet, a trickle of dark blood running down his neck onto his shirt.

A whole row of men slowly moved out of appel lineup as one. The commander kicked Country Boy in the face until he was a mass of blood, and lay still. An enemy and a friend, motionless, strangely close together. Jakob and Roelof could help Bevins now, and each put hands under his shoulders and lifted him, motionless like dead wood. No Japanese interference.

Dr. Akker rushed over. He put his fingers on Bevins' neck and immediately shook his head. The world spun in dizziness for Jakob. *Not unconscious. Dead.* Jakob widened his legs against the spinning and pulled Bevins higher, tying to get him on his feet, taller than any Japanese. Bevins had his heart, and his soul. Jakob didn't fight the blurring of his eyes, tears flowing, or sorrow stabbing. He yearned to vomit, to vomit the whole day away, and start again, detecting dangerous boots from afar. Men wiped away tears and shuffled with lowered shoulders, in half circles, not knowing where to go.

How could this happen on this day when rumor had it that a part of the Netherlands was freed, and Japan was being fire bombed? Was this the reason Country Boy hit so viciously? This war had to be over, yet it seemed endless, so far beyond the quick months of fighting they had told themselves in the first kamp.

They carried Bevins away. Seeing Bevins spirit immediately gone, Jakob remembered a Catholic Brother's words at Grogol. *Although it is outside of my religion, I wonder. A wise Indo man taught me that dying goes in stages. The body dies first, then the spirit lingers, then the spirit ascends to heaven. Too many needless deaths.*

They laid Bevins' body on someone's meager centimeters of wooden tier bed, eyes closed, arms folded. Men filed by, touching his shoulder. His face looked peaceful in spite of the boot shaped bruise on his upper left cheek bone, and the odd angle of his neck.

Jakob stayed with him, becoming as wooden as the barrack sleeping slats. What good was the hidden Bible now? No one would want to read it or see it. This man had been like their sanctuary-church and he was gone. He touched Bevins, still warm, one last time. He left for the punishment hut, which had become the talking hut, and counted up the days. He would know the date of Bevins' death, because it was his own sixteenth birthday, May twenty-second. He felt a spirit stage—his Bevins. Jakob scooted down and the breeze came again. He ceased fighting the battle to be like dead himself, and though of Sara's birthday on the veranda of their Billiton home. He always saw Sara in his mind as thin, yet her hair parted on the side, and somehow, a butterfly bow. Surely he would see Mammie, Pappie, Sara, and Wim again.

Men straggled to corvée, guards held back, and Jakob went too. All day there was little talk, and a dull ache replaced his heart. The emptiness pleased him, for it was a fact, it was real, not like shaky hopes. He had to hope for family, but he had hoped for Bevins, and he was gone. *We are indeed bent down.* He scraped his patjol in the dirt.

† † †

In the morning Jakob had nothing he wished to face, with no Bevins next to him. He was forced awake by a thud on his hip.

Roelof de Witt said, "Bevins left this for you." Jakob held the small Bible, desiring to throw it. But Roelof looked at him hopefully. "Hide it well."

Another man came to him. He had no idea of his name. "Hello boy, Bevins knew how weak he was, that he could die. He said for you to read Luke twelve at night."

The Bible felt warm in his hands. He sniffed it; it smelled of dust, and sweaty hands. When he opened it wide, it smelled of home, of ordinary pages without human death and sewage smells, and with some kind of sweetness. He felt Bevins with him, he felt calm. Luke twelve was marked. He looked up to the unfamiliar man. "You?" he asked, pointing to the mark.

"No, Bevins said, you."

That morning Jakob began to read out loud, aware for the first time that, like Bevins, he had a voice that carried. Nearby some men automatically stretched, moaned, got up, and went some meters away to talk. The usual routine, except it was daylight. Later they would do this in reverse, with listeners diverting, and the diverters listening. So there would be a next time.

Jakob read on, words that almost silenced everyone, even the diverters, "I tell you my friends, do not be afraid of those who kill the body and after that can do no more. But I will show you whom you should fear: Fear him who, after the killing of the body, has power to throw you into hell. Yes, I tell you, fear him. Are not five sparrows sold for two pennies? Yet not one of them is forgotten by God. Indeed the very hairs of your head are all numbered. Don't be afraid, you are worth more than many sparrows. I tell you whoever acknowledges me before men; the Son of Man will also acknowledge him before the angels of God."

Jakob stopped, although he was nowhere near done. They had no time to reverse the routine right now. Tonight, then. He nodded, and the others understood. He stowed the Bible in his own hiding place when everybody had turned away. Heading for the food line, he thought of what he'd read. If they were all sparrows, and more precious than sparrows, precious to God, the greatest hell was to give up all thoughts of hope. Not ordinary hope, but hope in God.

He turned to the new man, who gave his first name, Frederick, as if Jakob for some moments was an adult. "Where is Bevins' body?"

"We took him yesterday and put his body with some who just died in the hospital. They all looked peaceful in death; their spirits gone to a better place."

Jakob wished he had embraced Bevins one more time, after all the men had filed past him. He could remember instead his ears roaring with rage pulsating in him like a weapon and friendly hands pulling him away before he decided to hit. He only recalled leaning back against the hut wall alone an hour later, alternating between faith and despair. But now he had this new day, both fresh and terrible. He thought of Bevins' bible. *He left me his bible. I was 'his other' after all, and did not know.*

†††

Papa and I talked about Bevins over days. I repeat Papa's Bevins lesson. "He died so violently, a man courageous enough to remain peaceful. Even the Japanese respected him."

"Yes, they did. They must have thought that he had samurai spirit and that the guard who attacked him was acting out of cowardice, not outrage. There was more than one man beaten to death."

"Ja, so sad. And I used to think it was Albert that died from a beating."

"Well, I felt as if I had beaten him, that I couldn't assure life for my own brother once he became so ill."

"And what about your pappie, my opa?"

"Your opa, a hard story to live with. He too died at the end of the war. So many died in the last months, just before liberation. Soon I'll tell you about the happiest day of my life, until I met your mother. The day I made it through the open gates of Tjideng and there were my mammie and Sara."

Be at ease now Papa. We both say I love you, and I lower the phone as gently as if I'm squeezing his hand.

I know one thing about this world: there is no understanding it. Ironically, now that I'm old I'm part of recreating a different home and a different family for Baby, Vincent and Daniel. I understand that Papa is telling me with this story, that anyone who harbors rage inside will not be free, but reporting to a corvée of misery every day. I harbored so much rage for being stuck with moves all of these years, always leaving, always seeing life by looking back. I built my career on looking back, then coming into the present. Yet everyone has had to pull hard to teach me to truly live moment by moment. "Today is a gift, that's why we call it the present," Eleanor Roosevelt said.

480

The day Papa saw Sara and Oma, I muse. So many times I have seen Baby on sonogram. Life is good. I wonder about Matteus, so often mentioned by Papa. I wonder about Willem Vanderveer, the Opa I never knew. I am intensely grateful that the deceased and the survivors are so vivid to me. The vast majority of my life I was without Beppe and Pake, yet their determined survival, their way of talking about God, filled me with a faith I felt, and let go of. For thirty years now, I have returned to faith, and I have seen Papa's faith come to life again.

I call Kemble and make no excuses for my own old sorrows, no comparisons are necessary. Old pain is what it is, and I tell her that I won't call Alby to see how he is. She gives me the familiar AA advice to pray for him daily, until my own concentration camp of resentment is truly gone.

"But that's too easy," I say.

"For you, that's actually really hard." She laughs.

CHAPTER 27

Luce

Calabria, California
May 2005

Over the weekend, Vincent keeps me up late, working on a school paper, wriggling around on my current "office furniture" — the king-size bed in our master bedroom. Vincent has been glad to have me as his helper. I'm relieved he's not been shutting me out as he has been. Lovely to be useful too, after being so drained and yet alive with what I hope is the last death Papa has to remember. For nights now, Baby kicks so much that I can't fall sleep easily. Her kicking is the antidote to my worries however, so I trust sleep will come and celebrate every kick.

On Monday morning I am so tired of bed rest. Poor me; eventually I'll deliver a healthy baby, born to a mom with atrophied muscles. I wish I could get up on a ladder and paint Baby's room, like when I was pregnant with Vincent — Daniel wasn't moving quickly enough for me then. All I can do these days is tell myself, *if I'm good now, maybe I can get off bed rest soon* — weeks before Baby's birth. So I'm not going to fret; I'll just call Papa to see how he is.

"How's the treatment Papa?" I ask him.

To my surprise his tone is light. "Well, celebrated the last of this round of chemo. It's amazing to be able to hold food down. You can imagine how I feel about vomiting and diarrhea."

"Yeah." He's referring to the kamp years more matter of factly now.

"And then Cindy told me Alby wasn't going to his AA meetings. He hasn't been making his reach out calls either," he adds like an expert. "He's not cheerful like when he first checked himself out of rehab. So I thought, you and Dr. Ingstrom have a point about AA, and I formulated a plan."

I roll my eyes. Silly, as Papa can't see me. He must know by now that Alby is like a force of nature; no clever plan will change his path.

"I told him if he would go back to AA meetings, I would go with him, and he said yes." Papa's voice lifts. "So Alby checked his schedule and I met him there last night. He said it's one of the best men's AA meetings in Houston, over in Memorial, at a Catholic retreat center."

"I've been there. That place can be hard to find, and it's a long drive for Alby."

"Ja, that's why it was so good for him. 'Willingness to go to any lengths,' like you AA-ers say. And for me, worth finding. In the end it was like an adventure, and a great meeting."

Weird, having Papa admire a twelve-step meeting. Well, not so weird, I keep forgetting he liked parents' meetings at HOW, after I finally told him I attended. Still I have to relax my jaw from old anger that roils on up every time my parents are glad to get Alby into AA meetings. They wanted me to avoid my meetings, even as recently as a year ago. *Why do you still go to those meetings?* I would hear.

Oh, drop it, I tell myself. I'm just cranky from this bed rest. Papa must have struggled behind the wheel, weak from chemo, sweat trickling down his back, as he made sure that left turns didn't accidentally take him down the wrong side of the boulevards in the dark. I know the treachery of those streets, in the pitch dark of Memorial; for some reason fancy neighborhoods eschew streetlights.

I know the treachery of my thoughts too. I realize with a jolt I found resentments to justify my emotional distance from Mama and Papa. It left me in the pitch dark, like those blacked-out Memorial streets. I used to end up there in alcoholic blackouts, and as I wasn't even the driver during those times. I can thank God for getting me home. I didn't trust them to find out that they could have gone through a war with me too, like they did themselves, like they did with Alby's addiction.

I imagine Papa prayed, as we've all been referring to faith more now. Probably like me, his teeth clenched, praying and gripping the wheel. Finally he would have arrived to the crowded parking lot. "Heh," he would have grunted to himself as his sweaty hands slid off the steering wheel. He'd have sat for moments in the dark car, breathing slowly. His war-time trick for panic, Papa already told me, was to pair each breath with counts, to always exhale one more count than the inhale. He'd have hoisted himself out of the car, probably leaving his cane behind out of pride.

"So I will tell you the whole story. There's a lot I told the man at the meeting."

He makes it sound like every meeting has one particular man. Actually it's true, I suppose, that providence helps each person find that someone if they are ready. Papa must be ready, and he apparently thinks he can tell somebody at the meeting how AA should work, tell Alby how it all should work (again). When Papa thinks he is in charge, all is well.

† † †

Jakob

Houston, Texas
April 2005

Alby points to the seat next to him, grinning and directing as if he never objected to going to AA meetings at all, as if he is in charge of seating elderly men with canes and limps. Everyone sits in rows and rows of cushy chairs. This Catholic bunch must bring in the bucks.

Jakob wishes to cool off the sweat from the twisted dark roads he traveled, as bad as jungle roads. Alby's clear eyes make the effort worth it. *Yes, Son, I would do it again.*

"Why so many readings?" Jakob whispers to Alby.

Alby lifts his fingers to his lips, and rolls his eyes, annoyed. All three children always tell Jakob and Nikki that they are much too loud. Now that they are each hard of hearing, it's worse, they claim. But he's only whispering, such a small disturbance. Later he'll remind Alby about all the calls he fielded in the middle of the night. Alby would call knowing Jakob might be restless and awake, only to hang up, leaving the shrill telephone ring echo in his ears. If he called right back, his son never picked up. Once at 3:00 a.m. Alby called and didn't hang up successfully, leaving Jakob with his uneven trudging over gravel, and nearby a nickering horse. No one could rein him in all those years. *And now he's trying to rein me in?*

It's too much. He plays a silent minor scale on his legs, goes into "Begin the Beguine," stops.

Alby whispers annoyingly close to his ear, "These are AA Big Book readings, they are good reminders."

Normally Alby never listens to anything. Here he listens.

"And here's Brother John," a man finally announces.

How strange, a sober priest or monk. An unusually tall man, all bones, in his early sixties, rises. He wears a faded blue work shirt like the kids used to wear when they were teenagers, blue jeans, and running shoes. "Hi, I'm John, a recovering alcoholic and a visiting Christian Brother here."

Jakob's eyes twinge with pin pricks of pain. This is how he cries, so easily these days. One vague memory and off he goes: age, chemo. He stares straight ahead so Alby can't see tears welling up in his eyes. There were Catholic Brothers and priests at the men's and boys' kamps. So many lost, starving boys. He and Albert were raised Protestant, but it didn't matter; there was something steady about these men. First off, it didn't bother them that they never put up a fight like soldiers. That was their vow. Most of the Brothers' eyes were clear, whereas the other's supposedly godly eyes looked dark and empty.

The few Godly men were as steady as the heavy rocks the boys stacked for their play contests of strength–solid, real, there. *One Brother, Gerard, knew us by name, encouraged us, and came up with games to fight the long hours of boredom. That is until we became full-out slave laborers.* The good men let us speak to them with the informal *je*, a sign of respect that our suffering indeed made us men too. Ja, *the second we saw our fathers marched, beaten or snatched away, we were no longer children.*

Jakob missed Brother John's first words as surprise heat burst in his chest. Good heat, memories of Bevins and Gerard. Only a few times since then had he experienced this unbidden sense of faith, like being impaled by belief. Occasionally in the concentration camps, on his wedding day, the birth of each of his children, in the Utah desert with Tom, and now, like a reopened wound. *I may crack open, but there is still much nobody knows. The one thing I always still have, no matter how cracked, is secrets.* Yet the cracking open went on as Brother John spoke.

"I'll talk of faith in two ways, as a recovering alcoholic and a monk. I'll bet you can't guess which one gave me the most faith."

Alby and many others laugh. Jakob finds himself laughing too. He thinks of a recovery saying Alby told him: *Religion is for those afraid to go to hell. Spirituality is for those who've already been there.*

Brother John talked of the few good men he knew, who helped him find his way.

Were there really so few good men? *Am I really so bad myself?*

"I hit bottom before I ever had the first drink."

More words to sink in. *How many times have I hit bottom? I bet he doesn't know what it's like to starve. And let's face it, I did*

486

have drugs. Kreteks to dull starvation. The rare opium pipe to escape.

Brother John gazes all around the room, his hands in a relaxed grip on the podium. "So I have two hitting bottoms to talk about; the one from childhood and the one from booze. I was going to be so good when I grew up. I was never going to be an alcoholic like my dad. I thought that meant not drinking *like* my dad. I didn't realize that in my instance, that meant *not* drinking at all, so as not to be an active alcoholic like my dad. It took me a long time to talk about my worst secret from childhood." He nodded at the poster on the wall. "That would be steps four and five, up there, getting out our secrets."

Maybe that's why Alby stopped meetings; he's smart enough to not share all his secrets.

"I always got stuck halfway through the steps. Finally I told my sponsor the biggest secret I had." His hands grip the podium, like he doesn't know his own strength, moving it with a clunk, letting go. "My mom was knocked unconscious and later died from an aneurism. I thought it was my fault. 'Your fault?' My sponsor asked.

"'Oh yeah,' I answered. 'When he knocked her unconscious, I cowered on the cold linoleum floor, where he had slammed me down. If he saw me get up again, he'd beat me again. If Mom was dead, I soon would be too.'" Brother John's voice broke.

Oh, it is the worst, to not be able to protect those you love. The worst. He could leave this second, why dredge up the past, the worst? There are escape doors in every direction, but how to leave? Alby selfishly put himself in the aisle. Still, he will leave. But the warmth in his chest pins him down. And Alby needs him to stay, because he too leaves every place that tries to pin him down.

"I waited, feigning I was knocked out too. My body screamed to go to the bathroom, but I had to wait for him to pass out. Waiting was agony. I peed my pants, I waited for his even breathing. When I snuck out to call emergency services, she was already dead. My sponsor finally got it through to me, that I was just a kid, that it was not my fault, and that I had done all I possibly could. So, not my fault. I couldn't be God and save my mom's life. Maybe she even saved mine."

The room drops into silence as the air conditioning hums to life. A chair creaks. Brother John goes on, "Really not my fault. I guess the first thing we all learn here is that if there is a God, that it's not us, right?"

Alby and a few others laugh.

So we're all struck silent. The question of God when the horrific happens. The question of blame. Brother John witnessed only one death. He didn't see his own brother, like Albert flash before him, the horror of his death, his wasted face. *It was my fault.*

"So I stopped holding that deadly weight, of being the little boy who was supposed to risk his life to conquer his father and rescue his mother. Sobriety got easier."

Brother John wraps up with stories of friendship and his temporary travel assignment around to the retreat centers.

The meeting ends with a huge circle. Men's voices, saying, "Our Father, who art in heaven." *Grant me this day, my daily bread. I have said this prayer in many languages.*

Alby has a pen and notebook out. Phone numbers, good. *Ja, excellent,* Dr. Ingstrom would say.

He can go rest, settle his trembling insides, and then leave. Every muscle hurts, his chest still aches, his cane wobbles with every step. *Better no one knows, no one creates a fuss. Nikki is wrong when she insists that I always want attention.*

He wanders to the edge of the meeting room, to the lit-up patios; there will be beautiful grounds and pathways nearby. A jungle in the middle of Houston, an open slider door, frogs and crickets rumble and trill.

Relief, no one to talk to. *Like most places, I don't belong here, I am just a guest.* The sharp aroma of bad coffee as he falls

488

into a patio chair. Not a bad idea to load up on java, just like an alcoholic instead of booze. *I'll be ready for the drive home in the inky black night. The way home should be easier. It's the getting to anywhere else, safe and on time, that's so hard.*

Alby approaches, with only a ghost of his old limp. *At first Alby had the worst injuries from the accident, now I do. That is how it should be, and he is half a foot taller than me. Do my children know I would have been a taller man without the starvation? I looked up to older brother Wim after the war, because he did not starve for as many years. And Sara, the shortest of us, taking after Pappie's stature yes, but how tall would she have been? Ach, I should call Sara.*

"What's up, Pap?"

Jakob jumps even though he saw Alby coming. A strange panic rises inside, surely invisible on his face. But Alby widens his eyes; he sees. *Might as well tell him something.* "I was thinking of the *dominees*, you know priests, brothers, I knew in the kamps. One man might as well have been a *dominee*; he had true faith that one. The other was, actually a Catholic Brother. Such good men."

"What happened?"

"Well, of course, the really good one died, beaten to death into rock-hard ground by the Japanese. That was Bevins; the one I told you all helped me."

Alby's face flickers with shock, and then composes again. *See, you kids can't really take it when I tell you the worst, and this is not the worst.* "That's how it often went. Usually a man horribly injured on the ground, sometimes a man dead. Bevins was such a good man, that the Japanese commander himself came over to yell at the guard — and beat him almost to death. The Japs were cruel to each other too you know, which I always found to be a comfort, but not that day, no way. Bevins wasn't hit as hard and repeatedly as some. All our bodies were worn out by then, too vulnerable to death."

"Oh, Pap, I'm sorry." Alby drifts away. *Ja, you kids really don't like it, bodies on the dirt.. Kids, I had been a kid and thought*

Bevins an old man. Suffering aged him and the other men. I am now the one who is truly old and vulnerable to death.

He settles further into the chair, stirs in powdered cream and sugar, and keeps remembering. Instant Nescafé coffee, hot water, and sugar whipped into a forth of foam was one of the rare treats in the early years of the kamps.

Alby returns and jostles his shoulder. "Come."

"Heh, you'll make me spill."

Alby ignores as always. "Pap, John, this *dominee* is still here. You can make an appointment to talk to him; he is at this retreat center for a week."

"Oh." *Talk to him?* "Nonsense, no. What for crazy idea is that?" His heart beats worse than when he was peering through the dark for the tiny retreat sign. Talking to John would be like Bevins all over again, but not as a youth trying to stay strong, but as a weak old man, crying, giving up.

"Papa, you've been telling me never quit opening up. This will do you good. Now come on, *toe nou*. Here, I'll introduce you."

"No!"

But Alby drags him. He sloshes more coffee from the Styrofoam cup on himself and his good Hush Puppies. The expensive suede shoes will be ruined. Alby doesn't compensate for his slow uneven walk. Then he is in front of *Dominee* John, who has blue eyes, like Bevins. Jakob wants to run, but his chest warms again. Stay.

John reaches for the cup, steadies it, dries it off with an old-fashioned handkerchief, and passes it back. "So your name is Jakob?" he pronounces it correctly, *Yaahkop*.

"My dad's ready for an appointment," Alby jumps in.

"Okay, you. Let's hear what your father has to say." John turns away from Alby, who waves good-bye, a satisfied look on his face.

Too bad he's going already. Typical, but he does have the longer drive home.

"Let us walk over here, ja?" John says, as if saying *yaah* correctly is a joy for him. Blue eyes, Bevins' eyes, Dr. Ingstrom's eyes. None of these eyes could have escaped the chaos of *Bersiap* time; each would have to hide from the native Indonesians, or suffer attack or death. They end up on the patio together, walking to the seam between light and dark. John screeches two wrought-iron chairs together, and plumps the chair pads. "Tell me what is on your mind."

Jakob looks right into his kind eyes. The doorways to the soul. Nikki said in the early years of marriage, *Tell me*, and her father, Heit, when he first met him, *Tell me*. "You spoke of forgiveness."

"Some wonder if it is truly necessary … to forgive. What happened that you cannot forgive?"

"You don't run around the bush."

John grins. "No I don't beat around the bush. You heard I'm not here long, so I move fast. Do I detect a Dutch accent?"

"Ja, Dutch. I was in a Japanese concentration kamp. World War Two. You know some Dutch guys?"

"Sometimes I think those of us who have survived tough times feel like we all have our own country together, plus we recognize each other somehow. And yes, I have met others who are Dutch and survived. So you must have been in the Japanese kamps as a child?"

"Ja." *He makes it much easier to talk, than those who know nothing.*

"Let's settle back." They both eased into the chair cushions. "So, forgiveness?"

"Two things."

"Two things or two people?"

"Two people."

"Well, we might as well talk here and now," says John, leans back as if he has all night.

Jakob's heart stops racing, then warms again. "The man who was the kindest to me, the one who made me feel like I wasn't alone, as a completely unattached kid in the kamps; he was killed. I watched so many boys at least have fathers with them in the men's *kamp*en, I never did. Well, almost never. Bevins could somehow see that even if I was with my father later, it would not be like the others. Maybe it was because he knew us before the war. Maybe because he was the type who could see a lot. It was like I was old already, and Bevins knew this, and knew that in spite of that, I was still a kid without a father. How can I say? He fathered me, I wish you could have met him, he was such a good man."

"And do you tell everyone about him?"

"Well, no. Only my family, only this year."

"So let's let Bevins live through us."

A hand drops on Jakob's arm. Again Alby startles him. He's still here after all. John nods him away. Alby hovers and then retreats back into the brighter pool of light. "Okay, Pap, I have to go, it's so late."

He is acting like a good boy. "Good-bye." Jakob waves him away, his voice almost disappearing, thick with tears which constrict his throat, but can't flow. He turns to John. "Bevins was at the next to the last kamp I was in. I was a young cynic, not interested in anyone's direction and care. He was from my home island, Billiton. In the first kamp, Tjideng, I was with my mom, sister, and brother, and also Bevins' son and wife. He talked to me as if he could see right through me. For months he saved me from loneliness and starvation. Then he was beaten to death by the Japs."

"You saw all this?"

"Ja." His tears flowed, not as horrible as he had feared. He rubbed his hands over his wet face.

John's concerned eyes never changed. "I'm so sorry."

"And he was the only one I had talked to of my brother's death."

"Your son said your brother and father died in the kamps too," John says searchingly. "So much, Jakob. Let's keep a good man's memory alive, and you need to see the fine man you are. We will talk again, yes? About your brother and more?"

Jakob picks foam tufts out of the chair cushion, shredding them. "Not necessary." He grins as a cover. "It's nice that you actually know about Europeans in Japanese concentration camps. That's enough for me." John is mistaken to call him a fine man. He is a man whose own son has seldom felt comfort from him. A man, who, it could be argued, caused accidents. They might talk again of forgiving others, not the greediness of forgiving himself.

"It is necessary. Tomorrow?"

"I'm busy."

"Look, I'm sure you are retired and can find room in your schedule. I leave soon. If you don't schedule now, you may never come back, ja?"

"Ja, okay then, tomorrow." *He could let it go and not show up for this self-important man, so confident he already knows what Jakob has to say.* Yet he saw himself in daylight here soon, meeting with John, as if he was an old friend.

"Bevins would want you to come to find more peace. Drop this burden, and ja, even the other ones too. I did hear you; I know you wonder about forgiving. Will you pray?"

Jakob looks around. Alby has indeed left. John reaches out to hold hands as if they are little kids at the dinner table.

"Father," begins John. Jakob finds he is shaking. "The Holy Spirit has you," John whispers, and then louder, "Father, we cast all burdens on you. Help Jakob to know you never meant him to carry the burden of the world's cruelty. Help him to feel his own courage, to this day. Father, please grant him peace beyond all understanding."

John hugs him. "Drop the rock," he says. Must be another AA saying. A stupid one.

Jakob pounds John's back, quickly let's go. "Drop the rock? You never went through the kamps, and I bet you were never at war."

"Jakob, my so-called father beat my younger brother until he lost his hearing in one ear; beat my mother in front of me. You know he killed her, and he hit me too, all the time. Don't you think I felt guilty? Don't you think my household felt like a war zone? I was just a kid, I couldn't keep them safe. So yes, I know. What will happen if you do not let go? Notice I do not talk yet of forgiveness. You know you could just be your old self. Is that how you want to remember Bevins and your brother?"

"No." This was like warm ocean water washing over him on a safe shore. Yet he still would rather be alone.

"Let go, none of you prisoners should have had to live or die with that brutality. You survived for a reason."

Drop the rock, surviving for a reason. Surviving for a reason, words he hated much more than *drop the rock.* Poor Alby, was he supposed to stay sober with just words?

Jakob nods at Brother John, too tired to fight anymore. He could curl up and sleep right here. "Three tomorrow." John doesn't even have his phone number; he could still escape tomorrow's appointment with no harassing call.

John pulls him to his feet, hands him his cane. He makes it through the building, walking easier in spite of the fatigue.

"Hi, Pap."

Alby surprises him—instead of startling him. "You're still here?"

"Sure, time for me to take care of you. Maybe that's been Dr. Ingstrom's scam all along, to have us take care of each other. This way out."

They reach the parking lot together. As Jakob pokes his key in the car door, Alby throws his arms around him. "Pap, this has been a long time coming. You'll be back to see John?"

"Ah, watch out, you will knock me over." But Alby has him in a solid grip. He starts to pat his back.

"Hey, they say in treatment, 'Don't burp the other guy when you're hugging, just be close.'" Jakob relaxes, let's go of his cane, which falls with an aluminum clunk. His face is in his son's chest, he hears his strong heart. "Ja, I will be back. Now help me," he barks.

"Okay, well, good-bye." Alby opens the car door, lowers him in with easy, healthy strength, hands him his cane.

He acts like I'm old and feeble, probably thinks I'm feeble-minded too. But he's a good boy, he loves me after all. "Wait, Alby." His son turns. "Thank you. John is one in a million. It's as big a deal as the long ago when I saw my own pappie again. The right man at the right time. Actually, more right than seeing Pappie, I'll tell you sometime. This is a good thing you did today."

Alby drops his head, looks up with a shy smile, like his old report card days. "No problem, Pap. I like him too." Alby glows when he smiles. "Okay, good-bye."

Alby stands back and watches him drive away. Ah, his breathing is easy. He talks to God on the way home, about night blindness. *Get me home. If I die, Nikki will kill me.* He chuckles. Ja, she'd come to heaven and kill him for dying.

Night blindness was a side effect of no nutrition in the kamps. *Oh ja, Meneer de Haan thought he'd made it outside the barracks to pee in the middle of the night, when he had not yet left the building. Stupid we had a long rope hung to guide us out. Yet, he almost peed on me. How apologetic he was for just that one time, it was only an almost. Strange what shames people in war, and what doesn't.*

He peers at each curve, easing his foot on and off the gas. He's close to home by now. The peeing incident becomes funny, hysterical, keeping him laughing aloud. He thinks of Bevins, of his beautiful smile, of John with his firm voice—give your burden to God. Driving home is easy, and it doesn't matter too much if you are late, because home is the one spot on the map that won't disappear.

††††

"That's nice, Papa, that's so nice." My voice breaks.

495

"Oh, Lucie. Did I upset you?"

"No, not at all. I'm so happy that you have your special person to talk to, and more than that, just that you're happy."

"Yeah, that's all we want for family."

"And Papa, I can feel it now, everything is going to be okay."

"Of course," he says, as if this is what his message to me always has been. "You know, Liefje, let me see if Mama and I can visit, cheer you up. You must be so tired of being in bed."

"And soon I could be off of bed rest, it's not so bad," I hurriedly say. How awful could it be to have them come, and maybe even stay with us? The intensity of a Vanderveer visit is not what I need.

"Yes, we'll have a little talk, and we'll call you back."

"But,"

"No worries, our finances aren't so bad you know."

I started the day with atrophied muscles slow to walk and move briskly again, and now I'll be crowded with visitors. I stare at the phone in my hand. I won't tell Daniel yet. Maybe this will all go away. At least I'm sleepy. I arrange a pillow mountain next to me, heave to my side, and know I'll take a long, restful nap.

† † †

The next day I see Dr. Simonian and he says I'm officially off bed rest. Any labor starting now would deliver a healthy baby. We go over the date of the planned C-section, well after the family visit. Should I cancel the visit, with the dates being relatively close together, I ask hopefully.

"No," he says. "Although anything can happen, there are absolutely no signs of you going into labor sooner."

After dinner, the phone rings and Daniel picks up. I felt so well today, we went on a slow walk around the block, enjoying the variety of late spring roses, and for me the prospect of more life beyond our yard, block, and neighborhood.

"Oh, hi, Jakob," Daniel says.

Oh no. I should have warned him.

There's a lot of excited talking from the other end. "Well …" Daniel swallows, but actually looks neutral, not alarmed. "So you can all come here, even Dr. Ingstrom? Yes it is wise, I think, to stay in a hotel, so Luce doesn't feel she has to hostess. She's not quite off bed rest yet."

A good lie, that. Vincent is sitting with me, playing Scrabble. I'm teaching him Dutch words to add to the mix. Ja, he mouths at the mention of hotel, raising a fist with a pretend cheer. He's the one who has to give up his room if we have guests.

"Sure she can talk." He passes the phone to me.

Papa fills me in that Mama and he are offering plane tickets to the whole family. "You were willing to come to us, now we are going to come to you." Wade and Marina will stay with their other grandparents, but everyone else is coming to California: Alby, Cindy, Corrie, Mama, and Papa.

"And even Dr. Ingstrom?" I ask, still in shock.

"Yes, she happens to have a conference to attend, and she'd like to help us have a support meeting for us, all together. Alby did some research; there is a housekeeping hotel near you."

All I can say is *okay*.

I hand the phone to Daniel, to hang it up. "Aren't you going to freak out?" I ask.

"No," he says seriously. "You're still into your family history thing, and what could be better than them coming to you?"

"Really, I could hurry up and call them, have them cancel. And it's way too much for Papa, he shouldn't travel around airplane germs, he should take it easy."

"He talked about that. He's off of most restrictions to avoid infection. Don't be so stubborn. He says especially now that he's fighting cancer, he wants to see you. Most of all … he wants to hear *your* stories now." He smiles happily.

Ironically, this is what I always said I wanted: to be truly heard. I clench my fist under the table. Oh how I want to shove it all away. *It's too little too late. Now they're interested — finally. But Papa is only asking for what I asked from him.*

Does he think I'll lay out a beautiful story of healing like his Brother John? I can't imagine where to start and where to end.

† † †

Day by day I walk more and more. Surprisingly there is little or no pelvic girdle pain, nor back pain, nor pinched nerve pain radiating down my leg. All the rest must have alleviated the pressure. *My health is a gift, God's grace,* I write in my journal. But I don't write the same about my whole family coming to me in California. Guess I'm as terrified as Papa must once have been. They want me to talk.

CHAPTER 28

The whole family has arrived, and forbade me to host a visit the first night. I'm listening to a favorite CD, *Phantom of the Opera*, loud. I feel inspired to cook well for just the three of us, and to stop thinking about heavy family history. None of the past has to matter so much. I will focus on the present. I see it's a little later than we all like. It's definitely part of the Vanderveer family legacy, and Daniel's old family life too, to *always* eat on time, no later than 6:30.

I'm drizzling olive oil over salad when Vincent shuffles in, noisily of course. I turn around. His face looks stricken; he is pale as could be. "What?" is all I can say.

He's clutching the surviving part of his sketchpad. His hands tremble as he smoothes it out. What could it be? "You know there are some good sketches in here," he says.

I nod, adjust the simmering spaghetti sauce, and bring us to our favorite chairs. "Please, Vincent; don't worry an old pregnant mom, what's wrong?"

He shrugs, frowns, and stuffs the yellow baby booties I've had out again, back in the drawer. He reaches for the cell phone in his pocket. I want to grab his distraction away from him. He looks down again, still shaking. His appearance is that of an aged man who can't speak. Next, he crumples the paper on the end table and neatly drops it in the wastepaper basket, straightening the plastic liner.

"Vincent?" I say insistently.

"Grandpa yelled at me," he says. "Really, really loud."

Papa can alternate between tremendously kind, or explosively angry. I won't excuse it anymore with *it was the war-years* explanations.

I reach gently for his phone, although I'm furious. "Why would he yell at you? Honey, you don't deserve that. I'll call him, and we'll work this out." Papa yelling? More pangs of guilt. I should have insisted they all come over for dinner tonight, we could have avoided *ruzie* with all of us here.

"No, Mom, don't call him." Vincent says firmly. "I'll talk to him tomorrow. I deserved it. This wasn't bad yelling; it was good yelling. I asked him why he told me about his fighting during the *Bersiap* time like it was so much more than it was, and he said everything was hell, and I said, 'Yeah, I would have liked to have known,' just like that— sarcastically. Then he yelled at me and told me that to really understand you had to know the story from the beginning, and that's what you were trying to do. So I yelled back and asked what's so hard about that. He said it would be damned hard, harder than being a teen paratrooper. And I said I think I finally get it, and he said, 'Ja, that's good.'"

"Oh." I lean back in the chair, glad my belly feels so full of Baby's life.

"Yeah, Mom, and he made me realize that telling everything takes the most courage of all. I've always had you and Dad, never starved, never fought for bread, and never lost our family. So I'm sketching again."

I flip through the early pages of his sketchbook, not too bad off for the beating it got. It has been carefully pressed straight and the pages turn on their spirals with only a little bit of a hitch. I find a sketch of two thin women and a girl standing out from a crowd, all waving through barbed wire. To the side, a truck of bobbing boys' heads takes off through dust. Each set of eyes radiate love. The little girl must be Sara. She has the Vanderveer mouth and clutches her doll with one hand. Another woman, Oma, has soft eyes radiating love, and a mouth pulled into bereavement. I knew her only as the quiet woman permanently faded into gray; here she is brave, the woman who the Japanese once said had Samurai spirit. Tineke Bevins has eyes of love too, wide open, trying to take it all in. I touch each image softly. Each one is the only one left, the child, the moms.

† † †

The hotel conference room table reeks of lemon disinfectant, perfectly clean. A tiny refrigerator hums and everyone has fetched a Styrofoam cup of something to drink: tea, juice, lemonade.

Alby looks around with agitation and concern.

It's unlike him. "What's up?" I ask.

"We're waiting for Dr. Ingstrom."

"Really? No way."

Papa slurps his coffee, "remember we said she'd be in California to present at a conference?"

The door opens, and she walks in, looking funny in a casual jogging suit, because it's way out of style, and pastel pink is not her color.

"I can't believe you're here for all of us," I say.

"Actually Luce," Daniel squeezes my hand, "she's here for you."

How crazy. "How come?"

Alby responds. "This is like you getting help from all of us Luce. And we have a talking stick, so I don't do all of the talking." He pulls out a pencil wrapped in bright yarns.

"I roll my eyes, Dr. Ingstrom..."

"Clara," she says.

"I don't need special help from the whole family."

"Yes you do."

Daniel, the traitor, squeezes my hand. "Relax honey. You know everyone here loves you right? Try trusting your parents, they would only do what's good for you and Baby, right?"

"Yes." Do I fight or agree? I give myself a talking to— stay, rather than run away, I know I haven't fully trusted my parents in forever. I used to think I could tell Mama everything but stopped when she put her foot down—with me. I was always a Daddy's girl, enjoying my Papa, but you never knew when he would explode. "You've all been planning behind my back?"

Mama replies, "Liefje, I knew it was good for you and for Baby, that we had our phone calls lately, with much more openness. So I invited Dr. Ingstrom. You know she's the only one who's ever made us put down the walls."

Baby kicks. What can go wrong now, really? I nod.

Clara covers the ground rules, which of course include no yelling, and no running out of the room. We all solemnly agree.

Papa's in a crisp, pressed shirt, like he thinks today is an occasion. He's thinner from the chemo, yet maneuvered in easily with his cane, like a burden lifted. Mama told me about his joy to go walking and swimming again, appreciating his treatment-free days. Papa gave Vincent a ride here today in the rental car and they bump shoulders purposely from time to time, buddy buddy now. My son, with his height, looks particularly adult. He has black jeans on for this occasion, his nod toward appearing dressed up. Corrie rocks back in one of the comfy conference table chairs, obviously relaxed. Cindy and Alby lean toward each other, holding hands like I haven't see them do in decades. I take a deep breath, catching each family member's eyes. They are just people after all, very powerful people in my world. No sparks of *ruzie* in anyone's eyes.

I reach for the talking stick. "I've never said sorry. I'm sorry Alby I spoke to you in a nasty way for your whole recovery, when you've been so determined to stay sober. I want to be different today." Daniel makes a quick face at me. He rightly thinks I'm terrible at apologies. I could have added, *and I was wrong.*

"And you'll be different by being more open?" Cindy asks.

"Yes, open."

"And now," says Clara reaching for the talking stick and hands it over, "Jake, you asked to go next."

Yes, they all planned behind my back, and what a great sign that Mama and Papa are getting along. I glance at Vincent; he will want Papa to talk about the World War II fighting. But he looks absorbed, peaceful; like he's thinking, *what does it matter, we're all here.*

Papa points down to a worn brown bag at his feet, I've bumped into it several times. Oh this is the one he had at Montreal airport, and the one from the family library closet too. Old creased straps and buckles secure the scarred leather. "I think Luce and Mama know this bag. Luce, I didn't want you to worry about me, because this was my old escape bag—in case I ever had to evacuate again. Sixty years I've kept it. If pappies were rounded up again, like my pappie, I'd be ready, and I'd help all of you prepare for the worst. Inside I have old-fashioned vitamin drops, a tin of crackers, and secret items. Turns out I didn't really want to lose the past."

He hauls the bag up to his lap, shrugging away my help. Each buckle is unfastened, and he slides it to me. Then he nudges Vincent politely and says, "Let's switch seats." It's rare for him to ask rather than imperiously tell a grandchild to move.

They switch, and Papa slides out the contents one at a time. I feel chills, thinking that Papa brought us his past, items we can touch. Sure enough there's a tin in there and Papa holds a tiny bundle of plastic and tissue, opening it to reveal a fragment of red fabric.

He shakes his head as if to banish the old *it's too much, it hurts too much. They were cruel to each other too. I cannot tell you.* "Her number ..." Papa's voice breaks. "We all had them."

Mama finishes, "Ja, her kamp number. She had to sew dozens of them on to each family member's clothes, and this was hers."

503

He has Vincent and I touch frayed red fabric, the inked on prisoner number still visible.

My voice chokes. "She was always so elegant. Remember her fur coat, her perfectly pressed clothes? And this she kept, her reminder from when she had nothing."

Cindy has her turn to touch and pass along. "I wish I had known her."

When Oma's number reaches Papa again, he holds it in the palm of his hand.

He delicately unfolds the layers of tissue and plastic, tucking it back in. He smiles gently, "We have belatedly memorialized her, together, now." He reaches for the tin. "This used to hold emergency biscuits. Now this is what I most wanted to show you."

Inside is a small carved wooden-camphor box, which he hands to Vincent.

"For me?" asks Vincent.

"This is for your mama and you. Still mine, for now."

Wings are carved on the box, like an angel or bird. When Vincent opens it, a distinct smell lifts up to my nose recalling our own Vanderveer family camphor chest back in Houston. Boxes and chests keep bits of home safe, secure. Camphor wood's smell is what signals that some possessions have to be sorted out, important things selected from many.

Inside this miniature chest, something is wrapped up in a soft gray polishing cloth. Vincent unwraps the dull unpolished roundness, a simple, solid case—perhaps an old watch. Papa's hands reach to help, just as Vincent finds a button opposite the hinge, and opens it to the face. The watch has only the minute hand left. Scratched glass is intact and unusual roman numerals. Oh, not numerals, letters.

"A compass," Vincent says, not surprised. "Your compass!" He cups it in his hand like he would hold it forever.

It points to true north. "Never broken?" I ask with wonder.

"Ja, never broken," said Papa, "A miracle that it remained whole, and that it came back to me. It was taken away so early in the war. After all the kamps, moves, cruelty, it came back to me."

"It was yours when you were little?"

Mama answers for him, "This is the one thing your papa got from his pappie."

"I told you, our family had the last ship ride home one year before the Japanese invaded. This was right before Europe was cut off from us due to the Nazi invasion. Pappie sought me out. He and Albert had the botany book to discuss; Sara had paper dolls and their outfits.

"Albert and Sara received their gifts at breakfast. Of course I worried about being left out and that Pappie wanted to be with Wim, not me. Now I'm realizing that Pappie must have had a super active streak like me, and thought he had to tame that in me. He brought me to the captain's bridge, we strode around the boat, and then he gave me this. Brother John told me I needed to look at the past and realize my Pappie loved me, and I do. He loved me, and for those weeks he gave me the gift of his time."

"Matteus and I discovered it when we had each experienced transport again and ended up in one last kamp together. I found it just as we left that kamp after liberation. I didn't think how miraculous the return was then. Lately I have thought again about miracles, seeing Alby change so much, no matter how hard the circumstances, seeing him be the father he wants to be."

Alby blushes. This is the first time I've seen him respond so innocently in decades; we all need to know our papa loves us.

Tears have been streaming down Papa's cheeks; he pulls out a handkerchief and wipes them. "Almost everyone I grew close to died. Brother John also told me to stop thinking linearly like an engineer. Just because I was there when Albert, Pappie and Matteus died, I was of course not responsible for death. He helped me see that we all deserve this love."

I grip the table in sympathy, three deaths he witnessed? Indeed, too much.

Daniel says, "Jake, I wish you had known you were deserving, when the compass first came back to you."

"I wasn't ready yet then. Now I am."

Clara smiles, "You always thought you didn't deserve to be open and receive love, and that you would run out of time. We do have time. Let's all rest, and in two hours come back, right before dinner."

"Dinner," I say. "Time for some fun."

Papa smiles, "Of course, Luce, after you talk. No one's forgotten about you."

He shuffles away. To me he looks drained, all other deep talk could have waited. But he insists there's more to come, and the more is me.

† † †

Papa looks rested after all, as we are around the table. No adagio piano fingers, just relaxed.

"So what's up?" I ask.

The stupid talking stick has been discarded. Alby says, "Let's talk about your feelings."

"I've been doing just that since the day I didn't want you to die, Alby." My voice breaks, but my heart is better. He told me, eventually, that seeing me try to balance my love for Baby by coming to Houston again, for him, for Papa, was his final wake up call. Sure he went home, but he started to open up to his fellow alcoholics, like he never had before.

Clara's been quiet, mostly a witness. Now, she takes a deep breath, like getting ready to make a speech. "Yes everything you do for your family is about emotion, but not your own feelings — their feelings, their life."

"But—." I want to protest, but every part of me heaves with emotion around my huge belly. I look at Clara with desperation. *Stop, this can't be good.*

"Luce if you just make a start now, like Jakob once did in my office, it won't be bad for Baby, nor is it bad for you."

Daniel puts his arm around me and I nod. "I know you worry about stressing out Baby, its okay. Think about the stress of not speaking up all these years."

Clara fishes out the darned stick, and gives it to me.

"My toughest times, I was dazed. Remember Mama and Papa, when I smacked my head so hard against the glass wall when we all had to stay the night at Montreal airport?"

Papa looks particularly surprised, and caring, as if he would like to pick me up all over again to check out my head.

"My first night in the U.S., dazed. And I'm realizing more stuff, this back pain"—I arrange a pillow behind me—"is most likely the result of an accidental drunken dive down the side of the bayou, which I never told you about. I hope I don't have to hurt my head anymore times to get my life lessons."

Mama stares at Corrie and Alby. "There was another dazed time, and you two remember right?" They nod.

I feel the momentary rush of blood to my ears, I upset Mama. She says, "There was another time you smacked your head. I guess you don't recall. I was ready to bring it up today, so you could talk, but now I realize … "

Daniel turns to me and softly says, "You really don't know?"

I shake my head, and Mama goes on. "In nineteen-seventy, we had lived in Texas for a couple of years. You were only twelve years old and Papa and I hated to have to tell you Beppe had died; we knew you would take it the hardest. Remember? She had collapsed in her chair, while Pake did the afternoon milking?"

I nod yes, with a tingling in my ears, and hear a middle-of-the-night phone call, ringing a long time, then starting over, answered. Mama's eyes red in the morning, Papa home from work, on an oddly beautiful Friday, the beginning of a weekend, a false spring-like day, in the middle of Houston winter.

"You were in seventh grade and you set out on your bicycle to the place you said reminded you most of the boerderij, the place with the abandoned barn."

A foggy puzzle floats in my brain. "That's close to the same trails I went down the night I fell down the bayou before HOW."

"About twenty minutes after you left, someone pounded at the door. You had gone over a jump on your banana-seat bicycle, trying to pull a wheelie. But you pulled up too far and fell straight back, right on your head. Luckily some kids nearby recognized you. One of their moms loaded you into her station wagon and brought you home. They said you had lost consciousness for just a moment."

"What time of year was it again?" a child's high-pitched voice asks — me.

"February," says Mama.

Spit in my mouth feels like warm blood ready to ooze out. My head pounds. Daniel gently massages the back of my neck. I breathe deeply and pat my belly.

Vincent clatters his chair back, stands behind me and wraps his arms around me. Baby kicks, like she is saying *yes, yes.*

I speak softly. "I had plenty of reason to be sad, and I felt that way for a long time, especially in February. Bad days were grayer. Good days had only an edge of leaden gray. I went back to that barn again. I had been with Pake and Beppe on and off, two times here in America, one time there, and I thought, *this is it, this is all, and it's not enough.* There are some losses you don't get over. I don't remember the fall or being injured."

508

Everyone at the table nods.

"Why didn't we talk about Beppe every year on the anniversary of her death? And later, when he died, Pake too? The cold, cold Dutch winter. Dark for Beppe and Pake. Killed me to think about it."

"Me too. And I missed not just them, liefje; I missed you," says Mama. "I do know you're not supposed to need your kids to make yourself feel better, but I needed you during those long weeks into months that Papa and Alby were gone. You're right, for years we didn't memorialize Beppe, and perhaps you and I missed her the most."

"Ja." My fog clears. It comes together, how I wanted to get to that boerderij barn, and never making it. I remember my last escape, when Papa and Alby still had their hospital care from the accident, the deliciousness and fear of not facing any *ruzie*. One thing for sure, I still wish for a boerderij, and the peace it brings. "I really did disappear again when Papa and Alby were in the hospital." I hear the wonder in my voice. Yes, I ran away.

"Ja," says Mama, "and I'm sure I was horrible to be with, full of rage."

"Only the littlest bit," says Papa, his lip corners turning up.

"Full of it," says Alby.

Corrie looks at me. "I wish you would have told us Luce, any of us. You were actually great to me, when Papa and Alby had the accident, but you never told me how upset you were about Beppe and Pake, the accident, why you went to HOW, nothing."

Vincent pipes up. "Mom, that's like I tell you, you're gone too much, even when you're here."

"Listen to your son," Alby says.

"Listen to Marina and Wade," I shoot back, tired of being on the hot seat.

Daniel elbows me to be kind.

Cindy says, "He does, he listens now."

509

"I'm sorry," I say, and repeat the words. I mean it. "Okay, I thought when I was little," for a moment, I can't breathe, the worst lump ever in my throat. I swallow warm tea. "Okay, I thought when I was little, Mama, that I should no longer tell any of you how sad I was, because remember you got tired of hearing?"

She looks at me with puzzled love.

"I guess you don't remember. But when I cried every night, you looked too sad. Papa, you were angry all the time, wanting our excellent grades, yelling at us, smashing Corrie's face in her food if she didn't eat her spaghetti."

He flinches and nods.

"So I shut down. So how do I really feel. I wish they were here at the table now. I wish I had my own special bag, a magic bag to bring Beppe and Pake here."

Vincent reaches into his back pack. "Here you go, Mom." He hands me the coveralls.

"Ow, ooh," I cry. And I'm back on the boerderij. "This hurts. Why couldn't you send me every single year. Why couldn't we all go, why were we so stupid? Why didn't you all discover I visited that block with a sad excuse for a boerderij?"

Mama says, "Liefje, we lived through the pain too."

"And I'm sorry," Papa says. "Sorry you hurt so much, sorry we didn't go to Nederland all the time. Sorry only Mama went to Beppe's funeral. Sorry I didn't pack you all up for my Mammie's funeral there, so we could all remember and you would know the grandmother you only knew as a quiet shadow, who wanted everything *regeld*." He smiles faintly.

"And I just wanted to be there for every important moment, if I had to be gone. To be there when they left the farm, to be there when Pake was first alone. To see my cousins all the time, not just that one year I was eleven, and for Alby and Corrie to be more Dutch, and know Nederland as much as I."

They nod. Corrie wipes a tear, "Yes, I wanted to be more Dutch."

Mama comes to me. "You're ready now darling. Enjoy this time of just being a Mama, not doing so much. You can help Papa best by being happy, by showing him that you too are happy."

"I am. I'm happy." I'm crying with relief.

"You are all ready," says Clara. "Thank you. You were all the first to bring my own parent's war experience back me, and you helped me feel at home in Houston again." She can hardly see through her glasses. Her face is all wet.

EPILOGUE

I miss my family in a different way, once they are gone. Just like I used to wish I could scrunch together the world globe in big wrinkles and have Europe border North America, I now wish Texas bordered California. I don't talk to Papa, but get my reports from Mama, Cindy, and Corrie. He had a new outpatient surgery called radiofrequency ablation. He didn't want me to know he postponed it for the trip to California. Everyone in the family understood the postponement, because of course he said he couldn't have surgery if he didn't get to see me again before Baby is born.

Baby is due by C-section, only one week now. Daniel and Vincent think they are doing me a favor by being far too self-sufficient. Tonight I'm alone again as Daniel takes Vincent for driving practice in the dark.

Baby hasn't moved since dinnertime. To stave off worry, I reach for my book. My hands tremble as I flip to the ninth month. *You will notice a change in the baby's movement. This is no cause for alarm. By now the womb is a small space for a big baby who often moves his/her hands and head only.* Okay, panic gone.

† † †

Daniel leaves for a two day trip to bring in more cash for his own paternity leave. Tonight I hear plenty from Vincent about how his life is going. He's cooperative, although he delays coming home after school until dinnertime. I check off the slips from his teachers. He's keeping up and I verify it on the school computer system. He tells me more about Tania. I'm still a mom who's needed.

We take our plates of food to our patio table. Roses bloom everywhere.

"Almost time for my baby sister, huh, Mom?"

I nod. He knows where my suitcase is, has been to the hospital, and knows I'm preregistered there.

"What if Dad's not home when it's time?"

"Oh, he will be. No worries. That's the advantage of scheduling a birth."

† † †

I wake up whimpering. I dreamt of being at Hope Eternal OB-GYN unit. Alby, Mama, Papa, Daniel, and Vincent were all there. "Too soon, too soon," I yelled as labor pains hit repeatedly. Every time the doctor would say, *we have stopped them now, no more premature labor*, another contraction would hit, and I would moan, *No, no, no*.

Ah, so relieved it's just a dream. I curve my hands around my belly and the cinch grip of a real contraction hits. I must have been having pains for some time, till they finally woke me up. It's 6:00 a.m., half an hour before Vincent wakes up for school.

The pain melts away and I head for the kitchen, probably a false alarm. I decide to prepare morning oatmeal in a pan, gently simmered with whole milk as if I am a child with *havermout pap*—oatmeal on the boerderij. Another contraction, stronger this time. It's been ten minutes since the last pain.

I pad off to Vincent's room, knocking and poking my head in. The door will barely budge past his dirty clothes strewn on the floor. "Honey, wake up, I'm having labor pains."

"What?" he mumbles. "Okay, Mom, getting right up."

"I'll call Kemble, you get ready for school."

"No way, I'm okay with school now! I can drive you to the hospital."

"No way, you're supposed to have a calm adult with you when you drive. Not one in distress."

He jumps out of bed. "Come on, Mom. Otherwise I'll be a kid at school in distress." Always the smart aleck. He pulls on yesterday's jeans over the boxers he sleeps in, and then finds a clean T-shirt from the bottom of a stack. I want to call Kemble anyway, but Vincent has his determined happy look, like when he did page after page of Grandpa sketches. I realize I want him there, and if I were in his shoes, I wouldn't be able to pay attention at school either.

"Okay, you can drive. We have a little time. Get fully ready. You should have some real breakfast and don't rush. I'll be calling Kemble." I rush to the phone.

The oatmeal makes my mouth water; I would love to add more milk and then butter and brown sugar. But no food for me. The C-section could happen today.

Vincent usually avoids oatmeal as if it were rat poison. Today he just digs in.

When I moan during his breakfast and then again as we are about to leave, I realize he's been timing my contractions. "Nine minutes. They're closer."

I'm surrendering to both the pain, and the relief of the right kind of pain. This is very different from the intense pelvic girdle pain back at *Hope Eternal*. I breathe through the pain slowly. Not horrendous, but it will be a relief to get to the hospital. "Are you calm enough to drive us?" I gasp.

"What? After all this waiting, I'm so ready. No problem. I'll get the wehpuhns," he says in his never-ending Arnold Schwarzenegger imitation. I'm glad that for him this is an adventure, that he is not too freaked out, and that we're in this together. He grabs my suitcase from the closet. "Let's go." He wiggles from one foot to the other.

He drives gently, as if I have turned to glass.

"Oh, my baby is driving me and his sister to the hospital for her to be born. Wow."

"Okay, Mom, stop. You're going to cry. Hold it together."

We arrive, and both Vincent and I know where to go. The contractions are only six minutes apart. I've called ahead and Dr. Simonian is soon there. He's an old hand at births. This is like winning the lottery to have my primary OB-GYN, when needed. I tell him so and he replies with a shy smile like Papa's. "I told the staff to call me in if you went to the hospital early."

With his reassuring presence I discover I've been scared, and let it all go. I breathe through a contraction with Vincent next to me.

Dr. Simonian turns to him. Vincent has been along for appointments before. "Hi, buddy, how are you doing? Brought your homework along, I hope?"

"Heaaiil no," says Vincent.

"And your dad is just hanging out somewhere?"

"Mom called him when we got in the car," Vincent reports. "He's driving in, but he's got his big truck to park at the warehouse first, and that's after a four hour drive to get here."

"And we know the rules," I say. "No cell phones here."

"Oh, that's for the ER; turn your cell phones back on." Vincent's phone immediately beeps on, and he listens. "Dad is already only three hours away, in the big truck."

"Wow, I hope he's not speeding."

Vincent rolls his eyes. "No worrying, Mom." He positions himself strategically at my head. I know this routine; soon I won't have any real privacy. I moan with another contraction, Vincent gives me his hand. "Wow, Mom, you're squishing me." He wraps a towel around his own hand for padding and then lets me squeeze some more. "Okay, we're set for the next contraction."

Dr. Simonian finishes checking me for dilation, then comes over to my shoulder for discussion mode. "So you are now a candidate for a VBAC, vaginal birth after C-section. She's right at term and you are almost fully dilated."

I am amazed and dizzy. *No, no, don't hyperventilate, no asthma, breathe oh so slowly and deeply.* I look up at Vincent's intense but relaxed face, Doc's smiling face on my other side. I have taken a new C-section scar for granted. I'm picking between ordeal number one and ordeal number two, and think of Kemble reminding me to ask for help. "What would you recommend, Doc?"

"Well, it's great for baby's lungs, squeezing out those fluids due to birthing, and good for you too. We can help you prepare and push her out."

"Okay." The sun breaks through a cloudy sky and light is streaming into the room. Vincent, much like me, can wander through life missing a lot, yet notice the sun in my eyes.

"Only block the light a little," I say to Vincent, and gasp with the next pain.

Dr. Simonian's walking out. "I'll go get the team and your medical orders ready."

I do the deep breathing that is the only thing that helped the first time, before the unexpected C-section. Vincent's towel-wrapped hand is back in mine. I focus more on breath than pain.

"Honey, call Grandma and Grandpa."

Vincent does, and reaches his Grandpa, hearing a storm of words on his side of the phone call. "We are already in the hospital. No really, Mom is fine. Is Grandma there? Would you let everyone know? Everything is fine; she's not even going to have a C-section. No, no, that's actually good news, not bad. Is Grandma there? Okay, we'll tell you the news soon."

When Vincent was born, we had had a birthing plan, with deep breathing, focus points, homey touches, and no technology. That was soon gone in the world of induced labor, epidural anesthesia, and monitors. I was already almost a high-risk pregnancy then, and in the end I told myself to get over it, that after hours of pushing, he was born by C-section because it was necessary. Because baby

Vincie was at risk. I never had the satisfaction of knowing if a safe birth would have resulted from our natural birthing plan. On all the hospital roller coaster rides I ever have been on—the accident, Vincie's birth, and Alby's rehabs—I never could figure things out. I can only hope that natural childbirth is the best plan now.

Vincent is asked to leave and put on scrubs. Baby's head monitor is applied. I'm grateful for that much technology. My stuff is rearranged, and put in a bag in case we end up in surgery after all. Vincent comes back in. I got through one contraction without him, and now the next one arrives. Pressure builds; no one has even offered me an epidural.

A fresh-faced nurse reminiscent of my MaryAnn Hope Eternal nurse in Houston holds my hand, Vincent the other.

More pressure. "I have to push."

Another contraction comes in minutes, and Vincent says, "Wow, she is really in a hurry, not like my birth." He speaks expertly as if he can recall every minute of his own thirty-six-hour birth process, but he's starting to look worried and scared.

I glance at the clock; Daniel is still about two hours away, too soon to expect him. I asked Vincent to call Kemble again.

"I'll leave you the towel hand," he jokes and makes the call. His tone takes on a higher pitch, as if he is going to be very brave but wants to yell out, "Daddy!"

Another contraction strikes. I focus on every second, breathing, riding it like a wave. The pushing feeling is almost unbearable. The nurse has left, surely for Dr. Simonian. Back when my birthing plan for Vincent had been tossed out, I was in and out of my body, having difficulty imagining the baby coming out, just wanting it to be over. Daniel and I both still laugh, and sometimes cry, when we remember me saying, "Right now I hate everyone in this hospital except me and you, and I just want this baby to come out." Months later Daniel warmly greeted two women in the grocery store, who smiled my way. I, who had not been "doped up" during the birth, asked him who they were. They were two among the shifts of labor and delivery nurses who shared parts of the thirty-six-hour vigil before Vincie entered the world.

My now big teenaged son puts his hand back in mine. Another contraction and I feel in charge of the wave, ready to roar over the beach.

The nurse and Dr. Simonian are suddenly in the room. "It's time to push." Baby's monitor beeps more.

"She's in distress?" I ask.

The nurse's eyes widen as Dr. Simonian says, "Everything is fine, dear. You get to push now."

"Duh," I want to shout. I put the scream into the first push. Vincent squeezes my hand hard after. He is grinning and crying. I flash suddenly on sobbing during the return airplane flight from visiting Nederland ten years ago, wanting to be on two shores at once so much, wanting to have weekend reunions with any family I wished, knowing it could not be so. All the sorrow and joy strengthens me. All the women in our family go through this: my cousins in Nederland; Beppe, who could have only one baby; Mama with us three kids; and now me, delivering a baby with my baby Vincent.

Feet pound down the hall. Daniel rushes in, panting. The nurse hands him scrubs. He hugs Vincent, comes to my other side, and takes my other hand. "They're about to move Mom, or have her give birth or something," says Vincent.

"Have they prepped you for surgery?" asks Daniel.

"No surgery," announces Dr. Simonian, "and we're staying right here. Your stubborn wife can push this baby out. Your daughter is just about ready to enter the world." He laughs.

Daniel laughs, too, although the worry of racing here has left him pale and shaking. He calms himself. There are no reliable Lewis family members to call who can support Daniel, but we'll call them later with the news. I feel his protectiveness. All sense of time is gone, yet I know he got here in record time.

The door swings open again, and Kemble is here. Her hair sticks up fresh from a shower. "First you tell me I'm not needed, now I'm here." She and Daniel quickly depart to put on scrubs, return. "We raced in neighboring dressing rooms," she says. "Daniel won." She looks so sweet grinning her happiness. She puts her hand on Daniel's shoulder. Now he does have someone. I no longer feel a need to be a thousand miles away from any family member. Still, I'm so grateful this is my family for now. By now, Papa would have ordered Dr. Simonian around and would have been exiled to the waiting room.

The nurse finishes converting the bed into a delivery table. Light streams into the room and hits the opposite wall. Daniel has worked my focal point out of the bag, Papa's compass, and threads it up to hang from the TV support.

"You're staying right here for Baby's birth?" I ask Vincent. "Honey, you can switch your hand to my shoulder now." He hedged all along, *I don't know, seeing Mom all covered with blood and ick.*

Kemble studies him from the foot of the bed, alongside Dr. Simonian. "Heck yeah, he's staying."

Vincent nods. "Of course I'm staying. We got to the hospital just the two of us, Mom, and we're finishing this together."

Pains hits like swift sledgehammers. Dr. Simonian urges, "Okay, push, push."

I cry out, can't think, can't hear. I am one big push. I feel a tremendous heaviness, like my whole body is collecting to deliver. I yell, grabbing Vincent again, hard, on the wrist.

"Go, go," Vincent is saying. Daniel's hand is a warm rock in mine.

"Oh, she's already crowning," cries Kemble.

Dr. Simonian adds, "Yes, crowning. Don't push, don't push. First you'll birth her head and then her shoulder." The monitor beeps. "Don't worry, she's fine."

I growl, transformed into an all-powerful Mom. I know every cell in me needs to push. "I have to push, aah."

"Let her push," Daniel says urgently.

"Hold, breathe," says Dr. Simonian.

Pressure, instinct. It is all up to me. Faces blur around me, the room is full of energy. I wish I were squatting in a hut. "Daniel, hold up my back," I yell. I'll hold off to give my doc one more minute, no, one more second. I have to push. The pressure is as keen as the pain. I push, following my own orders.

"Here's her shoulder. Push again!" Doc sounds celebratory.

The pain and pushing come in rhythm.

"One final push, and out she comes."

Daniel moves to Vincent and says. "Go ahead, Vincent; you can be the first to hold her."

Daniel's large hands hold me up. "I love you so much."

"Me too," yells Vincent.

The final push is like body surfing in the Caribbean, a huge warm wave.

"A beautiful healthy baby girl," Doc announces.

Vincent is already holding her, her cry rings out. "Hi, baby sister."

"Hi, Baby." I'm sobbing.

Silence, snuffles.

"She knows us, she knows me, she stopped crying!" Vincent says.

She waves her thumb, which has a tiny callus on it, up to Vincent. He frees a hand, points the callused thumb at her mouth. She sucks.

Dr. Simonian says, "Here, Daniel, cut the cord."

Then she's laying on me, rosy-red, healthy. The nurse scoops her up and coos, "Okay, I'll wash you and check you." She begins the cleaning and Apgar score check.

The room's still so brightly lit. I'm alert, awake, alive in every cell of my being.

Daniel is murmuring on and on over by Baby. "Oh, so beautiful. Here you are. Welcome, welcome to the world. No more worries. No worry for you. There you are."

"Afterbirth push," Dr. Simonian says. No problem.

"What's her score?" Daniel asks our nurse. He loves numbers.

"Ten!"

"Woo-hoo!" we all stage-whisper.

I gaze at everyone, circled up in their scrubs. Baby is bundled and laid next to me. Vincent whispers to Daniel, and then he sits down.

"Does he need a rest?" I ask Daniel.

Vincent hears me. "No way, I'm just going to text and call everyone." He stretches out in the chair by a slightly darkening window. Baby was born at sunset. "All my friends are texting back already. They want to know her name."

"Yes, the name. Because now I have to make my calls," says Kemble.

"Hold on for the name everybody," says Daniel.

"Okay, mystery people," sighs Kemble, "she's not a puppy you know," and steps out.

"I'm calling Grandpa in Houston," Daniel announces. "He's the one we'll say her name to. Okay, honey?" He looks at me.

I nod, kissing Baby's head, holding perfect tiny fingers, each with its own little scalloped fingernail. We knew we would finalize her name at birth, so now Papa can be told.

Vincent shrugs. "Okay, let's see if Grandpa can stop all that worrying."

"Stopping all worrying, now that would be nice," I say.

Daniel calls, and Mama picks up. "Baby has arrived, and we are oh so well," he says, sounding Dutch in his phrasing. He passes the phone to me, after some loud protests from Mama that I am to rest.

"Yes, liefje, oh you are both well. I'm so happy. What's her name?"

"We have to tell Papa too, so get him on the phone."

He clicks on. "Oh *liefje*, you and Baby are fine."

"Oh yes, her name is Marijke, but pronounced and spelled as close as we can come to Marijke in English, Ma-ray-kah. You know, after your friend in Tjideng, Papa, in remembrance, and because it's a beautiful name."

"It's a good name," he says, "a proud and strong name."

Mama whispers sweet, lovey words like, *Oh liefje, schatje.* It's the Dutch way of saying, *I love you. My baby is having a baby. Oh, you little treasure.*

"And some people will think we played with the word *America*, since her name is spelled M-a-r-a-y-k-a, and that is just fine with us. After all, you and Papa in separate countries always prayed for the Americans and other Allies to arrive. She is beautiful. Come visit, but you don't have to rush. Vincent is insisting on doing all of the diapers, and he will be bringing Marayka to me for midnight feedings."

I watch Vincent frown, then grin.

The nurse adjusts my hospital gown; I nurse Marayka for the first time. Daniel grabs the phone.

"Marayka," I croon, "come to Mommy." I roll to my side and place her to my breast. Without much effort, she latches on. It's as if I had a detailed, carefully written birth plan this time, the kind of plan a thorough Dutch person would write, everything *regeld*. I never wrote such a plan, but God did.

Daniel holds the phone away from his ear. "So they are really both well?" I hear tears in Papa's voice.

"Yes, all is well. Luce and little Marayka will be home soon."

"Amazing. Good. And thank you for the name." I hear the click of the phone hanging up. Abruptly they're gone. I suppose they're ready to rest, and feel the peace of new life.

Marayka nurses with little kitten grunts.

Vincent murmurs, "Welcome, Marayka, welcome."

Daniel pats her head. She is home and so am I.

AUTHOR'S NOTE AND FAMILY

The World War II legacy to families, it seems, never stops hurting, and never stops giving. Millions gave their lives, millions had their lives torn away, and these sacrifices did buy the freedom much of the world is graced with today. My own legacy, generations after World War II, is to search for meaning, and faith. That is — the ebb and flow of faith vs cynicism and meaningfulness vs. senselessness.

My personal World War II legacy has the shadow of family secrets and the light of family pride. The Jobsis and De Vries families I grew up with took care to tell stories of the survival of World War II — especially before and after.

But how it was to survive six seemingly endless years in The Netherlands (Holland) and most especially how it was to survive four endless years in the Dutch East Indies (now Indonesia) was left solidly in shadows. I wondered. Is it too painful to share? Are the younger generations protected from the unspeakable cruelty which occurred in the Japanese Concentration Camps in Indonesia? Were memories buried along with those who died? What I have learned is yes, it's all true and the war was so wrenching that it's still difficult to explain these times today. Sadly, to some extent one can explain WWII suffering in the context of the suffering that still happens now: the holocausts, battles and refugee camps of recent times. As you know, after World War II, the world had a rallying cry, "never again." But there have been and are "agains."

Novels and memoirs related to war and survival offer us universal stories through the eyes of a few characters. Family and survivors of World War II inspired Following Shadows.

I could not have put portions of my daily life and daily earnings on hold, without the support of my immediate family. Thank you my dear ones: Donald Brown for always understanding the importance of family heritage and loving family; Dakota Brown for inspiring me with your own artistry as a writer, artist, graphic artist and musician; and Amy Brown Stapleton for your patience and love.

I treasured my early years with my maternal grandparents; it is to their memory I turned each time I yearned to give up on life as a child, teen or adult. My Beppe and Pake, Jantje Veenstra de Vries and Gerrit de Vries, knew all the fears of World War I, the Great Depression, the rigors of farm life, World War II, and persevered. Thank you for showing that love survives no matter the vastness of time, continents and oceans which separate us. My paternal grandparents Gerrit Jozef Jobsis and Anna Margaretha Gieben Jobsis, (Oma and Opa) kept courage during times of unspeakable suffering. Oma, thank you for showing us all grace after losing your husband, parents, home and security.

Most people living the life of a tiny family in the U.S., with relatives in other countries would not have the close bond with family I have enjoyed, and drawn inspiration from. I treasure the memory of Roelof de Haan, and thank you Mechtelina de Haan Jobsis for telling me your experiences, and reminding me to, "Fight for your happiness!" Thank you my Canadian family: Herman and Adriana "Jean" Jobsis for openly sharing your experiences in The Netherlands and the Dutch East Indies. I want to thank my Dutch cousins: Auke and Geertje de Haan Renssen, Teade and Dieuwke Punter-de Haan, Anne Marie and Rob ter Haar Jobsis, Pieter and Dorien Jobsis Stomp, and Michiel Jobsis. After decades you can pick me up at Schiphol Airport or a train station, and our love and laughter is immediately present. Without your hospitality, navigation skills and museum time this writing would never have achieved lift-off.

I have never yet had the privilege of experiencing Indonesian hospitality on Indonesian soil, however research has given me that experience right here in California. Each Dutch-Indonesian-American made me realize that to have at least one person to live for, keeps the human spirit alive. Fred Wilson, you "called me," when I was hesitant to call you. Thank you for breaking silence with speaking engagements, your memoir and our visits about your lost childhood in WWII Indonesia. Thank you Robine Andrau. Jan and Joyce Krancher, you opened your home and hearts regarding life inside and outside the concentration camps. Louis and "Jopie" Johana Furstner you shared so much of your story, and gave me atmosphere for the Vanderveers. Roger Boots, I appreciate your stories about growing up with parents who survived and I want to thank your aunt — Marijke De Ruiter De Wildt Creswick for leading me through the experience of growing up in the kamps.

My bonus Dutch family from De Krant koffie uur, offered wisdom, support and literature. I am grateful in memoriam for Chris Lyffyt, and wish to thank Adriana Lyffyt, Josje van Lieverlo, Jan and Henny van der Linde, Nellie and Peter Bol, and Ria Westerhof.

And finally, to my parents and sister, immigrating in the United States in the 1960's was like forming our own tiny country. We learned together, grew together, and loved each other fiercely. Boukje Jobsis de Vries, you always nurtured, encouraged every exploration, and instilled an appreciation of all the arts. You unflinchingly helped me try to understand a cruel world, as well as a loving world. Adrianus Cornelius "Kees" Jobsis, although you often talked of lack of faith, your ability to rise out of the ashes, like the Phoenix bird, made me see you as spiritual instead. Your strong love nourished me all my life, I still miss you. To my sister Anna Mechtelina Jobsis Johnson, thank you for your understanding, love and support. I'm grateful we greeted children together in each new country, state and neighborhood. Yes, I still like to hold your hand.

A. C. "Kees" Jobsis

Jobsis Home

Jobsis family with Gerrit and Jantje Veenstra de Vries,
immigration already planned

Mechtelien, Anna, Janneke, Kees, Bouk

Anna Margaretha Jobsis

Gerrit, Anna, Herman, Kees

Anna, Kees, Gerrit, Gerrit Jozef

Kees, Mechtelien, Anna, Herman
(Gerrit in the Netherlands)

Jobsis children and friends

Kees, Bouk

Bouk and Kees wedding day

Anna Mechtelien and Kees in Iran

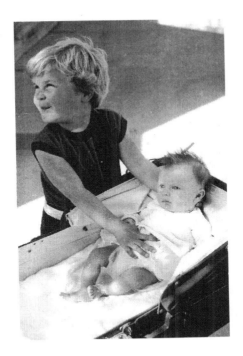

Janneke Margreet and Anna Mechtelien in Iran

Mechtelien, Kees, Bouk in Texas

Made in the USA
San Bernardino, CA
08 July 2017